Jackie Ashenden writes dark, emotional stories with alpha heroes who've just got the world to their liking only to have it blown wide apart by their kick-ass heroines. She lives in Auckland, New Zealand, with her husband, the inimitable Dr Jax, two kids and two rats. When she's not torturing alpha males and their gutsy heroines she can be found drinking chocolate martinis, reading anything she can lay her hands on, wasting time on social media or being forced to go mountain biking with her husband. To keep up to date with Jackie's new releases and other news sign up to her newsletter at jackieashenden.com.

Clare Connelly was raised in small-town Australia among a family of avid readers. She spent much of her childhood up a tree, Mills & Boon book in hand. Clare is married to her own real-life hero and they live in a bungalow near the sea with their two children. She is frequently found staring into space—a surefire sign that she's in the world of her characters. She has a penchant for French food and ice-cold champagne, and Mills & Boon novels continue to be her favourite ever books. Writing for Mills & Boon is a long-held dream. Clare can be contacted via clareconnelly.com or her Facebook page.

D0715995

91120000414164

If you liked *The Debt* and *Cross My Hart*
why not try

Faking It by Stefanie London
Forbidden Sins by J. Margot Critch

The Debt is the first instalment of
The Billionaires Club series, which continues with

The Risk by Caitlin Crews
The Proposition by JC Harroway
The Deal by Clare Connelly

Join an exclusive, elite, exciting world and meet the
globe's sexiest billionaires!

Discover more at millsandboon.co.uk

THE DEBT

JACKIE ASHENDEN

CROSS MY HART

CLARE CONNELLY

Printed and bound in Spain
by CPI, Barcelona

MILLS & BOON

THE DEBT

JACKIE ASHENDEN

MILLS & BOON

To Fra.

I wrote this book sitting in your bedroom.

Just thought you should know.

CHAPTER ONE

Ellie

I WIPED MY palms surreptitiously down my black trousers and adjusted my black suit jacket, briefly touching my head to make sure the chauffeur's cap was in place. Mentally, I went over the address the chauffeur company had given me: The Gustave Eiffel Suite of the Shangri-La, Paris.

Yep. I was in the right place.

I took a deep breath.

Okay, here went nothing.

It had taken me a month of careful planning to get to this point—including relocating from Australia to England—but now I was here I wasn't going to let the opportunity slip through my fingers.

I had two days to convince one of the UK's most difficult billionaires to give my father more time before withdrawing the venture capital his firm had invested in our family's company. It was capital we desperately needed in order to stay solvent. And it was not going to be easy.

Ash Evans, billionaire property developer, investor and slave driver, was as famous for his ruthlessness as he was for his temper, not to mention his unapologetic pride in the fact that he came from a poor background.

He was also notorious for never forgiving a debt.

Still, I liked a challenge and, apart from anything else, this was for Dad's sake and for Australis, our super car company, and that was more important than any qualms I had about confronting some self-important rich guy.

Not that I had qualms. I was a Little, and Littles were tough. We could get through anything. The key was to put your head down, not make a fuss, and keep going.

Keeping my fuss-making to a minimum, I gave my jacket another tweak then raised my hand and knocked sharply on the suite door.

There was no response.

There was also no one around, which was unusual.

I'd been driving for the rich and famous for a couple of years now—a second job to supplement my position as a designer at Australis because I liked driving—and I knew they tended to be always surrounded by people. Assistants, bodyguards and all kinds of hangers-on.

Apparently not Mr Evans.

But then, given what I knew about him from the research I'd done, that wasn't completely unexpected.

He was a self-made man who'd grown up in one of London's most notorious council estates and who'd risen to the top through a combination of ruthlessness, hard-headed business sense and a fight-to-the-death attitude that people whispered had come from his days as a street fighter.

A scary dude by all accounts.

Took a lot to scare me, though—I had four brothers after all—and I was prepared to do what I had to do in order to keep the company solvent. Dad was counting on me since he didn't want my brothers to know the true state of the company finances, and I was very conscious of the fact that I didn't want to let him down.

Mine was a ropey plan, but it was the best I could come up with: sign myself on with the chauffeur company that Mr Evans used and hope that I would be assigned to him. It had taken a month for that to happen, but a combination of luck and the fact that he was enough of a prick that no one wanted to drive for him had worked in my favour and I'd been given the assignment of driving him in Paris for two days.

It was a sneaky move, but I'd run out of options, not to mention patience. I'd tried all the usual ways to get a meeting with him to talk about the investment face-to-face, but apparently that was impossible and all I'd managed to score were a couple of interviews with some minor flunkey who hadn't given a shit about either me or my dad.

Driving for him was the only way I could think of to meet with him in person, to convince him somehow to give us more time before withdrawing his money, because, with the current state of Australis's finances, we would go under the moment he withdrew.

Yeah, and you know whose fault that is.

I ignored that thought and glared at the shut door instead, raising my hand to knock again.

It was suddenly jerked open.

A man stood on the threshold, the height and breadth of him filling the entire doorway.

I blinked, getting a confused impression of an expanse of bare skin and hard-cut muscle. Then a pair of fierce blue eyes met mine and all the air in my lungs mysteriously vanished.

He stared at me suspiciously for a second and it occurred to me that every single aspect of me had just been observed, catalogued and filed away for future reference.

Then, just as suddenly as he'd opened the door, the man turned and strolled back into the suite, talking to someone on his phone as he went, his voice a deep, gritty rumble. He appeared to be wearing only a pair of worn blue jeans that sat low on his lean hips, leaving his massively muscled shoulders and back bare. A Chinese dragon had been inked into the smooth olive skin, the colours all brilliant blues, reds and greens.

I blinked again, staring, oddly shaken though I had no idea why. Because it wasn't as if I hadn't seen a shirtless man before. I'd also seen a fair number of tattoos in my time—my brothers all had them, plus I was involved in the car industry where it was practically *de rigueur*. Still, I hadn't seen anything quite as beautiful as that one.

I swallowed, for a second unsure whether to follow him or wait. But since I wasn't the waiting type I stepped into the suite, shutting the door behind me as I followed him into the lounge area.

He stood with his back to me, still talking on his phone and so I took a moment to study him.

Okay, so this was the scary Ash Evans.

I'd seen pictures of him—who hadn't? He was built like a heavyweight boxer with the height of a basketball player, his face scarred all to hell from an encounter with the wrong end of a knife back when he'd been a teenager. He was an absolute beast of a man—at least according to one gushing female journalist who'd been granted the rare privilege of an interview and had obviously been bowled over by him.

I'd scoffed at all the over-the-top language in the article—honestly, the way some women got when it came to men, I couldn't understand it. But being in his presence now, I could see what she was talking about.

Even though he had his back to me, he stood in the middle of the lavishly appointed room as if he owned it. No, more as if he owned all of Paris. A fierce kind of energy radiated from him, kinetic and masculine and utterly compelling.

I knew what it was. Two of my brothers were race car drivers and they both had it in spades: pure male confidence.

Luckily, I'd had plenty of practice in dealing with it and my solution was simply to be as confident and in-your-face as they were.

I waited patiently for Mr Evans to wrap up his conversation, staring at his beautiful Chinese tattoo until finally he'd finished and turned to face me.

Intense blue eyes met mine and my breath caught for the second time that day.

The pictures of him were one thing, but the reality was a whole different ball game. His features were blunt, but roughly handsome and somehow made even more compelling by the famous scars that bisected them. One scar narrowly missed his right eye, while another caught one end of his mouth and twisted it, making it look as if he was sneering. A third highlighted his hard, square-cut jaw. But it was those eyes that really dominated his rough-hewn face. They were *so* blue, electric almost, reminding me weirdly of lightning in a thunderstorm.

Hot.

The thought came out of nowhere, hitting me like a gut punch. Because he was, and I couldn't remember the last time I'd even noticed a guy in that way.

Since the Mark incident I'd put my love life on hold because I simply couldn't be bothered dealing with all the drama involved, and, so far, I hadn't met anyone who'd made me want to change my stance.

Not that Ash Evans was even in my league.

I didn't actually have a league.

Conscious that I'd been standing there, staring at him like an idiot, I shoved my momentary fluster away and I stuck out my hand. 'G'day, Mr Evans,' I said, going full Aussie. 'I'm Ellie Little. I'm—'

'What do you want?' His voice was as rough and gritty as sandpaper, and his stare skewered me like a pin through a butterfly. 'I told the hotel I wasn't to be disturbed.'

Obviously I was getting a taste of Mr Evans's famous rudeness. So far, so billionaire. And to be honest, nothing I hadn't come across before either driving or in the Australis workshop.

'I'm not from the hotel,' I said cheerfully. 'I'm your chauffeur.'

'Chauffeur?' He ignored the hand I was still holding out. 'I usually have Bill.'

'He wasn't able to make it to Paris. One of your assistants okayed a replacement.' I lowered my hand since it didn't look as if he were going to shake it. 'Don't worry, sir. I've been given a full rundown of your—'

'Don't call me sir. I'm Mr Evans to you.' He shoved his phone into the back pocket of his jeans. 'And my assistant never mentioned this.'

With some dudes if you gave them an inch, they took a mile, and clearly Evans was in this camp. I'd found the best way to deal with it was to be as laid-back as possible, all the while making it clear that you were not there to be walked over.

'I'm sorry you weren't contacted, Mr Evans,' I said easily, giving him a wide smile. 'But that's not really my problem. I'm just here to do my job.' And to fix Dad's little investment issue. But I couldn't ask him about that now; I needed to build up a little rapport with him first.

There was a silence.

Clearly he did not like my answer, because his gaze became arctic, the electricity in his eyes taking on a bright, cold glint. A sense of threat gathered around him and I could suddenly see why people might be scared of him because that, combined with his height and scarred face, made him pretty damn intimidating.

I wasn't intimidated, though. I'd dealt with plenty of difficult men in my time and not making things into a drama was the way to handle it.

So I simply stared back and kept my smile easy-going. Letting him know that I wasn't a threat so he didn't need to bristle at me the way he was doing now.

His eyes narrowed and I had the oddest feeling that his focus had shifted, zeroing in on me like a laser sight on a high-powered rifle.

It was unnerving since I didn't much like being stared at, but I didn't let my unease show. Keep it fuss-free, that was the Little way.

'Do you speak to all your employers like that?' he demanded.

'Yes,' I said, with absolute truth. 'And they've all appreciated my laid-back attitude.' I grinned wider. 'That's a direct quote by the way.'

A deep blue spark glinted in his eyes for a second and for some reason I felt an unfamiliar heat rise into my cheeks.

Weird. Why was I blushing? I kept my smile pasted firmly on and hoped the blush would go away.

'Fair enough.' He gave me a brief up and down glance then reached out to pick up the black T-shirt that had been draped over the back of a luxurious white couch. 'Though if you speak to me like that again, you won't last the night.'

I wasn't listening. I was too busy being oddly mesmerised by the flex and release of the chiseled muscles of his chest and abs.

Which wasn't like me *at all*. It was only that he was just so very…powerful. Like one of the Pythons, Dad's latest model supercar. Super charged and sleek, with a big V8 engine. The most perfect design. Dangerous in the wrong hands, yet an adrenaline junkie's dream in the right ones…

'Do you understand?'

I nearly jumped as the edge in his voice caught me, making me realise I'd been standing there gawping at him with my mouth open.

Dude. Zoning out staring at his body? What is wrong with you?

Purely from a design perspective he was an impressive specimen. Built for strength and power, with not an ounce of fat on him. He could probably deliver the maximum amount of force with maximum efficiency too—

You're not in the workshop now, idiot, and he's not a bloody car.

Oh, hell. Of course he wasn't. And now he'd caught me staring.

I struggled to find my normal chill, trying to think of a jokey way to defuse the situation.

'Uh, yes,' was all I could come up with.

His gaze narrowed further. 'You'd better,' he said, his upper-class British accent completely at odds with the roughness of his voice, his scarred face and worn jeans. 'I'm not accustomed to repeating myself.'

Concentrate, fool! It's like you've never seen a man before.

Well, to be fair, I hadn't seen a man like *him* before.

'Sorry, Mr Evans.' I grinned like an idiot, pretending I wasn't still blushing furiously. 'I was thinking about something else.'

He stared at me with the same intense focus as when he'd opened the suite door earlier. 'What did you say your name was?'

'Ellie. Ellie Little.'

Would my surname mean anything to him? Probably not. Evans Investment, his venture capital firm, invested money in a lot of different projects so there was no reason he'd know about our company in particular.

Sure enough, there was no recognition in his eyes as he unexpectedly put out his hand. 'Good to meet you, Miss Little.'

Now, he wanted to shake? A small, rebellious part of me was very tempted to refuse, which would have been stupid given the massive favour I had to ask of him at some point.

So I ignored the urge, reaching out to take his hand politely instead. Yet as his big palm and long fingers wrapped around mine, the weirdest thing happened.

A jolt of electricity shot straight up my arm, making me jerk my hand out of his before I could stop myself.

Good one, fool.

'Sorry,' I muttered. 'Damn static.'

An odd expression I couldn't quite decipher crossed his face, making the unsettled feeling inside me deepen.

My heart was beating fast and my skin was tingling where he'd touched me. It felt sensitive, as if I'd been scorched by his fingers.

It wasn't static, you idiot.

But I didn't want to think about what else it might have been so I shoved that thought away and put my hands behind my back instead. 'Ready when you are, Mr Evans,' I said, as if nothing had happened.

He gave me another of those intense searching looks, though what he was searching for I had no idea.

'Go down and wait in the car,' he said at last. 'I'll be down in a minute.'

With one last dismissive glance, he turned away, the colours of the tattoo on his back flashing, leaving me with no other option but to do as I was told.

CHAPTER TWO

Ash

I LOOKED OUT of the window of the limo, watching a string of couture-clad people file through the entrance into the elegant historic brick building, and allowed myself a certain sense of satisfaction.

Finally. Fucking *finally*.

Here I was, outside the door to the most exclusive private members' club in the world: The Billionaires Club.

Joining was by invitation only—an invitation that only came once your bank balance reached a certain level. A cool billion, obviously.

Mine had come a week ago in the form of a hand-delivered black envelope with a simple gold seal on the back and my name, Mr Ash Evans, written in cursive on the front.

Inside was a heavy slice of black platinum the size of a credit card, embossed with the club insignia: an M with two bars over the top of it, the Roman numeral for billion.

An exclusive club for the rich and famous.

And here was I, the scum of the streets, with a key.

Dad would be turning in his fucking grave. He'd have hated the thought of his bastard son finally having access to everything he'd denied him over the years.

Correction. Dad wouldn't hate the thought, because, even if he'd still been alive, he wouldn't have thought of me at all. *Not* thinking of me was all he'd done from the moment I was born, the product of an illicit affair with one of his maids.

Still, I wasn't going to let happy memories of my prick of a father ruin my evening, not tonight. I'd worked too long and too hard to get to this point and I had other, bigger fish to fry.

Fish like my half-brother and chief competitor, Sebastian Dumont. He was one of the reasons I'd decided that my first appearance at the club would be at their burlesque event in Paris. I knew he'd be attending and I wanted to shove my membership in his rich and privileged face. He wouldn't be expecting it and seeing me, his undeserving, lower-class half-brother, showing up where he didn't belong, would piss him off in the extreme.

Petty? Yes. Satisfying? Completely.

But that wasn't the only reason. I was also hoping to sabotage his latest business deal, too, just for the hell of it.

John Delaney, a property investor who was looking to sell a couple of islands in the Caribbean that he owned, was also going to be attending the event tonight, and my plan was to corner him and make him an offer for those islands.

I had a luxury hotel business that I'd just got off the ground and the islands Delaney was selling were perfect sites for it.

They were also the same islands that Dumont just happened to be after for *his* luxury hotel business.

Oh, Dumont had tried to keep his intentions under wraps, but I had my ways of finding out things. And now my entire plan was to buy those islands out from under him.

Yes, we had a rivalry. And to say it was mild was like saying England and Germany were slightly at odds during World War II.

It had been going on for years and I had no plans to build bridges any time soon. Not after what he'd done to me.

I flicked a glance in the rear-view mirror of the limo and found my chauffeur for the evening, the sexy little Australian, staring back at me.

And for a second, all thoughts of my hated half-brother vanished.

When she'd come to the door of my hotel, I'd been expecting Bill, white-haired and grizzled and pushing sixty-five. Instead, what I'd got was brunette and fresh-faced, and pushing twenty-five, if that.

Not to mention small and curvy, with a pretty, freshly scrubbed face, glossy brown hair in a no-nonsense ponytail, the usual chauffeur uniform of black trousers, white shirt and a black tie doing its best to hide the fact that she was unequivocally female.

Oh, yes, and she had a sunny attitude to match.

She hadn't appeared to notice my scars or to be in the

least bit intimidated by my manner, and she had looked me in the eye, which most people never did.

Then there had been that smile. That pretty smile like a bright burst of sunshine. As if she'd never heard of my reputation and had no idea what a bastard I was.

Those things shouldn't have made her so immediately fascinating to me, because she was nothing like my normal type. I preferred them beautiful and expensive-looking, all the better to soil with my rough, dirty hands, not with a dusting of freckles, dressed in a chauffeur's outfit, and telling me with a cheerful smile how my assistant not briefing me on her arrival wasn't her problem.

Not many of my employees would have dared say that to my face.

Correction, *none* of my employees would have dared say it.

What made her think she could?

She stared at me in the mirror, hints of gold and emerald glinting from beneath long, silky dark lashes, and there was no deference in her gaze. It was full of curiosity and a certain boldness that I found…exciting.

Been a long time since you had a worthy opponent.

Yes, it was true. A *very* long time. Not that I was into physical fights these days, at least not outside the gym and never with a woman. But it had been a while since I'd met anyone who could hold their own against me. And every fighter needed a challenge to improve their game.

If you didn't get better you didn't win, and if you didn't win, all you got was your teeth kicked in.

I'd never been a fan of getting my teeth kicked in.

She grinned at me. 'Are you ready to go, Mr Evans?' Her tone was ridiculously chirpy, yet her voice had a soft, smoky edge that somehow made it sexy at the same time.

She could be your challenge.

Nice idea, but no.

I'd felt the chemistry between us the moment she'd taken my hand back in the hotel room, and when she'd jerked away, her skin pink, I knew she'd felt it too.

Normally that would be something I'd explore, since I never denied myself something when I wanted it, but fresh-faced, tomboyish little Australians who should know better than to smile at men like me were not worth the trouble of tangling with.

And besides, I had a golden rule: never screw the staff.

She might only be a substitute for Bill for a couple of nights, but she was still a staff member. Which made her out of bounds.

'I'll go when I'm good and ready, Miss Little,' I growled, irritated for no good reason.

'Of course,' she replied with the same chirpiness, apparently impervious to my annoyance. 'You can sit here as long as you like. I only asked so I could be ready to open your door for you.'

My irritation increased. She looked so bright-eyed and bushy-tailed and eager to please.

You could think of a few ways she could please you.

Yes, but again, not happening.

I stared hard at her, trying to put a dent in her insufferable cheerfulness, but she kept staring boldly back, apparently impervious to my game. And also, apparently, unaware of the blatant challenge she presented by doing so.

A certain tension began to gather in the car, one she also seemed blithely unaware of. At least until I noticed a hint of red glowing in her freshly scrubbed cheeks.

So. Maybe she wasn't as unaware as she seemed. Not that I was going to be doing anything about it.

'Then what are you waiting for?' I said, unaccountably irritated with the direction of my thoughts. 'I'm ready now.'

Once again, she didn't bat an eye at my tone, immediately getting out of the car, coming around to my door, and pulling it open for me with a little flourish.

Normally I didn't bother with that kind of theatre, but tonight I was making an exception.

I glowered as I got out, unfolding myself to my full height, looming over her like the hulking, scarred beast that I was.

She was very small, her head tilting back as she gave me a searching look. Her forehead creased, her smile turning sympathetic. 'Don't worry, Mr Evans. You'll have a great night, I'm sure of it.'

The comment was so unexpected that for a second I had no idea what she was talking about.

'Do I look fucking worried?' I said.

Either she didn't hear my sarcasm or ignored it, because she gave me another thorough scan, her expression becoming serious. 'Actually, on second thought, you don't. You just look really grumpy.'

No one made casual observations about me quite like that. Certainly no one said them out loud. To my face.

I opened my mouth to give her another lesson in driver etiquette, but she charged on, giving me another sunny smile before reaching out to pat my arm. 'Don't let the bastards grind you down, eh?'

People didn't touch me, not these days. In fact, the only people who did were the women I took to bed.

No one ever patted me sympathetically on the arm.

No one would dare.

To make matters worse, the brief touch sent a ghost of the same electricity I'd felt back in the hotel sparking through the leather of my jacket and straight into me.

Christ. That was all I needed.

My temper, already mean, took a feral turn.

I glanced pointedly down at her hand on my arm. 'I'm not a dog, Miss Little.'

Colour bloomed in her cheeks. 'Oh. Sorry.' She dropped her hand, her cheerful smile returning. 'No worries.'

For some reason that didn't make me feel any less irritated.

Trying to ignore my inexplicable annoyance, I turned away without another word, starting towards the entrance of the hotel and pushing her out of my mind.

The pretty, rich people in their glittering couture gowns and perfect tuxes were gathered around the doors and they all stared at me as I approached.

I scowled, staring them down in turn.

I didn't miss their looks of disdain and the whispers, their glances at the limo and then at me in my jeans and black T-shirt, leather jacket thrown over the top. I knew what they were thinking. They were thinking that I couldn't possibly belong in their rarefied circles. I wasn't handsome enough, glittering enough, rich enough.

Poor bastards. They were in for one hell of a shock.

The thought mollified me and I was cheered still further by how they all rushed to get out of my way like antelopes before a lion as I strode for the door.

The impressive-looking doorman, though, was not an antelope and there was not a whiff of disdain from him. He gave me a nod and pulled open the door as soon as I approached, ushering me into the foyer with a simple, 'Welcome to The Billionaires Club, Mr Evans.'

I hadn't been expecting to be treated with respect and it took the wind out of my sails slightly.

The foyer was a huge space with an impressive staircase leading to the upper stories and a massive chandelier that dripped jewelled light into the vaulted space.

Directly in front of me was an ornate and obviously antique table with a huge spray of white orchids in a glass vase on top. The simplicity of the arrangement was in direct contrast to the chandelier and the table it sat on, and the floor of horrifically expensive Italian black marble. A few chaises longues were strategically placed for people to sit on, covered in luxuriously ostentatious gold silk.

The whole place reeked of money, the scent of the elite, the entitled, the privileged. The lucky, lucky few.

Of which I was now one, despite my father's best

efforts to keep me in my place, and my own half-brother's betrayal.

Fuck you, old man. And fuck you too, Seb.

I smiled savagely at the thought.

There was a woman waiting for me beside the table, tall and slim, with long blonde hair and the kind of perfectly groomed appearance that only the very wealthy could achieve.

She ignored my smile, didn't blink at my scars, simply held out a hand and said, 'Mr Evans, welcome to The Billionaires Club. I'm Imogen Carmichael. Pleased to meet you.' Her accent was American, east coast.

I took her hand, reining in my temper, because I could be pleasant when I wanted to be. 'Likewise.'

She gave me a cool smile in return. 'I'm glad you could make it to Paris to join us. Would you like a drink to start with or would you prefer it after the tour?'

'After. Since I received precisely nothing in the way of information, I want to know how this place works.'

A flicker of genuine amusement crossed her classically lovely face. 'That's intentional. Part of the mystique, you understand.'

'Of course. It's also pretentious as hell.'

She laughed. 'You're direct. I like it. In fact, if I'm not much mistaken, you'll fit right in.' Stepping back, she gestured towards a grand set of double doors opposite the main entrance. 'Right, I'll show you to the ballroom. We're in the middle of a burlesque gala event right now, which will give you a taste for the kinds of things we do.'

The club was as exclusive as it got, with a million-dollar membership fee per year. It was an extortionate amount, but I'd already figured out that membership could only benefit me. Evans Construction and Development, my property development firm, was going from strength to strength as it was, but the club would open doors when it came to growing Evans International, my luxury hotel chain. Especially when it came to stealing my half-brother's business from him the way he'd once stolen mine from me.

As Imogen showed me into the ornate ballroom, with high ceilings and yet more chandeliers, I took a glance around, scanning the glittering crowd for any sign of Dumont or my other quarry, Delaney. Suspended above the crowd by a pair of red, silken ribbons, a woman clad in nothing more than jewelled bikini bottoms and nipple pasties performed a sensual aerial act. Music with a heavy beat played while both men and women in risqué jewelled costumes circulated with trays of drinks.

'We hold gala events like this one all over the world and throughout the year,' Imogen murmured. 'And all the proceeds go to various nominated charities, as does fifty per cent of each member's buy-in.'

'Of course,' I said, listening with only half an ear as I searched the crowd. 'You must need the tax breaks.'

Imogen clearly heard the cynicism in my voice, because she raised a brow. 'It's all completely genuine, Mr Evans, I assure you. And most of our members help out by attending each event, though you can come and go as you wish. Right now, I'm in the middle of arranging the Christmas ball that will take place in New York, the money from which will also go to a very good cause.'

From the expression on her face she believed every word that she said, and maybe it was true. Maybe my cynicism had more to do with me than with her and this club.

Whatever. I wasn't here to debate charity and privilege, or to hear about parties. I was here to find Delaney and my brother.

As if sensing my impatience, Imogen gestured to another door. 'Come with me, I'll show you something else.'

We went through into another area, a series of plush interconnecting rooms full of subtle lighting, clusters of deep, velvet-covered armchairs and low tables. People were sitting either in groups or pairs, talking intently in low voices. It was all brandy balloons and Scotch glasses, expensive cigar smoke in the air, and the scent of money, of big deals being done.

My favourite hunting terrain.

'Our quiet area,' Imogen said as we passed through. 'Where members can relax and talk business or whatever else they might like.'

'Sounds like my kind of place,' I murmured, finally spotting Delaney sitting in a corner chatting to a group of people.

Good. He was here. Now to figure out where Dumont was.

We came back out into the entrance hall and Imogen gestured to the magnificent staircase that led up to the upper levels. 'And up there are our intimate suites, if you want to take a look.'

I raised an eyebrow, curious. 'Intimate suites?'

Imogen's smile turned secretive. 'The club provides for anything our members and their guests might need or want, and that includes some private spaces for blowing off a little steam.'

She didn't need to elaborate, I got the idea. And I approved.

'Now,' Imogen went on. 'That concludes the tour. You're free to join the other members in the ballroom or adjourn to the bar, whichever takes your fancy.'

The bar, obviously, since Sebastian was not in the ballroom. Besides, although I was very much into pretty girls dancing while wearing not a lot, I wasn't keen on the pointless posturing that was happening in the ballroom. Give a person a billion and they thought they were God's fucking gift. Half those arseholes hadn't had to work for what they had, not like I'd had to, and I wasn't going to stand around pretending I was as good as the rest of them.

I was better. And I saw no need to pretend.

The bar was off the main ballroom and was just as gilded and ornate, with quite a few people gathered at the tables and sitting in the gold-velvet-covered booth seats that ran down one wall. Light glittered and dripped from the chandeliers that hung from the ceiling, sparkling on jewelled necklaces and glinting off cufflinks. The low hum of voices filled the room along with the heavy beat from the ballroom.

People stared at me as I made my way to the bar and I let them look, enjoying the attention. Me, with my knife-fight scars, in my jeans and T-shirt amongst all the jewels and tuxes.

I didn't need to imagine what they were thinking. I knew, since it was written all over their faces. They were thinking I didn't belong. That I was scum from the streets, their reminder that, though they might be insulated from the hard cold realities of life by their wealth, hard cold reality was now also here amongst them.

It amused me. I also didn't give a shit. They could think what they liked. I'd earned my place here and too bad if they didn't like it.

Strolling up to the bar, enjoying the way the crowd rippled to give me space, I took another scan around before ordering a drink.

A pretty blonde in a red dress with diamonds sparkling around her neck sidled up to me smiling, her intent very clear.

She was just my type: rich, sophisticated and beautiful. Definitely the kind of woman who'd never let a guy like me, rough and blunt and scarred all to hell, touch her if I didn't have a billion dollars in my bank account.

Definitely a potential cure for the burn of thwarted attraction and annoyance my little chauffeur had ignited inside me.

I bought her a drink and she put her hand on my chest, leaning in to whisper something filthy in my ear. And that was when I finally spotted him.

He was standing right down the other end, one elbow propped casually on the bar, his head bent to talk to a brunette in a tiny black dress.

A deep satisfaction pulsed through me.

Sebastian Fucking Dumont.

My half-brother and once my closest friend. We'd

ruled the exclusive school my mother had forced my father to shell out for—the only money he'd ever given her
for me—and we'd had plans. So many fucking plans.

Until he'd stolen those plans for himself.

They say you're supposed to forgive and forget, but
I wasn't a forgiving kind of man. I never forgot a betrayal, either—and I hadn't forgotten his.

His blue eyes—so like mine—widened as they saw
me and I gave him a savage smile.

*Yeah, you rich fuck. Here I am, despite what you did
to me. Here, in your territory.*

Shock gave way to anger, and he frowned. As I expected. He'd be wondering what I was doing here and
why the club had let riff-raff like me into its elite halls.
And then, no doubt, he'd be calling someone to have
me thrown out for daring to gatecrash.

The bastard was in for a couple of big surprises. Especially when he eventually found out the islands he'd
been angling for were already sold. To me.

I smiled wider and gave him a jaunty one-finger
salute. *I'm a member of your precious club, motherfucker, and what are you going to do about it?*

He stiffened, turning away to say something to the
brunette before pushing his way through the crowd towards me.

But I was done.

I'd showed my face. I'd proved my point.

Time to find Delaney and buy those fucking islands.

CHAPTER THREE

Ellie

I CHECKED THE rear-view mirror again to make sure the entrance to the fancy hotel Mr Evans had disappeared into was still clear and, again, it was.

I didn't expect him to come back out so soon—not that I'd been given details of the event I'd dropped him off at—but I wanted to be ready when he did. Anything to make up for my little mistake earlier, when I'd attempted to defuse his mood by cheering him up.

I'd thought he looked apprehensive when he'd stared at the crowd outside the doors, so I'd given him a pat and a rousing 'don't let the bastards grind you down' talk the way I did with Jason, my oldest brother, when he was racing and feeling nervous.

Not a great plan in hindsight, because Mr Evans was not my brother, nor had he been feeling nervous, apparently, given his grumpy response.

Which meant that now I needed to be on my best behaviour, especially if I was going to be broaching the topic of Australis with him.

I'd hoped I would have made a good enough impression by this point that I could ask him about it tonight, but maybe that was too soon, especially given his temper.

Now that I'd been given a taste of his fearsome reputation, it seemed as if he'd come by it honestly, and the curious part of me wanted to know why. Was he genuinely a grumpy bastard all the time or did he just not like people? Did it have something to do with his scars? Or was there something else going on?

My research hadn't given me any clues since he never talked about his private life. There were all kinds of rumours about how he'd made his initial start-up money, but the general consensus was that he'd earned it in illegal street fights, which naturally the media ate up with a big spoon.

They had quite a fascination with him and now I'd met him, I could see why.

He was quite…magnetic.

I frowned out of the front windscreen, reflecting again on when and how I needed to approach the question of his Australis investment.

It was important I get this right, since there wouldn't be another opportunity to get close to him and if I didn't succeed, the company was more than likely going to tank.

If only Mark hadn't been drunk at the Christmas party and thought I was fair game. And if only I hadn't got angry when he'd grabbed me and kneed him in the balls.

But I had. I'd committed the cardinal sin of turning something minor into a big deal, and Mark had complained to Dad about 'assault' and talked about lawsuits. Dad had had no choice but to pay him off, thus losing the best designer we'd ever had, not to mention a large portion of the investment capital we'd been given by Evans Investment.

I'd then compounded my error by showing Dad a potential answer to our financial worries—the design for an electric supercar that I'd been working on for the past five years or so.

But he wasn't interested. He'd already been disapproving of how I'd handled Mark and he liked my electric car suggestion even less. He was an internal combustion engine man all the way and 'fancy, newfangled' ideas had no place at Australis.

There'd been no point making a fuss so I'd quietly shelved the supercar project, turning to other ideas to fix our money problems instead.

Some days I wondered if he would have liked me more if I hadn't been born the spitting image of my pretty, womanly, passionate mother. If I'd been born a boy instead.

Mum had died of cancer when I was seven and Dad had been destroyed by her loss. He hadn't even been able to look at me in the days following her funeral, so I'd put away my pretty dresses and swallowed my grief, and tried to act like my brothers instead.

But I couldn't change the basic shape of my face. And of course, I had her eyes…

Dad had never treated me the same way since.

An old grief caught in my throat, but I forced the

emotion down, distracting myself by glancing at the hotel entrance again.

This time I saw the doorman move to pull open the door and finally Mr Evans came striding out, his arm wrapped around a pretty blonde woman in a skintight red dress.

I only just suppressed a groan.

Bloody hell. There went any opportunity for a quiet word about Australis. If he was going to be entertaining women, I'd probably have to wait until tomorrow.

Annoyed and trying to ignore it, I got out of the car and hurried around the side to open the door, pasting on my usual smile.

The woman was tall and lovely, her dress beautiful, her make-up perfect. Just the kind of woman men liked. At least, she was definitely a woman my brothers would have liked.

She didn't look at me as she got in and I was expecting Mr Evans to ignore me the way she had, but he didn't. As I stood there holding the door, he glanced at me and those electric-blue eyes pinned me to the spot.

An intense, hot satisfaction glowed there and it was so at odds with the cold lightning that had been in them before that I could only stare, my breath catching.

But it was only a moment. The next second, he'd got into the car leaving me standing there staring into space, my heart beating unreasonably fast.

God, what was wrong with me? He was just a man. A rich man, yes, and powerful, but a man all the same. And I knew all about men. They were either stoic like my dad and my middle brother, Dev. Or they were cheeky and fun like my two older brothers, Jase and Justin. Or quiet like George, my youngest brother.

Or pretending to be nice and ending up a sleaze like Mark.

But Mr Evans didn't fit into any of those categories. There was something burning inside him that none of the men I knew had, something that sparked and crackled like an arc welder melting metal.

I had no idea why that fascinated me or why I'd ended up standing there staring into space because he'd glanced at me…

It's not static, remember?

But the thought was an uncomfortable one, so I pushed it away before it could settle, shutting the door and going around to the driver's side, getting back behind the wheel.

I reached up to adjust the rear-view mirror, catching a glimpse of the pair of them as I did so.

Mr Evans's dark head was bent and he was whispering in the woman's ear. She was sitting very close, half turned towards him, her hand spread on the broad expanse of his chest, and she gave a soft giggle.

Ugh. Were they going to carry on like that the whole way? Not that it was any of my business what they did and not that I was at all bothered by it. I'd seen worse over the years I'd been driving.

Ignoring my strangely hot cheeks, I jerked my gaze away from the mirror and stared out of the front windscreen instead.

'Back to your hotel, Mr Evans?' I tried to sound

cheerful and professional and completely relaxed about what was happening behind me.

'Yes,' Mr Evans said.

His voice had gone even deeper and grittier, a thread of heat curling through it, and, despite myself, I glanced into the mirror again, drawn inexplicably by the sound.

He was watching me, a hot blue flame glowing in the depths of his eyes.

My mouth dried and my heart kicked in my chest, which was totally ridiculous, because him looking at me shouldn't affect me like that. Not after Mark and the way he used to stare at me from behind his computer in the workshop. Making me feel as if I'd had a bath in a tub full of grease.

So there shouldn't have been any reason why I felt restless and hot. Why the expression in Mr Evans's eyes connected to something hungry inside me. Something he saw that I hadn't realised was there.

Something I didn't understand.

I looked away before I could stop myself and then felt instantly annoyed. As if I'd retreated somehow, which was a mistake when dealing with a guy like him.

Get it together, Little. You shouldn't be playing games anyway.

I definitely shouldn't, not that I was a game player anyway. But there was a reason I'd managed to manoeuvre my way into driving for him and it wasn't because he'd turned out to be hot shit on a stick.

I had a mission and I had to keep that in mind.

Determined not to look again, I started the limo and

pulled away from the kerb, concentrating squarely on driving and not on the man behind me.

Except I found the low rumble of his voice distracting. There was a velvety texture to it, a kind of huskiness that made me feel shivery.

The engines of the Pythons sounded like that. A deep purr, like a giant cat. I loved the sound of those engines, loved those cars, sleek and dangerous and powerful.

Taking one of them for a spin around the track was a huge rush, an adrenaline hit I'd craved right from the first moment I'd sat behind the wheel and the engine had turned over, throbbing like a giant heartbeat.

The rush of speed had been the perfect way to deal with all the messy teenage emotions I hadn't known how to handle, the emotions that Dad hadn't known how to handle either, and so I'd taken to the track to drive whenever I was feeling upset or needing an emotional release.

Speed was better than crying and there was nothing like hitting the gas hard and throwing a powerful car around a few corners.

Ever since then, the revving purr of a V8 engine had made me feel good. Made me feel reckless and powerful. And listening to Mr Evans talk, his voice thrumming through me like one of those engines, a deep vibrating rumble that I could feel in my chest and lower, in my sex, made me feel that same way.

What would it be like to drive him?

What a stupid thought. He wasn't a car. He was a man and probably wouldn't appreciate being driven anywhere.

Yet try as I might to concentrate on the road ahead of me, the thought wouldn't go away.

He was muscular and powerful, just like one of the Pythons. Would he take me on a wild ride if I put my hand on him? He probably wouldn't be as easy to drive, but he'd certainly be as hot. And he'd be hard, too, and the rumble of his engine…

There was a throb between my legs, a hot, raw feeling that I wasn't sure how to handle. I'd never felt this before, not for anyone, not even for my one lone high-school boyfriend.

Still think it's static?

Okay, no. It wasn't static. It was attraction. But that didn't make things any easier, because I still didn't know what to do about it.

Sex is what people usually do about it.

I glared out of the front windscreen as I manoeuvred the giant car through the narrow Parisian streets.

Sex was not happening. I'd had it a couple of times with that one single boyfriend and it had been nice but forgettable. Certainly not worth trying it with Mr Evans, even if he had been interested, which I was sure he wasn't. Not given the woman he was with now.

Anyway, he was clearly a man who was used to being in charge and, after Mark and his handsy ways, I wasn't keen on letting any guy take charge of me.

Apart from anything else, I was supposed to be asking him for more time on the Australis investment, not…anything else.

The lights were red at the intersection ahead of me so I stopped, irritatingly conscious of Mr Evans's voice rumbling again, followed by more feminine laughter and then a soft gasp.

Don't look. Don't look.

I wasn't going to look. I wasn't curious. I didn't need to see what was happening behind me.

Of course I looked.

And the way the rear-view mirror was positioned gave me the perfect view of one of his large hands cupping her breast over the fabric of her dress, his thumb moving lazily back and forth over her nipple.

I blinked, a weird flashback hitting me. Of how Mark had grabbed me from behind, squeezing me and pinching me, and how it had hurt. He'd been rough and I'd been taken by surprise, unable to jerk away until it was too late.

Yet the woman didn't seem to find what Mr Evans was doing to her unpleasant. She was arching into his hand as if wanting more. And…it seemed as if he was holding her carefully, his thumb moving gently, lightly…

Unexpectedly, my own nipples hardened, pressing against the cotton of my bra, and I had to jerk my gaze away, my face flaming.

Bloody hell, what was I thinking? Staring at my clients wasn't at all professional. And as for getting turned on by it…

No. Just no.

The light changed colour and I put my foot on the accelerator, determined to ignore what I'd just seen.

But Mr Evans made another of those deep, purring

sounds and it shivered through me, making my mouth go dry and the throb in my sex even more intense.

Was it the blonde making him sound like that? And why? What was she doing?

Madness. I shouldn't even want to look again, let alone be battling the sudden and intense desire to do just that.

Another set of lights was up ahead, turning red as soon as I approached.

I wasn't going to look. I wasn't.

But I couldn't help myself. I did.

His hand had moved to her butt, curving around it possessively, while hers had shifted from his chest and down between his powerful thighs, her fingers spread as she cupped him through his jeans, her red nails standing out against the blue denim.

I swallowed, trying vainly to get some moisture into my bone-dry mouth.

Her fingers were lazily stroking up and down, tracing the outline of something very long and very thick, and his thighs were spread wide, giving her room, as if he was enjoying very much what she was doing to him.

A hungry feeling pulsed inside me, my palms sweaty as I gripped the steering wheel.

This time I couldn't drag my gaze away. I was glued to the view in the mirror, mesmerised and not even sure why.

There was something hypnotic about the way her fingers moved on him, about the shape of his cock beneath the denim, that caught my attention, twisting my curiosity tight and refusing to let go.

What did he feel like? Was he hot? Was he as hard as he looked? Would he make that soft bass rumble for me if I touched him?

Need throbbed between my thighs, my hands itching to touch.

I loved driving, and chauffeuring satisfied that need in me, but I also loved design. There was nothing that gave me as much pleasure as the clean lines and curves of a beautifully designed car, form and function perfectly melded.

I wanted to see Mr Evans's form. I wanted to see the lines and curves of him, and whether he'd be as beautifully designed for power and strength as he seemed to be. I already knew his torso was a work of art, but what about the rest of him?

My heartbeat accelerated like one of the Pythons, revving hard.

The mirror didn't show his face and suddenly I wanted to see it. Wanted to know what his scarred features looked like when he was turned on and whether those intense blue eyes were still full of heat and not just lightning.

With a hand that shook only slightly, I reached up to adjust the mirror so I could see. Then froze as his gaze clashed with mine.

Electricity sizzled through me and this time there was no static to blame.

It was all him.

'The light is green, Miss Little,' he said in his deep, rough voice.

And it took me at least five seconds to process what he was saying. And then I did.

Oh, crap.

My face burned and I wrenched my gaze away, pressing my foot down hard on the accelerator. Too hard. Much to my shame the car bunny-hopped a couple of times before I managed to bring it under control again. I stuttered an apology, keeping my attention resolutely forward this time.

He didn't answer, but I was just about combusting with embarrassment, angry with myself for staring when I knew I shouldn't, and also at my own reaction. At the pulsing, insistent ache between my thighs.

I didn't understand it. Australis's continued existence was on the line and here I was, letting some stupid sex stuff distract me. And now he'd caught me watching him…

He'll probably fire you.

Shit. The thought made my palms even more sweaty.

I tried to dismiss it, plaster my smile in place, get back into a more professional space, but I was still blushing furiously by the time I pulled the car up outside Mr Evans's hotel.

'Stay there, Miss Little,' he growled as I reached to undo my seat belt.

Oh, great.

He said something to the woman that I didn't catch, but I didn't dare look this time to see what was going on.

Instead I waited, staring out of the widow, listening to the rear door open and then close with a *thunk*.

There was a long silence.

Eventually, I had to glance in the mirror, because the suspense was killing me.

The blonde had gone, but Mr Evans hadn't.

He was still sitting in the back seat.

And he was staring straight at me.

CHAPTER FOUR

Ash

I HAD NO idea what Miss Ellie Little was playing at, but one thing I did know: she needed to stop.

Because I was finding that having my fresh-faced chauffeur steal little glances in the rear-view mirror, watching me while the blonde stroked my cock through my jeans, was surprisingly erotic. And that if she kept on doing it, she was going to find herself spread out on the back seat of the limo, naked, with me on top of her.

Which obviously could not happen.

I should be thinking about screwing my beautiful blonde friend instead, because she was sexy and experienced and definitely not working for me. Unlike Miss Little.

Which meant I should *not* be thinking about Miss Little's sneaky glances in the mirror, watching us from her place in the driver's seat, her gaze darkening as she realised what was happening. Colour flooding her clear skin, making her freckles stand out, and her lush red mouth open.

Or thinking about how watching the blonde and me was turning her on.

Or about the realisation that it wasn't so much what the blonde was doing to me that was making me hard as it was Ellie's reaction.

It was obvious she didn't want to look and yet hadn't been able to help herself, and I liked that very much.

Too much.

I'd got under her insufferably chirpy skin, flustered her; made her blush. And I found that incredibly satisfying, especially after she'd steadfastly refused to show any reaction to me or my temper.

Except there's nothing you can do about it.

Irritation gnawed at me. Even though she was only driving for me temporarily, she was still an employee and that was a line I never crossed.

And it irritated me still further that the thought she was forbidden only made me harder, perverse bastard that I was.

The lights from outside illuminated Ellie's face in the mirror and the deep blush still burning in her cheeks. I could even see the scattering of freckles across her nose. She was clearly embarrassed yet she didn't look away. 'Uh, so I guess I'm fired now, right?' she said, that cheerful smile trying to make an appearance again, though it wasn't as confident as it had been before. 'Perving at the clients isn't exactly a good look, I know, but—'

'Want to tell me why you were staring at my dick?' I demanded, not letting her finish, impatient with the attraction that burned in my blood and with the hard-on in my jeans that refused to subside no matter how unwanted it was.

Her smile faltered, green sparks of irritation flickering to life in her hazel eyes, and that didn't help. Because I did not need further signs that I was getting to her. Not given the state I was in.

'To be fair, I could hardly *not* stare at your dick,' she pointed out. 'Especially when it was in my face every time I had to check my rear-view mirror.' She tried again with the smile, though it was even less convincing this time. 'And hey, if you really didn't want me to see, you should have put the partition up.'

She might have been trying to make a joke of it, but I heard the note of challenge in her husky voice and it hit me like a shot of adrenaline, making my cock even harder than it was already.

Fuck, she had guts confronting me like that.

Respect stirred inside me even as my anger deepened, mostly at myself for not simply getting out of the car and going after the blonde, whom I could at least have in my bed without all these moral quandaries.

And it didn't help that she was right. I *should* have put the partition up. But I hadn't. Because I liked her watching.

My jaw ached, tension crawling through my shoulders.

I'd come out of the club so pleased with myself, because my meeting with Delaney had gone extremely well. My price for the islands was significantly more than what Dumont had offered him and he'd been into the idea. Though not without a few unexpected caveats.

The islands had been in his family for years and he had a certain sentimental attachment to them, going on to tell me that he'd hoped to sell them to someone who was family-minded, too.

I wasn't family-minded in the slightest, but to get those islands away from Dumont, I could pretend, so I'd muttered some nonsense about a girlfriend and how we were looking to get serious. Delaney had been surprised, but very positive, and told me he'd be in touch in a couple of days, likely with good news.

It had all been very satisfying. As had been the prospect of a couple of hours' pleasure with the blonde.

But not now. Now the thought of the blonde left me cold.

Get out of the car, you stupid bastard.

I should get out of the car. Not sit here, hard and annoyed because I wanted a woman I shouldn't touch.

But I didn't.

And she was still looking at me in the rear-view mirror, gold glowing through the green in her eyes, like the sun through leaves on a hot summer's day. Making me realise that I was cold and had been for quite some time.

Except the gold in her eyes now was different from the sunny cheerfulness of before. There was a smoky heat to it that was definitely not forced.

Where there's heat, there's fire.

Oh, yes, I could see hints of that fire now, glowing embers in her gaze that wouldn't take much to ignite…

'You shouldn't look at me like that.' My voice was rough and harsh in the dense silence of the car. 'Not if you're not ready to face the consequences.'

'What consequences?' Her hands were curled around the steering wheel, making me think of how it might feel to have those delicate fingers wrapped around my cock.

Did she really have no idea? Could she not feel this tension between us? Static, she'd said back at the hotel, a response that had seemed genuine. Which meant she was probably inexperienced.

Yet another reason for me to get the fuck out of the car and not sit here like a bloody fool, staring into her pretty gold eyes.

'What consequences do you think?' I snapped, my temper getting a mean edge. 'I don't want to fire you, Miss Little. I want to fuck you.'

Shock flickered over her face. 'What?'

'Don't act so surprised. Did you really think those little glances you kept stealing wouldn't get me as hard as a rock?'

She blinked rapidly. 'Uh… Are you sure you're not talking about the blonde chick? I mean, she was the one who had her hand on…um…you.'

Was she serious? Or was she playing with me? Some women liked that kind of game, but I didn't. I preferred straight-up honesty, especially when it came to sex.

However, there was no doubting the surprise in Ellie's eyes: she really had thought it was the blonde.

'No, I'm not talking about the "blonde chick",' I said, increasingly annoyed at the hard-on in my jeans and my apparent inability to get the fuck out of the car and away from her. 'You kept looking at me like you wanted to join in.'

Her cheeks turned an even deeper red. 'I didn't want to join in.'

'No? Then why did you keep staring?'

'I…' She looked away. 'I'm sorry. I shouldn't have. That wasn't very professional.'

'Screw being professional. Just answer the bloody question. And look at me when I'm talking to you.'

She stiffened then abruptly twisted around in her seat so she was facing me, the dusting of freckles across her nose even more fascinating close up without the distancing effect of the mirror.

Gone was the cheerful smile. Green sparks of anger danced in her eyes instead and they were every bit as interesting as her freckles.

'Look, you're being a bit bloody rude,' she said flatly. 'I'd heard of your reputation, but seriously, mate, you need to tone it down. I'm just doing my job.'

Mate? She'd really just called me 'mate'?

This pretty little thing in her chauffeur's cap, who didn't know what the hell she was getting into, thought she could talk to me like that? Because if so, she really did have no idea what she was doing.

I was a man who liked a fight, who was all about the challenge. And if that challenge was a pretty woman I could get down and dirty and sweaty and raw with? Who I could take apart with pleasure, make her beg, make her want all kinds of filthy things?

Fuck, yes.

Which made me too much for this sweet-faced girl, no matter how badly she called to the warrior in me.

The blonde would have been able to handle me. The blonde knew what she was getting into.

You don't want the blonde.

And that was the problem. I didn't.

'Say that again, and there will be consequences.' I didn't disguise the naked threat in my voice. It was explicit.

She didn't appear to hear it. 'So you keep saying. What exactly are these consequences, then?'

'You don't want to know.'

'If you're too bloody afraid to say them out loud then maybe you shouldn't go throwing vague threats around.' Gold glittered briefly in her eyes. *'Mate.'*

If that wasn't a gauntlet thrown down, I didn't know what was.

Exhilaration pulsed through me and I leaned forward, getting in her face, giving her a taste of what it would be like to tangle with me and enjoying the way her breath caught in response.

'You're a pretty thing, Miss Little. And pretty things shouldn't mess with men like me.'

'Pretty thing?' she echoed, incredulous. 'Dude, seriously?'

'You're pretty and you're a little thing.' I leaned forward even more, getting closer. 'And I eat pretty little things for breakfast.'

We were almost nose to nose, but she didn't move away or back down. She was so close. Close enough for me to see the fine grain of her skin and the sparks of gold and green glowing in her eyes. To feel the heat of her body and smell the warm, musky scent of her.

Her pulse beat fast at the base of her throat and her mouth looked soft and kissable. Fuckable, too.

'That's not at all patronising.' She glared at me. 'How would you like it if I called you…big dick or something?'

Oh, yes, I was getting to her. I very definitely was.

Desire spiked in my blood, a hot, raw feeling. 'I'd like it just fine,' I said roughly, trying to resist the urge to grab her hand, draw it over my fly and hold it down so she could feel how big I actually was.

She went scarlet and I didn't miss the way her gaze dropped to my groin, where my cock was pressing hard against the denim. 'Of course you would,' she muttered. 'But firstly, I'm not pretty or a thing. And secondly, you're not…uh…' She stopped.

'Big?' I finished. 'Are you sure about that?'

Her hazel gaze flicked up, the fire I'd sensed in her beginning to ignite. 'What? You want me to check?' She sounded defiant and angry, yet the heat in her eyes told a different story.

I went very still. 'Be careful what you ask for, Miss Little. Because you might just get it.'

She stared at me, no trace of that sunny smile evident now. 'You think I can't handle you?'

'I *know* you can't handle me.'

'Oh, yeah?' Heat flared in her eyes. 'Try me.'

I shouldn't have goaded her, because I knew what her reaction would be. And I knew myself. I knew what I liked. And the fact that she was responding without fear, without being intimidated by me…

Christ, it was the biggest turn-on I'd had in years.

I wanted to see what she would do, whether she'd rise to the challenge. Whether I could get under her skin as deeply as she was getting under mine.

'You want to touch me?' I said it out loud so there could be no mistake. 'You want to feel me for yourself?'

She didn't blink this time. Not once. 'Yes.'

The word was thick and breathed out, making my fucking cock ache, and I had to grit my teeth against the intense rush of desire.

'Give me your hand, then.' I tried not to make it an order.

Without hesitation, she held out her hand and I took it. Her palm was small, her fingers delicate, her skin very soft. Electricity bolted the length of my arm, a direct line straight to my dick.

And she must have felt it, too, because her breath caught, her eyes widening. But she didn't pull away. If anything, her chin lifted higher.

So I slowly drew her hand to where I wanted it, over the front of my jeans, holding her gaze all the while. And she never once looked away, the fire in her eyes burning brighter, hotter.

I held her palm down, letting her feel how hard I was. Letting the heat of her hand seep through the fabric and into me.

Her pretty mouth became a perfect O of surprise as her fingers closed over my aching hard-on. Then, finally, she looked down. 'Oh…uh…wow.'

I wasn't sixteen any more. I didn't need a woman to look in awe at my cock. So why I felt such pleasure at her reaction I had no idea and, like so many of my interactions with this fascinating woman, it irritated the hell out of me, even as it turned me on.

'I did tell you,' I bit out, my voice much rougher than it should have been.

The flush in her cheeks showed no sign of abating. 'Sorry, that sounded dumb. But seriously…' Her gaze rose to mine, searching. 'Does that…uh…feel good? When I touch you, I mean?'

I should have stopped her. I should have taken her hand off me and got out of the car. Because I was crossing a line here and I knew it.

But I didn't do either of those things.

'Yes.' I held her fascinated gaze. 'It feels fucking good.'

Her mouth curved, as if she was pleased with the news. Then she bit her lower lip, her fingers moving hesitantly over me, tracing the line of my dick through the denim, watching my face intently as she did so.

I'd never been looked at like that before, not even when I'd been street fighting and an opponent was sizing me up. Sex for me was usually about making my partner come and come hard, that was how I got off. They generally didn't pay me the same attention, mainly because I refused to let them.

So I didn't know why I was letting her now. But, Christ, it was good. Too good. My muscles went tight, my jaw aching.

'Wow,' she murmured for the second time. 'You're *really* hot. Like an engine.'

An engine? What the hell?

But then her fingers spread out and she gave me an

experimental squeeze, and all thoughts vanished from my head as a wave of pleasure rolled over me.

'Fuck,' I muttered hoarsely, my hands closing into fists to stop myself from reaching for her.

A crease deepened between her silky dark brows. 'Sorry. Was that too hard?'

'No.' I could barely get the word out. 'But you're done.'

My control was good but it wasn't limitless.

'Oh?' She frowned. 'But I haven't finished checking.'

I glowered, my prick throbbing, lust firing in my blood, my temper in no way helped by the firmness of her grip. 'Yes, you have. I suggest you take your hand off me now, Miss Little. I'm not made of fucking stone.'

There was an intensity in her stare now, as if she was weighing something up in her head, and she didn't take her hand away, the heat of her palm destroying me second by tantalising second. 'Are you sure? I mean... I could do something about it, if you like.'

Oh, Christ.

There were so many fucking reasons *not* to. She was my employee and I didn't want to cross that line as my bastard father had with my mother. She was also inexperienced and in no way ready to handle what I wanted from her.

Then again, it had been a long time since I'd been with a woman I'd actually wanted because of who she was and not because of what she represented. A long time since I'd been with a woman who looked at me the way Ellie Little was looking at me, as if she saw the dirty street fighter that still lurked inside me and wasn't afraid.

So, why not? It would be the perfect ending to a perfect night.

'Yes,' I said, staring at her, noting how the dusky red in her skin made those little freckles stand out. How the pulse at the base of her throat was fast and getting faster. The way her white shirt pulled across the full curves of her breasts as she breathed. 'I would very much like you to do something about it.'

CHAPTER FIVE

Ellie

I COULDN'T BREATHE. I *literally* couldn't. Not while Mr Evans stared at me as if he wanted to eat me alive.

And I wanted him to.

Or rather, I wanted to climb into the back seat, crawl into his lap and put my hands on him. Discover the contours of his body, get his engine revving hard, experience the thrill of being at the wheel, handling all that raw power. Speeding down the track…

I had no idea how I'd gone from being embarrassed and expecting to be fired to having my hand on his cock, but it was probably to do with the way he'd goaded me.

I'd tried not to make a fuss about how he'd busted me staring at him in the mirror, tried to keep it jokey and light instead, but he hadn't let me. He'd been all pissy and rude, and when I'd confronted him, he'd stared at me with those electric-blue eyes and told me bluntly that he wanted to fuck me.

I'd been as much shocked as I had been turned on.

Then I'd got angry at being turned on and things had somehow escalated from there until here I was with my hand on his cock, wanting to fuck him as badly as he apparently wanted to fuck me.

Thoughts of my father and Australis had vanished. The doubts I'd had about touching him, about the way he was looking at me, about memories of Mark had dissipated like smoke.

Because this was nothing like what had happened with Mark.

Mr Evans hadn't made a grab for me, even though I'd put my hand on him. Even though I'd goaded him as much as he'd goaded me.

No, he'd just sat there and let me touch him, the hard set of his jaw and the fire in his eyes telling me exactly what my hand was doing to him.

It was intoxicating. He was a supercar in human form. Powerful, sleek, dangerous and difficult to manage. But, oh, how I wanted to manage him.

And why not? I knew how to drive a car. Driving a man wasn't that different.

Are you sure that's a good idea? This isn't Davey and you're not at school any more.

No, I was a grown woman and Mr Evans was definitely nothing like my high-school boyfriend.

He was more than that, he was a challenge I simply couldn't resist, and wasn't going to. Because who knew when I'd meet a man like this again?

I might not ever. In which case this would be my only chance to take him out for a spin…

Mr Evans was sitting sprawled out in the back seat,

the whole car full of an intense, thrumming energy, like an engine at full rev.

And he was looking at me as if daring me to take him on.

God, he was mesmerising. Even sitting there apparently relaxed he looked dark and arrogant and powerful.

He wasn't a beautiful man—he was too rugged, too rough and scarred, for beauty. Yet he was phenomenally attractive all the same. Blue eyes and a hard jaw, powerful chest and lean hips. A long, thick ridge behind the denim of his fly...

A thought suddenly occurred to me. 'What about your blonde?'

'What about her?'

'She's waiting for you.'

His glower intensified, but without a word he reached into his pocket and drew out his phone, looking down at the screen to type in a quick message. Then he threw the phone carelessly down on the seat next to him. 'She's not waiting any more. The hotel staff will make sure she's looked after.' The ferocity in his face grew impossibly fiercer. 'Happy?'

I didn't respond. Instead, with no grace at all, I launched myself out of the driver's seat and into the back.

He reached for me before I'd completed the movement, catching me by my hips and pulling me into his lap so I sat facing him, my thighs spread on either side of his lean waist.

Right where I wanted to be.

For a moment all I could do was sit, my heartbeat

thundering in my head as the reality of the situation began to form around me, a cage of heat, of sensation. Of need.

Sitting on him was exactly like sitting directly on top of a V8 engine.

Hard. Hot. And so powerful.

Excitement clogged my throat and I put my hands out to press against the wall of his chest and, sure enough, that was hard and hot, too, power thrumming through him.

God, he felt amazing.

'Oh.' I breathed out slowly, my palms pressing harder, lost for words. 'Oh…wow… You're…like… wow…'

His gaze burned up into mine, the rough lines of his face tight and fierce. His hands tightened and he shifted, flexing his hips, the ridge of his dick pressing against me in the most incredible way, sending a bolt of pleasure right through me and making me gasp aloud.

But Mr Evans wasn't simply a machine waiting for me to turn the key. He was already running.

He lifted a hand, his fingers curling around my black tie, tugging on it at the same time as he leaned forward, catching my mouth with his.

Heat poured through me in an overwhelming wave.

I'd never had a kiss like it. Oh, I'd kissed my high-school boyfriend quite a bit, but comparing him to Mr Evans was like comparing a Mini Cooper to a Lamborghini. They were both men and both had mouths but, as far as similarities went, that was it.

Mr Evans took my mouth as if he owned it, his

tongue pushing inside, exploring, demanding a response. He tasted rich and dark, like my favourite chocolate, with a sharp, spicy edge that took my hunger and amplified it somehow.

I leaned into him, my fingers spreading out on his chest, kissing him back with a desperation I couldn't hide, unable to stop the moan that ripped from my throat.

His grip tightened on my tie in response, holding me still. Then he took the cap off my head and threw it on the seat next to him, before pulling my hair free of my ponytail and letting it spill over his free hand.

He made a soft, rumbling sound of approval before he took my mouth again in another hard kiss, nipping at my bottom lip, sending little electric shocks of pain jolting through me.

I groaned, the kiss intensifying the ache between my thighs.

Unable to keep still, I curled my fingers into the cotton of his T-shirt, tugging at it, desperate to touch him as I kissed him back, to feel his skin and the hard muscle beneath under my hands.

He didn't move, ravaging my mouth, his grip keeping me right where I was. But I was in the driver's seat and I wanted to drive.

Acting on an instinct I hadn't known I'd possessed, I ground myself down on his lap, twisting so the hard ridge of his cock was pushing against my throbbing clit, sending hard, sharp pulses of pleasure spiralling through my veins.

A growling sound escaped him, the vibration of it

echoing through my entire body, thrilling me, making me so aware of him and his power, his strength.

I'd never felt so hungry for something in my entire life. Hadn't known I could even feel this hungry, as if it had been inside me all this time just waiting for the right man to release it.

My hands shook as I clawed at his T-shirt, dragging it up, and then the hot, oiled silk of his chest was bare and I was touching him, prickles of hair a delightful abrasion against my skin, the rock-hard feel of his muscles a glory.

Oh, yes, he was just like one of those cars, smooth and sleek, the bass rumble of his engine a delicious thrum as I touched him.

I could handle this. Oh, I could *more* than handle this.

I opened my mouth, kissing him harder, shifting my hips impatiently, being demanding.

He bit me, a firm nip on my bottom lip that made me gasp, then let go of my tie and took his hand from my hair…before jerking my shirt open with one hard, sharp movement.

I trembled, the air cool on my heated skin, and then he was pulling aside the cups of my bra, his big, warm hands cupping my breasts, long fingers pinching my nipples.

I shuddered as sparks of pleasure and delicious points of pain electrified every nerve ending I had. It felt so good, I could hardly believe it. I had the distant thought that after Mark, having someone touching me should have been uncomfortable, but it wasn't. This made the throb between my legs more intense, the pleasure more acute. No wonder the blonde had been leaning into him.

'Oh, my God,' I whispered in amazement, arching into his hands as he flicked his thumbs over my achingly hard nipples.

'Yes, you like that, don't you?' His voice was as deep and dark as it could possibly get. 'Now who's boss, pretty thing?'

'Me,' I replied, gasping as he pinched me again. 'I'm the one driving.'

'Are you, now?' His thumbs circled around each nipple, gentle now, teasing me mercilessly. 'Then by all means, take the wheel.'

So I did, spreading my hands out on his chest and pushing him firmly against the back of the seat. Then I reached down to the button on his jeans, pulling at it, trying to get it open.

He was so hot and he smelled musky, with the bite of some dark spice that had me nuzzling down the side of his neck, biting it so I could taste his skin, kissing his collarbones and nipping at him.

He cursed, his powerful body tightening, and I clamped my thighs around his waist to let him know that I had no intention of moving and that I didn't want him to, either.

But his hands were moving too, finding the button on my trousers and deftly flicking it open as I fumbled with his jeans, then he was pushing beneath the cotton of my knickers, his fingers sliding against my slick flesh.

Stars burst behind my eyes as a whip of pure pleasure licked across me, tearing another gasp from my throat.

His other hand settled on the small of my back, urging me forward and against his stroking fingers.

'Oh...' I gasped. 'I... *God*...'

'Still driving, hmmm?' he purred in my ear, all arrogant male satisfaction.

I tried to pull myself together, tugging at his jeans, desperate to get them open and my hands on him so I could stay in charge, but he'd already found my clit and, for all his brute strength, his touch was so gentle, so light that, much to my horror, I felt the prick of tears.

No. How was this happening? I hadn't cried for years, not since my mother's funeral, so why was I crying now? Why was having someone else touch me so much more intense than when I touched myself? Because it was. And I had no idea why.

I shuddered helplessly, all thoughts about fighting him for control fading away, crushed by the weight of pleasure building inside me.

'Why don't you let me drive for a change?' His voice was a low, dark rumble, his finger stroking gently, making me rock against him, desperate for more.

'Yes,' I panted, barely aware of what I was saying, turning my face into his neck as pleasure gathered tight as a fist inside me. 'Yes, okay...please.'

There was something to this, to simply letting him do what he wanted. Like giving myself up to the machine carrying me, to the speed of it. Trusting that it wouldn't crash somehow.

Strange to give that trust to a man I didn't know.

But I did it all the same, shifting my hips against his hand as his finger slipped and slid around my clit, his other hand pressing hard against the small of my back. 'Oh, Mr Evans…'

'That's sexy, pretty thing. But I think you can call me Ash now.'

I shuddered as his finger eased inside me, testing me. 'A-Ash…'

'Better,' he growled. 'I like the way you say my name when my fingers are in your pussy.' And he pushed another in, stretching me.

I moaned, pleasure breaking over me in waves as his fingers slid in deep. Then out. Then in.

My fingers curled on his chest, digging into the heavy muscle of his pecs as I tried to move against him, impatient now and increasingly desperate. 'More,' I whispered. 'Faster.'

'Patience.' His fingers slowed. 'Remember who's driving.'

But I'd never been one for patience.

My hands were shaking as I made one last frustrated attempt to get his jeans open but this time I managed it. And then I was pushing beneath the denim and into his boxers, finding the huge, hard length of his cock.

He hissed as I wrapped my fingers around him and for a second I forgot what he was doing to me, the velvety feel of his skin so unexpected. But the heat was there—oh, God, so much of it.

I tightened my fingers, relishing the way he jerked in my grip.

But that was where I miscalculated.

One minute he was sitting there like a car before a race, engine rumbling, my foot on the gas and my hands on the wheel. The next he surged beneath me as if the flag had dropped.

With effortless strength, he pushed me back, holding me as he somehow stripped my trousers off, taking my underwear with them. I thought he was going to put me on my back and I opened my mouth to protest, wanting to stay in his lap, but before I could say a word he settled me back where I was, my thighs spread over him, the denim of his jeans rubbing against my tender skin.

Panting, I stared at him, for a second unable to move.

His blue eyes met mine with so much ferocity I couldn't breathe, and he didn't look away as he reached behind him, shifting to get something out of his pocket. His wallet. Then he took a small foil packet out of it. A condom.

'Still with me?' he demanded as he ripped open the packet, his gaze searching.

'Yes.' My voice was little more than a croak. 'Can I…?' I reached for the condom, wanting to put it on him, touch him, feel the rock-hard length of him for myself.

'Hell, no.' He ignored my hands. 'Not this time.'

And I didn't have time to be disappointed, because he'd rolled down the condom and lifted me before I could protest, setting me back down, something long and hard and thick easing into me.

I gasped as he put his hands on my hips, pushing me down at the same time as he thrust up, impaling me.

The pleasure was almost agonising and I cried out, overwhelmed by an intense feeling of fullness, as if he were taking up all the air in my body and there were no room for me.

I shuddered, the unexpected sensation making me feel strangely panicky, my eyes prickling again.

But he must have sensed my distress, because his hands were stroking down my back, soothing me. 'Easy,' he murmured. 'Take it slow.'

His blue gaze was a lifeline I could hold on to and I did, staring back, my hands on his shoulders, shivering as he began to move, surging up into me, his fingers shifting to my hips and moving me with him, showing me the way to go.

The panicky feeling receded, leaving me with the same breathless hunger I'd felt before and a pleasure that pushed at my boundaries, making me gasp and shake.

He kept moving, thrusting up into me, hard and deep, pulling away from me, like those big cars. Taking control.

And I let myself go, let myself feel the speed, moving with him faster and faster, the power of his hot, hard body pushing into mine, taking me with him, a race to the finish.

I could have raced for ever.

But then he took my hand and brought it down between us, putting my fingers against my own wet flesh and holding them down as he thrust, deeper, harder.

Then there was lightning behind my eyes, an explosion of heat inside me, petrol igniting and pleasure cascading through my body. So much pleasure…

I opened my mouth to scream but he covered it with his own, drinking down my release as he moved, faster and out of control, chasing his own ending.

Afterwards there was nothing but silence, the car

full of the desperate sounds of our breathing. I couldn't move, my body heavy and sated, happy to rest against his strength and immense heat.

Then the aftershocks of the orgasm began to recede and I began to feel cold and shaky. And somehow he must've sensed it, because he slid his hands from my hips and up my back, then down again, stroking me slowly, lightly, like a cat.

My family wasn't physical. A back slap here, a handshake there, and that was it. We didn't hug. Dad wasn't much for displays of affection. And since my mother had died, no one had ever touched me like this, gently, as if I needed soothing or comfort.

Again, I was horrified by the prickling of yet more tears, my throat getting tight and my chest sore as another weird emotional tide rushed in where the pleasure had been not moments before.

I didn't understand it. I'd never cried the few times I'd had sex. It had been nice, sure, but afterwards I'd only felt a bit awkward. Certainly not…whatever this was.

Maybe it was a girl thing. Either way, I did *not* want it, especially not in front of Mr Evans.

Moving quickly, I pushed myself away, wriggling out of his grip before he could stop me.

'Hey,' he said. 'Where are you going?'

I kept my face turned away as I frantically grabbed my trousers and underwear, inelegantly shifting around on the back seat as I pulled them back on again. 'Uh… gotta get back. You know, things to do.'

Thank God I sounded okay and not all husky and thick.

There was a moment's silence as I hunted around for my cap, blinking furiously against the tears that threatened.

'Are you okay?' The edge of command was in his voice, leaving me in no doubt he wanted a response.

Dammit.

Forcing away the thickness in my throat and ignoring the pricking behind my eyes, I made myself turn around and meet his gaze.

It was sharp, the expression on his scarred face fierce as he scanned me like a quality inspector looking for faults.

I forced myself to hold his stare. 'I'm fine.'

His eyes narrowed. 'Why don't you come up to my hotel room? I'll order dinner and run you a bath.'

The heavy emotion in my chest gathered tighter. 'Um, no, thank you,' I said quickly, ignoring the part of me that very much wanted to do just that. 'Like I said, things to do.'

'Miss Little—'

I leaned forward and kissed him before he could finish. 'Thanks for that, it was really fun.' I turned around, pulling the door handle so I could get out.

It would have been better if I could have walked away, but sadly, I had to deal with the limo, which meant waiting until he was ready to leave.

So I got in the driver's side, determinedly checking over my clothing to make sure everything was all buttoned up, resolutely not looking at him.

There was a silence in the back of the car. Then eventually, his voice curt, he said, 'Tomorrow. 9:00 a.m. Don't be late.'

I risked a glance in the mirror and found his searing blue gaze on mine again. It took effort to give him my usual smile, but I managed it. 'See you then, Mr Evans,' I said jauntily.

I waited until he'd got out of the car.

Then I burst into tears.

CHAPTER SIX

Ash

'WHAT DO YOU MEAN, you're rethinking the deal?' I demanded, staring sightlessly at the view of the Eiffel Tower from the hotel suite.

Delaney sighed down the other end of the phone. 'I told you yesterday that the islands have a certain…sentimental value. And I was very much hoping they would go to someone who has the same family values as I do.'

I scowled at the street outside, trying to get a handle on my already touchy temper. I didn't much care about other people's feelings in the normal scheme of things, but alienating Delaney would be stupid. 'If you're expecting Dumont to have the values you're looking for, you're sadly mistaken.'

'Actually, Mr Dumont told me that he's thinking of settling down and is looking for a place to raise a family.'

Like hell he was. My half-brother was a playboy extraordinaire and settling down was the very last thing he'd ever do.

The bastard.

If I wasn't careful, my little plan to buy his precious islands out from under him was going to go tits up. Not that it was just my petty-yet-satisfying revenge that was at stake. There was also the success of Evans International, my luxury hotel business, to consider.

It was my first foray into the market and I wanted it to work, especially since all profits were to go into the charitable foundation I'd set up especially for the purpose.

A foundation for business scholarships, leadership programmes and mentorships for kids from poor areas who didn't have access to the kinds of education and contacts that rich kids did.

All the things that I could have had if my own father hadn't washed his hands of my mother and me, relegating us both to a hand-to-mouth existence on a council estate.

I'd made it my mission to succeed despite him. To be better than him in every way. To help people who needed it and never deny them.

And if I got a bit of private satisfaction out of privileged arseholes paying an arm and a leg to stay on some island so that the money could go to helping the very people those privileged arseholes looked down on, then that was just icing on the cake.

Another one in the eye for the old man.

'I'll be settling down too,' I said. 'Eventually.'

There was a pause down the other end of the phone. 'You mentioned a girlfriend…?'

'Yes.' My gaze dropped from the famous view to the

street below, tracking a long black car moving down it and drawing up outside the hotel. 'What about her?'

'You said yesterday that you were serious about her.'

The door of the car opened and someone got out. Small and curvy and female in black trousers and a white shirt, a chauffeur's cap on her head. She moved to the front of the limo and pulled something out of the back pocket of her trousers: a piece of cloth. Then she leaned down and buffed the shiny black metal with it.

Everything in me drew tight.

Ellie.

My heartbeat began to accelerate, my jeans to feel a little snug, reminding me of why I'd had such a bloody terrible sleep the night before.

I hadn't been able to stop thinking about her.

How she'd come apart so beautifully in my arms. How she'd screamed as I'd made her come. How soft and silky her skin had felt, and how tight and hot her little pussy had been.

How she'd tried to take control, only to give it up to me in the end without hesitation. Trusting me despite my reputation for being the biggest bastard in England. Even though she'd only just met me.

Even though I'd not done a thing to deserve it.

Which either made her a fool or very calculated and I couldn't decide which.

What I did know was that I'd wanted to scoop her up in my arms and carry her upstairs to my room. Peel her completely out of her clothes and lay her across the bed, do lots of dirty, dirty things to her just so I could hear her scream my name again.

Except she'd very firmly refused.

I hated being denied anything and I couldn't pretend I hadn't been royally pissed off by it. But maybe I wouldn't have been *quite* so annoyed if I'd suspected that something had upset her. She'd determinedly avoided my gaze as she'd pulled on her clothing, giving me that incredibly fake smile again.

I should have pushed the issue, but had decided that, since I'd be seeing her the next day, I'd broach the topic then, meanwhile giving her the space she so clearly wanted.

'Evans?' Delaney's voice was sharp. 'Are you still there?'

'Yes.' I followed every one of Ellie's movements as she inspected the limo, giving the black metal small polishes here and there.

Something had been wrong after we'd had sex. Something had upset her. Had it been me? Something I'd done? I'd been rough, but she'd seemed to enjoy it and I'd given her plenty of opportunities to call a halt to the proceedings if she'd wanted to.

Then again, I was, after all, still me. And plenty of women couldn't handle my particular brand of rough dirtiness.

'Well, how about it, then?'

Shit. I'd missed something, hadn't I? I'd been too busy staring at my chauffeur. 'Sorry, had a call on another line,' I lied, still watching Ellie from the window. 'What did you say?'

'I said, why don't you bring your girlfriend to the club event in Dubai in a couple of weeks? I'd like to meet her. Then perhaps we can talk more about the islands.'

Oh, fuck.

I gritted my teeth, annoyed that I'd let myself get so distracted.

'Of course,' I said, left with no other option but to agree. 'That sounds like a great idea. I'll bring her along.'

'Excellent. I'll look forward to it.'

I disconnected the call and shoved the phone into my back pocket, my already foul mood turning even fouler.

Wonderful. What the fuck was I going to do now? I didn't have a girlfriend, let alone a serious one, and I didn't want one, either. Wives and kids were for other men. I was too busy and too damn selfish for either, and people had to take me as I came or not at all.

Except Delaney wasn't taking me as I came. He wanted me to bring my non-existent serious girlfriend to meet him and I'd agreed purely so I could buy his fucking islands.

My plan to sabotage Dumont was getting more and more complicated by the second.

Down in the street outside, Ellie had shoved the cloth into her pocket and was now moving to the driver's door. She glanced up at the hotel briefly but I couldn't see her face. She must not have seen me, either, because she looked away, getting into the car once more.

I had a day full of meetings before I flew back to London that evening, and no time to talk to a tempo-rary staff member about the sexual encounter we'd had the day before. Certainly no time to obsess about it the way I was doing now.

Christ, it was ridiculous. I'd double-check she was fine when I went downstairs, but then I'd ignore her the way I should have done the day before.

She'd be gone by tomorrow anyway.

I turned away, grabbed my jacket, laptop and the duffel bag that was the only item of luggage I'd brought with me, then went downstairs to check out.

Ten minutes later I strode out of the hotel and, sure enough, Ellie was already out of the car, hurrying around to open my door for me.

I'd planned to simply walk past her and get in, but for some reason I paused, looking down into her pretty face, searching for I didn't know what.

'Good morning, Mr Evans,' she said chirpily, giving me the same jaunty smile as the day before.

And it irritated me just as much.

Because there was no trace of the husk in her voice that I'd heard when I'd touched her. No sign of the blush in her cheeks and the gold flames in her eyes that I'd seen as I'd slid my hands between her thighs, the wet heat of her pussy against my fingers.

'Good morning, Miss Little.' I narrowed my gaze, scanning her for any signs of the upset I was sure I'd sensed the day before. For any sign of acknowledgement of what had happened between us at all. 'How are you feeling?'

'Box of birds, thanks.' Her expression was resolutely cheerful.

I tried not to scowl. 'You slept well?'

'Fantastically.'

Damn woman.

It was ridiculous to be annoyed at her cheeriness, though. Because it was good she wasn't upset. I didn't want her to be, after all.

But you don't want her to act as if nothing happened between you, either, right?

Bullshit. What did I care? The sex between us had been good, yet nothing more was going to come of it. I was flying back to London tonight and she would be driving for someone else and that would be that.

I'd have Bill back at the wheel by tomorrow.

'And you?' A small crease appeared between her brows as she studied me. 'Did you sleep well?'

I lost the battle against irritation and scowled. 'I don't appreciate small talk, Miss Little. Keep it to a minimum, please.'

Her mouth opened, but I'd already turned away, getting into the car before she could speak.

It was churlish of me to take my temper out on her, but too bad. I *was* churlish, and petty, too. Selfish to boot. I embraced my faults honestly at least, unlike others who pretended they were better, all the while being just as deeply flawed as I was.

Whatever. She'd be glad she only had one more day of putting up with me.

After she'd shut the door, I got out my laptop and fired it up, hoping to distract myself by dealing with the mountain of emails I got every day.

It turned out to be pretty effective and I'd been working a good five minutes before I realised that the car wasn't moving.

I looked up from the screen and, sure enough, we were still sitting right outside my hotel, while Ellie stared at me in the rear-view mirror.

'You do know I have a meeting in twenty minutes I have to get to, don't you?' I snapped.

Her small, pointed chin lifted, green gleaming in her eyes. 'You do know that you don't have to be an arsehole, don't you?'

People didn't call me on my behaviour normally; I was too rich, too powerful. Certainly they never called me on it the way Ellie was doing right now.

I didn't like it.

Perhaps because you know already that you're acting like a prick?

My temper pulled on the leash I kept it on, growling and snapping like a beast. Of course I was acting like a prick. I always acted like a prick. Did she really expect anything different from me just because we'd had sex?

She probably expects you to act like a human being and not a petty bastard.

I gritted my teeth, glowering at her. 'What? You don't like me snapping at you? Too bad. I snap at everyone. Don't take it personally.'

Her jaunty smile had vanished and I was bastard enough to be happy about it. 'Would it kill you to be nice? Even for a second?'

'Yes,' I growled.

There was a very disapproving silence.

'What?' I grumbled bad-temperedly, not sure why I was conceding this to her. 'You want an apology?'

The expression on her face was uncompromising; of course she wanted a fucking apology.

I let out a breath. I never apologised, not to anyone, not after spending most of my childhood feeling as if I had to apologise for my very existence. And certainly not after I'd discovered how much power anger and not giving a shit gave me.

But for some reason, I gave a shit now.

'I'm sorry for snapping at you,' I said, graceless and brusque. 'There. Happy?'

She frowned at me. 'Are you angry because I didn't come up to your room last night?'

The question was unexpected and abrupt, making something hot flash through me. I definitely wasn't angry about that. Was I?

'No,' I lied, very conscious of the tension gathering in my shoulders and the sullen burn of my temper.

She ignored my denial as if I hadn't spoken. 'Look, I'm sorry about yesterday, but I—'

'Couldn't get away from me fast enough?' The words came out before I could stop them and as soon as I'd spoken I wished I hadn't. Christ, I sounded pathetic. Like a hurt child.

But to my surprise, Ellie glanced away, colour creeping into her cheeks. 'I thought it would be easier if I didn't.'

'Easier for whom? Certainly easier for you.'

The long, dark lashes veiling her gaze were streaked with gold in the sunlight coming through the windscreen. 'I didn't think you'd care. It was only sex. No big deal, right?'

Good point. It *was* only sex and very much not a big deal. And yet, here I was, turning it into one. Great sex, sure, but ultimately sex I could get from someone else.

She wasn't special. I could get hunger and fire and desperation from any woman, it didn't have to be her.

But the kind of instinctive trust she gave you?

I shoved that thought away before it could take root. 'No big deal,' I echoed flatly.

An expression I couldn't decipher flickered across her face. 'Well, I guess you're ready to go, then?'

'I am.'

She turned the key and we pulled away from the kerb at last.

And I directed my attention back to my laptop, curiously unsatisfied and not sure why.

CHAPTER SEVEN

Ellie

THE DAY PROVED to be long and not only due to the driving I had to do in the interminable Parisian traffic.

It was also due to the presence of the man sitting in the limo behind me.

I tried very hard to pretend he didn't exist, but it was difficult when every time I looked in my rear-view mirror, I caught a glimpse of him.

Sometimes he had his attention on his laptop and sometimes he was looking out of the window as he talked on his phone. And then there were also times I found his gaze on mine, a burning look in it, as if he were waiting impatiently for some kind of response from me.

Except I didn't know what response he wanted.

I'd lied when I'd told him I'd slept perfectly well. I hadn't. I'd spent all night going over what had happened in the limo and why I'd stupidly burst into emotional tears afterwards like a silly virgin.

Had it been the way he'd stroked me at the end? Or had it been due to the sheer power of the physical release? Either way, I'd hated it and I definitely didn't want it to happen again.

Pleasure I could handle, but a big no to all that emotional bullshit. It only reminded me of how I'd felt after the Mark incident and how pissed off Dad had been at me at the way I'd handled it. Sure, kneeing Mark in the balls had been an instinctive reaction, but that had caused a whole lot of extra drama that had ended up with him making all sorts of extortionate demands.

No fuss, that was key, and yet here I was, making a fuss about the sex by crying, not to mention giving Mr Evans a piece of my mind for being rude to me.

I didn't know what was happening, especially considering I still needed to ask him about Australis and our debt.

Finding the right moment to broach the topic proved difficult, however.

When he wasn't in a meeting, he was on his phone, and it wasn't until I'd picked him up from his last appointment and was taking him to the airport that he finally put the phone away, directing his attention to the laptop.

Ideally I would have liked to pull the car over, but he was pressed for time since the meeting had dragged on, and the traffic to Charles de Gaulle was a nightmare, so there was no time to stop.

I was just going to have to ask flat out.

Trying to ignore the fact that I'd complicated matters first by having sex with him and then letting my anger get the better of me and calling him out for being rude, I swallowed my nerves and checked him in the rear-view mirror.

He had his attention on his laptop, his face set in lines of fierce concentration.

Bloody hell, this wasn't a good time, either. But what else could I do? He'd be flying out in a couple of hours and then my opportunity would be gone completely.

It was now or never.

'Can I ask you something, Mr Evans?' I asked, straight out.

He didn't look up. 'What did I say about small talk?'

'It's not small talk.'

'Bill doesn't talk at all.'

Well, this was off to a great start. Go me.

I gripped the wheel tightly, trying to hang on to my determination to keep this low-key and not a big deal. 'I'm not Bill.'

'No,' he said flatly, his attention still on the screen. 'You're not.'

Okay, well, I was just going to have to go for it. I didn't want to let Dad down, not again.

'I need a favour,' I said, throwing caution to the winds. 'I need to talk to you about an investment.'

That caught his attention.

His head lifted, electric gaze coming straight to mine. 'What?'

Time for my spiel.

'So, my family makes supercars, all built by hand in our workshop in Sydney, and we were lucky enough to get a cash injection from your venture capital firm a few years ago. But, business hasn't been great and we're not able to make the returns that were expected.' Shit, I was talking too fast; I needed to slow down. 'So, we tried contacting Evans Investment to give us some more time before the investment was withdrawn, but they weren't very receptive. I thought that if I spoke to you directly—'

'That I would automatically be fine with potentially losing my investment?' he interrupted, his voice sharp, hard, the look in his eyes cutting me to shreds. 'Is that why you had sex with me?'

A cold shock pulsed down my spine.

Did he really think that?

But there was no mistaking the icy blue light glittering in his eyes. Not just annoyance or irritation, but genuine anger.

Yes, he really did think that.

We'd come to a red light so I was able to give him my full attention. 'No,' I said fiercely, forgetting all about the need to keep things light and no drama. 'I had sex with you because I wanted to. Not for any other reason.'

But there were storms in his eyes, electric tension gathering in the air inside the car. 'Are you sure? It's been done before.'

Anger gnawed at me. How dare he think that? I would never use sex to get what I wanted and certainly not after Mark. 'No,' I repeated, with more force this time. 'That's…oh, my God, that's the last thing I would ever do.'

He ignored that. 'Do you know how many people have tried to use me to get what they want over the years?' His voice was cold and gritty as sleet, his accent even more cut-glass than normal. 'Many, many people, Miss Little. Believe me, you're not the first.'

Heat surged through my cheeks. 'I wasn't intending to have sex with you. I just wanted to talk to you.'

'But you didn't, did you? You liked the idea of my cock instead.'

I struggled to get a handle on my anger. 'So? It's just sex, mate. Like you said, no big deal. So, could we talk about the investment that Dad—?'

'No,' he cut me off, the word cold as an arctic frost. 'We will not talk about the investment. We will not talk about anything at all. This conversation, Miss Little, is done.'

Behind me someone honked their horn and I realised the light had turned green, leaving me no choice but to begin driving again.

I slammed my foot on the gas, trying to get a grip on my boiling emotions, very conscious that if I let rip the way I wanted to, I was in danger of screwing this up completely.

I couldn't do what I'd done with Mark and let my anger get the better of me. Certainly kneeing Mr Evans in the balls wouldn't help, which meant I needed to try something else, think of another angle that might interest him.

There is something else.

No, I couldn't tell him about my personal project, not after Dad had poured scorn on it. It wouldn't work and was going to end up being a huge waste of money, that was what Dad had said.

Still, I didn't have that many options. And besides, I had to fix this. Especially since it was my fault that this was a problem in the first place.

'I have my own project,' I said into the silence, ignoring the nervous tension in my gut. 'I'm designing an electric supercar. I think it could be a game changer, but Dad won't fund it because he doesn't approve. Not that he has the money, anyway, but if I could just get some backing for a prototype, it could turn Australis around, I'm sure of it.'

Silence from the back seat.

I didn't want to look in the rear-view mirror. I didn't want to meet his fascinating blue eyes, not again. 'I know you've got every right to withdraw your money,' I went on doggedly, 'but I'm asking you personally at least to put it on hold. If I get funding for my project, it has the potential to do really well and then I could pay you back with a ton of interest.'

Again, silence.

Dammit. I'd bloody well screwed this up, hadn't I? Sex had ruined it and then mentioning my stupid project probably hadn't helped.

There was pressure at the back of my throat, a heaviness in my chest. Shit, that was pathetic. Dad would be appalled. He'd tell me to pull myself together, that it was my mess and crying about it wasn't going to help anyone. I just had to suck it up and deal with it. That was the Little way.

The airport was coming up and soon I'd have to stop and let Mr Evans out. He'd walk away from me and that would be my opportunity gone.

'I can show you pictures,' I said uselessly. 'My design is pretty unique, so if you want to see an example of—'

'No.' The word was flat, unequivocal.

'Mr Evans—'

'I said no.' The was no mistaking the note of absolute authority in his cold, gritty voice.

The discussion was over.

Hot, angry words filled my mouth, but I kept it closed, my jaw aching with the strain.

Don't make a fuss.

'Hey, no worries.' I forced my mouth into a smile. 'Can't blame a girl for trying though, eh?'

He said nothing, the silence in the car becoming thick and suffocating. Full of his anger and something else I didn't understand.

I pulled the limo up in the drop-off area outside the airport and only then, gathering my courage, did I glance into the mirror.

But he was putting his laptop away and not looking at me.

I stared at him, unable to help myself. His face was guarded, the white seams of his scars stark against his olive skin. A muscle flickered in his hard, strong jaw. And I couldn't help noticing that he had the longest, darkest lashes I'd ever seen on a man.

My fingers itched to touch him, a throb between my thighs reminding me of what he'd felt like inside me, surging into me, taking me hard and fast, the wild thrill of having a man like that under my hands…

Abruptly he looked and the vivid colour of his eyes caught me, held me.

'Goodbye, Miss Little,' he said expressionlessly.

And then he was gone.

CHAPTER EIGHT

Ash

I STARED OUT from the empty floor of the tower building my company was in the process of constructing in Southwark, the Thames looking black and sluggish in the early afternoon light. Wind blew through the big empty space where the windows were going to go, while the site manager went through a list of excuses as to why the project had been delayed by several months.

I was only half listening. Despite the delays, the construction was going according to plan and I didn't care about the man's excuses. What I was concerned about was the upcoming trip to Dubai that I'd promised Delaney, and how I still hadn't sorted out the issue of the 'serious girlfriend.'

The solution, of course, was to bring someone with me and have her act the part. I had no shortage of women who'd be only too happy to pretend to be my 'serious girlfriend', but my real problem was that I couldn't act to save my life.

I'd never pretended to be anything but what I was, a

former street fighter turned property developer, and I seriously doubted my abilities to pretend to be 'serious' about a woman, no matter how lovely she was.

And I didn't see why I had to bother with this nonsense just to get those islands. But Delaney wasn't budging, which meant that if I wanted them, I had no other option. My only consolation was that he'd no doubt be doing the same thing to Dumont.

'Excuse me, Mr Evans?'

A female voice floated through the empty floor and I gritted my teeth, trying to ignore the lightning bolt that hit me every time a woman said 'Mr Evans.'

Christ, after a week, you'd think I'd have forgotten about one encounter in the back of a limo with a sexy Australian chauffeur.

Apparently not.

I turned from the site manager to see my chief assistant, Petra, exit the construction elevator and make her way towards me, adroitly skirting the piles of wood and steel offcuts, metal shavings and concrete dust that littered the floor, despite the skyscraper heels she wore.

'What is it?' I snapped, deciding my irritation had nothing to do with being reminded of my one-time chauffeur and everything to do with being interrupted.

Petra ignored my temper the way she always did, peering at me from underneath her hard hat. 'You wanted to know the moment I had that dossier ready. Shall I email it to you?'

Instantly the single lightning bolt down my spine became a storm, igniting me for no fucking reason that I could see.

It was just a dossier on a supercar company called Australis. Nothing major. And only for my interest's sake. It certainly didn't require me being interrupted in the middle of an important meeting with a site manager.

Yet that didn't stop me from saying, 'Yes, of course, email it to me. Immediately.'

Petra tapped her phone's screen and smiled sweetly at me. 'Done. Shall I finish up with Doug?'

But I'd already turned away, getting out my phone and opening my mail app, leaving her to finish up the meeting with Doug, the site manager. It didn't need me to be there, but I liked to visit a site at least a couple of times to get a feel for the building and the site itself, because you couldn't get that sitting behind a desk.

My boots crunched on bits of concrete as I came to a stop, staring down at the screen as the files Petra had sent me loaded.

Australis Supercars, an Australian company that designed and hand-built luxury sports vehicles. It was owned by a guy called Oliver Little, who managed it along with his four sons and one daughter.

I flicked through the pictures of the cars themselves. The Python model was the one garnering the big interest, apparently giving Ferrari and Bugatti, and some of the other big names, a run for their money.

I didn't keep track of every company I invested money in—I left that to my managers at Evans Investment—but according to the files we had invested quite a bit of money in this particular company.

Money that was not going to see the returns we'd anticipated.

So? Lots of companies don't make it. Why does this one matter?

It didn't matter, so why I was interested in it, I had no idea.

Yet I couldn't seem to stop flicking through more images, pausing at one particular photo. It was of the Python and had the family clustered proudly around it. And right at the back, almost hidden, was a smaller figure, her hand possessively on the roof of the vehicle.

Ellie.

The lighting storm inside me sizzled against my nerve endings, igniting them, making me curse under my breath.

I generally never regretted anything in my life—I couldn't, not if I didn't want to spend it being paralysed by all the shitty things I'd done—and had always believed the only way was forward. So there was no reason for me to be looking back at what had happened with a woman over a week ago.

A woman I'd only known a couple of days.

A woman whose relatively simple request you refused because you were being petty.

I glared at the picture of Ellie on the screen, remembering the dogged way she'd continued despite the reception she'd got from me, talking about some electric car project she was working on.

And I'd ignored her, too caught up in the rush of anger that had overtaken me the moment she'd mentioned that she wanted a favour from me.

An anger that even now I didn't understand.

Yes, the timing of her confession, right after we'd

had a one-night stand, left a lot to be desired, but, still, that didn't explain my furious reaction to her request.

You thought it was you *she wanted.*

The way she'd looked at me... Seeing the fighter inside me and not being afraid. Not being intimidated. Ready to take me on. And the sex had been incendiary...

But then she'd asked for money, just like all the others.

Not that all of them wanted money. Some of them wanted the cachet of having slept with the notorious bastard billionaire. It wasn't actually me they wanted. But I'd thought Ellie was different.

Christ, why was I still obsessing about this? I wasn't some sixteen-year-old kid hurt because some girl rejected him. I was thirty-two. I'd grown up on a grotty council estate with meth dealers in the stairwells and gangs roaming the hallways. My mother had spent her days constantly worried for me and my safety, grovelling to my father for money to at least send me to a private school—and he had.

But after that night when I'd realised how little he actually cared, I'd decided I was done apologising for myself. Done cowering with my mother, terrified she would get hurt.

I'd decided to make myself the biggest, baddest motherfucker out there. I'd have the drug dealers and gangs scared of *me*.

So that was what I'd done.

And then later, I'd had Seb. He hadn't yet shown me his true colours and I'd thought he had my back to hell and beyond.

Sadly, hell had come sooner than I'd thought.

You think that excuses you being shitty to her?

My jaw ached. Behind me I could hear Petra and Doug talking, Petra flirting a little in the way that she did when she wanted to get someone on her side.

Fuck, I was shitty to everyone. Why should Ellie be exempt?

Yet all I could see was her face as she'd talked about her family's company, genuine worry glittering in her eyes. Then she'd mentioned that special project, the one that pulling my investment dollars would put at risk.

It was important to her, wasn't it?

I was supposed to help people when they needed it, not deny them the way I'd been denied. That was why I'd set up my charitable foundation in the first place. And yet, what had I done?

I'd refused her.

If my company had been small and in its infancy, it might have been a different story, but it wasn't. Evans Investment was just one of a number of companies in my portfolio and giving someone some time before requiring promised returns would have absolutely no impact on my bottom line.

I shouldn't have denied her.

On the other hand, business was business and if she wanted a favour…

Something clicked into place in my head like pieces of a perfectly constructed building.

I could give her what she wanted, while at the same time solving my own problem. Not that I couldn't give her what she wanted without making it dependent on me, but I hadn't got where I was today by being soft. Everything was a deal. Everything was give and take.

I'd give her something and she could give something to me.

Such as her presence as my serious girlfriend in Dubai, for example.

I wouldn't have to act as if I was into her the way I would have struggled to with someone else. Our chemistry would take care of that. Certainly it should be convincing enough for Delaney.

Hell, I could even sweeten the deal by giving her access to The Billionaires Club and their contacts. There'd be plenty of people there who'd be interested in her electric car project.

In fact, the more I thought about it, the better an idea I found it.

All I needed to do was put the proposal to her.

I didn't waste any time, putting through a few calls there and then. Bill was more than happy to take an evening off and the chauffeur company was more than happy to accept my exorbitant offer for one night of Ellie Little's services. It was very late notice, but they could certainly accommodate me.

That sorted, I shoved my phone back into my pocket and turned to rejoin the meeting, trying to ignore the way the lightning in my veins had become hot, electric.

Nothing to do with the prospect of seeing Ellie again, definitely not. I was simply pleased to have solved the problem of how to get Delaney on my side.

Liar. You still want her.

No, I didn't. Been there, done that, and I didn't go back.

This was business. Nothing more.

CHAPTER NINE

Ellie

I WASN'T HAPPY when the job came through and I almost refused. I didn't even want to see Ash Evans again, let alone drive for him.

But I couldn't say no, not if I wanted to stay on the chauffeur company's books, and I did want to, because my options for money were few and far between.

I'd spent the week since getting back from Paris trying to figure out what my next move should be. I couldn't bear the thought of calling Dad to tell him I'd failed—not that I had failed. I just needed to…regroup.

Failure wasn't an option anyway, not when I was the whole reason the company was having difficulty in the first place.

So I accepted the job and tried to ignore my own personal doubts about seeing him again. Tried not to think about why he'd asked for me, especially given how angry he'd been back in Paris.

Perhaps it was for another encounter in the back seat, though if that was the reason then he was shit out of luck. No way I wanted to have sex with him again, not given how emotional I'd been after the first time. And then there had been him getting so furious with me…

No, definitely not going back for that. I wasn't a masochist.

Thoughts of what we'd done together that night in the limo wouldn't leave me alone, though.

The whole week I'd tossed and turned in my uncomfortable single bed in the Shepherd's Bush flat I shared with a few other Australians, my body aching. Unable to stop thinking about him. His hands on my skin, his cock inside me, pushing deep and hard. The weird sense of freedom as I'd given myself up to him…

And you crying like a fool afterwards.

Yes, there was that. I should have been able to put the experience behind me, and the fact that I couldn't disturbed me.

So, by the time I reluctantly turned up for my shift as Mr Evans's driver, I was already feeling restless and out of sorts.

The address for the pick-up point was odd into the bargain and I had to double-check it numerous times to make sure it was right, because it seemed very much *not* the kind of place from which to pick up a billionaire.

A large, featureless council estate tower block, it had a scraggly green lawn out the front with a couple of spindly-looking trees dotted here and there. A group of teenagers were hanging around outside, shouting and playing loud music, and being generally annoying.

There was a grim feel to the place, a kind of hopelessness that made me sad. I might have had a lonely upbringing after losing my mother, but at least I'd had a decent home and food on the table, and no drug dealers hanging around my front door.

I frowned out of the window. Surely Mr Evans wouldn't be here?

A young woman pushing a small toddler in a stroller approached the entrance to the building, prompting a swirl of attention from the gathered teenagers.

Tension crawled over me and I reached for the door, ready to spring out and go at them if they started threatening the woman.

Except at that moment a tall, powerful figure came striding out. And instantly the teenagers swarmed, clustering around him instead, hooting and calling out greetings, their faces alight.

I stared in amazement as Mr Evans gave out high fives as demanded then paused to chat, the group hanging on his every word.

The woman waved at him as she passed, entering the building unmolested as the air filled with the sound of raucous teenage laughter.

Then Mr Evans extricated himself from the crowd of youths, striding on to where I sat waiting for him in the limo.

And all of a sudden my heartbeat accelerated, my pulse so loud it just about competed with the beats coming from the teenagers' phones.

Somehow I'd reduced him in my mind. Made him not so large, not so muscular. Not so powerful. Not so compelling. Certainly I'd turned down the burn on the intense energy that trailed along in his wake like his own personal force field.

How could I have forgotten the sheer physical reality of him? How could I not have remembered how completely and utterly hot he was?

I stared dumbly, my mouth dry as he came up to the limo, pulled the door open and got in.

And when I looked in my rear-view mirror, there were those eyes. Those searing blue eyes.

'You didn't open the door for me,' he said, his familiar, deep, gritty voice vibrating through me. 'I really expected better service from you, Miss Little.'

Oh, hell. I'd forgotten about the stupid door. I'd been too busy staring at him.

I tried to find my usual laid-back, cheerful persona, but it had slipped away on me and all I managed to take hold of was anger. At him for being so ridiculously hot and at myself for being so susceptible.

'Sorry, Mr Evans.' I let a touch of acid tinge the words. 'I wasn't sure what temper you were going to be in this evening. Outright rude or merely mildly offensive.'

His eyes gleamed, as if with appreciation. 'Tonight I thought I might try pleasant.'

'Pleasant? You?'

'Drive, Miss Little. There's a bar I want you to take us to.'

Us?

I opened my mouth to ask what he meant by that, then decided against it.

Not my business. Just as it wasn't my business to

ask him why he'd chosen me to drive him for the night. Silence was probably the best response I could give.

It was a resolve that lasted all of two seconds.

'Interesting pick-up address,' I said, unable to contain my curiosity. 'Not your usual billionaire hang-out.'

There was something about his expression in the mirror that fascinated me, similar to the savage satisfaction that had burned there the night after he'd come out of the club in Paris. The look of a man who'd beaten all comers to win.

'Not usually,' he said. 'But it's mine. I used to live there.'

I blinked in surprise.

So that was the dodgy council estate he'd grown up on. Interesting. Was that where he'd fought too? I could imagine that, him with his fists raised, blood on his face and on his knuckles, that savage look in his eyes...

Hot.

A shiver went through me. I had no idea why I found the idea of him as a street fighter so damn sexy, but I did.

I glanced in the mirror. 'Really?'

'Yes. My mother still does.' His hard mouth quirked in something that looked very close to a smile, sending another shiver of heat chasing across my skin. 'I renovated a perfectly nice place in Chelsea for her but she refuses to move. Says she likes it there.'

'Why?'

'No idea. She's a stubborn woman, my mother.' His gaze caught mine. 'Perhaps that's why I like stubborn women.'

Surely he wasn't meaning...me?

Irritation needled at me. If he was trying to angle for another encounter in the back seat he needed to think again.

'Is there any reason you asked for me in particular tonight?' I asked, sounding more belligerent than I'd meant to. 'Because if you're hoping to get me in the back seat again—'

'No,' he said, before I could finish. 'Rest assured, that's not what I want from you tonight.'

'Then why?' I demanded, annoyed by the fact that I felt disappointed, which I totally shouldn't have.

'You'll see.'

There was a hint of smugness to the words that needled me even further.

I knew I shouldn't let him get to me, that I should be thinking of this as another opportunity to talk to him about Australis, but the irritation and disappointment sat inside me all the same. And by the time I'd pulled up outside the Covent Garden address he'd given me, it wasn't so much him who was in a foul temper, but me.

The bar looked exactly like the kinds of bars he'd be used to, complete with a long line of beautifully dressed hopefuls outside, an ostentatious-looking bouncer, and a velvet rope to sort the aristocracy from the peasants.

'Here we are,' I said unnecessarily, trying to force my bad mood away with a cheerful smile. 'Do you want me to get your door?'

'No.' Another gleam in those blue eyes. 'I want you to come and have a drink with me.'

'Excuse me?' This time I actually turned around in my seat.

The impact of his direct gaze was like a physical blow.

'One drink, Miss Little,' he murmured. 'I have a proposition I want to put to you.'

He sat there, dark and scarred and powerful, and so achingly compelling I couldn't look anywhere but at him. And, God, he was incredible. I didn't know how he managed to look so damn hot simply in a pair of jeans and a T-shirt—this time a dark blue one that somehow intensified the colour of his eyes—but he did.

'A proposition?' I echoed stupidly. 'What proposition?'

'Come and have a drink and you'll find out.'

Fighting the pull of his charisma, I gave him a narrow stare. 'You'd better not be rude again. I haven't bloody got time for that kind of carry-on.'

Again, his hard mouth twitched. 'I can't guarantee there won't be any "carry-on". But I can guarantee it will be worth your time.'

I didn't want to accept, not just like that. It felt like giving in.

'I'm supposed to be working,' I said, prevaricating.

'You are working. For me. Think of it as a business meeting.'

Huh.

I gave him a suspicious look. 'About what?'

'Australis. I've been investigating your family's company.'

Shock pulsed down my spine, my bad temper vanishing in an instant. 'Seriously? In that case, yes. I'd love to have a bloody drink. Though it'll have to be non-alcoholic. I'm still driving.'

I didn't want to get my hopes up too high, but I couldn't stop the excitement that gathered in my gut as we were ushered to the head of the queue outside the bar, the velvet rope being pulled aside so we could enter in front of everyone else.

Inside, the bar was dark, full of dimly lit alcoves and small rooms where people could sit and chat in complete privacy. Another room had a dance floor in it, but we passed it by, Mr Evans leading me to an out-of-the-way alcove furnished with a dark blue velvet couch and a low coffee table in dark wood. The lighting was atmospheric, the music low and seductive.

As we sat, a waitress came to take our drinks orders and I went with an orange juice while he had a Scotch.

I perched awkwardly on the couch while he sprawled out beside me, surveying me, the electricity in his eyes turning into something hotter and more potent, and I was very conscious of how close he was, his knee nearly brushing mine.

His proximity was insanely distracting, near enough to me to feel the heat pouring off his body. It made it hard to concentrate on anything else.

'Okay, so what's this proposition?' I asked when the waitress had gone. 'And why couldn't you ask me in the car?'

'Because I didn't want you to be distracted by driving.'

'Fair enough. This is about the investment money, yes? About what I asked you in Paris?'

'Yes.'

My heartbeat got faster. 'And?'

His gaze was very direct. 'I don't change my mind often, Miss Little. And when a thing is done, I consider it done. But I've had a week to think about what you asked me and I've decided that I was too hasty in refusing you.'

I swallowed, taken aback despite myself. I really hadn't thought he'd reconsider. 'You were?'

'Yes. I had a chance to look at your family's company personally this week and I'm willing to give Australis more time before we need to see some return on our initial investment.'

Yes!

Despite how I'd nearly screwed it up, my gamble in going from Paris to England to face Mr Evans personally had paid off. Dad was going to be so pleased.

Triumph glowed in the centre of my chest and I grinned like a lunatic. 'That's just fantastic, Mr Evans. I can't tell you—'

'But you're going to have to do something for me in return,' he went on, as if I hadn't spoken.

The triumph glowed a little bit less bright.

'If you're wanting sex—' I began.

'Sex is not required,' he said before I could finish, a spark of his usual bad temper glowing in his eyes. 'You must know by now I'm not that kind of man.'

'But I don't know,' I shot back. 'All I know is your reputation and, to be honest, that's pretty shitty.'

His gaze narrowed. 'Fair point. But understand me, I don't need a business deal in order to get sex and I certainly don't blackmail people into it.'

I refused to feel ashamed about it. After Mark, who knew?

'You can never tell,' I said. 'So what do you want from me, then?'

The scar pulling at his mouth was very white against his olive skin, his sneer pronounced. 'What do I want?' The scar twisted further as his mouth curved, making his smile seem savage. 'I have an event I have to be at in Dubai in a week's time. And what I want is for you to be my date.'

CHAPTER TEN

Ash

'YOUR DATE?' ELLIE ECHOED, her eyes wide. 'For…what?'

She was sitting on the end of the couch with her arms crossed, her shoulders hunched, clearly trying to keep what distance there was between us.

Which was probably a good thing.

I hadn't realised that seeing her in the flesh would be quite so problematic, though I should have.

She was in her chauffeur's uniform as usual—white shirt, black trousers, black tie and hat. And her glossy brown hair was tied back. Again, she wore no make-up at all.

Again, she was the fucking sexiest thing I'd ever seen.

She was staring at me suspiciously, hazel eyes narrowed, yet all I could think about was how she'd looked straddling me, with that white shirt pulled open, her bare breasts pressing against my chest. The tight clasp of her pussy around my cock. She hadn't been so suspicious then. No, she'd been full of hunger and demand, gripping onto me as if she couldn't bear to let me go, warming up the cold places inside me with her heat.

But you're not going to keep thinking that, are you?

Bloody hell, no. I wasn't here for sex. And besides, I'd been there, done that, and I never went back.

Fighting down the relentless pull of our chemistry and the anger of thwarted desire, I tried not to snap at her. Because that wouldn't get me what I wanted. Playing nice wasn't in my nature, but I'd do it. I knew how to play the long game, too.

'I'm a member of a very exclusive club that hosts a lot of charity events around the world,' I said. 'In fact, that event you took me to in Paris was one of them.'

'But you didn't need a date for Paris.'

'No, but I do for Dubai.'

'Why me?' she asked bluntly. 'You must have a hundred other women who'd jump at the chance. And why do you need a date anyway?'

I was conscious all of a sudden that I didn't want to give her the details of my plan to dupe Delaney. She was very…blunt. And there was an honesty to her that made me certain she wouldn't approve.

Then again, I had no idea why her approval mattered to me. 'Okay, here's the situation,' I said, deciding on the full truth and to hell with my ridiculous qualms. 'I have a luxury hotel chain that I want to get off the ground and I'm angling for a couple of islands in the Caribbean that would make for a perfect resort site. Unfortunately, the man I want to buy them from is getting cold feet about selling them to me. He wants someone more "family-minded" to have them.'

Ellie's gaze sharpened. 'And you're not…family-minded.'

It wasn't a question.

'No,' I agreed. 'But I want those islands. Which means I need to convince this man that I'm as family-minded as he hopes I am.'

Her silky brows drew together. 'How?'

I opened my mouth to tell her, but she'd already worked it out.

'Oh, wait,' she went on. 'You want to use me, don't you?'

She was quick, I'd give her that.

'I promised Delaney I'd bring my "serious girlfriend" to the next club event,' I said. 'And that's Dubai.'

'So just to be clear—I'm your "serious girlfriend", right?'

I leaned back against the couch, meeting the challenging look in her eyes with one of my own. 'You have a problem with that?'

'With essentially lying to someone to get your hands on their property? Kind of.'

Her disapproval was palpable and it irritated me, no matter that I'd already prepared myself for it. 'It's business, Miss Little, and people lie all the time in business. It's not a big deal.'

She kept frowning at me. 'But why not find some islands you don't need to jump through so many hoops for?'

Damn. I didn't want her asking questions, not when the answers involved Dumont. Because there was no way I was going to talk about him and how he'd not only broken my trust, but my mother's too.

You had a hand in it, too, don't forget.

Yes. And didn't I know it?

'Those specific islands are the best sites,' I replied dismissively, glancing around at the dim bar. 'Where the hell has that Scotch got to?'

But I should have known she wouldn't be distracted.

'There must be other good ones,' she insisted. 'It's the Caribbean. Aren't there hundreds of islands just lying around waiting to be bought by billionaires?'

Persistent little thing, wasn't she?

My smile started to slip, the leash on my temper starting to fray. 'I don't want any other islands. I want those ones.'

'But why?' she asked, relentless.

'Because I want them. That's why.'

'That's not a good enough reason.'

'That's all the reason you're going to get,' I snapped, losing my temper. 'Will you do it or not?'

'No,' she snapped back. 'And don't get shirty with me. It sounds dodgy and I'm not doing anything dodgy.'

Desire shot through me, thick and hot. She was rousing the warrior in me, making me want to fight. Take this to the bedroom where we could work out our disagreement in a more private and ultimately more satisfying way.

Mercifully, at that point the waitress delivered the drinks, giving me a moment to get my temper, not to mention my rapidly hardening cock, under control.

What I should not be doing was sitting here with her as though we were on a date, but that would be to admit she was getting to me and I wasn't going to do that.

Besides, she hadn't accepted my proposition yet and

I wasn't leaving until she had. It had become a matter of pride now and I never conceded a fight.

'Not even if it meant saving your family's company?' I asked casually, playing my ace.

'Oh, I see. So this *is* blackmail, then?' Green sparks of anger glittered in her eyes, making my dick twitch in response.

Christ, the fire in her was sexy. The way she refused to back down got me hard as much as it irritated the shit out of me.

'No, of course not.' I gritted my teeth. 'But I promise you there isn't anything dodgy going on.'

'Lying sounds pretty dodgy to me.'

You're going to have to tell her about Dumont.

Because clearly she wasn't going to agree to anything until I did. Fuck.

Lifting my glass, I downed the Scotch in one go, scowling.

I didn't relish the idea of telling her about Dumont, but then not telling her made it seem as if I gave a damn about her opinion of me and I didn't.

At all.

I put the empty Scotch tumbler down on the low table in front of the couch and met her gaze.

She had those pretty, slender fingers wrapped around her glass, and I had to drag my focus away from them, my brain helpfully replaying memories of how those fingers had felt stroking my cock through my jeans, then adding fantasies of how good they'd feel if there were no denim between us. If they were wrapped around my dick…

Focus, arsehole.

'Fine, you want to know why I want those particular islands?' I didn't bother adjusting my surly tone. 'Because my half-brother, Sebastian Dumont, also wants them and I don't want him to have them.'

Ellie frowned, studying me over the rim of her glass. She still had her chauffeur's cap on and there was something vaguely endearing about how she was sitting there so primly in her uniform in a dark club with thumping music.

'Okay,' she said slowly. 'So why don't you want him to have them? I mean, I have four brothers, so I sort of understand.'

Yes, she might. Then again, her family had a certain level of privilege. Her father built supercars, for fuck's sake. You didn't do that without money, regardless of his financial difficulties now.

She must have seen something in my face because suddenly sympathy flooded through her expression. 'Oh, hell. Is this painful for you?' She leaned forward and put one of those delicate hands on my arm. 'I'm sorry. You don't have to tell me, if you don't want to. I just get curious. Tell me to piss off if it's too much.'

The concern in her eyes jolted through me like an electric shock, the light touch of her bare skin against mine only deepening the sensation.

People never looked at me like that, as if my feelings mattered to them. Usually because I was too busy showing them how little theirs mattered to me.

Yet right here, right now, despite how grumpy and

rude I'd been, Ellie was looking at me with sympathy and concern.

As if I mattered to her.

Which, given the way you've been treating her, is absolutely undeserved.

A muscle flickered in my jaw, my chest feeling suddenly tight. 'You'd better not touch me like that, Miss Little,' I said brusquely. 'Not if you don't want to be naked and on your back right here on this couch.'

That's right, make it about sex.

I wasn't making it about sex. It *was* about sex. Certainly it had nothing to do with the constriction in my chest, the ache in the vicinity of my heart.

Something flickered in her eyes, but then her lashes came down, veiling her gaze, and her hand dropped from my arm. And I couldn't get rid of the sense that my response had hurt her in some way.

Unexpected shame crept through me.

She does matter.

I had no idea why or even how she'd managed it. But that didn't change the feeling inside me. I didn't like that I'd hurt her.

Ellie was looking down at her orange juice, fussing with her straw, and I noticed that her hand was shaking a little. 'Okay, so anyway,' she said quickly. 'You don't have to tell me if you don't want to. No worries at all.'

You bastard.

Well, technically, I was a bastard. And it had never bothered me before that I acted like a bastard, too, not when caring about other people's feelings and what they thought of you was a vulnerability I could never allow.

Except, I was bothered now.

'You want to know where I got these scars from?' I asked abruptly, following an impulse I never normally listened to.

She looked up from her drink to the scars on my face. 'I heard you were a street fighter or something.'

The media loved my background; the story that I'd been into illegal street fights to get my start-up money was great fodder for them. The reality was a hell of a lot less romantic.

'I was. And one day my opponent brought a knife to what was supposed to be a fist fight.'

She looked aghast. 'So…you fought him?'

'Of course.' I smiled, feeling the pull of the scar. Remembering the pain and the blood, and how everyone had roared my name afterwards. 'I never backed down from a fight.'

Her gaze followed the lines of my scars, her hand twitching as if she wanted to touch them. And quite suddenly I wanted her to. Wanted to feel her cool fingers on my hot skin with a desperation that took my breath away.

The crease between her brows was deep. 'But you could have been killed.'

Something pulled inside me, like a muscle that hadn't been warmed up properly, and it hurt. I wanted to snap at her all of a sudden, the pain and the strange desperation for her touch making me angry.

But I didn't want to hurt her, not again, so I bit back

my retort. 'Maybe,' I said mildly enough. 'But I was very good at fighting.'

'So...' Her gaze roamed over my scars again. 'You won?'

'Oh, yes, I won.' A ghost of that familiar savage satisfaction echoed through me, the power I got from winning. From pitting myself against the odds and coming out on top. 'I always won.'

'You didn't care about getting hurt? Or losing your life?'

I shrugged. 'I needed the money. And that was more important.'

It always had been. For my mother's sake.

'My brothers like to win, too,' she said quietly. 'Which makes sense given that they're racing car drivers.'

'What about you?' I watched her lovely face, shadowed by the brim of her cap. 'Do you like to race cars and win as well?'

Slowly she shook her head. 'I don't race. I like driving, don't get me wrong, but my talent is design.' One corner of her mouth lifted in a shy kind of smile. 'I do like speed, but I'm all about making things go faster more efficiently from the ground up. The whole machine rather than simply putting your foot down.' There was a certain sparkle in her eyes as she spoke, an excitement that for some reason caught me by the throat and refused to let go.

'Your electric car,' I said, suddenly desperately curious. 'Tell me about it.'

Her smile turned from shy into something a whole

lot more forced and fake-looking. 'No, you don't want to hear about that. Anyway, you still haven't told me why you want those islands.'

But I didn't want to talk about me. I wanted to talk about her. Because it hadn't hit me until now what a fascinating collection of contrasts she was. Direct in a way that was very masculine, yet she was sitting primly in a way that was very feminine. She called me mate, pointed out my rudeness, and yet she blushed. Looked horrified at the knife scars on my face and yet had seemed pleased when I'd told her that I'd won.

She was interesting. But getting interested in her was not at all what I should be doing.

Which was getting her to agree to be my date.

Which she still hadn't.

'Fine.' I tried to mask my irritation at the change of topic and failed. 'I took on those fights for a reason. I needed the money.'

'Right. To start up your business.'

'Partly. I also needed it to pay back a debt.'

She sipped at her drink, watching me. 'What debt?'

'I already had that start-up money. In fact, by the time I left school, I had a nice little nest egg stashed away. Money I'd saved over the years through jobs here and there.' My chest tightened but I forced myself to say it. 'But mostly the money came from my mother, from the retirement savings I convinced her to give me. I was going to invest it in property and by the time she actually had to retire, she'd have millions. At least, that's what I promised her.'

She hadn't wanted to give me that money, either, but

I'd convinced her. I'd told her she'd get it back and with interest. And she'd believed me.

Ellie grimaced. 'Oh, no. Don't tell me…'

'I lost it. I lost every penny.' My jaw ached. Christ, this should not be so hard to say. 'My half-brother took it all.'

'Hell,' she muttered. 'What did he do?'

I wanted another Scotch, but I ignored the urge, concentrating instead on Ellie's face. 'About the only thing my bastard father did for me was to pay for a private school, the same school Sebastian went to. We became close friends and had plans to go into business together. He had money, plenty of it, but I didn't and so I had to work hard to get my share of the cash together.' My hands had closed into fists at my sides and I had to take a breath to unclench them. 'There was a property we were aiming to buy and I thought we'd agreed on it, but soon after we left school, he decided on a different site that he thought would be more profitable. I told him the deal was shady—believe me, growing up on the estate, you get a sixth sense for that kind of thing. But he refused to listen. He went ahead and shelled out the cash without my agreement and, sure enough, the deal fell through and we lost everything.'

More sympathy flickered in her eyes, making something inside me ache. 'Oh, that's awful.'

'I was furious.' And I had been. I could still feel the rage coursing through my veins to this day, boiling me dry. The sheer betrayal of it. Seb had been my closest friend and he was supposed to have my back. He wasn't supposed to completely ignore me, treat me like I was just a know-nothing kid from a shitty council estate. He'd been shocked when it had all fallen apart, as if he hadn't been warned that something like this was going to happen. Warned by me.

After my father's rejection of me, Seb's refusal to listen had been too much.

You could have talked to him at any time over the years. You didn't have to turn your back on him so completely. But you did, didn't you?

'If it had been only my money that had been lost, it wouldn't have been so bad,' I went on, shoving the thought of my own culpability in the destruction of our friendship aside. 'But it wasn't. It was all my mother's savings, too. He told me to relax, that we could get more money from somewhere else, but he was rich. Of course he could get what he wanted, whenever he wanted it. He even offered to put in my share for next time, but I refused.' The embers of that anger burned sullenly inside me, turning my voice into a growl. 'I didn't want his fucking money. I didn't want to have to be beholden to someone who didn't listen. Someone who should have been my friend.' I stopped, trying to get a handle on myself. 'Anyway, I swore I'd make it on my own from then on. So I went out and tried to raise as much cash as I could, doing what I could. Street fighting was lucrative, paid cash, and I could earn it relatively quickly.'

Plus, you enjoyed it.

Yes, there was that. The gangs and the dealers threatened and intimidated everyone on the estate, my mother and me included. And it had given me immense satisfaction when I'd finally grown into my height and build, and I'd earned a reputation for being a mean son-of-a-bitch, to pay back that intimidation in kind.

After that knife fight, no one had messed with me again.

'What about your mother?' Ellie asked. 'She can't have thought fighting was a good idea, surely?'

I bared my teeth, remembering Mum's disapproving face. 'No, she didn't. She said the money didn't matter, but she was wrong. She's always been wrong about that. Money *always* matters.'

Especially when it had been money she'd worked hard for. Money that would have given her the kind of life she would have had if she hadn't had me.

There was a brief silence, Ellie's gaze uncomfortably sharp. Uncomfortably knowing.

Shit, I'd been too vehement, hadn't I? Too angry. Betrayed too much.

'Anyway, I got the money back,' I went on, too quickly. 'And I made my fortune. And I want those islands because Dumont wants them, too, and so I'm aiming to buy them out from under him.'

'So…this is revenge or something?'

I smiled. 'It's a reminder. That I'm still here. And that I haven't forgotten.'

She looked at me for a long time, not saying anything.

Then she put her glass down on the table and said, 'If I do this, you'll give Australis some more time, right?'

'Yes. I'm a man of my word.' That was the one good thing people could say of me. When I gave my word, I stood by it. 'Plus, I can introduce you to a few key

people at my club. You might find future sources of in-
come for your own project.'

Strangely, colour rose in her skin and she looked
away. 'I need to get Australis back into the black before that happens.'

Her response wasn't what I'd expected—given the
sparkle in her eyes when she'd spoken about it before,
I'd thought she'd be excited to talk about it. But again,
this wasn't about her as a person. This was about her
as my date.

'So, do we have a deal?' I asked, leaving the subject
of the car alone. 'You'll come to Dubai?'

She glanced back at me, her expression unreadable.

And a word escaped me, a word I never said to anyone. A word that I didn't need to say to her, not given
the power I had over her. Yet it came out all the same.

'Please.'

Her expression softened. 'Yes,' she said. 'Okay. We
have a deal.'

CHAPTER ELEVEN

Ellie

THE FIRST THING I realised on accepting Mr Evans's deal was that I had nothing to wear. Or at least nothing that a 'serious girlfriend' would wear to a billionaires event in Dubai.

I didn't wear dresses or skirts or make-up—I hadn't since my mother had died—and had never seen any reason to start. But even I knew that I was probably going to have to scrub myself up for this. Sadly, my chauffeur's uniform—the nicest, most professional clothing I had—was probably not going to work.

Which meant I was going to have to buy something nicer.

However, that required a level of female know-how I did not have.

A couple of my flatmates could have helped, but I was reluctant to tell them what was going on. They knew me as Ellie the chauffeur and the thought of asking them to help me buy dresses made me feel strangely self-conscious.

Luckily, Mr Evans had an assistant called Petra, who soon took charge of Operation Get Ellie Ready for Dubai by taking me out on a shopping spree the Saturday before we were due to leave.

It took me all of two seconds to realise that the shops she was taking me to were so far out of my price range they might as well have been the sun to my poor, poverty-stricken Pluto, and that there was no way I could afford it. I quickly told her the situation but she informed me crisply that this was a business trip and that Mr Evans would cover any and all expenses. Then she ignored my protests, dragging me into yet another designer shop on Bond Street.

She was very good at getting her way. Some of the dresses and skirts she made me try on I protested about, uncomfortable at seeing myself in the mirror looking so… female. But again, she ignored me. She even got me into a gown—a green thing made out of some gossamer-like fabric that wrapped around me like a second skin—and then bought it, not even blinking at the outrageous price tag.

Business expenses. Bloody hell.

Eventually I gave up protesting. If Mr Evans wanted to pay for all that bullshit, who was I to argue? He could probably pass the dresses on to his next girlfriend any-way and, besides, I had bigger things to think about.

I called Dad that night with the good news that Mr Evans wouldn't be pulling his investment from Australis any time soon, and he seemed pleased, though, as al-ways, it was difficult to tell.

He didn't thank me—both of us knew that if it hadn't

been for Mark we wouldn't have been in the position of me having to go to Mr Evans to start with.

Yet, even though I'd expected it, Dad's response sat in my gut like a small piece of glass, cold and sharp. He didn't ask how I'd managed to get Mr Evans to listen and I didn't tell him.

He didn't need to know that in return for doing what I had for Australis, I had to promise to go as Mr Evans's date to some billionaire event in Dubai.

I still didn't know why I'd agreed. I'd demanded at least that Mr Evans tell me his reasons for lying to some guy so he could get a bunch of islands and also get one over on his half-brother.

I hadn't expected him to tell me, but he had. And it was clear that as much as he was angry with his half-brother for losing the money his mother had invested, he was also angry at himself, too.

The blame game was something I was familiar with myself, and I couldn't help feeling for him. But that wasn't why I'd agreed in the end.

It was the way he'd said 'please.' As if the word was foreign to him and he didn't know its power, but had said it anyway.

And because he'd needed something from me and it had been far too long since someone had needed anything from me.

Still, I couldn't help but feel a little bit of trepidation.

Being his girlfriend would probably involve some… physical closeness. And I wasn't sure I was ready for that.

Watching him talk about his fights, knowing the

reasons for his scars, seeing the ferocity in his face as he'd mentioned how he'd won...

The man had a chip on his shoulder the size of a redwood and I don't know why that fury fascinated me so much, but it did. Like a moth drawn to a burning bonfire, I was compelled towards him.

He was so fierce and passionate. So unlike the reserved, laconic men I'd been brought up with and worked with at Australis.

Sex might not be part of the girlfriend deal but there was a part of me that hoped it would be.

A few days after the shopping trip, my bags packed and ready, I was in the weird position of being the one picked up for a change.

Mr Evans insisted that we go to the airport together—and since we were supposed to be a couple, he had a point.

He drove his own car this time, a massive Land Rover that seemed appropriate given he was a property developer and into construction.

Automatically and by instinct, I headed towards the driver's side only to have him give me a narrow look. 'I'm driving, remember?' he reminded me. 'It's my car.'

'Oh, right. Sure.' I gave him a sheepish grin.

It felt strange not having the wheel in front of me and I didn't know what to do with my hands. So I gripped onto my seat belt as he took us to London City Airport, where we'd catch his company's jet to Dubai.

He drove with the kind of aggressive confidence I'd expected of him, talking via speakerphone the whole time, dealing with site issues, property concerns, something legal to do with a contract and then some kind of staffing problem. He dealt with it all with authority and a bluntness that probably added to his fearsome reputation, yet I found myself admiring it.

No wonder people didn't know how to deal with him in the UK. He wasn't polite and he didn't play by the normal rules, and I found that incredibly attractive. That he didn't care what other people thought of him was also apparent, and, as someone who did care, I found the fact that he didn't fascinating.

Dad would have been appalled.

We got to the airport, boarded the jet, and were in the air within a couple of hours and even then Mr Evans was still dealing with calls.

He paced impatiently around the cabin, filling the space with his own particular brand of vibrant electricity, and even though I sat in one of the plush leather seats, ostensibly looking through a magazine, I couldn't help but watch him instead.

That energy was anger. I knew that now.

Given how he'd been totally shafted by his half-brother and how responsible he felt for the loss of his mother's money, I understood how driven he was.

I was curious, though, as to why she was still living in the council estate, not to mention why he was still feuding with his half-brother, when all of that had happened so many years ago. Also, the few times he'd spoken of his father it was with nothing but contempt, and I wondered what the story was there.

Being curious about him was probably a bad thing, but I was all the same.

It was a good half hour into the flight before Mr Evans finally finished up his calls and threw himself down into the leather seat opposite mine, his blue gaze like a slap of ice water across my hot skin.

He stared at me for a full minute at least, then said, 'So, tell me how Australis got into trouble.'

Every muscle in my body gathered tight. 'Wh-what?'

'I've been looking over the financials and it does seem as though there are some issues.' His stare became sharper. 'Which is odd because it seemed like a good bet when we made our initial investment. You want to tell me what the problem is?'

I should have expected him to ask, especially considering it was his money he'd invested, but that didn't change the sudden and intense need to change the subject. Because I really did *not* want to have to explain to him about how my mismanagement of the Mark incident had turned what should have been a minor problem into a giant mistake.

'There was a…staff issue,' I said, deliberately vague. 'We lost one of our best designers.'

'And why was that?'

'He had to be let go for…certain reasons.' My hands had crept into my lap, my fists clenched.

Mr Evans frowned. 'What reasons?'

It was stupid to feel so tense about confessing the truth to him. So I'd made a mistake in my handling of it. So what? Anyway, I didn't have to say it was me, did I?

I swallowed. 'He harassed a staff member. There was a fuss so Dad paid him to keep quiet and go away. It was a lot of money.' Too much money. But Dad hadn't wanted it to become public. He'd met Mark's demands without protest and hadn't said a word to me about it. But I knew he was angry at how I'd handled it. If I hadn't gone and hurt Mark, it wouldn't have been such an issue.

Mr Evans's gaze had got very narrow, sapphire glinting from beneath his thick black lashes. 'And Australis struggled after that?'

'We couldn't get another designer that good. I tried to fill in, but…' I trailed off. No need to tell him that Dad had never been satisfied with my work after that, no matter how hard I'd tried.

A silence fell and it wasn't a comfortable one, not with Mr Evans's gaze on me, concentrated as an X-ray.

'It was you,' he said suddenly. 'You were the person who got harassed.'

Of course he'd guess. He wasn't a stupid man by any stretch.

Who cares that he knows? You shouldn't. It was nothing, remember? Nothing at all.

I forced myself to look at him. Forced myself to smile. 'Yeah, but it was no big deal.'

Mr Evans didn't smile. He went very still instead, a feral light glowing in his eyes. 'Did he hurt you?'

But I didn't want to go into it. 'It wasn't a drama, honestly.'

'Did. He. Hurt. You?' Each word was bitten off, a rough thread of anger running through his voice.

I wanted to ask him why he cared so much, but I was afraid of the answer for some reason, so I didn't. 'Not physically.'

'And your father paid him off? Why? He didn't defend you? Get the police involved?'

'No,' I snapped, feeling defensive. 'Dad didn't want any fusses made. And I'd made it into this big deal already.'

Mr Evans's expression settled into forbidding lines. 'And how exactly did you make it a big deal?'

'Mark grabbed me, so I… I kind of…kneed him in the balls.'

An electric-blue flame leapt in Mr Evans's eyes and it looked suspiciously like approval. 'Good,' he said fiercely.

'No, it wasn't good.' I tried to ignore the warmth that approval had ignited inside me. 'I shouldn't have done anything. I should have just…handled it. But Mark told everyone that I'd assaulted him and Dad didn't want to deal with it. So he paid Mark to be quiet and leave.'

'He shouldn't have.' Mr Evans leaned forward abruptly in his seat, his voice low and savage. 'He should have hauled that motherfucker down to the station and booked him.'

I blinked at his vehemence and the ferocity in his gaze. 'Well, he didn't. Why does it matter to you, anyway?'

'My mother was my father's maid. He seduced her and she ended up living hand to mouth in a council estate with a child she got no support for.' Bitterness edged each word. 'I know what workplace harassment can do to a woman. And yes, I care about it.'

His ferocity was a physical force. A shock wave pushing against me. 'Apart from anything else, I don't like people taking advantage of others more vulnerable than they are.' He put a hand on each of the armrests on either side of my seat, a wall of hot male anger. 'In fact, you're damn lucky I wasn't anywhere around this Mark bastard when he grabbed you. Because if I had been, he wouldn't have had any balls left for you to knee.'

He was threatening like this, his anger not directed at me but *for* me. A protective anger. An anger that Dad had never displayed, not once. No, his had always been *at* me. As if Mark grabbing me had been my fault.

I didn't know why desire hit me so hard in that moment, a surge of it spiking in my blood. Because it shouldn't have. I didn't need a man getting protective of me—hell, I'd kicked bloody Mark straight in the family jewels, hadn't I? I could protect myself.

But some part of me liked that Mr Evans was angry on my behalf. I could imagine him at the Australis Christmas party, standing behind me, big and scarred and dangerous. Scowling that famous scowl. A wordless threat to anyone who thought touching me was a good idea.

And he wouldn't have cared about making a fuss as Dad had.

No, he wouldn't have cared about that one single iota.

He would have been on my side.

I wanted him suddenly and very, *very* badly.

And he must have seen it, because his gaze became very focused. 'You like that idea, don't you?' His voice dropped almost an entire octave.

'Yes.' Very purposefully, I put my hands over his

where they rested on the armrests of my seat, his skin searing my palms. 'I do.'

'That's very bloodthirsty.'

'You have a problem with a woman being bloodthirsty?'

'Fuck, no. But fair warning, pretty thing. It turns me on.'

I shivered. I shouldn't goad him and yet I couldn't stop. 'I don't mind if you're turned on.'

The expression on his face got taut. 'You might. Because if you keep touching me like that, we're having sex. Understand?'

Oh, I understood. I was very clear. And the more I stared into his eyes, the more I wanted him and the less my doubts about it seemed to matter.

I couldn't even remember why I hadn't wanted to have sex with him again in the first place. It was only sex. Not a big deal.

'That's going to be difficult in Dubai,' I said huskily. 'I mean, presumably couples who are serious have to touch each other. And it'll look weird if we don't.'

The look in his eyes became scorching. 'You want to get in some practice, then?'

If I thought about this too long I'd get cold feet.

I needed to stop thinking.

I leaned forward, running my hands up his strong forearms, trailing my fingers over hot skin and powerful muscle.

And kissed him. Hard.

CHAPTER TWELVE

Ash

ELLIE'S MOUTH WAS HOT, her delicate touch against my bare skin making my breath catch.

I shouldn't have responded. I should have pulled away, especially given what she'd just told me about the prick who'd touched her, who'd hurt her no matter how she'd downplayed it.

Because I was just another prick who would hurt her.

Because that was what I did. I hurt people.

But I couldn't have pulled away from her in that moment if my life had depended on it.

I'd warned her, though. I'd warned her that if she was going to touch me like this, we'd be having sex. And I was a man of my word.

Despite numerous invitations, I'd never had sex in the company jet—I preferred to keep the line between my company and my pleasure *very* separate.

Today, I didn't give a shit about that line.

Her tongue was tentatively exploring me, her nails beginning to dig into my biceps. She tasted so sweet, strawberries on a summer day, and the heat of her body was temptation incarnate.

She was wearing shorts today, instead of her uniform. Just a simple pair of blue denim shorts, with a green T-shirt. Nothing spectacular.

Yet I hadn't been able to take my eyes off her.

I'd had to busy myself with a whole lot of business just to stop myself from gaping at her like a love-struck teenager. I'd thought I'd had myself well in hand. But when she'd started talking about her family's company, about the situation with the harassment and some motherfucker who thought he could touch her; about how her father had paid that prick off instead of supporting his daughter...

I'd wanted to kill someone over that.

If either her father or the prick who'd touched her had been there I think I would have literally strangled them.

But since they weren't, I'd have to take the sex.

What a fucking hardship.

I shouldn't touch her again, but she was kissing me quite desperately and I couldn't refuse her. I didn't want to refuse her.

I lifted my hands to her face, sliding my fingers along her delicate jaw, her skin silky and soft beneath my fingertips.

A kiss was great. But her mouth wasn't where I wanted to kiss her.

Holding her carefully, I pulled away.

She blinked, her eyes a pure dark gold, looking at me as if she'd never wanted anything so badly.

My cock, already hard, ached like a bastard.

'Lie back,' I ordered. 'Let me give you something.'

'But I—'

'I'm not asking.'

As I expected, the order ignited her fighting spirit. 'Oh? You think you're driving again?'

'Yes.' I dropped my hands to her bare thighs, stroking, her skin just as silky and warm as her jaw had been. 'And as I recall, you very much enjoyed it when I drove the last time.'

She was already a very pretty shade of pink, and when I stroked her again she went even pinker. 'But I'm always the driver.'

'I know. So let me do the work for once.' I kept my gaze on hers as I reached for the buttons of her shorts, watching her reaction. 'All you need to do is lie back and enjoy the ride.'

'Oh.' She chewed on her bottom lip a moment as if considering it. Then she let out a breath. 'Well, I guess when you put it like that.' Slowly she sat back in her seat.

Raw triumph flooded through me, along with something a little more uncomfortable. Because she wasn't one of my socialites, or an aristocrat I could sully. She was different. She was a fighter who was conceding me the advantage by choice. Because she trusted me. Even after that arsehole had hurt her, she trusted me.

The heady eroticism of the knowledge caught me by the throat at the same time as it unsettled me.

I had no idea why she would trust me, even why she had the night in the limo in Paris, especially given what kind of man I was.

You're not good enough for her. You're not good enough for anyone.

I shoved that thought away. This wasn't about me. This was about her. About giving her pleasure and making sure she'd never regret the trust she put in me.

I undid the button of her shorts and pulled down the zip. Then I slid my hands into the waistband and began to ease the denim down, taking her underwear with it, watching her face the whole time.

Her gaze had darkened, but I didn't miss the hint of uncertainty in it.

I stopped. 'What? Changed your mind?'

'No.' She sounded sure, at least. 'I haven't changed my mind. But…' She glanced at the door that led to the galley and cockpit. 'No one's going to interrupt?'

My tense muscles relaxed. Thank fuck for that. Shyness I could deal with.

'My staff know better than that,' I said. 'I like to do work when I fly long distance so they leave me alone. No one's even going to knock for another couple of hours.'

'Oh, good.' She gave me a small smile, her flush deepening beautifully. 'I didn't much care about it in the limo, but this is…I don't know, different.'

She was right. This *was* different. Because this wasn't us being at the mercy of our chemistry. This was us being very purposeful.

This was me doing something for her.

I wasn't used to reassuring people, but I tried. 'Don't worry. I would have told the stewardess to stay put if I thought it would be a problem.'

Her uncertainty melted away entirely. 'Okay, good. Well…' She lifted her hips. 'Come on. Get going.'

Impatient girl.

I was generally a selfish man but not sexually, and especially not now, with her. This was about what Ellie wanted. And I was going to give it to her. Slowly.

I tightened my grip on the fabric still covering her and tugged it down, easing it over her butt, down her thighs and off, before discarding it onto the floor of the cabin.

She'd gone the loveliest shade of pink and I put my hands on the armrests of her seat, taking a moment to look at her, because she was a fucking gorgeous sight. All silky pale skin and the dark nest of curls between her thighs.

The pink became scarlet as a tide of red washed over her skin and her hands lifted as if to cover herself, but I caught her wrists before she could, gripping and holding them lightly. 'You don't want me to look?'

She shifted uncomfortably but didn't pull away. 'No… I just… Mark used to look at me and I didn't like it.'

'I'm not Mark.'

'No, I know, but I—'

I released one wrist and caught her chin in my fingers, holding her so she had no choice but to meet my gaze. 'I'm not Mark,' I repeated. 'And this is different, understand? Yes, I like to be in charge, but the only reason I am is because you're letting me.' I tightened my grip, because this was important. No, this was vital. 'You have the power here, pretty thing. And you have it because your pleasure matters. It didn't matter to him, not one fucking iota. But it matters to me.'

She didn't say anything, her attention focused on me as if she'd never seen me before in her entire life. And that made my cock even harder, my body liking the way she was staring at me very much indeed.

'Let me look,' I went on, letting her see the desire in my gaze. 'Because you're beautiful and I like looking at you. And I think there's a part of you that likes me looking at you, too. A part that you don't want to let yourself acknowledge.'

Emotions flickered through her expressive face, gone so fast that I couldn't decipher them. But then I felt the slight resistance drain from her arms, her wrist going lax in my grip. And she eased herself back in the seat, her chin lifting, the expression glowing in her eyes very clear now. A challenge. Because of course, she was a fighter.

'Shall I show you how much you like it, then?' I asked, to be certain.

She lifted a shoulder, as if she didn't much care. But the gold flames in her eyes told a different story.

So I let go of her wrists and reached for the hem of her T-shirt, tugging gently on the fabric to indicate what I wanted, keeping my attention on her face.

Another flicker of uncertainty, but then she leaned forward and slowly raised her arms, letting me pull the cotton up and over her head, taking her bra with it, so at last she was sitting in her seat completely naked.

Then I put my hands on the armrests again and I looked, taking my time, letting my gaze track down, over the slight, sweet curves of her perfect tits with their pretty pink and rapidly hardening nipples. Then the graceful indentation of her waist and the curving plane of her stomach. Down further to the flare of her hips and her rounded thighs.

Beautiful. Absolutely fucking beautiful.

She trembled, but didn't move. Didn't cover herself. She'd gone bright red, but she didn't look away, either.

Brave girl.

But I wanted to see more.

I put my hands on her knees, spreading them apart, watching for any sign of resistance, but there was none. So I pushed them wider, my gaze falling hungrily to the tantalising nest of dark curls and pink flesh.

So fucking pretty. And she was wet, too, I could see the slick gleam of moisture on her skin.

Desire pulsed through me, thick and hot, the ache in my groin becoming demanding.

'Yes,' I said roughly. 'You like me looking at you, don't you?'

She shifted on the seat, her chin lifting higher. 'Maybe. And so?'

'So?' I let the hunger show in my voice, throwing the challenge right back at her. 'Show me more. Show me that pretty little pussy of yours.' I rested my weight on my hands and leaned in, the scent of her arousal sweet and musky in the air, the heat of her body making me ache to touch her. 'Show me how wet you are.'

Her skin was a fiery red, but her chin firmed, the gold in her gaze leaping higher.

Desire wrapped its hands around my throat, choking

me, because if that wasn't the look of a woman accepting a challenge, I didn't know what was.

Christ, she had courage. And a backbone of pure steel.

She lifted her hands and then—little witch—put them on her hips, sliding them down slowly and watching me as she did so, as if gauging my response. I didn't hold back, showing her what her sexy show was doing to me and she liked that. She liked that a lot, desire flickering over her face as she stared at me.

As if that was a goad, she slid her hands lower, between her spread thighs, her fingers firm on her own slick flesh as she gently eased apart the wet, pink folds of her pussy, holding them there.

My fingers dug into the leather of the armrests, the need to dive right in, put my mouth on her, my hands on her, almost all-consuming. I ached like a motherfucker and my mouth watered. But I stayed where I was, enjoying the view.

'Beautiful.' My voice had gone low and rough. 'All pink and wet. You *really* like me looking, don't you?'

She shivered, her breathing uneven, her gaze hot and focused on mine. 'Yes. Seen enough, yet?'

'No, not nearly enough.' I glanced down at the lovely sight of her spread thighs, at the petal pink of her sex and the gleam of moisture on her skin, the sheen of it on her fingers. 'Is this all for me?'

'Y-yes,' she said thickly.

My own heartbeat was loud in my head, a thudding, insistent rhythm. I was used to taking what I wanted when I wanted it. I never had to wait. But now, here with her, I wanted to.

If it added to her pleasure I'd wait till kingdom fucking come.

I met her hazel eyes. 'And what would you like me to do about it?'

CHAPTER THIRTEEN

Ellie

MY HEART WAS beating so loudly I could hardly hear anything, and I was shaking, hardly able to breathe through the intense hunger that had me in its grip.

Mr Evans was kneeling in front of my seat, gripping onto the arms, his knuckles white. His scarred face was fierce with the same hunger that was rising in me, his eyes electric on mine.

Sitting there with my legs spread, holding myself open for him, I'd never felt so vulnerable and yet so weirdly powerful in all my life.

Doing this was pushing him hard and I knew it. In fact, I could see how close to the edge he was—he didn't hide it. Yet he wasn't moving.

He had all the strength and yet, strangely, I had all the power.

I'd been hesitant about him looking at me at first, and, to be honest, uncomfortable and a bit scared. Because I'd hated how Mark had done the same thing, staring at me as if I was something he wanted to eat.

But I didn't hate Mr Evans looking at me.

I didn't hate it at all.

Not when I could see how hard he was holding himself back. All that strength was tightly leashed, the power of him humming in the air around him like a force field, yet he didn't release it. He kept it in check.

Kept himself in check.

He'd said this was different, but I hadn't realised how different until now. I hadn't realised how much I liked him looking at me until now either.

Being desired wasn't something I'd wanted, and yet… I wanted to be desired by him. More, I wanted to keep pushing him, to see how far I could go, where his boundaries were, because he must have them.

A dangerous game, perhaps?

Maybe, but then I'd always been a fan of danger and the adrenaline rush.

'Well?' he demanded, the rough edge in his voice making me shiver in delight. 'Tell me what you want.'

'I want you to keep looking.' I sounded just as rough as he did. 'Keep watching.'

A muscle flickered in his impressive jaw. 'What are you going to do, pretty?'

'I'll show you.' And without taking my gaze from his, I shifted one of my hands, sliding my finger over my clit, sending electricity firing through my body like a switch being thrown.

Instantly his attention dropped to my hand and what I was doing, that muscle in his jaw jumping again as I slid my finger around my clit once more, rubbing gently.

Pleasure uncurled inside me, a sweet ache made all

the more intense by the way he followed every move I made.

I'd done this in bed at night, when I couldn't sleep, when I was feeling restless. Before Mark it had been for fun, but after, I'd done it to try and make myself feel better, to reclaim my feelings for myself.

I thought it had worked, but right now, with Mr Evans watching me, I knew it hadn't. This was better than anything I could give myself. Because Mr Evans's electric gaze didn't simply blaze over memories of Mark staring at me fixedly during that horrible Christmas party, it replaced those memories entirely.

Instead of powerlessness and an oily, sick feeling, I felt strong, pleasure humming in my veins. Making me want to keep going, push him even more, wipe out those memories so I'd never think of Mark again.

I'd never backed down from a challenge, so I kept going.

I slid one finger inside, going slowly, making sure he watched as I did, lifting my hips and spreading my thighs wider so he got a good view. It felt incredible, pleasure licking up my spine as I watched the flames in his eyes leap high.

His expression was taut, his jaw hard, and I could almost feel the tension in his body myself. He was still holding himself back and yet it was getting difficult for him.

Satisfaction unwound inside me and I slid my finger out then back in again, feeling my own wetness and heat, allowing myself to give in to the sheer pleasure of it. To having this powerful man watch me as I touched myself, taut and hungry and not able to touch me. Because I had said so.

I arched back in my seat, moaning as I moved my finger faster, rubbing at my clit with my other hand, watching him from beneath my lashes, his gaze fixed between my legs.

I added another finger and he growled, a rumble coming from deep in his chest, a rough, hungry sound. 'You like to push, don't you?'

'No fun otherwise.' I panted, shifting again, moving my hips in time with my hand, electric ripples of pleasure moving through me and making me gasp.

The blunt, scarred lines of his face became set, his knuckles white where he gripped the armrests. His nostrils flared as if he'd scented me, his focus intensifying.

Was he near the edge? Was he going to go over like I was? Because I would and very quickly if I wasn't careful. Watching him watch me was unbelievably erotic and it wouldn't take much to send me flying.

But I wanted to see him break first.

I lifted one leg, hooking it over the armrest, brushing the back of his hand, opening myself up wider so he could get an even better view. And he growled again, a low, rough warning, flashing me a brief, electric glance that told me he was hanging by a thread.

Exhilaration gripped me, like throwing a car around the track, foot to the floor, seeing how fast you could go and still stay in control. Stay in command.

Go faster.

I arched in my seat, sinking both fingers deep inside, moaning softly at the pleasure that rolled through me, letting my thigh rest heavily against the back of his hand.

He cursed, filthy and low. 'Miss Little, keep playing with fire and you're going to get burned.'

'Why?' I panted. 'Am I too much for you?'

And just like that, the warning in his eyes blazed into intent. He shifted, reaching for the hand between my thighs and pulling it away. Then he lifted my slick fingers and drew them into his mouth.

The suddenness of the movement and the heat of his tongue around my fingers stole every breath I had.

I gasped as he began to slowly and methodically suck, his gaze on mine. The pressure was gentle and yet I felt it intensely, as if he were sucking on something else. Something far more sensitive.

I shuddered, my breathing getting faster, the unfulfilled ache between my thighs acute. I wanted to come but suddenly I didn't want to make myself do it. I wanted him to do it for me.

And he must have known that, must have read it in my gaze, because he took my hand from his mouth and placed it down on one of the armrests. 'Hold on,' he ordered. 'Don't let go.'

Excitement wound through me and part of me wanted to argue with him. But I wanted his touch more, so I obeyed, shivering as he did the same with my other hand, before holding both hands down by covering them with his own. Then he gave me one blazing glance, before he leaned forward and buried his head between my spread thighs.

Fire burst along every nerve ending I had.

I arched in the seat, crying out as he pushed his tongue into me, a hard thrust that nearly tipped me over the edge. But not quite. I groaned, shivering all over, the pleasure of it indescribable.

I'd never had a man do this to me, had never felt the rough prickle of his stubble against my inner thighs, or the pressure of his tongue in my pussy. It was incredible, the pleasure almost painful in its intensity.

Then he pulled back, his tongue beginning to explore me, licking me with broad, flat strokes, before finding my clit and teasing.

He seemed to know exactly how far to push without giving me exactly what I wanted, stopping before I fell over the edge, pushing me every bit as badly as I'd pushed him.

It was payback, I got that. But it was the kind of payback I was more than happy with. Well, if I hadn't been so impatient, that was.

'Please…' I gasped as he flicked my clit with his tongue. 'Oh, Mr Evans, please…'

His voice was a low vibration against my inner thigh. 'Ash, pretty thing. You're going to have to start calling me Ash, because no one calls their boyfriend Mr.' A blaze of blue met mine. 'Unless it's in bed.'

Through the haze of pleasure, I understood. Just. 'A-Ash,' I managed, trying it out as I squirmed and shifted beneath the pressure of his tongue. 'Please…' I tried to lift my hands but he was holding them down and didn't let me.

'Please what? You have to tell me what you want.'

'Please make me come. Oh, please…'

He didn't reply, merely turned his attention back between my thighs, covering my pussy with his mouth. Then he went to work on my clit, teasing and licking, nipping too, just a little, the pain slight and yet so sweet I couldn't stop the cry of pleasure it dragged from me.

And then one more flick of his tongue and I was gone, bucking in my seat, arching and shifting as the pleasure rocketed through me, turning me into a human firework, bursting me into flames right where I sat.

I didn't know how long it was before I came down from the high, my body pulsing, my heartbeat roaring in my ears, my breathing wild.

But then his hands were on me and I was being gathered up from the seat and into his arms, taken over to the low couch on the opposite side of the cabin. He bent and laid me carefully down onto it before putting one hand on either side of my head and leaning over me, staring down into my eyes. The expression on his face stole my breath, the hunger for me burning bright in his gaze.

Yes, I'd pushed him. I'd pushed him right to the edge and over it. He'd broken. He'd touched me and I couldn't help feeling as if, somehow, I'd won this round.

It made me want to test him again.

'I want you,' he said roughly, without any preliminaries. 'In fact, I don't think I've ever wanted to fuck anyone as badly as I want to fuck you right now. But this is about you, not me. Your pleasure, not mine. So if you don't want—'

I reached up and put a finger across his hard mouth, silencing him. Then I said huskily, 'Fuck me, Mr Evans.'

Wildfire blazed in his eyes and for a second I thought he was going to take me there and then. But he pushed himself away and straightened to his full height. Then he began to get rid of his clothing, watching me all the while, stripping his T-shirt off and dropping it to the floor, his hand dropping to the buttons of his jeans.

I couldn't drag my gaze from him, running over the wide, powerful planes of his bare chest, the hard, cut muscle of his abs, the flex and release of his biceps as he undid his jeans.

He was a beautiful man and I couldn't stop looking as he took his time undoing his fly, teasing me as I'd teased him.

'This is payback, right?' I asked thickly as he shoved his jeans down and off.

'It might be.' He straightened, naked now and totally magnificent, the whole cabin full of his fierce hunger and electrical presence.

My mouth dried as I looked down his brutally powerful body to where his cock stood out, hard and huge, curving up to his corrugated stomach. I pushed myself up, my hands itching to touch him, but he must have known what I wanted because he gave one firm shake of his head. 'Just lie there, pretty thing. No touching me quite yet, not if you want my cock.' He bent to get his wallet out of his jeans, extracting a condom before tossing everything back down on the floor. Then he ripped open the packet with his teeth and rolled down the latex with a couple of powerful, efficient movements, before coming over to where I lay on the couch.

I was panting now, the ache between my thighs

building once more, desperate to touch him, to feel him against me. I spread my legs as he got onto the couch, reaching up to him as he positioned himself over me, my hands sliding over the smooth skin of his powerful shoulders.

God, he was amazing. All that strength leashed and contained for me. All of that pleasure for me, too.

I didn't know why I was important enough that my experience with Mark mattered to him, but I wasn't going to question it, not now. The fact that it did matter was enough.

That what I wanted mattered enough. Because it had been a long time since that had happened, too.

I couldn't read the look in his eyes as he slid his hands beneath my butt and lifted me, fitting the blunt head of his cock into my body. But something in it burned. He was so intense, almost too much to look at directly.

But I watched him as I felt him push inside me, thick, hot and hard, feeling my own flesh part before his, straining to accommodate him. I shuddered, gasping, digging my nails into the hard muscle of his shoulders.

He didn't look away from me, not once, sinking deep and making me shudder and groan because he was big. But I'd taken him before and I took him now, tilting my hips so he could go deeper, wrapping my legs around his lean waist and arching up. My nipples scraped deliciously over his hard chest, the prickle of hair an added delight.

'God,' I whispered, looking up into his eyes. 'You feel amazing...'

The ferocity in his expression stole my breath. He didn't answer, only leaned down and covered my mouth with his, kissing me hard, an edge of desperation in it that I didn't quite understand.

I could taste myself on his lips, but I didn't care. It was like spice added to an already hot dish, building the heat even higher, and I kissed him back, hungry as he was.

He nipped on my bottom lip as he moved, lifting his hands to the arm of the couch behind my head and gripping it, then using it as leverage as he thrust hard, then harder still. Deep then deeper.

I could barely think now, the pleasure getting larger and larger inside me, the pressure of it becoming more and more intense.

Too much.

Dimly in some part of my brain I heard the warning. But I was too far gone to listen to it. The ecstasy of having him inside me, the furious pace he was setting too irresistible. I didn't want to stop it.

I didn't want it to end.

The heat of him was all around me, inside me. The heady musky scent of male arousal and clean sweat was an aphrodisiac that I'd never dreamt would turn me on as much as it was doing. And it was.

I slid my hands down his powerful back, feeling his hard body surge into me, digging my nails into his skin, holding on tight as he drove us both to the edge.

This is going to make you cry again.

I shut my eyes, kissing him hungrily, trying to lose myself in the taste of him and the feel of his cock thrusting into me, trying to lose myself in the pleasure and not think about the ache in my chest that was building as much as the pleasure was.

An ache I didn't understand.

Just sex, huh?

I shoved the thought from my mind. 'Harder,' I whispered against his mouth. 'Fuck me harder, Mr Evans.'

He made another of those low, sexy rumbling sounds, his rhythm intensifying until the cabin was full of the sounds of his flesh hitting mine, my gasps of pleasure and his own rough groans as we came closer and closer to the edge.

I dug my heels into the taut muscle of his butt, my nails scratching him as lights began to burst behind my eyes.

He moved harder, deeper, and something began to shift inside me, beginning to crack under the weight of all that pleasure. I felt tears begin to start behind my eyes, pinpricks of emotion stabbing through me.

I fought it, fought the release instinctively, not wanting to give away anything, but it was too late. He shifted his hand between my thighs and found my clit, stroking me as he thrust until I cracked apart completely and all the pleasure came flooding out.

I screamed into his mouth as it hit, my whole body arching and going rigid against his, electrified.

His grip tightened, holding me together as I fell apart in his arms, before getting even tighter as he slammed into me, chasing his own release. His thrusts got wilder, falling out of rhythm, before he tore his mouth from mine and turned his face into my hair, giving one last hard thrust, his body going rigid as he came.

I shut my eyes, blinking furiously to hold back inexplicable tears as he shuddered against me, my name whispered in a rough, dark voice against my skin.

God, what was wrong with me? Why was I getting so emotional again? It didn't make any sense.

I felt good, *so* good. I shouldn't want to cry about it.

Swallowing hard, I managed to keep the tide of emotion at bay, content to let his big, hard body anchor me to the couch, his breath hot in my ear.

Eventually, though, he lifted his head and his blue gaze pinned me. 'Petra booked us a suite with adjoining rooms in Dubai, but I'm telling you now that the moment we land, I'll be wanting to take you into that suite, spread you out across that bed, and keep you there the entire bloody night.' He paused, searching my face. 'If you don't want that, you need to tell me now.'

What could I say? I'd crossed the line and I didn't want to go back, no matter the raw feeling that stuck in my chest.

I could ignore that. It was just sex, right?

'I want it,' I said without hesitation.

And hoped I didn't regret it.

CHAPTER FOURTEEN

Ash

THE FUCKING LIMO felt too goddamn small.

Ellie was sitting beside me, dressed in a green gown that appeared to be constructed out of nothing but tissue. It had a neckline that plunged almost to her belly button and fitted like a glove around her hips and thighs, the skirt falling silkily to her ankles, and I wanted to rip it off her body, and bury myself inside her.

Again.

I thought I'd be satisfied after our first night in Dubai, screwing each other senseless in the suite Petra had booked for us as soon as we got off the plane. But apparently not.

Apparently screwing her only made me want to screw her more, and now I felt nothing but hungry and possessive and feral, all of which were a bad combination.

Especially since we were on our way to the club event where I was supposed to be talking Delaney out of his precious islands. I was going to need my focus for that and couldn't afford to be distracted by my lovely chauffeur.

Except she didn't look like a chauffeur tonight. She looked like one of my expensive socialites, with her brown hair lying gleaming and glossy over her shoulders, her face newly adorned with make-up.

It was strange seeing her like this, but not at all unwelcome.

She looked gorgeous and I'd already decided I liked her just as much in a gown as I did in her uniform, though the shorts won because they showed more skin.

However, she was obviously nervous because when she wasn't tugging up the neckline of her gown, she was touching her hair or straightening the fabric of her skirt. Small gestures that betrayed her.

'You don't need to be nervous,' I said into the silence. 'You look beautiful.'

She gave me a quick glance. 'And you look hot in that tux.'

I grimaced and tried not to pull on my tie; I hated wearing a suit.

'Anyway,' she went on, 'I'm not nervous.'

'Yes, you are. If you pull at your gown one more time, you're going to rip it.' I reached out and took her hand from where it was tugging at her neckline for a fourth time, threading my fingers through hers and drawing it away from the gown to lie on my thigh instead.

Touching her was probably a bloody stupid thing to do, especially when the chemistry between us was so volatile, but I thought my touch might reassure her.

She stared at our linked hands for a long moment, her fingers looking small and delicate compared to mine.

'Okay,' she sighed. 'Maybe I am. I'm not used to wearing dresses.'

'Really? You don't wear dresses at home?'

'No. After Mum died I got out of the habit.'

There was a slight catch in her voice as she said the words and I found myself searching her face. 'Why? You don't like wearing them?'

'Not really. But also I look like her.' She hesitated. 'Dad found that…difficult.'

Her father sounded like a piece of work—hell, he hadn't protected his own daughter from someone who wanted to hurt her. But given her defensiveness about it in the plane yesterday, I kept that opinion to myself for now.

'Difficult?' I asked.

'When I say I look like her, I mean I'm the spitting image of her.' There was a certain sadness in her eyes that made me tighten my grip on her hand. 'Mum also loved dresses and make-up and all kinds of girly things, and after she died, he was so upset that I just…thought it was easier if I didn't look so much like a girl.'

'You wanted to protect him.'

She sighed again. 'He was so lost without her and he doesn't do emotion. He couldn't deal with losing her and I wanted to help him.'

'And what about you?'

'What about me?'

'Did anyone help you?' I didn't know what made me ask. Maybe it was that sadness in her eyes, or the way her fingers had tightened around mine. The sense that I knew the answer to that question already: no one had.

The lights from the city outside glided over her face, a flash of something raw in her eyes, and I felt my chest constrict. 'No,' I said, annoyed with myself. 'Forget I said anything. You don't have to answer.'

She gave me a long look, then said eventually, 'I had my brothers. But they were all older than me. And Dad had no idea what to do with a seven-year-old girl. So... no. I guess I didn't have anyone.' She smiled, but I'd never seen anything so forced. 'Anyway, it was fine. I coped.'

Of course she had. Because she was tough—at least on the surface. But underneath she was vulnerable, I could see it in her eyes. Hell, I'd seen it up in the plane yesterday, too.

I stroked the back of her hand with my thumb, trying not to give in to the anger I felt on her behalf. She was loyal to her family, but it made me wonder if they were as loyal to her.

Certainly there were issues with her dad and his handling of the harassment problem. I got the feeling that he blamed her for it, which was so wrong I wanted to hit something. Hard.

'It wasn't fine,' I said roughly, not liking how she dismissed herself and her own needs so easily. And with a smile that was in no way natural. 'I'm sure you did cope, because you're tough. But that doesn't mean you didn't need anyone to be there for you.'

Her forced smile faltered. 'Dad didn't like fusses. He didn't know how to deal with them.'

'Well, as you probably know by now, I don't mind a fuss.' With my free hand, I gently brushed a finger along her lower lip. 'But what I really don't like is pretence. You have a beautiful smile, pretty thing. You don't need to fake it.'

She blinked and the smile slowly disappeared. Her hand tightened in mine. 'What about you? Did you have anyone?'

I didn't want to talk about me. But then, it was my own fault. I'd introduced the subject and this was where the conversation had ended up. And I couldn't not tell her now, not after what she'd told me.

'I had my mother,' I said, somewhat reluctantly. 'My father wasn't part of my life in any way. He got rid of Mum once he found out she was pregnant and wouldn't pay a cent towards helping her with anything. The only time was when she begged him to pay for my schooling.' I stroked my thumb over Ellie's skin. It was very soft against mine and very warm. 'I tried once, when I was thirteen, to get something from him myself. Mum was having difficulty covering rent and I thought I might be able to convince him to help us. But…' I didn't know why I was telling her this story, not when it ended in nothing but humiliation. Nevertheless, I found myself going on. 'I went and stood outside his house, and when someone eventually came to the door—I don't know who it was, but not Dad—they told me he didn't want to see me. That I wasn't his problem.' Even now, the anger of that moment burned inside me, no matter how many years went by. How I was dismissed. As if my mother and I meant nothing and were nothing to him.

The slight pressure of her fingers around mine made

me realise that she was squeezing my hand. As if I was the one who needed reassurance this time.

It made me want to put some distance between us, but I couldn't pull away. Not without hurting her and I didn't want to hurt her.

'It's fine,' I said brusquely. 'It was a long time ago.'

She gave me a small, shy smile. 'Now you sound like me.'

'It's not quite the same. You lost your mother. I still have mine.'

'But you did lose your dad in a way, didn't you?'

Something shifted inside me. An ache. I ignored it. 'His loss. Anyway, you can't lose something you never had.'

She gave me a searching look. 'It's the potential though, isn't it? The potential for there to have been something more.'

The ache deepened into pain and I gritted my teeth hard. 'There was never any potential for something more. I wasn't good enough for Dad. I wasn't his problem.' The words sounded bitter, like something a petulant teenager would say, which was galling. 'But like I said,' I went on quickly, before she could say anything, 'that was years ago. Anyway, we weren't talking about me. We were talking about you.'

Ellie scowled. 'I don't want to talk about me. I'm bloody boring.'

The tight feeling in my chest eased at the grumpy expression on her face. 'And now you sound like me,' I said, amused.

That got a smile from her, an easy, natural one that seemed to light up the interior of the entire car.

'That's better, pretty thing,' I murmured, watching her. 'That's the smile I'm talking about.'

She flushed. 'How did you meet him?'

The question was so out of the blue that I didn't quite understand what she was talking about for a second.

'Him?'

'Your half-brother. I mean, you didn't have contact with your dad, so I've been wondering.'

My amusement vanished. Fuck. I didn't want to talk about Dumont, either.

No, because then she'll know what a petty bastard you are. How you destroyed the only friendship you had because you can't let go of the past.

No. Maybe she should know what a petty bastard I was. I'd told her how Seb had lost my money, but I hadn't told her how I'd spent the last twelve years competing for his business. Or how I'd preferred my anger to all the olive branches he'd tried to hold out.

'I met him at school,' I said at last. 'My mother finally got Dad to pay for my schooling at a private prep school and I met him there.' A memory floated through my head, of how I'd been shunned by the other boys, because I was poor, because at that stage I was skinny and short and I didn't belong with them. Of how they all drew away from me as I sat that first day in the ancient hall where they ate. And how one lanky kid had dropped onto the bench opposite me and had given me a grin. 'Hey,' he'd said. 'This seat taken?'

I'd glowered at him, wanting him to go away and leave me alone.

But he hadn't. He'd simply stuck out his hand and introduced himself. Then he'd said, 'Brothers have to stick together, right?'

'He didn't care that I didn't belong,' I said aloud. 'He didn't give a single shit where I'd come from. We were brothers and as far as he was concerned that was all he needed to know to be my friend.'

Ellie squeezed my hand again. 'No wonder you were so angry with him when he lost your money,' she murmured. 'He broke your trust.'

She saw through me. She saw through me too well.

'And so I went after his business.' My voice was rough and I made no effort to hide it. 'He tried to mend fences, but since he'd ignored me, I ignored him.' I bared my teeth at her. 'Don't make the mistake of thinking I'm totally the wronged party here, pretty thing. I'm a petty bastard and I'm fully aware of that fact.'

She gave me a long look. 'Is that supposed to be a warning?'

'No. Just the truth.'

Her hazel gaze turned intent. 'You're very uncompromising about certain things. Why is that?'

Something shot down my spine, a bolt of heat. 'Because I don't apologise for who I am and I don't hide it, either. You take me as I am or not at all. Understand?' I didn't know why it felt important to say to her. Perhaps because I didn't want her thinking I was something I wasn't.

Like, someone better?

I ignored that thought, holding her hazel gaze instead.

And slowly she gave me a nod. 'I understand.'

I hoped she did. Because if she wanted me to be someone else, she was out of luck.

CHAPTER FIFTEEN

Ellie

IT WAS STRANGE being a passenger in a limo. Even stranger for the limo to pull up outside the venue we were going to and for the door to be held open for me the way I usually did for other people.

We'd pulled up outside some hotel that was the very epitome of an *Arabian Nights* fantasy, all arches and domes and gardens. The space in front of the entrance was full of other limos dropping off expensively clad guests, ladies in couture gowns and men in tuxes.

Mr Evans—no, *Ash*—had surprised me by wearing a tux tonight and I found it surprisingly difficult to look at him in it.

Because if he was gorgeous in jeans and a T-shirt, in a tux he was absolutely mesmerising.

With his height and his broad build, his scarred face and the electric blue of his eyes, the formality of the clothing seemed only to enhance the raw masculinity of him, a kind of untamed earthy energy that had made my breath catch the moment I'd seen him in it.

He held out his hand to me now as I got out of the limo, the warmth of his fingers closing around mine as I took it. The reassurance of that warmth made something I hadn't realised was nervous inside me settle.

Back at the hotel, we'd talked a little about what our cover story as a couple would be and had decided that we'd go with meeting at a charity event a couple of months ago and keeping our relationship on the downlow to avoid any media nonsense. No, we hadn't been dating long, but we already knew that it was going to be something that would last. Yes, we were contemplating marriage, and kids were a definite possibility.

His gaze was intense on mine as I stepped from the car, attention turning to us, the paparazzi already gathering.

Except I wasn't thinking about the paparazzi. I was thinking about what he'd said earlier, about his father and Dumont, and about how he was a petty bastard. He'd flung that at me almost like a challenge, daring me to contradict him, and I'd wanted to.

Because the man who'd reached out and held my hand, who'd talked to me about how I should have had someone when my mother had died, who'd told me my father should have protected me against Mark, wasn't petty in the slightest.

But I knew he'd argue if I tried to contradict him and it wasn't the right moment for an argument. I didn't understand what made me want to convince him he was wrong, anyway. After all, why did I care whether he thought he was a petty bastard or not?

He was certainly a grumpy one, that was for sure,

though his temper didn't bother me. It only made me curious as to why he was like that. Because he struck me very much like a bear with a sore paw, swiping at people who came too close.

Do you want to get close?

Maybe I did. I was curious about the bitterness in his voice when he'd mentioned his father. The throwaway line about him not being good enough.

But it wasn't a throwaway line, was it? And it kind of explained why he was so driven to succeed and why he was so uncompromising that people had to take him as he was. Why he was so bluntly honest about himself.

He really was afraid he wasn't good enough.

But I didn't like that thought and I didn't like how it hurt him, because it did hurt him. He just covered that hurt with anger.

It made me want to help him in some way, though how I didn't know. It wasn't my place to do so anyway.

Well, you are supposed to be his girlfriend, so... maybe it is tonight?

The emerald gown swirled around me as we walked towards the entrance, a reminder of my role: Ash Evans's girlfriend.

I didn't know how to be a girlfriend—hell, I was barely used to being a lover, and we'd only been lovers for a single night. Was I even going to be convincing? I could talk about cars for ever, but anything else? Plans for the future and weddings and perhaps a family?

I hadn't thought about those things. I wasn't really interested in those things. My life was all about Australis.

What about after this is over? What are you going to do about him?

That, at least, was easy. I would do nothing about him. He'd been a lovely and unexpected interlude while I'd been in Europe, but that was it.

In the meantime, I'd have to play the part I'd promised and hopefully do it well enough that he'd get his precious islands.

'Don't look so nervous,' he murmured in my ear as we turned towards the entrance of the hotel, curling one arm possessively around my waist and drawing me close. 'Just stick to our story and you'll be fine.'

I leaned into the heat and hard muscle of his body. 'I feel like an imposter,' I murmured back. 'I don't know how to be anyone's girlfriend, let alone yours.'

People stared at us as we entered the hotel, flashes going off as the paparazzi swarmed. Not used to it, I tried to ignore the attention.

'You don't have to know.' He reached into his jacket pocket and brought out a matte black card that he flashed at the doorman. 'All you have to do is act like you can't wait to rip my clothes off. That should do it.'

My mouth went dry at the thought of ripping off his clothes. Or rather, of pulling open his white shirt and touching the warm skin of his chest, sliding my hands over all that hard muscle.

God…

'Yes,' he rumbled softly and approvingly as the doorman pulled open the door and we went inside. 'That's exactly the look I mean.'

I flushed. If that was all it took to look like a girl-friend then this was going to be a piece of cake.

A poised and beautiful blonde woman—Imogen Car-michael, apparently—greeted us at the hotel entrance, an American from the sounds of her accent, explain-ing about the various facilities in the hotel and giving directions. She greeted me without a flicker, her hand-shake firm and cool, just like her smile.

'Right,' Ash said, steering me down one high-arched hallway floored in white marble. 'Time to find Delaney.'

A flutter of nervousness collected inside me, but I tried not to think about that or how out of my depth I felt in my dress.

Imogen had given us directions to the bar area—a big open space intended to give the feeling of a Bedouin tent, with lanterns of coloured glass hanging over ornate tables in heavy dark wood, and low divans covered in brightly coloured silk cushions. A fountain played in the centre, the splashing water in counterpoint to the murmur of voices and the low pulse of music.

Ash steered me in the direction of one of the tables, where an older man sat, his white hair expertly coiffed, his smile welcoming as he stood to greet us.

'Evans,' he said warmly, reaching out to take Ash's hand. 'Glad you could make it.' His attention turned to me. 'And this is…?'

'Ellie Little,' Ash said. 'Ellie, this is John Delaney, a business associate of mine.'

I swallowed my nervousness and tried for a smile, shaking his hand. 'G'day, Mr Delaney.'

Delaney smiled. 'Oh, you're Australian. How charming. Please, call me John.'

'Good to meet you, John.' I gave his hand a firm squeeze.

Ash's arm stole around my waist again, pulling me close, his hand splayed on my hip, the heat of it seeping through my gown as if there were nothing between his palm and my skin.

It was a very possessive hold and obviously for Delaney's benefit, though some part of me found it thrilling in a way I wasn't expecting.

Was it weird to like the thought of being his? To enjoy the way he held me? As if he wanted the entire bar to know who I belonged to?

It's fake, though.

Yes, it was. Which, in a way, made it okay for me to like it. If it wasn't real, I could let myself enjoy the sensation of being protected, of having someone at my back in a way I hadn't had before.

Delaney's gaze lingered on the positioning of Ash's hand on me. 'Don't worry, Evans. I'm not going to steal her from you, though…' there was a sparkle in his eye '…maybe if I were twenty years younger I might.'

Ash's smile was little more than bared teeth, the pressure on my hip increasing. 'Try it.'

Delaney grinned. 'Relax and have a seat. I want to know how you two met.'

We sat down on the divan, Ash not allowing an inch of space between us, the heat of his powerful thigh pressing against mine. 'It was at a charity event in July,' he said gruffly. 'We got to talking, one thing led to another and the rest is history.' He sounded impatient. 'What else do you want to know?'

Delaney watched us from his seat opposite. 'I must say, I was surprised to hear you had a serious girlfriend. I haven't heard anything about it in the media.'

'No, because I wanted Ellie to stay out of the spotlight.'

'Which I prefer,' I added, putting a casual hand on Ash's hard thigh. He was hot there, too, powerful muscles tensing under my palm, making me want to squeeze them, test them.

Delaney leaned back in his seat. 'So what brought you to London, Ellie?'

'Work,' I said truthfully. 'I design luxury cars for my family's company.'

Delaney's eyes widened. 'Do you indeed? Impressive.'

'I thought so.' Ash's arm tightened around my waist, the muscles under my hand flexing yet again. 'At least, she impressed the hell out of me.'

There was an element of certainty in the words that made me blush like a fool. As if he was telling the truth.

Delaney clearly saw my reaction because he smiled. 'I can see that. So…forgive me for asking, but what are your plans together? I like to know these things,' he added, clearly for my benefit, 'because Evans here is wanting to buy some islands of mine that have sentimental value. I wanted them to go to someone who is family-minded. I hope you understand.'

'Of course I understand.' I gave Ash what I hoped

was an adoring glance. 'So, our plans? Well, at the moment I'm considering moving to London permanently.'

Something I didn't recognise glinted in Ash's blue eyes. 'Perhaps I want to move to Sydney, pretty thing. Did you ever think of that?'

The use of his silly pet name in public jolted me, the teasing note in his deep voice making me blush harder, the blood flowing hotter in my veins. 'No, I didn't.' I tried to pull myself together, flicking him a look from beneath my lashes. 'But you know I don't mind where we live as long as I'm with you.'

His gaze flared in a way that I was becoming familiar with, his competitive instinct rousing. 'As long as there's a bed, right?'

I could feel my cheeks get hot, but I wasn't going to let him win so easily. 'I wasn't aware we needed a bed.'

There were flames in his eyes now, one corner of his hard mouth curving in acknowledgement.

Delaney cleared his throat. 'Well, please don't let me interrupt,' he said, sounding amused. 'But I think you might be pleased to hear this news, Evans.'

'What news?' Ash didn't look at him, his gaze on mine.

The rest of the bar was beginning to fall away, the only thing in it the man sitting in front of me, staring at me with open hunger.

And I could feel myself beginning to respond, the ache between my thighs intensifying.

'I'm going to sell you the islands,' Delaney said.

'Good.' The curve of Ash's mouth deepened.

'It wasn't a hard decision in the end,' Delaney went on. 'Not after Dumont withdrew his offer.'

Ash froze, the fire in his eyes dousing instantly. Then he turned his head sharply in Delaney's direction. 'Say that again,' he ordered, his voice rough.

If Delaney was surprised at the change in Ash's mood he didn't show it. 'Your half-brother called me a couple of days ago to tell me he was withdrawing the offer. Mainly because he knew you were keen on the property and he wanted to clear the field for you.' Delaney smiled. 'He said he owed you, which is such a generous gesture given how much he wanted to purchase them as well. But I thought, well, if that's not family-minded, what is? And given that, plus your lovely Ellie here—' he gestured at me '—I don't think I could sell the islands to a better person.'

Ash had gone statue-still, tension gathering around him like a storm cloud. I could feel it crawling over me, too, tightening my muscles and making me catch my breath.

And I understood. The whole reason he'd come to Dubai, with me, was to steal those islands out from under Dumont. And now Dumont had just denied him. He'd conceded the fight.

The warrior in Ash would hate that.

Sure enough his blue eyes blazed like gas flames in his face, his scars vivid white against his olive skin. He didn't just look angry. He looked furious.

But… I got the sense that something else was going on here.

His thigh under mine was like iron so I squeezed it, wanting to give him some kind of reassurance. But he stood, a sharp, jerky motion, then without a word he turned and strode away, leaving me sitting there with Delaney, both of us staring after him in shock.

'What's happened?' Delaney turned to me, frowning. 'I thought he'd be pleased.'

I shot to my feet, the urge to go after him, to find out what was wrong and whether he was okay, filling me. I should probably have stayed to smooth things over with Delaney, but I couldn't. If Ash was a bear with a sore paw, then someone had just stomped on that paw, making him roar.

And I didn't like that. I didn't like it at all.

'Sorry,' I muttered. 'I'll just…uh…go see what the problem is.'

Before Delaney could speak, I picked up my emerald green skirts and rushed after Ash.

CHAPTER SIXTEEN

Ash

I STRODE THROUGH the ostentatious, overblown nonsense of the hotel, paying no attention to the people scattering in my path, fury pounding in my blood, feeling absolutely fucking feral.

I'd thought I'd won this petty little fight with Dumont. I'd thought I'd got one over on him, stolen those fucking islands out from under him, made life a little bit harder for him.

But no, apparently not.

Apparently he was the one who'd got one over on me. Because by simply handing those islands over to me, he'd won.

He owed me, so Delaney had said.

Over the years, he'd tried to pay me back the money he'd lost, but I hadn't accepted it. Because he'd thought it was just about the money and it wasn't. It was about the years of working hard, the long hours of all the various jobs I'd had in order to save that money. And my mother, the long hours she'd put in to earn her nest egg.

The nest egg she'd lost because of me.

Dumont couldn't give me those hours back. He couldn't give me back my mother's broken trust, either.

It's not just about Dumont, though, is it? You don't deserve any of this and you never have.

My jaw ached, the pounding fury propelling me down another gleaming white marble corridor and up some stairs.

No, fuck that. Of course I deserved it. I'd worked for everything I had. Fucking everything. My whole business was literally based on the blood I'd shed. My blood.

I'd fought for it and I'd been expecting to fight for this too. Except he'd denied me. It wasn't the money he owed me, it was the fucking battle.

I strode down yet another corridor, not knowing where I was going. I had to walk off this rage because I wasn't fit for any kind of polite company right now.

The corridor was full of doors and I opened one at random, entering a lavishly appointed suite that had a huge canopied bed pushed against one wall, French doors opposite leading out to a balcony with lots of white marble fretwork.

The parquet floor was covered with silk rugs and cushions, curtains of brightly patterned fabric billowing in the breeze coming through the open French doors. Another door led off the bedroom, probably into a bathroom.

Obviously I'd stumbled into some of the Billionaires Club intimate suites.

I turned around, intending to stride out again, only to come face-to-face with a flushed Ellie.

She was standing in the doorway, one fist holding a bunch of green fabric out of the way, breathing hard, as if she'd been running to catch up with me.

'What are you doing here?' I snapped before she could speak, furious that she was here when I was angry and no doubt dangerous. 'Have you been following me?'

'Of course I've been following you,' she said breathlessly. 'You just upped and left without a word. I wanted to see if you were okay.'

'As you can see, I'm fine.' I took a couple of steps towards her, hoping she'd get out of my way, but she didn't.

'You're not fine.' She tilted her head back to look up at me. 'You're furious.'

'Move, Ellie,' I growled, in no mood for her to argue. 'You don't want to be around me right now.'

She didn't move. 'What's going on, Ash?'

No, I did *not* want to have this conversation with her. Not in any way, shape or form. I didn't want to explain the rage that sat inside me, not when I could barely explain it to myself. And I certainly didn't want her floating around in her gown with its plunging neckline and tight-fitting bodice, outlining the lovely shapes of her breasts and hips. How the green made her skin look creamy and her eyes glitter like emeralds.

How it made me want to get rid of this rage by ripping that dress from her body and taking her down on the silken rugs right here, right now; to unleash myself on her lovely body, hold her down while I fucked away the fury that I could never quite seem to escape.

But I didn't want to do that. Not after what she'd been through with one man who'd hurt her already.

And besides, I wasn't in any mood to hear the word 'no' from anyone.

I took another step towards her, making myself seem as big and as intimidating as possible, hoping to scare her into getting out of the way.

But she only frowned, coming into the room and shutting the door behind her.

Silly, silly girl.

'What the fuck do you think you're doing?' I demanded, trying to get a handle on myself. 'Get away from me.'

She sniffed. 'I don't think so. You're really pissed off about Dumont and I want to know why.'

'I'm not explaining myself to you.'

'No, well, of course you don't have to if you don't want to.' Her chin lifted. 'But I'm not going anywhere until you do.'

'You're a fool. You don't think I won't just pick you up and move you out of my way?'

'Come on, then.' Challenge burned in her eyes. 'I dare you.'

If she expected me to hesitate, she was wrong.

I strode up to her and put my hands on her hips, preparing to pick her up and move her out of my way physically.

But she only lifted her arms and wound them around my neck, her body leaning into mine. 'Ash,' she said softly. 'Tell me what's wrong.'

And I felt myself freeze in place as the warmth of

her began to penetrate, making the fire inside me burn hotter, turning it from anger into something far hungrier and more volatile. A seething mass of desire that somehow was only encouraged by the soft note in her voice.

Her eyes were the most perfect blend of gold and green I'd ever seen and framed by long, thick, dark lashes. They were full of concern, and I wasn't sure why. In fact, I wasn't sure why I mattered to her at all.

'You know what I want to do, don't you?' My voice had gone deep and guttural, my grip on her hips no doubt punishing.

She didn't look away from me, nor did she try to escape. Her body was hot and pliant against mine as if she were exactly where she wanted to be. 'No. Why don't you tell me?'

'I want to fuck you. Hard. On the floor. And I don't want to be told no and I don't want you to even attempt to take the wheel.'

There was no fear in her eyes, not even a flicker. 'It's the fight you want, isn't it? You need it.'

I don't know how she understood, but she did. 'I'm going to be rough, Ellie,' I growled. 'I'm not going to hold back. So if that's a problem for you, you need to leave now.' Before her musky scent and the heat of her body stole what remained of my control.

Her arms around my neck tightened. 'I'm fine with it.'

Something inside me pulsed hard.

'You should be afraid of me.' My voice was raw and rough. 'You should be fucking scared.'

Her eyes widened in genuine surprise. 'Why?'

I reached up and buried one hand in her hair, curling my hand into a fist, pulling her head back, and not gently.

She gave a gasp but I couldn't see any fear in her eyes, only small sparks of green and gold. Her lips parted and she touched her tongue to the bottom one, her gaze drifting down to my mouth then back again. 'Is that supposed to scare me? Because I have to tell you, it's having the opposite effect.'

She didn't know what she was taking on. She had no idea. Me in this mood? I was the baddest bet there ever was, though not if you were betting on me to win a fight. In this mood, I always won.

I held tight onto her hair, the strands silky and soft against my skin, and leaned in, my lips almost brushing hers. 'I suggest you change your mind.'

She sighed, her breath minty and warm, the press of her tits against my chest making my head spin. 'Are you kidding me?' she murmured. 'Not a chance.'

Of course she wouldn't. She didn't understand. So maybe it was time I showed her.

I tightened my grip and held her still as I closed the distance between us, devouring the sweetness of her mouth utterly.

She shivered, stilling as I thrust my tongue into her mouth, taking it, ravaging it as if it was mine to do what I wanted with.

But then her arms constricted like a vine around my neck and she was kissing me back, her tongue meeting mine, thrusting and devouring, twining and tasting.

It was raw and desperate and I was down on the floor with her before I'd even realised what was happening.

Fabric tore as I put my hands on her, ripping away the tissue-fine silk of her gown, exposing golden skin. She didn't stop me, her own hands struggling with the jacket of my tux, then giving up to find the buttons on my shirt, jerking at them in a frenzy.

But she wasn't in charge of this now. I was.

With one last rip, I got rid of the remains of her gown, taking her underwear with it. Then when she was naked, I flipped her over onto her stomach and pulled her hands behind her back. She gasped, struggling against my hold. 'Let me see you,' she said thickly. 'I want to touch you.'

'No.' I used my weight to keep her pinned, holding her hands at the base of her spine. 'I told you that you weren't in charge.'

'What are you going to do?'

She didn't sound afraid in the least, only curious.

'This,' I growled and grabbed at a length of the green fabric, tying it around her wrists to keep them where they were.

'Oh…' The word sighed out of her in a moan, her naked body soft and hot beneath mine.

Now her hands were tied, I put mine on the floor on either side of her head, grinding my aching cock against the soft curves of her bare arse. 'And then,' I snarled, hungry and feral, 'I'm going to fuck you hard the way I told you I would.'

She moaned, shuddering, her hips rising to meet

mine, pushing herself back against me like the little warrior she was.

And something inside me growled in deep satisfaction.

Of course she'd meet me in this. She wasn't weak and she wasn't a coward. And she enjoyed the fight as much as I did.

My hands were shaking as I got my trousers undone and it took longer than I would have liked to get the condom on, too, but then it was done and I put one hand beneath her, my palm on her stomach, raising her so she was perfectly positioned to take my cock.

Then I flexed my hips, rubbing the head of my dick through the slick folds of her delicious little pussy, the friction making me growl in pleasure.

She shuddered again, bucking her hips against mine, urging me on. 'Ash, please…' she panted.

I'd never managed to resist that throaty plea and I didn't now, pushing hard and deep inside her. But then I had to pause, the tight clasp and the slick heat blanking my brain entirely. The pleasure was unbelievable and for a good few seconds I simply couldn't move. I hadn't been this close to coming prematurely since I'd been an overenthusiastic teenager.

She was trembling beneath me, her breathing wild and uncontrolled. 'Oh…' she moaned, her back flexing and arching as she tried to take me deeper. 'Oh, God…'

Fuck. No. She wasn't going to take control of me that easily. Not tonight. Not after fucking Dumont had taken my victory from me.

I shoved her hips down flat to the floor, letting my

weight slowly rest on her so she was pinned. Then I gave her a couple of shallow thrusts, which was a little of what she wanted, but not everything.

She gave another moan. 'Ash…please…'

I gripped her bound wrists, teasing her with a few more shallow thrusts, while I kept my other hand on one hip to stop her bucking up. She cried out in frustration but I ignored her, teasing myself as much as her with her heat and slickness.

Pleasure licked up my spine, twining with my rage to become something more intense, something stronger.

I snarled like an animal and pulled her up on her knees, thrusting hard into her, driving myself into her as deep as I could get. She was panting now, the feel of her beneath me mesmerising, the slap of her flesh against mine more arousing than any aphrodisiac.

I looked down at her writhing body trying to keep pace and then managing it, synchronising with me, her panting breaths matching the sound of my own. Then we were surging together, neither one of us trying to get the upper hand this time, but moving with one another, perfectly aligned, perfectly in time.

Travelling together to the same destination.

The edge of my anger became less raw, less ragged, and something powerful tightened in my chest. She'd come after me, she hadn't let me frighten her away. No, she'd simply wrapped her arms around my neck and given herself to me as if I weren't a bitter, angry man. As if I were more than that.

And for a moment I wanted to believe her. I *wanted* to be something more, something other than myself.

The kid my dad hadn't wanted. The teenager who'd broken my mother's trust.

The man who'd burned a deep friendship on the altar of his pride.

I didn't want to be any of those things.

I wanted to be someone who was worthy of the trust she'd placed in me and who could bring her pleasure.

So I curled my body over hers, thrusting deeper, reaching around to cup the softness of her tits, pinching her nipples, increasing the speed and rhythm. She began to shudder, writhing up against me, twisting around, her hungry mouth trying to find mine. So I let go of her breasts and grabbed her hair in one fist, tugging her head around so she could kiss me.

Her mouth was hungry and desperate, and I kissed her back hard, reaching down with my free hand, sliding down across the trembling plane of her stomach to the slick flesh of her pussy. Her clit was swollen and hard and she cried out as I stroked lightly over it, her whole body trembling in response.

'Oh, Ash… I need you…please…*please*…'

All my aggression and anger fell away, all my focus on her and what she needed.

I rumbled my appreciation of her, stroking her clit in time with my thrusts, fighting the unbearable pleasure that was pulling at me, determined that she was going to come before I did. And sure enough, another touch and one deep thrust, and she gave a high, thin scream as the orgasm hit, the convulsion of her pussy around my cock unmistakable, releasing something feral inside me.

As she trembled and gasped beneath me, I unleashed

myself, thrusting wildly and hard, driving myself inside her, until the climax hit me, too, like a bomb going off in the confines of my body, blasting me with pleasure so intense I couldn't do anything but roar as lights burst behind my eyes.

It took a long time for me to come back to myself and when I did, I could hear some muffled sobs. A second later, I realised it was Ellie and she was crying.

My chest went so tight it was painful.

Jesus, was it something I'd done? Had I hurt her?

A cold feeling wound through me, the languid heat of the orgasm disappearing.

Pulling out of her, I dealt with the condom in a nearby and cleverly disguised bin, then bent and gathered her trembling body into my arms. She tried to push against me, turning her face away, but I ignored it, tightening my grip as I took her over to the bed and laid her down on it. Then I stripped off my clothes and climbed in beside her, drawing the thick, soft velvety quilt over us as I held her small body close to mine, using my touch to soothe her.

She pushed against my chest. 'Don't,' she muttered even as more sobs caught in her throat. 'I'm fine.'

'You're not fine.' I held her tighter, not even sure what I was doing, something deep and instinctive inside me responding to her tears. 'Did I hurt you? Because if I did—'

'No,' she said thickly. 'You didn't hurt me. It's just… I don't know what's happening. That was just so… amazing. I can't… I don't know…'

I stroked her hair, wanting to give her some reassurance, the strands silky and soft against my palm. 'What did I say about not minding a fuss? You can cry if you want. Tears don't bother me.' Although I was beginning to think that her tears in particular bothered me. As in, I didn't like them if it meant she was in pain.

She sighed, some of her resistance receding. 'It just makes…this seem like a big deal.'

'This being the sex, you mean?'

Another soft sigh escaped her. 'Yeah.'

I looked down at her pink face, the fierce protectiveness that had hit me earlier gripping me again. Her life seemed to be full of her being concerned for other people's feelings, while no one was ever concerned with hers. Certainly her bloody father hadn't been and I suspected her brothers weren't overly involved either.

Perhaps today, right now, someone could show her that her feelings mattered. That they were important.

And that someone was going to be me.

'It is a big deal.' I ignored the warning that went off in my head as I spoke. 'It's a fucking huge deal.'

Her hazel eyes were wide and dark from beneath lashes glittering with moisture. 'You think so?'

I stared back, letting her see the truth in my eyes. 'It certainly doesn't feel like any sex I've ever had before.'

A wave of colour washed through her skin. 'But you've had a lot, haven't you? A lot of sex, I mean.'

'Yes, I've had a lot. And no, this is not the same. Not in any way.'

'Oh.' She blinked a couple of times, looking shocked.

I narrowed my gaze. 'Just how often have you had sex?' Obviously it wasn't going to be much.

Her chin lifted, but the flush in her skin betrayed her.

'A couple of times. With my high-school boyfriend. I mean, after Mark…'

She didn't finish the sentence, but then she didn't need to. I knew already. And I could understand. She hadn't wanted to be with anyone after him. Except me.

I wouldn't have been human if that hadn't satisfied me on some level, while at the same time a small part of me was appalled.

Violent and angry and selfish. Yeah, you're a great choice.

The cold threat inside me pulled tight through the heat of my triumph.

'What?' Ellie's gaze sharpened on my face, her warm palm pressing against my chest.

It was disturbing how easily she could read me, though I should have expected that by now.

'You shouldn't be letting me touch you,' I said gruffly, not in a position to be able to deny her anything, not when she was naked and locked in my arms, with tears on her cheeks. 'You need someone patient and gentle. Someone kind. Christ, someone less angry at least.'

Her brow wrinkled. 'I don't want someone patient and kind. Sure, you have a few issues with your anger and you've snapped at me a few times, but you've never been violent. You've never made me feel afraid. Mark was supposed to be a nice guy and look what he did.' She began to trace circles on my skin with her cool fingers. 'You're take-charge, Ash. A bit arrogant, but I kind of like that. I like that you're passionate, too, and how you don't care who knows it. How you don't care what anyone thinks of you. I really admire that about you.'

I ached, a longing I didn't know it was possible to feel tugging at my heart. She admired me… God help her.

'Ellie,' I began roughly.

'Patient and kind, I'd eat for breakfast,' she went on, totally ignoring me. 'I like arrogant and bossy and grumpy. And I really like sexy and hot and tattooed.' She shot a coy glance from beneath her lashes. 'But you know what I'd like most of all? If you told me what pissed you off so much before.'

CHAPTER SEVENTEEN

Ellie

I COULD FEEL the tension gathering in Ash's hard, muscled body. His scarred face was full of his usual ferocity, but there was something else burning in his eyes, something other than anger for a change.

If I hadn't known any better I would have said it was longing, though why he'd be looking at me that way I had no idea.

Though it all vanished the instant I asked the question.

I shouldn't have asked it, not when the post-sex warmth between us had been so wonderful, but I couldn't let it go.

I had felt the force of his anger when he'd pinned me to the floor and taken me hard. My poor bear with his sore paw…

He didn't want to tell me and he'd been trying to distract me ever since, but something had hurt him, and I had a feeling it wasn't simply the fight he'd been denied. It was something more and I wanted to know what it was.

I was betting it had something to do with the strange thing he'd said to me, about how I needed someone patient and kind, which was such obvious bullshit, I didn't even know what to say.

'Come on,' I said crisply, digging my nails into the hard muscle of his chest and meeting his glowering look without flinching. 'Tell me.'

'I don't know,' he said after a moment and with great reluctance. 'I was expecting a fight. I wanted it. And then Seb just took it away.'

'I think it's more than that, though,' I said, stroking him carefully.

For the first time, his gaze avoided mine, the tension in his body palpable now. 'I've done nothing but burn bridges with him ever since I lost that money. And yet, he just gave up those islands. After twelve years of me making his life difficult. It doesn't make any sense.'

'Why is that such a bad thing?' I asked carefully. 'So you didn't get your big fight. So what?'

His gaze came back to mine, fierce and hot. 'Don't you see? Mum didn't want to give the money to me, but I convinced her. I told her it would make our lives easier. And it didn't. I broke her trust, Ellie.' A muscle flickered in his jaw. 'Like Dad did.'

I saw it then, why he was so angry and so bloody driven. I reached up and touched his face gently. 'You're not like him, Ash.' Because that was what he was afraid of, wasn't it?

'You don't know him so you can't tell me that.'

'That's true. But honestly? Your father sounds awful. He got a woman pregnant and then threw her out, not caring one bit what happened to her. And then turning away his own son? By telling you that you weren't his problem?' I stared right into his eyes. 'You're protective and possessive, Ash Evans. Are you seriously telling me that's what you'd do to anyone you care about?'

That muscle jumped in his jaw again, the fierce blue glow in his eyes getting fiercer. 'I did to Mum. And I did to Seb. He kept trying to pay that money back to me and I refused to take it. Hell, I refused to see him at all. And as for Mum…' He paused. 'We never spoke of it again.'

It didn't surprise me in the slightest. And I thought I knew why.

'You pushed them away, didn't you?' I brushed my fingertips over his cheekbone. 'So they wouldn't reject you like your dad did.'

He shifted beneath me, clearly uncomfortable. 'I appreciate the psychology, Miss Little. But I assure you, it's not necessary.'

So, he was back to being a grumpy bear again, was he?

I stilled my fingers on his face, pressing lightly. 'The islands sound to me like an olive branch, Ash. And as for your mother, you should talk to her.' I held his gaze. 'It's not too late. None of it is. If I still had my mother, that's what I'd be doing.'

He blinked then turned his head so his mouth brushed over my fingertips instead. 'That's a low blow, pretty thing.'

It was, but too bad.

'If you can't handle it, don't deal.' I traced the line of his lower lip, revelling in the softness of it, then grazed over the stark line of his scar.

He stilled as I did so, watching me. 'I was hard on you,' he murmured after a moment. 'Are you sure you're okay?' He lifted a hand and cupped my cheek gently, his big palm warm against my skin. 'I shouldn't have been so rough.'

I couldn't help myself, leaning into that hand, loving the warmth of it. 'No, I'm glad you were. I'm not made of glass, Ash.' I gave him a level look. 'I don't want to be treated like a victim just because some dumb bastard thought he could put his hands on me. I mean, I might be a woman who cries after sex, but I'm tough.'

His thumb stroked the side of my cheek, his gaze unreadable. 'Why do you trust me? I don't understand it. Not when I haven't done one fucking thing to deserve it.'

The question took me by surprise and for a second I didn't quite know how to answer. 'I trust you because… well, I just do. Maybe it's an instinctive thing.' I flushed, remembering. 'That first night in the limo, well, I kind of thought you were like a car and as long as I was driving nothing bad would happen. And then I wasn't driving any more and you were in charge and I just felt…' I struggled to find the right word. 'I suppose I felt free. There's something quite liberating about giving yourself up to the speed, you know?'

An intense expression flickered across his face. 'Ellie, you should know right now that I would never do anything to make you regret that trust, understand me? Not a single thing.' He was absolutely serious, I could see it in his eyes. He meant this.

I put my hand over his where it rested against my cheek and gave him back a smile. 'I know you won't.'

He didn't smile back. If anything, the look in his eyes intensified. 'I don't know what you want after to-night is over, but I think we should stay on in Dubai for a couple of days.'

Something bloomed inside me like a flower. 'You mean, you want me to stay with you? And not to drive you around, I take it?'

His hard mouth relaxed, curving into one of the sexiest smiles I'd ever seen. 'No, not to drive me around. I want you to stay with me as my lover.'

Heat pulsed through me. To stay with him, in that lovely hotel by the sea, as his lover…

I couldn't think of a single reason why I shouldn't. Not one.

Sure you can…

But I pushed the thought away before it could form. No, I could do with a couple of days in a nice hotel with a hot AF billionaire. I'd be returning to Australia pretty soon anyway, so why not take the chance while I could?

And apart from anything else, I hadn't had a holiday for ages.

And when it comes to say goodbye?

Then I'd say goodbye. It wouldn't be a problem.

'I would love to.' I ignored the strange ache in my chest. 'I can call the company and tell them not to schedule any jobs for me for the next week.'

'That means you won't get paid, though.'

He was astute, I'd give him that. 'No, but I've put some money aside to cover holidays and sick days.'

His thumb brushed over my skin again. 'Just a few days, yes?'

I put my palm flat on his chest and reached up to kiss him. 'That is an absolute, yes.'

We didn't leave the room immediately after that.

I pushed him back onto the mattress and straddled him, indulging my need to touch him, and he let me. Then he found another condom from somewhere and made me ride him, and I loved the growls and curses I brought from him. Then, when we were sweaty and sated, I made him turn over so I could examine the beautiful Chinese tattoo that covered his back.

He'd got it done after his first fight, he told me. Because one of the people who'd bet on him was a tattoo artist who'd won a lot of money and was so pleased he'd offered Ash a free tattoo.

Luckily the artist was good and the tattoo amazing, and after I'd explored it thoroughly, as a reward for his patience, I made him turn over and lie there while I kissed my way down his body and turned the same attention I'd given his tattoo to his cock, taking it into my mouth and sucking him until he roared my name, his fingers clutching tight in my hair.

After that, we thought we'd better move, which turned out to be problematic when I remembered that he'd basically ripped my dress from me and now it was nothing but emerald green bits of fabric on the floor.

We solved the dilemma by Ash ripping down one of the silk curtains from the window and draping it sari-like around my naked body.

I didn't care what it looked like. There was something wild running through me, the same kind of recklessness

I'd felt when I was driving one of the Pythons, wanting to go faster and uncaring about the consequences.

The Little madness, my mother had called it once, slightly disapprovingly.

But she wasn't wrong. It was a kind of madness. As we left the suites, people stared at us, me in my improvised dress, and Ash in his rumpled tux, and I didn't care.

In fact, I enjoyed the attention, relishing it even more as Ash put his arm around my waist and pulled me tight against him, making no bones about the fact that I was his.

And this time it was almost real. For the next few days at least, I was his.

Ash took us back to the bar so he could firm up the deal with Delaney, acting as though him leaving abruptly and us both being away for a couple of hours hadn't happened.

Delaney was delighted and after a handshake and the numbers of their respective lawyers had been exchanged, we left the bar and headed towards the exit, both of us eager to get back to our hotel and resume what we'd started up in the private suites upstairs.

Imogen stopped us as we left, murmuring something to Ash about the next club event that was supposed to be held at one of his new luxury hotels in Monte Carlo. Then she mentioned something about supercars, which made my ears prick up.

'What do you mean the supplier fell through?' Ash demanded.

Imogen was frowning, her poise not quite what it had

been when we'd met her at the beginning. 'There was some production issue. The cars had to be recalled and they won't be ready in time.'

Ash flicked a glance at me. 'I think I might know where to get some more.'

Something moved like lightning through my whole body. Imogen had turned to look at me expectantly. 'You know someone?' she asked.

'Actually, I do,' I said, the wild recklessness still burning inside me. 'My family makes hand-built supercars.'

Imogen frowned. 'We have a certain market—'

'They meet the market,' Ash interrupted flatly. 'I've seen them. The club members will love them, I guarantee it.'

'Well, we need them in a month in Monaco. That's not a lot of time.'

I could feel my excitement deflating slightly. Of course it wasn't. Not when the cars were built in Australia and we'd need to ship them.

'Not a problem,' Ash put in again. 'We'll get them to you.' His gaze burned as he looked at me. 'I can work it so we'll meet the deadline.'

Imogen gazed at the pair of us sceptically. 'I'm not so sure. But seeing as how I don't have a lot of choice… Fine. I'll need to be kept in the loop, though, since I'll have to adjust the marketing.'

'No problem. Give me a couple of days to sort a few things and I'll get back to you with the details.'

This appeared to satisfy Imogen and a minute or two later, I found myself being tugged along as Ash pulled me towards the entrance.

'What the hell are you doing?' I asked worriedly as we walked.

'Taking advantage of an opportunity.' The blue of his eyes burned incandescent and not with anger this time, but with excitement. And I could suddenly see why his mother would have given him all her money—why many people did. When he was like this, he was mesmerising.

'An opportunity? I can't get a bunch of cars to Monaco in a month,' I protested. 'Not when we have to ship them from Aus.'

'Don't limit your thinking, Miss Little.' He flashed me a grin as the limo came for us. 'We don't need to ship them from Australia, not when I have a factory in France. We can build them there and drive them to fucking Monaco.'

I stared at him in shock. 'What? You just happen to have a factory vacant in France? Really?'

'I have lots of different companies doing different things. And yes, one of those things is a factory in France that just happens to be vacant. Or rather, it produces automotive parts and I'm sure we can make a few adjustments for your Pythons.' He frowned and I could almost see him sorting through all sorts of ideas and plans, weeding the wheat from the chaff. 'I'm happy to fly your father and any engineers he might want to bring out. In fact, I'll get Petra to contact him. No, scratch that, I'll contact him myself.' He had his phone out already, his thumb moving swiftly over the screen, obviously typing out some notes to himself.

I kept on staring, dumbfounded at how quickly he moved when he wanted to. 'But I—'

'Unless you want to call him?' Ash suddenly lifted his gaze to mine. 'After all, you were the one who came here to solve his debt problem. If this works out, he'll be making some returns even sooner than we anticipated.'

It was true. But the thought of talking to Dad felt wrong. I would be excited and he wouldn't. He'd try and damp it down somehow, turn a big deal into something small. And I didn't want small. Not yet. Right now, I wanted to enjoy the excitement of it all.

'You can tell him,' I said. 'He'll like that you called him directly.'

Ash scowled. 'He should be fucking grateful that I thought of him at all. And I only did because of you.'

I flushed, feeling a little disloyal at how pleased that made me, but feeling it anyway. 'I think he will be,' I said. 'Anyway, I'll be helping—'

'No, you won't.' Ash's eyes gleamed as he waved away the chauffeur, opening the door to the limo for me himself. 'I've thought of something else that you'll be doing.'

'Oh? And what's that?'

There was a hot, feral light gleaming in his eyes. 'Get in the car, Miss Little. Monaco can wait, but my cock can't.'

CHAPTER EIGHTEEN

Ash

IT TURNED OUT to be longer than a few days in Dubai.

It soon turned into a week.

Yes, we had stuff to organise but it wasn't anything that couldn't be managed via email and phone. The rest of the time we spent either lounging naked beside the suite's private pool and sipping cocktails, or in the bedroom fucking each other senseless. Or sitting comfortably in the suite's lounge, just talking.

A couple of times we went out into the city and I showed Ellie around since I'd been to Dubai a lot. She wasn't at all fazed by the heat and loved the cultural differences, the markets, as well as the high-tech luxury playgrounds. We even spent a night in the desert, in a well-appointed tent, where I made her scream at the stars high above us.

There was only one issue: spending time with Ellie only made me want to spend even more time with Ellie.

Her honesty and directness I already knew about, but I soon got to know her dry sense of humour, too.

She was ridiculously easy to tease and blushed adorably when I did, which meant I spent quite a lot of time teasing her. To which she responded in kind.

Apparently—or so she told me—I was easy to tease, too, though my response wasn't to blush. It was to take her to the floor and have my way with her, which meant she ended up on the floor quite a lot, given how much she liked teasing me in return.

I also managed to slowly draw her out about her electric supercar project, which she was very reluctant to talk about. I soon found out why—her father thought it was nonsense. Which incensed me, since I thought it was brilliant. No, I thought it was visionary.

I made no bones about my opinion, too, and though it took a couple of days and several rounds of convincing in bed, soon she was telling me in intricate detail about the five-year design process she'd gone through to get the car to the prototype stage.

Her passion for it shone in her eyes, coming slowly but surely, like the sun rising.

'I honestly don't understand why your father wouldn't even contemplate a prototype,' I said on our last night as we watched the sunset from the pool area. 'Why is that?'

She was lying on one of the sun loungers, her naked body gone a lovely deep gold after days in the sun, the sunset gilding her like a statue. She sighed, swirling the tall glass of lemon, lime and bitters she liked drinking in the evening. 'He prefers internal combustion engines. He thought the technology wasn't good enough to get the kinds of speeds people like these days.'

I'd already talked to Oliver Little at length, a laconic Australian who'd been pleased to hear the news I'd given him of the Australis coup in Monaco, though not overly effusive about it. He and a couple of his sons were already in France getting the factory I'd set aside as a Python workshop up and running.

He hadn't mentioned Ellie once in any of the conversations I'd had with him, and I could imagine him not knowing how to deal with his ebullient and honest daughter, whose passions ran deep and yet bubbled up no matter how hard she tried to keep them down.

'Yet you kept working on it,' I said.

Her eyes gleamed. 'Yes, of course. I wasn't going to give it up just because he didn't like it. Electricity is where the automotive industry is heading and he really needs to get with the programme.'

I liked how stubborn she was, rising to every challenge that was set to her.

No, I loved it.

The real challenge is going to be letting her go afterwards.

Sadly, it was. Because no matter how much I liked spending time with her, the days of our affair were numbered. I had other things to do and so did she, and there was no room in my life for more than what we had right now. There never had been. I wasn't a man built for relationships. Not given how severely I'd mismanaged the few relationships I did have.

She'd told me it wasn't too late, but she didn't understand. Of course it was too late. The money I'd lost for Mum was gone and with it her trust in me. And as for Seb…twelve years of me being a bastard would be too much for anyone, let alone him.

It had been tempting to throw the gift of the islands back in his face, but Delaney had been so thrilled at selling them to me that I hadn't been able to refuse.

Careful. You're getting soft.

The rays of the setting sun slid over Ellie's tanned and golden skin, bringing out the gold lights in her brown hair. It was damp and had dried with a slight wave to it, and lying there naked, toying with her glass, a smile playing around her lovely mouth, she looked like a goddess.

No, fuck, I wasn't soft. I was hard. Especially looking at her.

Oh, really? And the surprise you organised for her in London isn't soft?

No, it wasn't. It was a parting gift, nothing more.

Tomorrow we would leave and I was absolutely fucking fine with that.

A strange feeling of pressure pushed against my heart, an ache that I couldn't seem to get rid of.

I ignored it.

'Speaking of the programme,' I said, a part of me reluctant to broach the topic, but knowing I needed to. 'We're leaving tomorrow, remember?'

Instantly the light that had been in her eyes died and she looked away, fussing with her drink. 'Oh, yes, of course.'

The pressure in my chest became painful. 'We need to leave it here, Ellie.'

Her gaze came to mine then flicked away again. 'What happens in Dubai stays in Dubai, you mean?'

'Yes.' The word sounded heavy and there was a part of me that hated the finality in it. 'It was only ever meant to be a few days and it's been a week already.'

She looked down at her drink again, her lashes lowered, the light catching in the small golden strands. 'Sure.' Her lashes lifted again and she looked at me. 'No drama.' Her mouth curved in a smile that for some reason made the twisting sensation in my chest twist tighter. It wasn't forced. It was completely natural and somehow that made it worse. 'It's been great, Ash. I mean…really great.'

This was her brave face, wasn't it? I knew. I could see the currents of pain in her green eyes. The currents she couldn't quite hide. She was so laid-back and easy-going on the surface, but underneath there were passions in her that were vast and powerful.

Passions like mine.

I met her gaze, bearing her pain, ignoring the way it echoed inside me. 'Better than great. Even sensational wouldn't cover it.' I let her see how much I meant it then went on, 'But all good things must come to an end.'

She gave a small laugh that sounded less like amusement than any laugh I'd ever heard. 'I guess they must.' After a second she lifted her glass and drained it, putting it down on the little table next to her. 'One question I've been meaning to ask you. Why do you talk the way you do? You don't sound like a guy brought up on a council estate.'

My pretty little thing. She was always curious about me, wasn't she? 'It made school easier. And then I found out that it puts people off balance. I'm scarred and rough and yet I talk like an aristocrat. People find it very confronting.'

Her gaze was direct. 'It must get boring confronting people all the time. Don't you ever get tired of it?'

I felt something shift inside me. Something I didn't particularly want to pay attention to. 'What do you mean?'

'Your whole life, Ash. It's basically one big fight, isn't it? Against your brother. Against your mother. Against your father. Against the entire world, really. Don't you ever want to stop proving yourself to everyone all the time?'

I didn't know why all the muscles in my body tightened, as if I'd just taken a blow. 'I'm not proving myself to anyone,' I snapped, scowling. 'I'm being who I am. And if people can't accept that then that's their problem.'

Ellie rose gracefully from the lounger, and my cock, ever hungry for her, hardened.

She came over to me, glancing down at my unapologetic hard-on, then back up at me. 'I accept you for who you are. Even when you're being rigid and uncompromising and arrogant.'

'You especially like me when I'm rigid.' I reached out and grabbed her hand, guiding it down to my aching cock to prove my point. 'Stop trying to pick a fight with me and do something else with that sassy mouth of yours.'

Her fingers closed around me and the combative light

left her eyes and she smiled. But there was something wistful in her smile. Something painful.

She doesn't want this to end.

No. Which made it even more imperative that we end it. Because the longer this went on, the worse it would be for her when it came to a close.

And for you, too.

Maybe. It would hurt a little. But I was good at bearing pain. It was like a gut punch. At first it would take the air from your lungs and you'd fight to breathe, and then, once you could, the pain would set in. But it never lasted. Pain never did.

Only anger, right?

No. I was starting to see another way. And so I used it on her and the pain she was trying to mask, pulling her down with me on the lounger.

And as the sun went down, I used pleasure to make her forget.

At least for a while.

CHAPTER NINETEEN

Ellie

THE FLIGHT BACK to London was miserable, even though I tried to tell myself I was fine with it. That of course I was going to be feeling slightly sad about our affair ending, but it was only post-holiday blues. Soon it would pass.

I had lots to look forward to, after all: the unexpected thrill of the Monaco opportunity and the chance for a new market for Australis.

I was planning on going to France when I got back to London and visiting Dad at the new workshop Ash had set up. I wanted to check it out and see what Dad thought of the opportunity.

Apparently he was pleased with it, or so Ash said, but it was always difficult to tell with Dad.

You always want his approval. What do you hope he'll say?

It wasn't true, though. I didn't always want his approval. I just…wanted to connect with him. And it wasn't wrong. And as for what I hoped he'd say… 'Well done, Ellie' would be nice, though probably a bit much to hope for.

Ash spent most of the long flight on his computer or on the phone, and I could sense that he was purpose-fully putting distance between us. I didn't mind. It was good he was putting that distance there. We were not, after all, an official couple.

We'd both agreed that once we'd got back to Lon-don, we'd wait for a month or so and then let word get out that we were no longer 'officially' together. Purely for Delaney's benefit, of course.

I felt bad for deceiving the old man, but since Du-mont had basically given Ash the islands he'd wanted and Delaney had seemed to find that more convinc-ing than me being Ash's girlfriend, I was okay with it.

After a few hours in the air, I was feeling tired and, since I'd hardly had any sleep the night before, too busy drinking my fill of Ash before we ended it, I curled up on the couch with a blanket over me, trying not to re-member how he'd taken me here.

He'd made me feel so good that day. So powerful…

I curled in on the ache in my heart and tried to pre-tend it wasn't there, shutting my eyes determinedly.

I didn't think I would sleep, but I did, only waking when Ash shook my shoulder lightly and told me we were coming in to land.

It didn't take long and with customs formalities sur-prisingly quick, we were in Ash's Land Rover and on the way back to my flat before I was ready.

A heavy silence had fallen between us and I didn't know how to break it. I didn't want this to become too heavy or too dramatic, because it shouldn't be. This was only the end of an affair. A really wonderful affair, but only an affair nonetheless.

Certainly it had been about more than sex, yes, I'd admit to that. But nothing worth extending. Nothing worth making permanent.

Permanent? What the hell?

I swallowed, staring out of the window as the grey streets of London slid past the glass.

Why was I thinking that? I didn't want permanent. I didn't want deep and meaningful. My passion I kept for the cars, because machines were easy to love. They weren't like people who could simply ignore you whenever they felt like it, who didn't seem to care no matter how hard you tried to please them. They simply accepted whatever you wanted to give them.

Yet the silence settled around us, deeper and darker, and I tried desperately to think of a joke or some mundane comment that would ease the growing tension.

And then I noticed something.

This wasn't the way back to my flat.

'Where are we going?' I asked, glancing at Ash.

'You'll see,' he said shortly. 'I wanted to show you something first.'

That something turned out to be an old brick warehouse in Hackney.

Ash drew up outside and turned off the engine.

His eyes had gone electric, the way they did when he was aroused or angry or excited. This time it was excitement. As if he had a secret he was desperate to share. 'Come on. Time for one last surprise.'

'What surprise?'

But he wouldn't answer and I was left with no choice but to trail after him as he got out of the car and walked to the entrance of the building, pausing to tap a code into the keypad on the door.

The lock clicked and he pushed the door open, gesturing at me to go in, his eyes glowing.

Mystified, I took a hesitant step inside.

It was an open white space full of what looked like workshop benches. Computers were set up on various desks and there was a hydraulic jack for a car in the middle of it. A whiteboard stood in a corner, along with a stack of tyres. There were also rows of shelves full of boxes and tools and lots of other fascinating-looking bits and pieces. Familiar bits and pieces.

Car parts. And car tools.

I stared, suspicion clenching hard inside me.

Behind me Ash hit a switch and the lights came on, illuminating the workshop space.

Because it was clearly a workshop space. A car workshop space very like the ones I'd been around all my life. Except cleaner and newer.

The suspicion became certainty and my eyes filled with sudden, sharp tears that no amount of blinking would get rid of.

'This is yours.' Ash's voice was a deep rumble behind me. 'Your workshop, Ellie. You need to build your prototype. I took the liberty of getting a team together that will help you—I hope you don't mind. I'll give you the list of specialists and you can add to or subtract from it as you see fit. They're good, though. And if everything goes smoothly, you might even have the prototype ready for Monaco.'

The tears overflowed, rolling down my cheeks, and I couldn't stop them, my heart an aching ball in my chest.

My workshop. *My* team.

'But I have no funding,' I croaked, keeping my back firmly towards him, not wanting him to see what this meant to me. 'Please don't tell me you paid for this.'

'You have the funding. Some of it is mine because I like your ideas and I want a stake in them. But the rest is from some other contacts in the club that I gathered over the past week. They liked your ideas, too, and your vision.'

I didn't know what to do. For so long I'd put this passion of mine away; ignored it because it didn't fit with Dad's. And he'd thought it had no future and so I'd thought it didn't either.

Of course that hadn't stopped me playing with it, putting little touches on my plans here and there. Investigating workarounds with various engineers, drawing and redrawing designs. Always fiddling with it, always tinkering.

But I'd been realistic. There was no way my dream could ever be a reality and I'd told myself I was fine with that. I didn't care. It wasn't a big deal.

Except I did care and it was a big deal. And that was why I was standing there with tears rolling down my cheeks, feeling as if Ash had broken open a cage inside me and let the powerful, intense creature out.

He had done this for me. He had done this for *me*.

He believed in me in a way no one else had done since my mother died.

Not even my dad.

I turned suddenly and met his fierce gaze.

'Is it all right?' His stare flicked over my tears and for the first time I saw hints of uncertainty in his expression. 'Ellie, if this isn't right—'

'No, it's perfect,' I interrupted hoarsely. 'This is just what I wanted.'

He frowned, his hand coming up as if to wipe away the tears on my cheeks before checking himself. 'You're crying, though.'

'I know. Because I can't believe someone would do this for me. I can't believe you think it's worth putting the time and money into.'

Blue sparks leapt in his gaze. 'Of course it is. I told your father I was going to be investing in your idea and if he knew what was good for him and his company, he would, too.'

My throat squeezed tight. 'He thinks it's no good.'

'Who cares what he thinks?' There was ferocity in his voice. 'It's what *you* think that matters. And this is important to you, I know it is. Anyway, he did help me put together your team, so I suspect he might have at least heard what I was saying.' Ash stopped, looking at me. 'I'm not trying to muscle in on your territory, Ellie. You understand that, don't you? You're the one who has to build it. I'm just providing you with the tools you need.'

I did know that. I knew exactly what he was trying to do. What he'd done ever since I'd met him: giving me a challenge and daring me to rise to it; daring me not to be afraid of what other people might think.

And just like that I felt something hot pulse through

me. An acknowledgement of something I'd been too afraid to examine closely. Because I'd been afraid for a long time.

Afraid of my own feelings and the power of them. The strength of them that Dad had never been able to deal with. Not when I'd been a small girl grieving my mother and not as an adult, when I'd been hurt by a man who'd had no right to hurt me.

He didn't know what to do with my grief or my excitement or my anger.

He didn't know what to do with my love.

So I'd put all those feelings away in a cage and locked the door, pretended everything was fine.

But Ash had broken that cage wide open and I realised that I couldn't deny it any more.

This was a big deal. *He* was a big deal.

He would never be a comfortable, easy-going, laid-back man. But that wasn't what I wanted. I wanted fierce and hot. I wanted the burn, the speed. I wanted his merciless brand of angry protectiveness and his passionate, rough caring. And the moments of tenderness he showed in the gentle, light way he touched me.

I wanted him to be exactly as he was.

Because I'd fallen in love with him.

'What?' he demanded, intensity burning off him. 'If you don't like it—'

'I love it, Ash.' I stepped towards him, my heart full and aching in my chest, fear in my veins, but I was in the driver's seat now and I was speeding along the track. There would be no stopping me. I was surrendering to the momentum. 'And I think I love you, too.'

His expression froze and something bright burned in his eyes. So bright that for a second I could hardly look at him.

Then it went dark, his expression shuttering like a door to a furnace closing, cutting off all light and heat.

'No.' The chill in his voice was absolute. 'No. That's ridiculous. You can't.'

Perversely, his coldness only made the fire burn brighter inside me, an anger that I'd been keeping inside for far too long. 'Why can't I?' I demanded. 'Give me one good reason.'

'Christ, haven't I given you enough reasons?' He drew himself up, as if he were bracing himself, the lines of his face becoming set and hard. 'I told you I wasn't going to give you anything more. That this affair was only for a few days.'

'Did I ask you for anything more?' I took a step towards him, emotion flowing through me in a deep, hot flood, making me strong. Filling me with power. 'I didn't ask to feel this way about you. I didn't want it. But I'm not going to lie about it, I'm not going to pretend I don't feel it. It's too important, Ash. Because it *is* a big deal.'

'Why?' Anger flared in his eyes, his usual go-to emotion. 'Because I gave you a workshop? Because I'm funding your project?'

'No.' I closed the distance between us and put my hands up, cupping his face between them, watching as he flinched back from me as if my touch had burned him. 'I love you because you're arrogant and bossy and demanding. I love you because you're uncompromising. I love you because you're dangerous and passionate. I love you because you make me feel powerful and I haven't felt that way for years.'

He dragged my wrists away from his face, his expression forbidding. The scars were white against his skin, a reminder of his violent past. A reminder of his drive and determination, his ferocity.

But that was not what I saw, not now. All I saw was his vulnerability. The pain of a thirteen-year-old boy being told he wasn't his father's problem. The anguish of a young man who'd thought he'd broken his mother's trust.

A lonely man who pushed people away rather than risk his heart.

What makes you think he even wants you?

I didn't think he did. But in a way, that didn't matter. Because whether he returned it or not wasn't going to change the feeling in my heart. Vast, powerful. My very own perpetual motion engine.

'I don't want anything from you,' I said, before he could say anything. 'I just wanted to tell you how I feel.'

'Why?' he demanded, fury glowing in his eyes and vibrating in his voice. 'Why the fuck would you want to tell me that? Why the fuck do you think I would be interested?' His hands were clenched into fists at his sides, his knuckles white. 'Don't you dare put that on me.' His face was as white as his scars now. White with fury. 'I don't want your love, Ellie. And I certainly don't fucking need it.'

I'd overstepped the mark and I knew it. I shouldn't

have said anything. I should have kept quiet. Because of course he wouldn't know how to deal with this.

He didn't know what to do with something he didn't have to fight for.

My heart was nothing but a raw ball of pain, because even though I'd suspected that this would be his response, I couldn't quite get rid of the stupid hope that perhaps it would be different.

But it wasn't different. I couldn't force him to feel something he didn't. This was one thing I couldn't fight for. If he didn't feel the same, he didn't feel it.

'Okay,' I said thickly. 'It's okay, Ash. I'm sorry. I shouldn't have said anything.'

He stared at me and the expression on his face defeated me. I had no idea what he was thinking in that moment. His scars were vivid, his blue gaze even more so. 'I'll leave the car for you.' He chucked the keys carelessly down on a nearby desk. 'You can drive yourself home.'

And then he turned and walked out.

Leaving me standing in my brand-new workshop, my heart bleeding in my hands.

CHAPTER TWENTY

Ash

FURY PULSED IN MY VEINS as the cab I'd called delivered me straight to my mother's council estate. A raw, hot feeling. A familiar feeling.

The same feeling as when Delaney had told me that Seb had given up his claim to the islands.

The feeling of being given something I wanted without having to fight for it.

Something I didn't deserve.

Ellie, standing in the workshop I'd got ready for her, with tears streaming down her face. Telling me she loved me.

It was the workshop that had done it, that was what it was. It wasn't me. Just like two weeks ago when we'd had sex in the limo in Paris, and the next day she'd told me about her father's financial issues.

She'd told me she'd wanted to have sex with me, that it wasn't anything to do with Australis, but I'd had my doubts then. And I had them still.

Of course it wasn't me.

None of this was me.

And it didn't fucking matter. I didn't care what she thought of me. I didn't care about the tears on her face or the way she'd said 'I just wanted to tell you how I feel.'

I didn't care about the fact that she loved me at all.

The usual group of disreputable teens were gathered around outside, bored and with nothing to do. Once, I'd been one of them.

Today, though, I stormed past them, ignoring their greetings, anger burning like a fire in my gut, beating at the walls of the cage I kept it in, clawing to get out.

I bypassed the shaky lift and headed straight for the stairs, virtually running up the fifteen flights to Mum's floor without pause, working out my anger the way I preferred, with physical exertion.

Ellie had backed down in the end, so of course she hadn't meant it. She'd gone ahead and told me she loved me, and when I'd shouted at her, she'd turned away without even a protest.

I'd told her I didn't want it and she'd simply...accepted it.

And that was a good thing, wasn't it? That was how it should be, because I wasn't a man to be messed with when I was in this mood.

Her fault entirely.

She should have accepted my last gift to her, thanked me, and then walked out of my life. But no, she had to make everything so much harder by telling me she loved me.

Fucking love always ruined things.

I stormed down the hallway and up to Mum's door,

knocking on it as if I wanted to batter it down with my fists.

Mum opened the door and scowled. 'Ash? What the hell do you think you're doing breaking my door down?'

Without waiting for an invitation, I stepped into the tiny, dingy apartment I'd been brought up in. The apartment I couldn't understand why my mother hadn't left when given the opportunity. And then stood there as I realised I had no fucking idea why I was even here.

She shut the door behind me, still scowling. 'What is it? You look upset.'

'I'm not fucking upset,' I said belligerently. 'Why would I be upset?'

Mum folded her arms. 'You tell me. You're always pissed off about something.'

I glowered at her. 'Are you surprised? After the kind of upbringing I had?'

For a second Mum didn't say anything, only stared at me. Then she said, in a softer tone, 'What is it, Ash?'

'Why?' I demanded, not realising I was going to say it until it came out. 'Why do you not want anything I give you?'

She blinked then let out a sigh. 'Why don't you sit down? I'll get you a cup of tea.'

'I don't want a fucking cup of tea. Just tell me. You refused the house, you refused any kind of money I wanted to give you. Why? I just wanted to give you back what I lost.' My heart was beating furiously, the blood echoing loudly in my veins. I couldn't understand myself, why I wanted to know this bullshit. I didn't care about it, did I?

A strange expression crossed her face. 'Ah, this.'

'Yes, this.' My hands were in fists, my fingers aching with the tension, a strange kind of fear pulsing in my veins along with the anger.

'You worked hard for what you have,' Mum said quietly. 'And I know you blame yourself for what happened with the money. But…' She let out another sigh. 'I didn't care about that. I cared about you.'

I stared at her. 'I broke your trust, Mum. You never want to talk about it, so I—'

'No, *you* didn't want to talk about it. You were so angry and so betrayed. And so I decided to let it go.'

Shock echoed through me. 'But—'

'And as to why I'm here,' Mum went on, ignoring me. 'Well, it's home. I have friends here, good friends.' She smiled unexpectedly. 'I belong here, love. And I don't think you ever understood that, did you?'

'No,' I said automatically. 'You should want more. It wasn't your fault that you had me and had to settle for—'

'I never settled for anything, love.' Her expression became searching. 'I accepted the situation. It was you who couldn't accept it.'

Everything in me tightened. 'Why should you have to accept it? You didn't ask to be pregnant with me. I ruined your life.'

She snorted. 'Don't be so arrogant, Ash Evans. No one ruined my life. I made my own choices. No, they weren't the best, but I stand by them.' She gave me a penetrating look. 'You were the best thing that ever happened to me, though.'

My chest felt sore and it ached at the look in her eyes. 'I went to see Dad when I was thirteen,' I said hoarsely. 'We had no money and I thought—'

'I know. I found out about that.' An expression of sadness flickered through her grey eyes. 'I'm sorry, love. But your father had his own issues and they had nothing to do with you.' She crossed the distance suddenly and put a hand to my cheek, looking up into my eyes. 'You know that, don't you?'

'Yes,' I said. 'Of course I do.'

'Oh, Ash,' my mother murmured, seeing straight through the lie. 'It wasn't you. He didn't want anything to do with either of us and he never told me why. But I let go of him a long time ago. And so should you. He was a selfish man who didn't deserve to have you as a son.'

I felt nothing but instant negation. 'How am I any better?' I demanded, my voice rough and raw. 'I'm just like him, Mum. I'm just as selfish. I hurt people. I hurt you.' Ellie's white, tear-stained face loomed large in my memory. 'And I hurt someone else I shouldn't.'

My mother's hand against my cheek was warm, her gaze searching. 'Who?'

'A woman. A woman who didn't deserve it.'

She searched my face. 'The girl you were with in Dubai?'

'How did you know about her?'

'I read the news like everyone else.' She gave me a censorious look. 'You should have told me you had a girlfriend.'

'She's not my girlfriend.'

'There's only one reason you're here in a rage. And that's because you're hurt. You always get angry when someone hurts you.' My mother's gaze narrowed. 'What did she do to you?'

That was Mum. She'd always been protective of me.

I gritted my teeth, a strange hot feeling running through me. 'She told me she loved me. And I...walked away.'

Mum's eyes widened. 'That's it? That's why you're so angry? Because she told you she loved you?'

'Because she didn't mean it.' I lifted my hand and shoved it through my hair, restlessness and anger winding through me. 'I did a few nice things for her, that's all.'

My mother was silent a long time. Then she said, 'Then why are you so mad?'

You know why. Stop being so fucking stupid.

Something was clawing at my chest, an intense, painful pressure. It felt like an animal wanting to get out of a cage.

'I—' I couldn't finish, my breathing too fast, the words getting stuck in my throat.

An unbearably gentle look entered Mum's eyes. She was a tough old bird—as she liked to call herself—and she didn't do affection readily. But it was there in her face now. All the love she tried, in her own way, to show me. 'Ash Evans, are you in love?'

I opened my mouth to say no, of course I wasn't. But the lie wouldn't come. Just goddamn wouldn't.

The pain in my chest wouldn't go away either or the sight of Ellie's tears. Or the sound of my own voice, furious and loud, echoing off the walls of the work-shop, telling her I didn't want what she'd so bravely offered me.

You hurt her, you bastard. After you swore you wouldn't.

A violent heat poured through me, closely followed by something icy, and I stood there unable to move. Unable to speak.

But I had to. I had to say it aloud because I wasn't a fucking coward, even though everything in me wanted to hurl it away.

'Yes.' The word came out of me cracked and broken. 'Yes, I think… I think I am.'

'Of course you are.' Mum snorted. 'Only love messes with a person this badly.'

And the truth flooded through me then. The enormity of what I'd held in my hands and what I'd done with it.

'She's…too good for me,' I said, the knowledge sudden and blinding. 'She's everything I'm not. She's bright and beautiful, and I'm just a violent, selfish man who doesn't want to change.'

Mum snorted again. 'Oh, what bullshit. Those are excuses. You're just scared. You're scared of being hurt. And fair enough. You know what that's like and so do I.' Suddenly something burned in her eyes, something fierce. 'But you have one thing I never got from your father. You know that she loves you.'

I froze, something deep inside me shifting, like an undersea earthquake. A crushing weight. A vast pain. A current that wouldn't be denied.

Mum had never had that, but she'd loved Dad, I knew she had. Even though he'd kicked her to the kerb as soon as I was conceived. A love that, God knew, he didn't deserve.

What made me any better?

She already told you.

That day in Dubai, in the club, in that bed. Her telling me what she saw in me. Things I'd never seen in myself.

She'd been so brave, my pretty thing. Telling me what she felt, opening her heart up to me like a fighter opening themselves up to take that last punch. And she had taken it, straight to the heart. Only it had been me she'd KO'd.

But I hadn't taken it like a warrior.

I'd turned and run like a coward.

'What do I do?' My voice was a harsh scrape of sound as I tried to draw some air into my lungs. 'I hurt her.'

Mum gave me a disbelieving look. 'What do you think? Go and apologise, then kiss her and make it better.'

The weight was crushing. I wasn't going to survive it.

But Mum was right. There was only one way to make this any easier.

I had to apologise. Kiss her, heal the hurt I'd given her.

And hope like hell she didn't simply punch me in the face the way I so richly deserved.

CHAPTER TWENTY-ONE

Ellie

I took a flight to France that night. There was one seat left and, since my bags were packed already, it didn't seem like the most insane thing to do.

I couldn't bear the thought of going back to my flat and I couldn't stay in London one second longer. For once in my life, I wanted my dad and his no-fuss, no-nonsense presence.

For once I wanted it to be no big deal.

It was late by the time I got to the little town near Nice where Dad and his team were located. Ash had even hired a house near his small factory for the duration of their stay.

I took an Uber from Nice airport and got dropped off at the house they were staying in, my heart racing as I raised my hand to knock on the door.

I hadn't told Dad I was coming. In fact, I hadn't spoken to him at all. I'd just left Ash to handle it.

I could see Dad's shock in the way his white eyebrows rose into his hairline when he answered the door to find me standing on the doorstep. 'Ellie? What the hell are you doing here?'

My chest ached and my throat was tight, but Dad wasn't one for emotional displays so I swallowed it down and forced a smile. 'Thought I'd come and check out what was happening with the Pythons. Hope that's okay.'

It was okay, as it turned out, though, since it was late and he could see I was obviously tired, Dad told me that we'd talk in the morning, showing me to one of the unoccupied bedrooms.

I didn't sleep well. I couldn't stop thinking about Ash and his fury. About how he'd walked out. About how wrong I'd been to show him the contents of my heart.

I'd made a mistake in my comparisons of him to a car. Yes, he was large and powerful, but he wasn't simply an engine. A machine I could drive wherever I wanted. He was a man with his own will, and that will didn't include loving me.

Because no matter what I'd told him the day before about not wanting anything, the pain in my heart told me otherwise.

If I'd wanted nothing from him, I would have stayed in London. I would have been content to be near him—even if that meant just being in the same city.

But I didn't want nothing.

I wanted everything.

The next day, after coffee and croissants, Dad took me to the makeshift Python workshop where we had a miniature family reunion with two of my brothers.

They were excited—not that you could really tell

if you didn't know them, but I could tell. There was a certain sparkle in their eyes as they showed me around and introduced me to some of the team helping them. Even Dad had the sparkle.

'You did good, Ellie,' Dad said at last, quietly, as we stood beside the first of the cars that were beginning to take shape, the chassis gleaming under the bright fluorescent lights. Men in overalls swarmed over the car like ants, while one of my brothers barked orders from his place near the computer.

The praise hit me hard, making more tears prick at me. 'Aw, Dad,' I said, going for jokey. 'You're going to make me cry with that mushy nonsense.'

But he didn't respond as he normally did, with a smile and a nod. Instead, he said, 'You saved the company. Don't think I don't know that.'

I didn't look at him. I couldn't. I shoved my hands into my pockets instead.

'I know I haven't been the best father.' His voice was gravelly and gruff. 'I should have stuck up for you with that…other business. But when your mother died… Well. I didn't know how to deal with a girl.' He cleared his throat, obviously uncomfortable. 'That doesn't excuse me, I understand that. But… I just wanted you to know that I'm grateful for what you did for the company.'

I swallowed, my throat thick, unable to speak. The bright lights of the workshop ran like paint in my vision. 'Thanks, Dad,' I forced out, my voice hoarse.

'So, what's happening with your project?' he asked, as if he were asking me what I was doing for lunch.

'Evans told me you were going to start building a prototype.'

But I couldn't face that right now. I couldn't even imagine going into the workshop that he'd bought for me. 'Not right now,' I said.

'Look, I don't know what's going on with you and Evans—'

'Nothing,' I interrupted, the pain in my chest spreading like wildfire. 'Nothing's going on.'

'Ah,' Dad muttered, as if that answered a question. 'Well, it's only that he—'

'Hey,' Justin, my brother, said. 'There's some French guy on the doorstep wondering if you're here, Ellie.'

I turned, blinking the tears away hard. 'What French guy?'

Justin shrugged. 'He's at the door. You'd better go see.'

The guy turned out to be a man in a freshly pressed chauffeur's uniform and behind him, waiting in the street, was a long black limo.

My heart gave one hard, painful beat.

Justin, who'd followed me, whistled. 'Looks like someone important.'

The chauffeur gave me a professional smile. 'A gentleman wishes to know if you'll come for a ride with him, *mademoiselle*.'

My heartbeat picked up speed, my breathing coming shorter, faster. 'What gentleman?' I demanded, anger rising inside me, along with a ridiculous hope.

'He did not want me to give you his name. He only said that if you want to know who he is, you'll have to get in the car.'

But I already knew who it was and I'd stormed past the chauffeur before he'd finished speaking, heading straight towards the limo.

I was breathing fast by the time I reached it, anger becoming rage and hope and a thousand other things all rolled up into a big emotional storm that I had no hope of resisting.

So I didn't.

I flung the door open.

A man sat in the interior. Tall and broad. Black hair and scars. Blue eyes the colour of my heart. The colour of the love and rage and hope and despair and everything in the entire world pulsing through my veins.

'Don't you know you shouldn't get into a car with strange men, Miss Little?' Ash said, his gaze intense on mine.

There was white lightning in my bloodstream, lighting me up, making me incandescent.

'Why the hell would you think I'd get into a car with you?' I said, my voice cracking, my body trembling. 'After you walked away from me?'

'I know.' His voice was as cracked as mine. 'And you have every reason not to get in. But I'm asking you to anyway.'

I didn't want to. I wanted to.

And somehow my heart must have made a decision, because then I was inside the car and the door was shut. And I could feel the heat of him and his familiar electric energy. And there was relief in his eyes. As if he hadn't thought I'd get in. But he didn't reach for me. He stayed where he was.

'I'm not sorry,' I said fiercely before he could get a word in, every piece of me shaking. 'For saying all those things to you back in London. I shouldn't have said it was okay, that I was sorry I'd said it, because it's not okay. And I'm not sorry. I meant every single word.'

He didn't even blink. 'I know you did. And that's why I'm here. I'm here to apologise, Miss Little.' He paused then shut his mouth as if he'd been going to go on and had thought better of it. 'No,' he said at last. 'I'm not here to apologise. I'm here to grovel. I'm here to tell you that I was wrong to walk out. That I handled what you told me badly and I have no excuses for the way I spoke to you. None at all. But…you took me by surprise, Ellie. You…uncovered a vulnerability I wasn't expecting. And I did what I normally do when an opponent finds their way under my guard. I attacked.' He took a ragged breath, the fabric of his T-shirt stretching tight across his broad chest.

I didn't know why I was still sitting there when every instinct I had was telling me to punch his stupid, handsome face. To show him how badly he'd hurt me. To demand why he was here telling me all of this when every second of his presence burned my skin as if it were being held over an open flame.

But I didn't move. I wanted to hear what he had to say.

'I hurt you,' he went on, his gaze not moving from mine. 'I was angry and I hurt you. Because the weakness you uncovered was one I'd been trying not to think about. One I've been trying to ignore since that night in Paris.' He took another laboured breath like a runner forcing himself through the last, tough miles of a marathon. 'You asked me once whether I ever got tired of proving myself and I told you that I never had to prove myself. But of course I was lying. I've been trying to prove myself my entire fucking life. Because the truth of it is that I've never felt good enough. Not for my father. Not for my mother. Not for Seb.' His gaze burned. 'And not for you. Never for you, pretty thing. In fact, I've been desperately trying to prove I'm not in love with you since that night in Paris. And failing. And then you told me that you loved me... Christ, Ellie! I know it's not because of the workshop or the sex, you're too honest and direct for that to be the truth. But I told you it was because—' He stopped, his breathing faster, harder. 'I'm fucking terrified. You scare the living shit out of me. Because no matter how hard I try to prove to myself I'm not in love with you, I am.' He was so still, his body almost vibrating, as if he were trying to hold himself back. 'And I don't know what to do.'

I saw the bewilderment in his eyes and the shock. And my heart clenched hard in my chest.

Because he was here and he'd given me the truth. And he was afraid. A man like him, a warrior, a grizzly bear, didn't show their underbelly to just anyone.

This was a gesture of trust, I understood that.

I was shaking. 'You could just love me.'

His indrawn breath was sharp, the look in his eyes intensifying, narrowing. 'You still want me? After the way I hurt you?'

'Love doesn't go away just like that, Ash. You'll have to try harder if you want to get rid of me completely.' I opened my mouth to say more, but then he surged suddenly towards me, his arms around me, dragging me into his lap and holding me hard against his chest. 'I'm sorry, pretty thing,' he said thickly, burying his face in my neck. 'I should never have walked away from you. I was angry and I should know by now that anger isn't the best way to handle things, but it's just been my default for so long. And I'm going to try to be better. I want to change, to be different—'

'No,' I said fiercely, threading my hands through his thick black hair and tugging on it so his head lifted and his gaze met mine. 'I don't want you to change and you don't have to be different. I love you as you are, Ash Evans. Sure, you might have difficulty with being nice and you're a grumpy bear of a man, but your heart is in the right place. You want to do right by people, help them. All your charity work and investments in small companies... Hell, even your bloody revenge against your half-brother had a charitable purpose.'

He blinked at me. 'Grumpy bear of a man?'

I growled. 'Listen to me, idiot. I'm trying to tell you that you're an amazing person. You don't have to do anything but be yourself with me.'

The look in his eyes took my breath away. 'You don't either, understand me?' His hands cupped my face, his big palms warm against my skin. 'I love your honesty and your bluntness. I love your excitement and your smile. And I love your passion, Ellie Little. Because if there's one thing you are it's passionate and I don't ever want that to change.'

There were more stupid tears in my eyes, but I didn't

do anything about them, just as I didn't do anything about the ache in my heart, that was no less painful and yet had become sweeter somehow, an ache to cherish rather than fight against. 'I don't think I can change that, so you're stuck with it.'

He smiled and the ache got sweeter still. 'I won't be an easy man to live with, pretty thing. But I'm yours if you'll have me.'

'I will have you.' I reached up to kiss him. 'You should know by now that I love a challenge.'

He laughed, a deep rumbling sound. 'Then strap in, baby. I may not be easy, but I can guarantee one hell of a ride.'

That was the thing about Ash Evans. He was a man of his word.

And it ended up being the best ride I'd ever had.

EPILOGUE

Ash

SEB MET ME in The Billionaires Club London and we sat down for a drink. It wasn't easy to apologise for being a complete bastard for twelve years, but I managed it.

I'd been practising with a certain ex-chauffeur, after all, and it turned out that she was right. It wasn't too late. And sometimes when you'd burned a bridge, you could, if you were willing, find a way to rebuild it.

Seb and I talked long into the night and at the end, we shook hands. The bridge might have been built, but it was still a bit shaky and required some careful walking.

I stepped back out into the street, ready to get a cab home, only to find a long black car waiting at the kerb.

I smiled, my heart already starting to accelerate.

Without hesitation, I strode to the limo and got in, settling myself in my seat. Then I looked at the rear-view mirror to see a beautiful pair of hazel eyes staring at me from underneath the brim of a chauffeur's cap.

She'd promised me a surprise tonight; clearly this was it.

It was almost a month we'd been together and my breath still caught whenever I saw her, the sense of wonder that she was mine filling me like sunlight.

Her prototype was nearly finished and soon, with luck, we'd be showing it off at the next club event in Monaco, along with the Pythons.

I knew nothing about cars, but I knew hers was fantastic.

As beautiful and as visionary as she was.

'Where to, Mr Evans?' she asked in her gorgeous husky voice, a thread of amusement running through it.

I held her gaze. 'You choose, Miss Little.'

She smiled, the gold in her eyes beginning to glitter. 'How about to heaven and back?'

'That sounds perfect,' I said.

But she didn't need to take me to heaven.

With her, I was already there.

* * * * *

CROSS MY HART

CLARE CONNELLY

MILLS & BOON

For Jagger—who completely stole my heart at first sight
and whose smile lights up the world.

CHAPTER ONE

'YOU KNOW WHAT you need to put the wedding out of your mind? That. That guy right there.'

Penny points across the restaurant and my eyes follow the direction of her finger. I presume she's not talking about the high-powered businessmen sitting one table over. After Gareth, I'm giving suits a wide berth. Suits make me sick. I look beyond them, none the wiser. A family, an older couple with greying hair and three well-dressed younger people; two of them look to be a couple, one a sibling. My gaze lingers on them for a moment and a familiar pang of sadness sparks inside of me.

I miss my family.

Swallowing to clear my suddenly thick throat, I shift my gaze onwards, skating over the figure of a man standing at the bar, his back to me. Every fibre of my being goes on high alert.

Nothing about this man says 'suit.'

He's wearing low-cut denims, dark, scuffed at the arse in an 'I've worn them to death' rather than an 'I paid hundreds of bucks for them' kind of way, and a fitted white shirt that shows off the contours of a back that is muscular and sinewy. His arms are tanned, his neck thick, and beneath the white stretch cotton of the shirt I can make out the ghost of writing running across his centre—a tattoo?

My pulse leaps, pounding faster, and there's a twisting low down in my abdomen. His hair is thick and pale, blond, close-cropped.

I want to stare at him. I want to stare at him all night, ideally as he strips his clothes from his body.

All the more reason not to. I jerk my gaze back to Penny, a sardonic smile touching my lips. 'I don't think a one-night stand is going to make me forget that my ex is getting married tomorrow.'

'I don't know,' she coos, unashamedly watching the man in a way that makes envy spurt, unwelcome, in my gut. 'I think that guy could drive Gareth out of your head for a while.'

I look down at my drink, stirring the paper straw— half-disintegrated—in clockwise circles, watching as the ice chips against the edge. 'I think this is the only way I'm going to forget.'

'To this, then,' Penny agrees, chinking her glass to mine, lifting it to her lips and throwing it back in one fell swoop. 'Another?'

I laugh, despite myself. We've been best friends since primary school, when Marcia Adams called me fat and pushed me into the tennis nets, and Penny came running over and shoved Marcia—three years older than us—so hard she fell backwards and landed in a delightfully placed puddle. 'I can't have a big night, Pen. I've got that gazillionaire flying in tomorrow to inspect the golf course. And you know how much I need to sell it. That commission is… I need it.'

'You don't have to tell me how much you need it,' she says, crossing her arms over her chest. Her anger and hatred for Gareth know no bounds.

'I'm giving you until midnight,' I say, 'and then I want to be back in my own bed.'

'It's only six o'clock!' She laughs.

'Yeah, but I also need to not be hungover!'

'Babe—' she leans closer, pressing her forehead to mine '—do you trust me?'

'Of course I do.'

'Then let me help you put that fuckwit where he belongs—that is to say nowhere. He doesn't deserve even one minute of your attention. Got it?'

'I know that. I'm not… I don't still think about him.'

'Sure you don't.' Penny rolls her eyes. 'You're doing a great job of moving on, but, unfortunately for you, you still co-own the same bloody real estate agency.'

'More to the point—why I need this sale tomorrow!'

'Yeah, I get it.' She sighs. 'It's early. Whatever happens tonight, I promise I'll get you home by midnight. Okay?'

I bite down on my lip, nodding slowly.

'The same again?' She slips her slender body out of our booth, her eyes falling to my still half-full glass with disapproval.

I lift the glass and throw it back, slamming it on the tabletop before meeting her eyes. 'You betcha.'

She winks her approval and then sashays away,

oblivious to the way the table of businessmen watch her as she goes. But then, that's Penny. Stunning, sexy, unselfconscious, smart, and totally uninterested in flattery and praise. She's just happy going about her own business.

I'm not still hung up on Gareth. I couldn't care less that he's getting married.

Okay, that's a lie. I *care*, but that's normal. We were together two years—not that long in the scheme of a whole life, I suppose, but *two years*. We started a business together and were talking about moving in together, and yet he always said to me, from the first date, 'I'm not the marrying kind.' And I accepted that, I got used to it, because I wasn't even sure if *I* was the marrying kind—so why would I die on that hill?

And then we got more serious and our friends started getting married and I had this vision of our future, and suddenly it seemed strange to say we'd never get married.

Stranger still when he broke up with me. Ugh. I try to push that memory way, way back in my mind. The words he used I'll never forget.

'I love you, Gracie, but just not enough. Not in the way a guy should love a woman. I'm sorry.'

And he cried, because he's a good person and I think he felt like absolute shit to be pulling the rug out from under me.

'Everyone says they want to stay friends, but I mean it, Grace. Look at what we did together.'

He waved his hand around our office, and my stomach twisted because so much of who we were was in that place.

I agreed with him—we couldn't let anything destroy the business our blood, sweat and tears had turned into a multimillion-dollar real estate agency specialising in high-end property. Sydney was a tight market but we'd forced our way in and never looked back. We owed it to ourselves, each other, our clients and our reputation to get over this speed bump.

That seemed a lot easier to do before he hit me with 'part two' of the break-up.

'I've met someone.'

Those words! God, I'd heard them in movies and read them in books and they're just an innocuous collection of syllables, but when they were spoken to me I felt like my ears had been jammed with crickets. Everything hummed and buzzed and suddenly the guy I'd spent two years with, who'd seemed happy and content, was a part of someone else, something else, and I was on the outside of him and that, strangely adrift, as though whatever had anchored me to my place in this life no longer existed.

'His name—' Penny pushes a drink across the tabletop to me '—is Jagger.' She rolls the 'r' like a tiger, and I laugh.

'Of course it is.'

'He's only in town for tonight,' she continues, sliding in beside me. 'And he'd like to meet you.'

'Oh, for God's sake.' I roll my eyes, sure now that she's making it up, and look towards the bar. But he's facing us and my heart jolts in my chest. His elbows are lifted onto the bar so that he can recline casually, and he's watching me with a curiosity that sparks flames in my blood.

My lips part involuntarily and, even though I desperately want to look away, to blink, to *anything,* it's weirdly impossible. I am staring at him and he's watching me and no one else in the bar seems to exist.

His eyes are green, with thick black lashes, and he's tanned, a deep caramel colour, as though he's spent a heap of time at the beach lately. I wonder if he's brown all over? My eyes drift downwards and, holy crap, he's got a very, very nice body. Pecs clearly defined by that white shirt, toned forearms, lean hips.

Shit.

Pants that show a promising bulge. His hands are what really grab my attention, though. I like nice hands and his are…perfect. Neat nails, long-fingered with coarse hair on the knuckles, tanned, and he wears a scuffed gold ring on his middle finger and some loose leather strings around his wrist. He's a sort of devil-may-care surfer kind of guy. He's very, very easy on the eyes.

Heat stains my cheeks and now I jerk my gaze back to Penny, my expression one of mutiny. 'What did you say to him?'

'That you're looking to be distracted for the night,' she grins impishly.

'Penny!' I reach for the drink, taking a gulp to cool my flaming insides. 'How do you know he's not…?'

'What?' She leans towards me conspiratorially. 'It's a one-night stand, Gracie. What do you care about, beyond the fact he's hotter than Hades and undoubtedly great in bed?'

'Okay, for a start, how can you possibly know that?'

'I can tell. I'm good at this.'

'What, like some kind of sexual psychic?'

'Exactly.'

I purse my lips. 'Pen,' I sigh softly. 'He could be God's every gift to women and I still wouldn't knee-jerk my way into his bed.'

'That's a shame because, like I said, he's interested.'

Against my will, my eyes drag back to him. He's finishing his drink, but his eyes are still on Penny and me. My pulse ratchets up a gear and out of nowhere I imagine him naked, that shirt thrown across some hotel room somewhere.

'I'll tell you what,' she purrs. 'I'm going to go talk to that guy.' She jacks her thumb towards a group of men further down the bar and I can guess which one she means. Silver fox at the head of the group—Penny's got a thing for older guys, always has. Our take-it-to-the-grave secret is the fact she slept with our high school science teacher on grad night.

'And I'll come back in twenty minutes to check on you.'

'Pennyyyy…' I groan, shaking my head in exasperation.

'Six months ago, the bottom dropped out of your world. Gareth fell in love with someone else while you were busy building your business and planning a future with him. He went and fucked some bar girl.'

My heart spins at this frank assessment of our break-up. 'Yeah?'

'So at least have a drink with the hottest guy I've ever seen. Take a step towards remembering who *you* are. The you you were before Gareth, the you who built a multimillion-dollar business and is smart and funny and curious and loves to meet new people. He's from overseas; just chat to him. Have *fun*. I beg you!'

And not because she's right, and he's hot in a way you never see outside of Hollywood, but because she's my best friend and has never once steered me wrong, just as I have never counselled her badly. The science teacher would never have happened if I'd known about it in advance. I trust her. I believe she's right and some-how the timing of this, of at least opening myself up to the possibility of flirting with another guy on the eve of Gareth's marriage, would be strangely meaningful and important and…cathartic.

She's right. Pre-Gareth, I used to have fun, I used to flirt with guys, hook up. I'm in my twenties—why am I acting like someone's grandma?

I expel a breath and look towards him once more. He's turned away and if I have any doubt about whether or not I want to talk to him, the surge of disappointment to see his back answers that.

I stare at his tattooed spine with a frown on my face, but a second later he's spun back around, two drinks in his hands, and our eyes lock and certainty locks in my chest.

'That's my cue,' I say. Penny grins and I shoot her one last look of bemusement before I'm alone at the table. I have seconds to run my tongue over my teeth, making sure no trace of the beer nuts we shared earlier remains, to wipe my hands on a napkin beneath the table, and then he's standing on the edge of the booth, his green eyes—aquamarine, up close—boring into me.

'May I?' He nods to the seat beside me and I nod, grabbing my hair and pulling it over my shoulder.

'Grace?' he prompts, passing a drink towards me.

I smile belatedly, holding a hand out towards him. Our eyes meet as his fingers curve around mine and warmth spears through me. It's a handshake, the kind of thing I do all the time, but the way he's staring at me layers an intensity over it that changes everything.

'Yeah.'

'Jagger,' he says, the name on his lips so much sexier than when Penny purred it like some kind of wild animal.

'Jagger.' I'm unable to resist the feel of his name in my mouth.

He smiles when I say it.

'American?'

'Yeah.' His grin's completely disarming. He braces an arm on the edge of the booth behind me and, even though he's not touching me, I kind of feel like he is. I feel enveloped by his warmth and nearness.

'Whereabouts?' I prompt, lifting my drink towards his in salute.

He chinks it back. 'New York.'

'Nice.'

'You ever been?'

I tilt my head to the side a little, considering. 'Once.'

'Did you like it?'

'What's not to like?'

He lifts a brow. 'The traffic. The weather. The noise. The pollution...'

'Resident problems,' I say, deliberately moving forward a little so our knees brush under the table. I'm thrilled by the sense of power that gives me—the idea that this is all on my terms. That I know what I'm doing, where we're going.

'Not tourists'?' He doesn't miss a beat.

'Nope. Not this tourist. I love the snow.'

'And you don't get a lot of that here, right?'

'Not for long, and not in Sydney.' I sip my drink thoughtfully. 'I would have loved to move to New York. I used to think I would.'

'Why didn't you?'

I pull a face. 'It's not that easy. Life...can get in the way sometimes.'

'Sure it can.'

I appraise him, my heart racing, blood pounding through my body. 'Penny says you're only here for a night?'

He nods. 'Yeah. Had meetings today and I fly out tomorrow.'

I nod slowly.

'And you live here?'

'I moved here for uni,' I agree. 'But I grew up farther north.'

'How far north?' he asks with curiosity.

'A little town in Queensland. You know, the kind of

place where everyone knows everything about one another, with one main street and not much to do at any time, even less when you're a teenager.'

'Sounds like heaven.' He grins.

'Yeah, it kind of does.'

'Your friend says you're looking for someone to distract you for the night,' he murmurs, taking a slug of his beer, his eyes holding mine over the bottle.

I nod slowly. 'I guess I am.'

'Why?'

I didn't expect the question, even though it makes perfect, absolute sense. Only a monkey wouldn't ask. 'My ex—who happens to be my business partner as well—is getting married tomorrow.' Somehow, saying those words feels cathartic. So I say more. 'It was sudden. He's in love.' I spit the word with some distaste, earning a wry smile from my companion.

His teeth are so white, his face stubbled in a way that makes me imagine running my fingers over it.

'And you still love him?'

The question is a good one, one I haven't asked myself. I shake my head slowly from side to side. It feels good to admit that. 'I don't think so.'

'Then you don't believe in love?'

I gnaw on my lower lip. 'No. I mean yes, I do.'

'You sounded angry a moment ago.'

'Did I?'

He nods slowly. 'You sounded like someone who wants to fuck someone else out of their mind.'

'He's not on my mind,' I say, determined on this point. I'm not turning my first one-night stand in for ever into petty revenge sex. This wouldn't be about hurting Gareth so much as rediscovering myself, my agency, my right to think of myself as 'single,' just like he did—only we were together.

'It's...symbolic,' I say finally. 'Like a way to mark the date or something.' I shrug. And then, with bald honesty, 'Also, I don't particularly like the idea of him being the last guy I slept with when he's off on his honeymoon.'

He lifts a brow at my truthfulness. 'That's valid.'

'I'm glad you think so.' I wrinkle my nose. 'I'm not sure it's not a little bit fucked up.'

Beneath the table, his hand curves over my knee. 'It's not.' Desire jolts directly up to my thighs, and higher still. Heat pulses between my legs.

'Really? Speaking from experience?'

His expression is guarded. 'You could say that.' His fingers trace a little higher, to the flesh of my thighs. I grab my breath, hold it in my lungs a second, waiting for it to infiltrate my body.

'How long were you together?'

I can hardly think straight. His fingers creep a little higher and I stare at him beseechingly. It's not late enough in the night for this—people are still having civilised conversations at nearby tables. I am beyond grateful for the tablecloth that offers some discretion, but if he moves his hand any higher I think I'm going to make some kind of noise to show exactly what he's doing to me.

He moves his body closer and the arm around the

back of the booth curves over my shoulders. Holy crap, this feels good. Better than good. Ah-mazing.

His hand stops mid-thigh.

He's waiting for me to answer.

'Two years.'

He nods.

'And you broke up when?'

'Six months ago.'

He lets out a low whistle.

'So this wedding—whirlwind? Or was he with her the whole time he was seeing you?'

'No!' I shake my head, the idea sharper and harder than the truth. 'Just at the end. He met her a week before he broke up with me. Love at first sight.' Again, my words are derisive.

'Love at first sight is a juvenile concept.'

I agree with him completely. I hate that I do, that the girl who stared her sensible, conservative parents in the face and told them she'd rather be penniless and happy, chasing her dreams, than to give up on them because they seemed so unobtainable—that girl would never condemn 'love at first sight' as juvenile.

But he's right.

Love at first sight is a construct. Maybe love is in general. Desire isn't, though. It's real and it's flooding my limbs, bringing parts of me I didn't realise were dormant back to life.

I drop my hand to his beneath the table and I fix him with a determined stare. 'You know what?'

He moves his head closer. 'What, Grace?'

'I really—' I drag his hand higher '—really—'

higher '—*really*—' I place it between my legs, at the apex of my thighs, my eyes challenging him '—don't want to talk about him.'

'No?' He moves his thumb just a tiny bit, but enough for it to brush my clit through the flimsy lace of my thong, and my breath escapes in a shuddered, tortured exhalation.

'No.' I shake my head from side to side, burying my face in his shoulder for a second. Fuck. He smells like… heaven. Sunscreen, sweat, strength. I lift a hand to his side, digging my nails into his toned hip.

I don't know anything about him besides the fact he looks like a god and smells even better. His name. His country of origin. And the fact he's blowing out of town in twenty-four hours.

It's perfect.

'What I want,' I say into his shoulder before lifting my face and forcing my eyes to meet his, 'is to get out of here. Right now.'

CHAPTER TWO

I WATCH AS she walks into the hotel room, wondering what she thinks of this place. I think you can tell a lot about a person by the way they appraise hotels, and her eyes skim the simple, small room. A comfortable king-size bed—a prerequisite—a small en suite bathroom, a view of another city high-rise. The harbour is down at the rocks and I'm up near the park.

I remind myself she has no reason to be surprised by the somewhat meagre accommodation.

She doesn't know who I am.

She doesn't know what my bank balance is.

She knows nothing about me.

Except that she wants me.

And, God knows, I want her.

I've been with precisely three women since my marriage ended. An ex-girlfriend in Berlin for old times' sake—even though the old times weren't actually that great—a lawyer from Stockholm, and Katrina, who lives in the subpenthouse beneath me. That was a dick move, because every time I see her in the lift it's like she's angling for an invitation back to my place and nothing fills my veins with ice more than the idea of a relationship right now.

The ink on my divorce papers is barely dry—I got the notification from my lawyer last week—and I plan on staying single a goodly while. Possibly for ever.

This kind of thing—casual sex with fascinating and enchanting women—is all I need. Companionship, satisfaction and no strings—or iron chains, as was the case with Lorena. And this can't be more than it is—one night. I'm leaving in the morning, flying north to check out a golf course I'm toying with buying before heading home to the States.

This is my one night in Sydney.

One night with Grace.

I don't even know her last name, and I want to keep it that way. Last names lead to expectations and I expect nothing of women now. I expect nothing at all. I thought I was different, that my marriage was different, but here I am, twenty-nine with a divorce under my belt. Who knows how many I could rack up if I wasn't determined to not become Adrian Hart?

My father screwed up in a billion ways—but by far the worst, the one I run from every day of my life, was his ability to suck people in, chew them up and spit them out. Time and time again I saw him make women love him, but he never loved anyone. Not even us, I think. He was proud of his sons, proud that he had three boys to raise and carry on the Hart name.

But he didn't love us.

He didn't love anyone.

How else could you explain what he did to Holden?

I think of my brother and the news he learned only a month ago—that Hart blood does not run through his veins—and anger slams into me. Our father was a bastard, but keeping the truth of Holden's parentage from him was the cruellest, strangest decision he made.

Grace's eyes have stopped inspecting the room and now she's looking at me with a mix of curiosity and desire. I like the latter.

'Would you like a drink?' I offer, moving to the minibar and scanning it.

'God, no, those things cost a fortune. Don't waste your money.'

My lips twitch involuntarily, imagining how my brothers would react to that comment. With over thirty billion apiece, it's been a long time since any of us has worried about the overinflated cost of the minibar. Then again, isn't that part of why I choose to stay in places like this? Because I hate the assumptions people make when they know who I am. I hate everything people think about me when they know who I am.

'It's fine,' I assure her. 'Champagne?'

She moves towards me, the skirt she's wearing kicking a little as she walks, so my eyes drop to her legs of their own accord.

'I don't need a drink.' She presses a hand to my chest and then pushes me backwards, towards the bed.

I laugh, a husky sound from low in my throat. Her forwardness is different but, fuck me, I like it. She pushes again, her eyes holding mine, and I fall onto the bed, pushing up it until I'm in the middle. I watch as she stands at my feet, her fingers moving to the bottom of her shirt. For a second she hesitates, and then she lifts it up, over her sides, towards her head and she drops it to her side. I don't see more than the swish of the fabric, though, because my eyes are locked to her breasts as though they're some kind of glue or magnet in effect.

They are *nice* breasts.

My hands tingle with a need to touch them, to feel their weight in my palms. She reaches around behind herself for the bra strap, and I hold my breath, watching as she undoes it, her eyes still on mine. There is challenge in them and pride, a mutinous look of sheer determination, as she does something that perhaps she thought she might chicken out of.

Grace's hands drop to her skirt, and my cock is like granite in my pants. I am desperate to touch her, for my hands to be doing what her hands are, but somehow I feel like this matters to her. That taking charge of this is a big part of what she needs, and so I stay where she's pushed me, I lie there and I watch her and I tell myself, *soon.* Soon I will touch her and taste her and kiss her and drive myself deep into her body, burying myself balls-deep in her wetness, making her cry my name again and again into this tiny room.

She moves slowly, too slowly. I want to see her, I want to see her naked, but she teases the skirt over her narrow hips, her eyes almost laughing as they watch me, and then, realising she's enjoying this, I hiss out a breath, but still don't move. Finally, *finally,* she's wearing just about the most delicious scrap of lace I've ever seen. It's barely anything—fine and delicate, it covers her vagina but at the hips it's just lace, narrow bands that wrap around to the back.

'Turn around,' I command, my voice throaty.

Her eyes hitch to mine and she bites down on her lip again, drawing my attention to the full pillow of her lower lip. It was one of the first things I noticed about her. That, and the long blond hair that tumbled over one shoulder. And the way she kept stirring her drink and darting her eyes around the bar.

With the same speed, or lack thereof, she used to remove her skirt, she begins to spin, turning her back on me, and I can't help the groan that escapes me. 'Fuck me,' I mutter, because the lace is just a T between two perfect peach-like arse cheeks.

She tosses a glance over her shoulder. 'Isn't that the plan?'

Okay. I get that she wants to be in control here, but suddenly my dick is like a torture device in my pants. I move my hands to my belt but she turns back to me and I'm hit with the realisation of her beautiful rounded breasts and I don't know if I'm an arse or tit man any more, but just that Grace is whatever I need and want.

She straddles me, her hands on mine. 'Let me.'

She's really doing the whole 'take charge' thing, but I lie back, not caring if it's her or me who gets my clothes off, just caring that somehow we're naked together, soon.

But, instead of unbuttoning my jeans, she leans up to my shirt, which means wriggling her body higher up my frame, so suddenly her G-string-clad body is pressed right over my dick.

She moves her hips provocatively and I am done with the passive lie-still thing. I grab her hips, holding her on my cock, staring at her while I move my hips, as though I really were inside of her and she were naked, her legs spread, taking me into her wet core.

Her eyes flare wide and I grunt as I move her body up and down my length, through my jeans, and she's not passive here, either; she begins to grind her hips, using me to get off, her hands balling in my shirt front before pushing it up my body, and I lift my head so she can get it off completely and then she's dropping her body forward so her breasts, her soft, round breasts, run over my hair-roughened chest and she moans, low in her throat. Her nipples are puckered and hard and I thrust against her and she whimpers, her fingers digging into my shoulders as she cries out and trembles, pleasure filling her in a way that is more erotic than just about anything I've ever known.

Fuck me sideways, she's hot.

Her breathing is loud, tortured. Her mouth is hot, and she drops it to my shoulder first, nipping the flesh there with her teeth before dragging it lower, to my chest. She finds a nipple and flicks it; my dick jerks in my pants.

I bring my hands around and cup her arse, pressing her against me, and then slide a hand in front of her, finding her clit, and then her seam, pushing inside her, rejoicing at the feel of her muscles, so tight, so wet, so hot. I swirl my finger around her and she whimpers and then her hands are on my belt and she's moving away from me, she's looking at me with white-hot hunger as she pushes her thong down her thighs and steps out of it, then rips my jeans apart, pushing them.

She works fast, but not fast enough. The second I'm naked I feel like it's taken ten years to reach this stage, but hell, it was worth it.

I'm desperate to roll her onto her back, to take over, but there's that look in her eyes that speaks of a desperation, as though she's proving something to herself, and far be it from me to stand in the way of whatever challenge she's facing.

We've only got one night, but I plan on using the whole night, every goddamned minute, to enjoy Grace as much as I can before I leave. This first time, though, it's like slaking a ghost. There's a need humming through her that's more than just physical.

'Condom?' she asks, panting, her eyes sheened with the haze of her desperation. For a second I'm jarred out of this sexual fog and into reality because I was very close to forgetting to use protection and I would have said, until two minutes ago, that safe sex is reflexive for me—as much so as brushing my teeth or walking my dog.

'Yeah.' I push out of bed, using the chance to get rid of my jocks, and reach for my wallet. I always travel prepared, even though I didn't come here expecting this. Seeing those divorce papers made me contemplate celibacy.

Briefly.

Her eyes are devouring me, my ink, my muscles. I watch her watching me and wonder what her ex was like. It's a thought out of nowhere; it doesn't belong. I shove it aside, using my mouth to tear open the wrapper, and then unfurl the rubber over my length. Slowly, so slowly it's almost agonising, but I want to pay her back a little for her own sensual tease. I cover my dick and keep my palm wrapped around the base of my cock.

Her breath is the only sound in the room, hot little rasps that make me feel like I could come any minute. And then she's moving towards me, around the bed, her beautiful naked body something I'd love to just stare at, but, instead, she barrels against me and her mouth finds mine, hot and insistent, determined. Sweet Jesus, we haven't kissed before and this is all so backwards that only now, after I've had my finger inside of her, do I realise she's a great fucking kisser.

If we'd kissed in the bar I would have known this would happen—you can tell a lot about your chemistry with someone from the way you kiss, and this kiss is burning me up. Or maybe it's the feel of her generous, soft breasts pressed against my chest, or the little moaning noises she's making.

Fuck me.

I lift her arm, needing more of her, all of her, and wrap her legs around my waist, just needing to be as close as possible to her, and spin her so her back is against the wall. My desperate, hungry cock nudges at her rear without design and she arches her back, breaking our kiss for a second but giving me access to her breasts. My mouth, my ravenous, seeking mouth, drops to her nipple and sucks it inwards. Rolling my tongue over her swollen nipple, tracing it, sucking it, my hand seeks the pleasure of the weight of her other breast.

I feel it in my palm, my fingers brushing over her nipple, and she's crying my name and it feels so good to hear her say it I am bursting inside. Fuck this, I need her. No. I have a ravenous need for all of her; all she offers I will take and take again.

But there's heartbreak in the room, too, and as I pull away from her, kissing my way up her chest towards her throat, where I flick her pulse with my tongue, I ask, 'You're sure?'

Because I'm not a total arse, and she's mourning her ex and using sex to deal with that. Don't get me wrong, I'm happy to be used, but I want to hear that she's sure before we do this. I'm not my father—I'm not someone who exists in a bubble, not caring who he hurts.

Her eyes latch to mine and I don't think her ex is anywhere in her mind right now. This is her and me and the tornado of desire that's swallowing us up whole.

In answer, she digs her heels into my back so she can push up my body a bit, and rearranges herself, moving over my length. Her eyes are wide as she takes my tip inside herself and every bone in my body wants me to push inside of her all the way, but I don't. I wait, letting her get used to this, to the size of me, the feel of me.

She digs her nails into my shoulders as she goes down lower, and my hands cup her arse, holding her there, supporting her, and just feeling her beautiful roundness. Lower, and my cock is half-buried in her and she feels so tight, she's squeezing me in a way that is insanity inducing. Lower, and I see stars at how good this feels. She moans, tips her hips, rocking forward a little, and heat stains her cheeks. She's riding a wave and I still, watching her pleasure herself on my body for the second time that night.

Her responsiveness is some kind of catnip.

Lower still, until finally all of me is deep inside her, so deep, and we are melded together completely. And now, only now, do I thrust, lifting my head to watch her as I hold her hips still and push, deeper, harder, and she cries out, biting down on her lip, moaning, and begging me for more, please, more.

'Your wish is my command, baby.' I laugh, but it's husky because I haven't felt this turned on since I was in school and sex was still new and illicit. I thrust into her again and again and her back hits the wall and her legs stay tight around me so our bodies are like one, and my hands hold her arse, her beautiful butt, and I ache for everything, for this and so much more. I find her nipple again, the other breast this time, and I take it in my mouth, rolling her with my tongue, then clamping my teeth down so she cries my name into the room and I laugh, but it comes out strained because my own wave is lifting me up and I feel like I'm losing any grip I have on my control.

I take a breath, keeping my mouth on her breast, listening—feeling—the fast rushing of her heart, the beating that's like a cacophony of wild horses, pounding hard, and I know I'm the cause for that. Male pride swells inside of me, but I want more. I want to make her come again. And again and again and again. I want to give her so many orgasms that she can't even remember her ex's name. Or maybe it's that I want to give her so many orgasms I forget what a lying bitch my ex-wife was, I forget how much of our relationship was a fake.

Nothing about this is fake.

Grace is giving me everything, all of herself, and this moment, even though it's just physical, is the most intimate I've been with anyone in a long time.

Fuck. Stop thinking so much and just enjoy this!

I pull her away from the wall and cross to the bed; my legs are shaking, desire and adrenaline pumping through them. I drop her onto her back, falling with her so we don't have to come apart at all, and the second she connects with the mattress I push into her again. She stares up at me, her eyes huge in her face as she looks at me, as though she's high or drugged or completely blissed out.

I pull out of her so just my tip is teasing her clit and she pushes onto her elbows, her blonde hair falling over her face. 'Don't you dare stop,' she demands, fixing me with a look that is at once frantic and totally desperate.

The fact she doesn't mind showing how turned on she feels is another form of catnip.

'Wasn't going to,' I promise, not sure I could, even if a thousand wild horses tried to drag me away from her.

'I'm so close,' she says, and her cheeks flush pink and her beautiful, full lower lip gets dragged between her teeth. The thing is, I don't want this to be over yet, not even for a moment, and I think I'm at the edge of my control myself.

I keep my tip at her seam and she writhes beneath me, desperately trying to pull me back inside of her, the keening noises she's making something my mind will

replay often. My mouth drags down her body, finding
the underside of her breast and flicking at it. She's salty
and sweet and my gut clenches with a wave of desire—
more like a tsunami. Down I go, all the way, crouching
off the edge of the bed and pulling on her legs, pulling
her lower. I kiss her thighs, the skin there so soft and
pale, creamy and raw.

She isn't moaning now, but her breathing punctures
the stillness of the night. She's waiting. Waiting quietly, uncertainly.

I smile to myself as my hands curve over her thighs
and separate her legs a little wider, clamping them
where they are, and her beautiful sex is right there before me.

'Jagger…' My name falls out of her mouth—a plea,
a question.

'You're close?' I ask, my tongue running up her
seam.

Her harsh intake of breath is loud and primal.

Her hands scrape as they run over the duvet, digging into it.

'Uh huh,' she exhales. I find her clit and suck it into
my mouth and she cries out louder now, and I laugh—
despite the fact I'm as hard as I can get, the fact we're
surrounded by thin walls and God knows who else on
the other side of them doesn't seem to have entered her
head and I'm glad. I love her lack of self-consciousness.

I flick my tongue over her and she trembles beneath
me—I kiss her harder, faster, my tongue tasting her
until she explodes and I keep her legs right where they
are, when she might have pulled herself away, because

I want to enjoy every damned thing about her release. As she rides that wave, I push a finger inside of her and she bucks hard, her muscles squeezing me, and I groan then because my cock is more than a little jealous to be missing this party.

But there's time. We've got all night. Just this one night…and I'm going to make it count.

CLARE CONNELLY

CHAPTER THREE

HE IS SOME kind of sex god. Some kind of kinky, wild sex god. I can barely breathe. I think pleasure has taken up every square inch of my body, leaving little room for other optional extras such as oxygen and blood. No, the blood is there. It's rushing through me, reaching every tiny little cell, filling me up with heat and fire and flame and need.

More need—how is that possible? It's like I'm one of those stock market charts and every bloody release I get just pushes me down for a second before a new need swiftly kicks in and takes over.

I scramble onto my elbows so I can look at his dark blond head—between my legs—and I moan again because the sight of him like that should make me feel… squeamish or embarrassed, but it doesn't.

'You can just stay there all night,' I joke, smiling like the cat who got the cream—the girl who got the best head in the world, at any rate.

He looks up my body, over the curves of my breast to my eyes, and he grins then drops his mouth to my clit while he's watching me and I watch him as he lashes me again with his clever, clever tongue.

And I jerk because I'm so sensitive that the slightest touch feels like he's attached live wires to me.

He eases up, kissing me instead, just a gentle, soft kiss, and then he stands.

His cock is so hard, so beautiful, and I stare at it, wanting him inside me even when my body is still burning up from what we've just done.

'I want you,' I say simply, because what's the point in lying to a one-night stand? I don't care if he thinks I'm some wanton, sex-addicted hussy. I'm never going to see him again and hell, I *do* want him.

I'm already kind of high on the fact I've pushed my idiot ex way out of my mind, or at least erased his touch from my body. It feels kind of ceremonial—especially the timing.

'Stand up.' The command is gruff. I swallow, doing as he says, my eyes holding his as he takes my hand in his and pulls me towards the window.

'I like this city.' He positions me so I'm looking out of the glass.

'Me, too,' I say, my pulse thready as he spreads my legs from behind, my temperature skyrocketing. His hands on my hips steady me as he thrusts into me from behind, and I groan because I have missed him, the feeling of him buried inside me. He's so big—my muscles had to stretch to accommodate him at first but now I feel like I'm made for this. I brace my arms on the glass, thankful for the heavy tint and the fact we're high up above the city.

He thrusts into me hard and then one of his hands comes around to my breast, cupping it, and I call out because my nipples feel like they've been coated in extra nerve endings or something, so sensitive are they to his touch.

From this angle he reaches so deep inside me, my body is burning up with this.

'I want to feel all of you,' he says simply, as he pushes into me and his other hand comes around to my clit, brushing over it, as his cock pushes deeper and harder and I moan.

'I am all yours.'

He stills for a second, and then the hand that was on my breast drops to my hips and comes to my arse, curving around it, his fingers digging in slightly, and I whimper because the pressure feels so damned good.

His thumb inches closer to the middle of my backside and I hold my breath as he brushes over my butt.

Fuck.

Desire surges inside of me and I push backwards a little, encouraging him, not even wondering what the hell has gone on in my mind that I'm contemplating this.

He moves his fingers faster over my clit and I cry out as pleasure begins to break against me again and just the tip of his thumb pushes into me as he thrusts and I am losing all of myself in this moment, and gaining myself right back too. I look out at Sydney as I crest high above the earth and I lose my breath and my all.

I don't know what words tumble from my mouth, only that I am saying things over and over again, sounds and syllables, and then the hand that was on my clit clamps around my belly, holding me tight to him and, with his thumb pressed to my arse and his dick deep inside me, he comes, a fast, guttural thrust and a noise—low and so impossibly sexy. He throbs inside me and my muscles squeeze him tight, their euphoria undiminished, undaunted and, yes—even now—terrifyingly insatiable.

He is strong and moves me easily, angling my body so I can see our reflection in the mirror across the room. He doesn't speak, but his eyes hold mine and something surges inside of me because this is so, so intimate.

I am completely open to him, naked, wanton, wild and uncaring. My hair looks like it's been teased in some kind of tribute to the eighties, my cheeks are stained pink, my mascara has run around my eyes and my lips are swollen and full from the way I've been biting them non-stop.

He straightens, pulling out of me, turning away, and something like fear slices through me, that he's done with me, with this, but it's only so he can dispose of the condom, and then he's back, smiling, his eyes lined at the corners in a way that makes him seem so…nice.

I swallow, not sure I want to know anything more about my one-night stand.

'Now, I need a drink,' he says, moving to the bar fridge and pulling it open. He lifts out an ice-cold beer. 'You?'

'Yeah, thanks.'

He passes it to me then pulls out another, lifting his to mine in a gesture of salute, as he did in the bar.

I'm trying not to feel self-conscious, but what we've just done is…unlike anything I've ever experienced. There was some kind of whirlwind and it consumed me and spat me out and I'm a little unsure what to make of it. I sip the beer and then put it down on the bench top.

'Mind if I use the bathroom?'

'Go right ahead.' He nods towards the en suite bathroom.

I smile at him as I pass and he grabs my wrist, holding me still, his eyes searching mine.

He drops his mouth to mine, kissing me gently this time, slowly, tasting me, and I surrender to that kiss, my body arching forward, my tongue tangling with his. He groans into my mouth and his hands lift to my hair, thus explaining why it's such a bird's nest, as he weaves his fingers against my scalp, locking me where I am, completely imprisoned by his delicious kiss.

My hands curve around him, finding his arse and then, out of curiosity, I move one hand to his dick, feeling it like I wanted to ever since he undressed. He's semi-hard again and I am consumed by relief. Even as I know I need to unpack what just happened and how I feel about it, I know I want him again, too. I know I need him.

And the fact he obviously feels the same is reassuring and delicious.

I run my hand along his length, higher, my fingertips brushing over his tip, and his breath snags as he sucks it in and I smile against his mouth. I am totally here for whatever this night is going to be.

One night, no strings, and we'll never see one another again. Or a few hours, I think with a hint of regret as my eyes shift quickly to the cheap bedside clock that proclaims it to be just after nine. Like some kind of sexual Cinderella, I have my midnight curfew in mind and I *must* remember it. I've worked too hard to let anything come between me and success—and this sale means freedom! Freedom from Gareth, my parents' doubts over my ability to succeed—and their knowing nods that they were right. That I can't do this, after all.

Midnight's it—I'll go home, have a good night's sleep, ready to face the trip to the Whitsundays fresh, ready to wow this buyer.

And yet…for now…for the next few hours, there's this, and I want to enjoy all of it.

With that in mind, I move my hips from side to side, tempting his hands lower, and he doesn't disappoint, moving one palm from my hair, down my body, to my butt. I pull his cock in my hands, feeling its weight and strength as it grows harder, and his hand slaps down on my arse and I jerk and moan. It's not hard; it doesn't hurt, but hell, it makes my nerve endings fire with a heat I didn't know possible.

I move my hips closer to him so his cock is close to me, and he laughs into my mouth, lifting his hand and slapping my arse cheeks again. I move my hands to his back and pull him closer and he lifts his head, breaking the kiss, his eyes piercing mine but with desire and need. 'I thought you needed the bathroom.'

'Nope. I just wanted to take stock.'

His eyes widen a little; perhaps my honesty surprises him.

'And now?'

'I want to take something else,' I say simply, pulling at him, pulling him back towards the bed. He laughs again, but doesn't demur. I push him onto his back and look around for his wallet, grabbing it up off the bed-side table. Somewhere, in the periphery of my mind, I note the way he stills as I grab it, but it's not until I open it and see dozens of one-hundred-dollar notes in there that I understand why.

I flick past them, grabbing out another condom and unfurling it over his length, my eyes on his. 'You ever heard of credit cards?'

'I like cash,' he says simply.

Fair enough. His unique ways aren't of interest to me—it doesn't matter if he's some kind of conspiracy theorist who doesn't even believe in bank accounts. None of that matters.

I lift up and take him deep inside me again and it's quick and desperate—how can it be after what we've just done? I have no idea, but I feel like I've gone ten years without sex and this man is my dying meal. I take him deep and my muscles scream out with delight and relief. He digs his fingers into my hips and drives his own upwards, thrusting into me as I push down on his length, his possession of me absolute, and absolutely intense.

We explode together, our bodies mingled and tied, and as my nerve endings quiver with the force of this pleasure, I drop forward, onto his body, surrendering to the tidal wave of absolute release, surrendering to this and him.

I lie there, listening to the drumming of his heart, hearing its echo within my own, hot and too full of physical sensations to even think about emotions, about the fact Gareth is getting married in the morning and I'm in some cheap hotel room with a guy I don't know from Adam.

I don't want to think about that.

I don't want to think about the fact the last two and a half years of my life might as well have been erased, because I'm right back where I was as a twenty-one-year-old, with no commitments, no plans, no idea who I was.

He shifts a little beneath me, tumbling me off his chest and pulling out of me; I almost groan at his desertion.

But he pushes up on one elbow so he can look at me, and I feel like he's *really* looking at me. As though he's looking deep within my soul, into my very core, as though he's pulling me apart in a way that is...unwelcome.

I drift my eyes shut, like that might help a little, but his fingers curve around my cheek, stroking my skin gently, and I blink open reflexively. His eyes pierce me, to the depths of my soul. But he smiles and it's casual and easy-going so I tell myself I'm being pedantic or paranoid or both.

He says nothing, but I feel a thousand and one questions swirling between us and, for lack of answers, or for lack of answers I care to frame, I smile curtly and stand up. He doesn't stop me this time. I move to the beer I discarded a little while earlier and pick it up around the neck, drinking half of it with my eyes shut before replacing it quietly and moving into the bathroom. I click the door shut behind me and move to the sink, staring at myself in the mirror.

As I saw before, I am some kind of sexual being brought to life. I look like I exist for this and this alone. My chest is covered in a faint redness from where his stubbled face has dragged over my sensitive flesh. A quick inspection lower shows my thighs have undergone the same fate. I start the tap running and lather my hands in soap, then douse my face, washing off the relics of my make-up. It's better to have no make-up than the trashed wasteland I was sporting. I look around for the standard issue hotel cosmetics, pulling open a cupboard and seeing, instead, a travel pack of luxurious toiletries.

With a slight frown, I skate my fingers over them, noting the brand names with mild interest and growing curiosity before reaching for the next door. The usual products have all been shoved in here. I grab out the hotel branded moisturiser and run it over my face, then return my thoughts to his toiletry bag.

I know luxury brands.

I'm in the business of knowing them, after all. We sell some of the most prestigious commercial real estate in Australia, Gareth and I. Our clients are multimillionaires, and our job is to speak their language.

I recognise that he's carrying probably hundreds of dollars' worth of miniature toiletries and frown, because he doesn't strike me as vain, and he definitely doesn't strike me as someone who's got that kind of cash. And yet he literally does have a wallet bursting with cash, and now this?

But, no.

This room…his clothes…

Maybe they were gifts? I shrug; it's the last thing that matters. You know how sometimes your mind throws up strange distractions to stop you from thinking about what you should really be focusing on? I think there's an element of that going on.

Because I came here tonight wanting to erase him from my mind—Gareth. Wanting to push him out of my body, to replace him with someone else, and holy crap, did I achieve that! I don't know at what point this became less about Gareth and more about a plain and simple desire for Jagger, but that's what this is. I feel a surge of need and know what's responsible.

It's all him.

I lift my face to my reflection again, shaking my head. Smeared make-up is gone, but I still look like I've just done exactly what I have done. I finger-comb my hair, pulling it over one shoulder, then turn back to the door.

When I wrench it inwards I'm disappointed to see he's pulled his jeans on. They sit low on his hips, un-done.

He's on the phone, his back to me, but when I enter he turns and his eyes lock to mine and then scan my face, as if he's cataloguing the changes and simulta-neously making sure I'm okay.

And I'm more than okay. I smile brightly because this—this one night—is exactly what I needed.

'And a pizza. Large.' He covers the mouthpiece. 'Is there anything you don't eat?'

It's a perfectly normal question, but, given the context, heat stains my cheeks and he arches a brow, obviously understanding the direction of my thoughts. 'Food-wise?' he prompts again and I laugh, shaking my head.

'And I'm starving.'

He grins, holding a hand out to me, and I walk to him without a moment's hesitation. I put my hand in his and he squeezes it then pulls me closer to him, putting an arm around my body. 'Some fruit, and a couple of salads. Maybe some pasta, too.'

He disconnects the call, replacing the handset, then turns to face me properly.

'I'm so glad your friend picked me up for you,' he says seriously, and I burst out laughing, dropping my forehead to his chest.

'Penny's always had great taste in men.' I look up at him once more.

'Better than you?' His eyes scan my face in that intensely watchful way of his.

'Oh, definitely,' I agree. 'I was looking to go home with the bartender.' It's a joke, a sarcastic rejoinder, and he smiles but says nothing, and the silence stretches between us so, after a moment, I say, 'I've never been here before—to this hotel. It's…nice.'

He laughs. 'It's three-star at best, but my secretary booked it last minute.' He shrugs. 'And there's a bed, a bathroom, a good gym. What more do you need?'

'What more, indeed?' I lift my hand to his chest, running my fingers over his ridged muscles. 'And you work out a lot, I'm guessing?'

His breath speeds up a little as my hands go lower. 'I like to get my heart rate up.'

I arch a brow. 'I can tell.'

'I run ten miles, most mornings.'

'I can't even imagine running three miles,' I say with a shake of my head, pulling away from him and moving to my beer. I sip it, then look around for my clothes. He's picked them up and placed them neatly on the chair. It's such a small gesture but it does something strange inside of me. I move to them but he forestalls me, handing me a white fluffy robe instead.

'Don't bother getting dressed,' he says simply, but with a deep, husky promise in the words that makes my pulse quiver.

Shit.

I bite down on my lip and his eyes drop to my mouth, and desire is sparking around the room once more.

'Running is a habit, and one that gets easier the more you practice it,' he says, the words incongruous in the heat of our lust.

I swallow, trying to tamp down on my sexual heat, to keep my feelings at bay for a moment. 'I don't know,' I say, shaking my head. 'It's not my thing.'

'What is your "thing"?' he asks seriously.

My eyes skim his face, noting now that he has a slight bump in the middle of his nose, suggesting it has been broken at some point. 'For exercise?'

'Yeah. Or letting your hair down. Blowing off steam. You know, that kind of thing.'

I hesitate for only a moment and then speak with confidence and defiance. 'Pole dancing.' That defiance is hard fought for. My parents, my then boyfriend, everyone was askance when Penny and I took up the disreputable hobby. *It's amazing for your fitness*, Penny cooed and, as always, she was right.

He regards me cynically, as though I might be lying. 'Really?'

'Yep.'

I can feel his curiosity and turned-on-ness pulsing towards me. He moves to the narrow wooden desk and props his hips against it. 'Care to give me a demonstration?'

I eye the room and shake my head. 'I don't think anything in here would be strong enough.'

His disappointment is palpable. 'You can't pretend?'

I laugh. 'Not easily.' The robe is soft around me. I cinch the belt at the waist and move to sit on the edge of the bed, watching him.

'How'd you get into it?'

'The same way I get into most unorthodox parts of my life.'

'Penny?' he prompts, smiling.

I nod. 'Oh, yeah, you betcha. I suggested we join a ballroom dancing club—I wanted a hobby, and to move my body, to feel limber and flexible.' I smile distractedly. 'I work really long hours and even though I get to be out and about a lot of the time, I still feel more... sedentary...than I'd like. So dancing felt like a health kick, or a kick-start to a health kick...'

'Naturally.' He nods, his eyes skating over my body, which must look like a fluffy duck in this robe.

'She picked me up on the allotted night and we talked

the whole way there. It was only when she pulled into some dodgy car park out in the western suburbs that I realised we weren't at Miss Clarence's Ballroom Blitz.' I smile at the memory. 'Penny said she presumed that because ballroom dancing was for senior citizens, I must have meant pole dancing and just got mixed up.'

He arches a brow. 'You weren't keen?'

'I wasn't *not* keen; it just hadn't occurred to me before. But that's me—and that's so very Penny.' I shake my head. 'If I hadn't met her, I suspect I'd be running my life on a very narrow, very straight line.'

He nods thoughtfully, and his silence encourages me to continue.

'I guess I'm born with more than my fair share of the conservative in my blood.' His expression flickers with something I recognise: curiosity.

'Is that a bad thing?'

I'm confused for a moment—the curiosity or the conservative tendencies?

'Being conservative,' he prompts, as though he's read my mind.

I shake my head, compressing my lips. 'It's almost a prerequisite in my family,' I say simply. 'Mum and Dad have had the same jobs all their lives—good, reliable government jobs. Civil servant salaries and pensions, guaranteed security. My brother and sister followed suit.'

'It wasn't for you?'

I shake my head. 'Nope.' I look towards the window, my eyes sweeping over the high-rises beyond the small window of his hotel room. 'I always wanted to come down here. Growing up in a small town is—I guess I see it differently now, but, as a kid and a teen-ager, I hated it. I just wanted to travel and see the world, and not to have everyone I bump into know everything about me.' I pull a face of distaste. 'Sydney seemed like some shimmering oasis on my horizon. I couldn't be-lieve it when I got accepted to uni here.'

'So you're conservative in a different way,' he hedges, and again I feel like he's weighing me up, ana-lysing me cell by cell.

'Yes and no. My ex and I started our business from scratch. We were broke as a joke for the first six months, and my parents thought I'd lost the plot. There's no job security when you're running the show.' I shrug. '*But* the rewards are also potentially so much greater.'

'You went into business with your ex?'

'He wasn't my ex at the time,' I say with a droll shake of my head. 'My crystal ball wasn't working the day we signed the papers.'

He opens his mouth to say something, but I shake my head, my eyes sparking when they meet his. 'I don't really want to think about him right now,' I say hon-estly. 'Tomorrow will be for that, him, the real world out there. Tonight's just this…'

CHAPTER FOUR

I WAKE WITH a start.

Where am I? My phone is buzzing. And there's a body beside me. A warm, powerful, tanned body with tattoos on his hips and chest.

I lift a hand to my forehead as the events of last night—no!—I check the time—it's just before midnight—the last few hours—come rushing back to me.

Jagger.

I sigh his name in my mind, my eyes devouring him in this unobserved moment. For he sleeps deeply, exhausted by all the sex.

And I mean *all* the sex. We ate together, a mountain of food, and then one thing led to another and we were in bed again, and somewhere after that we must have drifted off to sleep. The lights are still on.

I grab my phone off the table, my eyes bleary, and squint at the screen.

Penny's face smiles back at me.

Frowning, I push my feet out of bed, stumbling towards the bathroom and shutting the door behind me. I push the toilet lid down gently then sit on top of it, swiping my phone to answer at the same time.

'Penny?' My voice is a hoarse whisper.

'Gracie?' She imitates it.

'Why are you calling so late?'

'I promised I'd get you home by midnight, didn't I?'

I smile slowly, her dependability never in doubt. 'That you did, lady.'

'So? Where are you?'

My smile is self-conscious. 'Not home yet.'

'Oh my god,' she squeaks. 'You went back to his place?'

I nod, then, because it's a phone conversation and nodding is pointless, clear my throat and say, 'Yes.'

'Gracie! I'm so proud of you! And? Was he every-thing those abs promised he would be?'

'And more.' A smile tickles my lips. 'But I can't talk now. I'm going to turn into a pumpkin unless I get out of here…'

Regret spirals inside of me. I don't want to go. Not yet. But tomorrow is a hugely important day for me; I can't mess it up. The whole future of my company is riding on it. This deal has the power to wrest me free of Gareth, to buy him out once and for all. Everything's organised. I just need to show the buyer around the golf course, spend a few days showcasing the best the region has to offer, and then present the contracts…

I have to be fresh-faced and quick-witted; I've heard the buyer is a hard nut to crack and I am absolutely going to crack him.

Penny sighs. 'As much as I hate to agree with you,

I don't want you working with that fuckwit Gareth for a moment longer. Away with you, Cinderella. Get thee to a taxi and texteth me when you're home at your palace.'

'Cinderella lives in a dungeon, I think.'

'Fine, your dungeon.' I can hear her epic eye-roll. 'Just text me. Love you.'

'You too.'

We hang up and I stare at my phone for a few moments, cradled against my naked legs.

I know I have to go, and yet I sit there for a few moments longer, bracing myself for the inevitable. This is just a sex thing, by the way. I've always known I'm a pretty sexual person—way more so than Gareth—but I never knew sex could be quite so…exhilarating. This went beyond sheer satisfaction. I felt like Jagger pushed me in every way possible and I abandoned myself to him, and this, in a way I wouldn't have said was at all likely.

There's nothing for it, though. I've worked too hard to potentially ruin a deal of this magnitude just because I'd really rather fall asleep next to his warm body and wake up in his arms…

With a sigh, I slip into the hotel room and dress as quietly as I can. And even though I'm barely louder than a mouse, I kind of wish he'd wake up and catch me in the act. Then I could explain in person. I could kiss him and one thing might lead to another, *again*.

He sleeps soundly and I stare at him for a few more

self-indulgent seconds before grabbing the standard-issue hotel notepad off the desk and a pen from my bag.

Thanks...you were great. Grace.

It is short and to the point, but what else could I say? I'm never going to see this man again and soon this will be a very nice, very distant burn-me-alive memory.

Sydney is baking hot and here, on the private runway to the west of the airport, it feels like Satan's waiting room. I stand at the base of the jet's steps and cast an impatient glance at my watch.

She's late.

Whoever Gareth is sending in his stead is five minutes behind schedule and it takes my mood from bad to worse.

I suck in a breath of the sultry, tarry air, reminding myself it isn't this person's fault that I woke up harder than rock with my erstwhile lover nowhere to be seen.

I should be grateful—I hate the 'morning after,' the awkwardness of extricating myself without leaving a phone number, the conversation about, 'Thanks, I'm just not in a place where I can commit to anyone right now...'

I'm glad I didn't have to go through that with Grace because, even though we both knew the score, she was...nice. And the ex-getting-married thing sucks, and I'm not sure how I would have gone letting her down gently *if* she'd shown even the slightest inclination to *not* be let down.

But she didn't. She walked away, she got it. She gets it. I'm not relationship material. Probably never was.

My eyes drop to my left hand, to the finger that up until a year ago had worn a simple gold band. I think about the ways I tried to make my marriage work. I think about the ways I tried not to be my father, and the fact I was sure being married would prove to everyone, and particularly to me, that I was free of his destiny. Except I wasn't. I think about the fact 'character is fate' and my fate is to be as much of a failure when it comes to commitment as he was.

The hum of an engine draws my attention skyward— a jet taking off. I follow its trajectory to when it's high against the cobalt blue sky, a streak of white far above me. Where the hell is this real estate agent? Hardly an auspicious start for a multimillion-dollar transaction…

Crappety, crappety hell. 'Can you go around it?'

'Sorry, love. Police've got it cordoned off right to the intersection.'

'Shit.' I blink apologetically at the driver. 'I can't be late for this. And I'm so, so late. Is there anything you can do?'

'A car's rolled into the intersection.' The driver shrugs, his thick grey brows shooting skywards as he meets my gaze in the rear-view mirror. 'We just have to sit it out. Won't take long to clear the crash.'

'Shit.'

I sit back in the seat, glaring at the digital time read-out on my phone.

Shit.

I'm a bundle of nerves. Why? Pick your reason.

Gareth's wedding? Sure. Imagining my ex dressing in a tux, his family, his mum—who I was so incredibly close to—all dressed up and ready to welcome someone else into the fold. My stomach is in knots, acid lining my gut. Because it should have been me.

Why wasn't it me?

From day one he told me he wasn't into marriage, but he was. He proposed to her—Alicia—within a month of dating. So it was just marriage with me he didn't want. Or maybe he didn't want marriage with anyone until he met her, and he realised she was the only person who could get him down the aisle?

How can you go from someone you've been with for two years—a happy two years—running a business together, living together, working as a team together in every way—and end up with someone else entirely? And so fast.

So blindingly, breakneck fast.

But it's not just the fact that right now the guy I thought I'd spend the rest of my life with is currently making that pledge to someone else.

There's also the fact my body is feeling *all* the things this morning. I'm sore between my legs in the best possible way, my breasts are tingling beneath my bra and every time I close my eyes, I see him, Jagger, going down on me, taking me from behind. I feel the ghost of his touch and my stomach loops into knots and it's like I've crested over the high point of a roller coaster.

So there's that.

But then there's the question of Silver Dunes. It's not just one of the most beautiful properties I've ever seen, though it is. It's also my ticket to a whole new life. If only I can get this sale through before the owner gets impatient and takes the listing away—if only I can get this sale through within the week, contracts signed, deal done, I'll be able to go to the bank and borrow what I need until the golf course settles... I'll be able to buy Gareth out while he's on his bloody Mauritius honeymoon and, with any luck, never have to see him again.

My mum would say I'm counting my chickens before they're hatched, and I am, but I know this deal's so close to being done. The golf course is ah-mazing. There's no way anyone could see it and not love it.

And I'm going to make sure this investor agrees with me. The first time I saw the course was in the evening. The lights were warm, leading us from the five-star restaurant at the clubhouse to the twelfth hole, for which the course was named. For here, at the right time of night and the right time of year, so long as the sky is clear, the moon casts the sand dunes in a perfect silver light, making them look like moondust.

It's magic.

My driver beeps the horn, jolting me away from the idyll of Silver Dunes and, thank God, we're moving forward. He's weaving around a small purple car and pushing us onto the footpath.

'Bloody jokers don't know how to drive,' he grunts, and I smile because, whatever has pushed his patience, I'm glad for it.

For the tenth time since getting in the car, I check

my bag for the brochure, our itinerary, the financials, the contracts and the brief bio I've got on the investor.

J Ryan Hart, one third of Hart Brothers Indus-tries. 29. Estimated personal worth $152.7 billion USD plus investments.

Can you even imagine having that kind of money? Maybe I should just ask him to float me a loan to buy Gareth out—I only need a million, Aussie. Small change to someone like him, right?

I skip my eyes further down the page.

Has bought three golf courses in five years. No property in Australia. Preapproved by FIRB.

That's it. Black and white, neatly collated by Gareth and our assistant Bianca. With any luck, this will be the last joint deal I do with him. My eyes drift to the bottom of the page, where Gareth's signature is scrawled, and my heart does a funny little tremble because in a few short hours he'll be signing his name like that on a wedding certificate.

Nausea perforates my belly and I blink furiously. *I will not cry.* I've done that. I've done more than enough. I think I spent the first three weeks after he left me curled in a ball whenever I wasn't at work.

No more.

I want to put him behind me, I want to live my life and I want to be happy. I'm never going to let myself depend on anyone else again. I'm never going to let myself care for someone more than they care for me. From now on, it's me against the world. Okay, me and Penny.

'Which way, love?'

'Oh—' I scan the green road signs above the busy six-carriageway entrance to the airport '—left—private tarmac.'

'La-di-da.' The driver grins. 'Going somewhere fancy?'

'Work,' I say with a grimace, skimming my eyes over the road as he turns into a separate lane and then steers us to the private terminals.

I suggested I meet Mr Billionaire J Ryan Hart in the Whitsundays, but he had business in Sydney and suggested the flight would be a good time to go over the financials—who was I to argue? It's my first time on a private jet. And while Old Me might have balked at the very idea—I'm not exactly a confident flyer—New Me is saying 'yes' to new experiences. Even this one.

'Only ten minutes behind schedule,' my driver chirrups as he pulls the car to a stop on the tarmac. 'Here okay?'

I look at the jet and a kaleidoscope of butterflies launches in my gut.

'Perfect,' I murmur. This isn't a little twin-prop plane. This is a proper Airbus or Boeing or something. It's *big*. With HART BROTHERS emblazoned down the side in gold lettering. And while there's no red carpet on the metallic stairs, I seriously feel like there could and should be.

This is a whole other world.

'Thank you.' I offer the driver cash and step out of

the car, moving to the boot. He clicks it open and I pull my suitcase out myself, barely able to take my eyes off the plane.

There's a solitary staff member at the bottom of the steps, wearing a generic airport staff uniform.

'Miss Llewellyn?'

I nod, and the airport worker takes my suitcase from me. 'Do you have identification?'

I pull my driver's licence from my purse, holding it for inspection.

'Great. Plane's all ready. Head on up. Mr Hart is waiting.'

Mr Hart is waiting. Crap.

I hoped he might have been caught up in the same traffic jam I was, but apparently I'm just not that lucky.

'You'll take care of that?' I nod to my suitcase.

'Of course, madam.'

'Thank you.' I smile, over-bright, trying to appear more confident than I feel. But it's silly to be nervous. This is what I do. What I'm good at. *Really* good at. I match people to property. I see what's special about something, and someone, and I match those qualities together.

The traffic couldn't be helped, but everything else is within my control. Mr J Ryan Hart has no idea I'm a bundle of emotions today because of my ex's marriage and my very hot, very kinky one-night stand. I'm going to walk onto this jet and be the consummate professional I actually am.

This is business.

All business.

Pep talk firmly in place, I take the steps, smiling at a steward just inside the doors. 'Good morning, Miss Llewellyn. Mr Hart asked you to join him in the boardroom. Halfway down on the right.'

I resist an urge to laugh. A boardroom on a plane? I'm definitely not in Kansas any more.

'Sure.'

'There's coffee and tea in there. Would you like anything else?'

'Stiff drink?' I joke, and shake my head to show I didn't mean it. 'Thanks.'

I turn away from him and move through the plane, the realtor in me taking in the pertinent details as I go. White leather seats and pale beige carpet, muted overhead lighting, bleached timber detailing. It's the last word in understated opulence.

Steeling my nerves, I go deeper into the plane. The doors are shut with a loud, telltale sound. Halfway down on the right there's a wooden door with a frosted glass panel. It must be the boardroom.

I hesitate for the briefest moment as the plane begins to push off, moving down the runway, then knock loudly.

'Yeah?'

A deep voice, but definitely impatient, and I wince because I really wish I hadn't started these three days off by arriving late. What a stupid mistake to have made.

I should have left twenty minutes earlier. Except I *had* left plenty of time—the traffic was unusually heavy. It was out of my control.

I push the door open, not seeing him at first.

I clock the details of the room—the enormous, highly sheened meeting table, the white leather seats that are set around it and, at one end, at the head, the man I've come all this way to see. The man I need to sell this golf course to. The man who, indirectly, holds my future in his hands.

The man who last night held my pleasure, and my body, in his hands.

It's him…

Him, Jagger.

Him, last night.

Him…

Oh, God.

At least I'm not the only one who's shocked by this. He looks like he's seen a ghost.

'Miss Llewellyn?' he asks, the words raw in his mouth. '*You're* Miss Llewellyn?'

'*You're* J Ryan Hart?'

He stares at me like maybe I'll disappear or maybe he's imagining this. He stares at me in a way that is cold and confused where last night every look was brimming with fire and flame.

'The J is for Jagger?' I ask, quickly collating all the facts and coming up blank. Nothing about this makes any kind of sense.

'Yes.' He stands up belatedly, moving to the seat beside his. 'Have a seat, Grace. We're about to take off.'

I stare at him and wonder if it's too late to back out of this. If it's too late to get my assistant Bianca to take the kind of promotion she's desperate for and accompany this handsome squillionaire to the Whitsundays in my place.

But I'm not going to compound the shitshow my life is right now with unprofessionalism.

'Fine,' I say crisply, taking the seat beside him. 'Let's go, then.'

CHAPTER FIVE

'YOU HAVE THE financials there?' He buckles a seat belt around his waist and I realise all these seats have belts. Of course they do. We're in a plane. Still, nice touch. I echo his movement, clipping in and tightening it, then reach for my bag.

'Yes, I do.' I pull out the manila folder but leave it in front of me, forcing my eyes to meet his. 'What should I call you?'

Something sparks between us, a hint of what we were last night. 'Mr Hart is fine, Grace.'

God, how the hell am I going to do this?

'Okay.' I'm pleased with how my voice sounds. Crisp and cool. 'These are the records of the last five years. A tropical storm damaged the clubhouse three years ago, so you'll see the rebuilding costs have made a dent in the P & L for the subsequent two years—'

'Yes, I'm aware of that,' he interrupts, all business, not a hint of anything more between us.

I frown because I'm playing catch-up here and I don't quite know how to reconcile what we shared less than twelve hours ago with this.

'However,' I continue, digging my nails into my palm beneath the table, 'there's a silver lining there for the new owners.'

'Oh?'

'The vendor, Karakedes Corp, used the opportunity to do a complete structural overhaul of all the buildings. Steel frames have been inserted to reinforce what was there. All the glass is triple glazed and tempered, like what you'd find on a naval vessel. The roofs are triple pinned. It would take two Category 5 storms to rip the roof off the clubhouse, plus a bunker's been built as a "just in case" for staff or players who get caught in its wake. The Karakedes Corp wanted to offer safe haven to local residents—not just club members—in the event of future catastrophic events.'

'You make it sound as though I should brace for cyclones every wet season.'

I dig my nails in deeper. The pain is excruciating. 'Not at all, Jagg—Mr Hart. But tropical storms are part and parcel of life up in North Queensland. I'm sure you're aware of that.'

His lips twist in what I think might be a smile, but he's stern again immediately afterwards.

Frustration zips inside me. 'How come you didn't tell me who you are?'

He regards me with consideration for a moment, then drops his pen onto the table, steepling his fingers beneath his chin. 'And who is that?'

'A Hart.'

He continues to stare at me and I'm unnerved by it, but I don't show it because I'd bet my bottom dollar on the fact he *wants* me to be off-kilter, and I don't like that. I can't reconcile that with the man I went to bed with last night.

'Would it have made a difference?'

'In whether I went back to your hotel room?'

He dips his head in silent agreement.

'Absolutely.'

His brows lift heavenward.

'I've never slept with a client before.'

He looks relieved for a microsecond and then he fires back a quick rejoinder. 'Just your business partner.'

It's a low blow and for a moment my businesslike façade drops. My chest hurts. I drop my eyes to the folders in front of me, taking in a breath and trying to think of something to volley back—but drawing a blank.

'I shouldn't have said that,' he offers, the words softer. 'I'm sorry.' He reaches out then, curving his hand over mine, and a zap of electricity sparks in my veins. I pull my hand away quickly. 'I was surprised to see you again today. I don't…like surprises.'

'That makes two of us.' I smile at him, a tight smile but a signal of a truce, nonetheless. 'I wouldn't have gone back to your place last night if I'd known we were going to be doing business together for the next three days.' God, that sounds kinky. My cheeks flame but thankfully he has the decency not to react.

'I wouldn't have invited you,' he says softly, 'if I'd known you'd be trying to sell me a sixty-million-dollar piece of property the morning after.'

My eyes lift to his.

'But rest assured, Grace, I never mix business with

pleasure. What happened between us last night will have absolutely no bearing on my decision. I'm a facts and figures man, so show me what you've got.'

I wish I was a little more facts and a little less figures—specifically, her figure—but from the moment she stepped onto the plane, wearing a simple cream suit with a pale pink silk blouse underneath, I wanted to strip it off her and lay her on this tabletop. Pink and cream, like her beautiful body, her breasts, her clit, all of her.

Fuck me.

Suddenly, three days of work feels like it could be more fun than I anticipated. My mind moves quickly, going over the situation.

I fly back to New York on Tuesday morning. That's non-negotiable. I never like to be away from Brinkley for more than a week—golden retrievers are loyal and Brinkley especially so. Besides, Theo takes care of him grudgingly and more than a week would be pushing our sibling relationship.

I have nothing to offer Grace. I can't possibly make her any kind of promise, nor do I want to. If my parents' explosive, disastrous union, and their subsequent failed marriages, didn't teach me how flawed the concept of monogamy and commitment is, then my own freshly sealed divorce does that perfectly.

After the example of my father, there's no way I'm making any promises to any woman—ever. I am not him and I will not make a habit of hurting people like he did.

This isn't about wanting anything from Grace; I don't. If I'd never seen her again after last night, I wouldn't have minded. Except that we're going to be spending the next three days together, in each other's pockets and, given that our chemistry is so…satisfying…wouldn't it be stupid not to explore that again? And again, and again, and again?

Beneath the table, my knees brush hers and she jolts away from me, her cheeks heating up. Her skin is like crushed pearls, pale yet luminescent, except beneath her wide blue eyes, which are marked with a silver grey.

She's tired.

Because of me?

My pride likes that. But then what about her ex's wedding? Is it possible she left me and cried into her pillow all night? All the more reason to bring her back to bed. I liked helping her forget. I liked it a lot. And she's not the only one who wants to use sex to put their past in the shadows for a time.

I watch as she lifts out more financials, opening them on the relevant pages. She begins to run through them, her fingers moving down the columns as she speaks. I focus on what she's saying with almost all of my mind, the part of me that's capable of rational thought taking note of how all over this she is. The detailed breakdown is complex, but she's explaining it to me calmly, patiently and diligently, as though she wrote the damned reports. I listen, impressed.

But a small part of me is wondering how I can proposition my real estate agent. How I can tell her I want more of what we shared last night.

She lifts a hand to her hair, pushing a pin back in more tightly. She's wearing it in a bun today and I ache to reach over and undo it, to let it fall down her back as it did last night.

Her eyes lift to my face and her cheeks flush pink.

'Mr Hart and Miss Llewellyn, Captain Morris here. We've reached our cruising altitude. We've got good tailwinds into Hamilton Island today, so we should complete the flight in a little over two hours, making up for the delay at take-off now that we're in the air.'

Her blush deepens.

'However, we'll experience a bit of turbulence as we get closer. I'll try to fly above it as much as possible.'

The intercom goes dead. I return my attention to the papers.

'You were saying?'

'Did he say turbulence?'

'Yeah. Why?'

'Oh, nothing.' She bites down on her lip; it's the last straw. I reach out and stroke my thumb pad over her mouth and she startles, jerking her face away and staring at me with eyes that show confusion and desire all at once.

'We both agree last night wouldn't have happened if we'd known who we were,' I say logically, calmly. 'But it did. We can't close Pandora's box now.'

To her credit, she doesn't flinch from my calmly voiced explanation. 'I know.'

'I don't want you any less now than I did when I woke up looking for you this morning.'

Her harsh intake of breath fires in my bloodstream. 'What are you saying?'

'I'm saying, I'm here for three days. Then I fly back to the States and we never see each other again.'

She nods, her eyes impossibly blue. 'And?'

'I'm here for three days.' I reach for her hand now, stroking my thumb over her flesh, my eyes locked to hers, boring into their crystal clear depths, my intention impossible to misread. 'And you're here for three days. We're going to be together, in the Whitsundays. Do you really want to ignore this?'

A small groan escapes her lips and my cock strains against my pants because I remember every single one of her delightful cries; I remember how vocal she was as we made love and I want to drive her to those levels again.

'You're my client,' she says quietly. 'I can't… Last night was amazing, but…if I'd known… It wouldn't have happened. We can't undo it but I won't make that mistake again, Jagger.'

I like it when she calls me Jagger, but I fucking loved it when she called me Mr Hart. I fight an urge to insist upon it, to insist upon it as she fucks me.

'This is too important.' She swallows and the fine column of her neck moves and I ache to press my lips to the pulse point at the base there, where her pulse flutters wildly.

'I told you,' I murmur. 'Nothing about us will have any impact on what I decide to do.'

'You say that, but I can't believe it.'

'I don't lie. Not about business.'

'I don't think you're lying,' she murmurs, a sad smile ghosting over her features. 'But people do stupid stuff once it gets personal.'

'What if it's not personal so much as physical?' I say, moving forward, cupping her face with my hands. I feel her pulse beneath my fingertips and it's going wild. 'What if it's just raw, animalistic sex? But only after five o'clock?' I run my eyes over her face, my expression undoubtedly as hungry and haunted as my voice. 'What if between eight o'clock and five o'clock we're Mr Hart and Miss Llewellyn, and after hours we're what we were last night?'

She's tempted. She's looking at me as though she wants me to throw her a lifeline, a way to make this okay.

'I can't,' she whispers, closing her eyes. 'I can't risk it.'

'Risk what?'

'I can't have that doubt in my mind, if you don't buy Silver Dunes, that it's because of some stupid decision I made. I can't risk it—this means too much to me.'

I drop my hand to her knee then and another small moan escapes her lips. 'Why?'

'It's…a big deal,' she says, and all my years in business tell me she's holding something back. But I'm not sure I care in this moment. I don't need to know her life's secrets. My hand creeps higher, my eyes locked to her face, waiting for her to say or do anything, to ask me to stop—and I will. I don't want to, but if she tells me to stop I'll put an end to this right now.

'Jagger…' She grinds my name out and it's a plea, a

hoarse, hungry plea that tells me everything I need to know. My hands inch higher, beneath her skirt, finding the lace of her thong, and I push it aside, my fingers brushing her feminine lips lightly, so lightly that she moves forward in the chair, giving me greater access, her knees wider.

'Three days' business,' I say, pushing a finger inside her sex. 'Jesus Christ, you're wet,' I drawl, distracted, as I feel her pulse around me. I slide another finger in and she moans now, low and sweet, and so perfect that my cock jumps in my pants. 'And three nights' pleasure. Then I leave Australia, and you, and we both get on with our very separate lives. Deal?'

'You're my client,' she says, but she moves her legs a little further apart and, fuck it, I'm so hungry for her. I unclip my seat belt, crouching down between her legs, pulling her belt loose then jerking her legs a little so she's further forward, on the edge of her seat.

'Jagger,' she cries, as I pull her thong down her legs, my palms squeezing her silky-smooth calves. I leave her underwear at her ankles, loving the debauched sight of them just above her stilettos. I want to make love to her later tonight wearing nothing but these shoes.

But for now, there's this. I push her legs apart, then bring my mouth down on her beautiful, sweet vagina, my tongue running over her, sucking her clit in my mouth and rolling it with my tongue. She jerks in the seat and inside I smile because she's as powerless to resist this as I am. Or maybe, like me, she just doesn't want to. Doesn't see a need to.

I slide a finger back inside her as my mouth drives over her and she whimpers now, her fingers digging into my hair, running through it wildly as she gets closer and closer to orgasm. And I want to drive her over the edge so damn bad. I want to tip her right over the edge but, more than that, I want to show her—and me—that I can control every single bit of this. That I can keep our sex separate to our work—that I can compartmentalise.

She cries my name and I pull backwards, rocking onto my haunches, my finger still inside of her but perfectly still. Her eyes show anguish.

'Jagger, don't you bloody stop,' she demands, looking at me with abject need.

'It's daytime, Miss Llewellyn.' Despite my intentions, the words come out husky. 'That means business.' I lift up, removing my finger and putting my arms on either side of her chair, surrounding her with my body. She stares up at me, bewildered and obviously feeling shitty.

'Say "yes" and I'll give you the best orgasm of your life tonight, Grace.'

She's still riding the wave, her body quivering, her lower lip dark pink from how she's been biting into it.

'Say "yes" and I'll drive your fuckwit ex out of your mind for good.'

This isn't about Gareth.

At least, not directly. This is about me reaching for what I want with both hands, not making excuses. This is about me having the courage of my convictions.

And, okay, it's a little bit about Gareth and the fact he's getting married today and going on his honeymoon. Why the hell shouldn't I have some truly incredible sex? Why not?

Sure, he's my client, but he's okay with this. I'm okay with this. I really am. I believe he can keep business and pleasure separate and I sure as hell know I can. Besides, Orion Karakedes isn't going to budge on price, so it's not like I could ever be accused of a conflict of interest. If Jagger lowballs his offer, my vendor says 'no.'

That's it. That's all she wrote.

I feel like I've swallowed a hive of bees. My nerves are jagged inside of me. Temptation simultaneously drags at me and lifts me up.

'We're two people who got screwed by our exes,' he says, and I'm jolted back to the present, to this aeroplane, to the fact I know nothing about him really, and a thousand questions spawn in my mind. 'So why don't we have fun screwing each other for a few days?'

'Finish what you just started and I'll think about it,' I murmur, my eyes hooded.

He laughs, a soft sound, and shakes his head. 'How else will you know I mean what I say?'

I purse my lips. 'I'm happy to act on faith there.'

He grins. 'No need. I'm a man of my word. I'm telling you—in the daytime we'll be all business, and afterwards…all pleasure. Deal?'

No! I want to scream. Because I need him to get his mouth back down there and make me come. I could do it myself. I could drop my hand right now and within seconds I'd be falling apart. And I'm so tempted. But I don't want to do this without him—I want it to be *him* that tips me over. I want him.

'You drive a hard bargain,' I say with mock annoyance.

'You'd better get used to it, Miss Llewellyn.' He turns away from me, moving back to his chair. But as he sits down I smile, because his cock is at a right angle to his body and I take great pleasure in staring at him, in showing him I see him.

When I lift my gaze to his, he's watching me. 'I'm going to fuck you hard tonight, Miss Llewellyn. All. Night. Long.'

My pulse trembles, my heart races. 'I'll hold you to that, Mr Hart.'

I'm divorced. She's not the first person I've slept with since my divorce. But she'll be the first person I've slept with over consecutive nights. The first person I've entered into a relationship of sorts with—albeit an unconventional one.

But it *is* unconventional—that's its saving grace. I'm laying all my cards on the table—I've told her what I want. And she's okay with this. Better, she's happy. She wants this as much as I do.

'If you look out of that window, you'll see the golf course on the northernmost tip of the island, the resort just beyond it.' I shift in my armchair seat, looking towards the window, bringing my attention back to the reason we're here. The manicured course is impossible to miss. It stretches from the east coast to the west coast, an impressive expanse of gentle undulations, water courses, crisp white bunkers and palm trees. The clubhouse is a modern building, visible from our descending altitude, all white walls and expanses of glass, perched high on the course to offer spectacular views of the Coral Sea.

The golf course itself takes up almost a third of the small island, and accommodation is offered as part of the package. A hotel, offering four hundred rooms and twelve luxurious bungalows, each with two bedrooms, spa bathrooms, private pools and offering in-room chefs and masseuses.

Even before this, before flying over the stunning island, I thought this would be a decent investment. The figures stack up enough, and with some fine-tuning in how it's marketed, the course could become truly world class. It's expensive, though; it's hard to say if there's value here or if I'd be better off buying a less prestigious course and getting a renowned designer in to reinvigorate the place.

'It looks like a golf course.' I turn around, the smile on my lips dropping when I notice that Grace is sitting in the chair across from mine looking as though someone's turned her to stone. Her eyes are shut tight and her hands are curved around the edges of the armrests, her skin pale, a fine bead of perspiration dotted across her brow.

'Grace?'

She opens her eyes and stares at me in what can only be described as an accusing manner. 'Yes?' Her teeth are clenched.

'What's happened?'

The plane pitches a little, the wings moving us from side to side.

She lets out a moan and then clamps her lips together. 'Nothing.' Her smile is a pathetic attempt. 'I'm fine.'

'You're a nervous flyer!' I laugh a little, shaking my head, but sober at the look she throws me, one of pure hatred in that moment.

'I am not.'

The plane lurches again and she makes a little squeak that has my smile dropping. This isn't actually funny at all—she's terrified. I lean forward, put my hand on hers.

'Close your eyes,' I murmur. 'And count, in twos, to a hundred.'

She glares at me with raw scepticism.

Of course she's going to fight me on this. 'I'll do it with you. Two, four, six...'

She mutters something under her breath and, while I don't catch the words, her tone is cynical. But she begins to count with me. The plane drops and steadies and she opens her eyes, staring at me, but I keep counting and she starts up again.

We make it to two hundred and eighty-six before the plane touches down and her expression is one of pure, unadulterated relief. She stares out of the window, as if scarcely believing we actually made it, then pulls her hand out of mine, wipes her palm on her knee and unclips her belt.

'Thank you.' Her voice is stiff.

I'm tempted to tease her but she's clearly defensive about this, if her closed-off expression is anything to go by. It just doesn't make sense—the woman I met last night was kind of...fearless, I would have said. A pole-dancing, sexy, sophisticated, funny, erudite woman.

'I've had hypnotherapy,' she says, standing, reaching for her handbag and hooking it over her shoulder. 'Flight immersion courses, counselling—you name it, I've done it. I just don't like the idea of being in a big tin can up in the sky with weather and flocks of birds and God knows what kind of maintenance crew and mechanical defects and fuel quality...'

Her admission touches something inside of me, I think because she's the last kind of woman I'd ever expect to have such a neurotic fear. I know flying phobias are common enough, but to this degree?

'Hart planes are serviced every time they fly. They're maintained meticulously, refit completely every six to twelve months depending on air time. Our pilots are ex-marines, capable of starting a Boeing in a mid-air stall—and routinely trained on it. If you're ever going to fly and not be afraid, it's on this jet.'

She doesn't believe me, I can tell. But the part of her that sees me as her client makes her nod. 'If you say so.'

'You don't agree?' I push, because I don't want our relationship dynamic to change to that degree.

'I think the statistical unlikelihood of something happening is no guarantee it won't.'

I feel like there's so much more she wants to say, but now she's all business. 'I've arranged for a driver to take us to the accommodation now, where you'll have an hour or so to freshen up before we tour the course. I presume that meets with your approval?'

An hour to freshen up sounds like a waste of time—time we could be doing something far more pleasurable. But didn't I promise we would keep our boundaries in place?

'That sounds fine, Miss Llewellyn. I look forward to it.'

CHAPTER SIX

'THE SIXTH AND ninth are blind tee shots, where angle
is more important than distance. Otherwise, each hole
is visible from the tee. The course was designed in the
1920s by Owen Moorsman, but redesigned in the '80s
to reflect the changing skill of the game.'

He lifts a brow, a smile tilting his lips. I'm not sure
my heart has ever raced so hard nor so fast.

'Go on,' he drawls, his accent seductive.

I take the golf buggy forward a little, over the im-
maculate green, finding it as breathtakingly beautiful
now as I did when I first viewed the course.

'It's marram grass, and these greens are mostly flat.
As you head around the course there's a gentle undulation that favours a bounce-and-run style of play. The
course attracts serious golfers, though its location in the
Whitsundays and the reciprocal membership scheme it
has with top clubs around the world means it's also fa-
voured by more recreational or tourist golfers.'

He's staring at me in a way that sets my pulse skit-
tering. My knee bumps his as we crest over the top of a
hill and sparks simmer in my blood. I don't look at him.

'Do you play?'

I shake my head a little. 'Golf? No.'

'Why not?'

'I never had any interest,' I say simply. 'Do you?'

'Do I what?' His eyes linger on my face. I'm pretty sure he's enjoying this. Enjoying the heat that simmers between us—the heat that's making my tummy zip and my gut twist.

But a deal's a deal and I'm not going to fall down in ours so early on. Daytime is for work. Night-time…fun.

'Do you play golf?' I keep my tone crisp, business-like. 'Because I think a game's scheduled, but I can cancel it…'

'I play. I spent a lot of time at my father's country club. It was practically impossible not to pick it up.'

'And when you say your "father's country club", you don't mean the club he's a member of, do you?'

There's a pause. 'As opposed to?'

'Owning it?'

'Yeah. He owned a chain of them, up the East Coast of the States.'

I let out a low whistle. 'Quite the property legacy you've got there.'

He shrugs. 'It's just business.'

I have a million questions but I shelve them for now. Maybe later, when we move into the personal side of our…whatever this is. For now, it's work.

'The course is irrigated with a newly installed state-of-the-art Japanese sprinkler system, and maintained every three weeks to ensure peak performance.'

It's an eighteen-hole golf course and it takes us al-

most two hours to tour properly. As I pull the buggy up
to the clubhouse the sun is still bright in the sky, even
though it's well on its way to the ocean.

'I'd be more than happy to take you out on the greens
again tomorrow, for another tour. I understand you'll
want to think through what you've seen today, and that
you might have more questions in the morning…'

His smile is a flash in his handsome face. 'I'm sure
I will.' He lifts his hands in the air, stretching, exposing an inch of tanned midriff, and desire kicks me in
the side, swift, so my mouth goes dry and my insides
quiver.

'Join me for a drink?' he offers, waving towards the
clubhouse.

I'm not sure I can speak just yet. My tongue feels
thick in my mouth. I shake my head instead.

He lifts his brows and moves ever so slightly closer.
'But the business part of our day is done…'

I swallow and nod slightly. 'For you, maybe. I have
to go back and do some paperwork.'

'Paperwork?'

His scepticism annoys me. 'Yeah. You know, email
clients, check on ads, a little something called running
a whole business single-handedly.'

He eyes me curiously. Fuck it. I've completely overstepped the line. We're meant to be in our business
personas and I've just ranted at him *and* made out that
he's not the be-all and end-all of my life.

'Besides—' I try to backpedal '—the sun's still up.
That means you're off limits to me for another hour or

so.' I smile slowly, meaningfully. 'Why don't you swing by my room later?'

He grins, and my pulse shimmers. 'Sure thing, Grace. I'll see you then.'

It's nine o'clock when he comes to my room and I am beyond ready. Okay, I had to work, and I definitely needed to get all my ducks in a row for the morning—I'm not going to risk coming off as anything other than uberprofessional while we're working this weekend. Still, nine o'clock is a lot later than I expected.

I wrench the door inwards, fighting an urge to say, *Where the hell have you been?*

He stands there and the world spins a little because I'd almost forgotten how gorgeous he is. He's changed into beige chinos and a white shirt. I'm disappointed, because he looks more country club than rock star and I liked him the way he was yesterday, all dirty denims and unkempt hair.

Hell, I like him any which way, though.

'Hungry?'

'Starving.' I pull the door wider. He strides in and lifts a bag between us. The unmistakable fragrance of fries wafts towards me. I take the bag from his fingertips and put it on the table behind me.

'Food can wait.'

He goes to say something but I don't hear it because I'm launching myself at him, pushing him back towards the wall. He laughs as I kiss him, into my mouth, rumbling humour into my belly, and I hold it there, my hands pushing his shirt up, my nails running over his chest, feeling his ridged abdomen, his hair-roughened nipples, his biceps, as I push the shirt up, over his head, breaking the kiss for the shortest possible time.

I'm still in the same clothes I wore on the plane. He groans as he pushes my shirt out from my skirt, bunching it in his palms and then lifting it up, his mouth finding my shoulder as soon as it's bare.

'I wanted to do this the second you walked into my conference room.' He grins as he tosses my shirt aside and cups the lace of my bra. I shiver at the feel of him, the feel of his palms against my breasts, the way my nipples harden and tighten and strain against the lace. He reaches behind me, unhooking it effortlessly, and then his mouth catches one of my nipples, rolling it with his tongue as his hands push at my skirt. I step out of it as he unzips it and slides off my thong, and then he's lifting me, easily, urgently, his hands fumbling at his zip as he strides across the room towards the bed.

He drops me into it and then crashes onto me, his mouth a torment on my body, his kisses hot, like fire, each one setting off sensations like fireworks beneath my skin.

He pushes out of his pants and then his naked body is on top of mine—his naked body so impossibly toned and sculpted, so deliciously tempting. I run my hands down his back and then curve them over his cock so he swears softly and laughs, dropping his head to my shoulder, breathing in and out.

'I need you,' he says simply.

I push him up a little so I can look into his eyes. 'That makes two of us.'

His face shows amusement as he lifts up, just enough to grab a condom and slide it on, and then he takes me, he drives himself into me with urgency and desperate imperative, as though everything he has in life is riding on this coming together.

'I wanted to fuck you this morning,' he grunts. 'I wanted to fuck you so hard, and you weren't there.'

'I had kind of an important work day ahead,' I defend between groans, smiling over his shoulder as pleasure swirls around me.

'I wanted to fuck you and instead found your note.'

I laugh, pushing at his chest so he flips onto his back. 'At least you can't fault my manners.'

'Yeah, you're right.' He holds my hips still, pushing into me, and I arch my back, swaying, tilting my head and staring up at the ceiling as his huge cock fills me right up. His hand drops to my pussy and runs over it, his fingers stroking me in time with his thrusts.

I drop forward, biting his shoulder as stars explode against my eyelids, as time stands still and speeds up.

'Bitch!' He laughs, shifting a little—whoops. I bit hard.

Nothing diminishes my pleasure.

He holds my hips and rolls me so I'm on my back again, and he keeps thrusting inside of me, even as I'm coming, so I ride this wave again and again, my body quivering with the force of this release.

I lift my hands to his sides, digging my nails in, scratching them over his back as I become incandescent with pleasure and he grinds his hips and then spills all of himself into me, his voice a guttural, hoarse moan.

It is fast, frantic, passionate sex. No niceties. No pleasantries. Kind of like a hurricane touched down between us. I blink, waking from some kind of sexual fog, to air that's filled with the aroma of the dinner he brought, and a lover on top of me, his weight pleasing, who I've physically marked with signs of my madness.

'I'm sorry,' I say, but smiling, because I'm not really. I push up, pressing a kiss to the small indentations on his shoulder—indentations that are already fading. 'But you really are too good at that, you know.'

He catches my mouth, kissing me then dragging my lower lip between his teeth and pressing into it lightly. I moan. 'You can bite me any time, Grace.'

I collapse back onto the bed, my breathing laboured, my body hot and a little sweaty from the sultry night air and the rapid-fire fucking.

'What'd you get us?'

'Chips, burgers, soda.'

'Healthy,' I tease.

'Tasty,' he corrects, winking. He stands up then and I watch unashamedly as he crosses the room, disposing of the condom in the en-suite bathroom before picking his jocks up off the floor. He pulls them on, then turns to face me.

I'm naked on the bed and not at all self-conscious.

'And here we find ourselves in yet another hotel room without a convenient pole,' he murmurs.

I grin. 'Design flaw.'

'Perhaps if I buy the place I'll have them installed in all the rooms. Just in case.'

'It's a great form of exercise,' I say, winking at him.

'I'm still looking forward to a demonstration.'

I laugh then, shaking my head. 'I think you're probably imagining something hotter than the reality.'

'I doubt that.' He approaches the edge of the bed and holds his hands out to me. He doesn't move when I stand up; his body pulls mine towards him. I stand, grabbing a sheet and wrapping it around me, toga-style, as I do.

'My mission is clear. To find a pole in the next three days.'

'You'd be surprised by how difficult that is.'

'You've got one at home?' he prompts.

'In my garage.' I grin.

'And your fuckwit ex still left you?'

Gareth.

It's like a ton of bricks landing on my head. I blink, disorientated for a second, nothing making sense.

'That wasn't the most sensitive comment I could have made,' he apologises.

'It's fine.' My smile feels sticky on my face. I spin away from him. 'Thanks for bringing dinner. That was thoughtful of you.'

'He was getting married today?'

He's not picking up the vibe I'm giving out. 'Yeah. This morning.' Another smile; it still doesn't feel right. 'So by now she'll be Mrs Gareth Clarke-White and I'm just a fragment of his past.'

I reach into the bag and pull out a box of chips, taking one then handing it to him.

The burgers are next.

'Vegetarian?' I prompt, reading the writing scored across the top.

'For me.'

'Are you?'

'A vegetarian? Yeah. All my life.'

'Seriously?'

'Sure. Why? You find that hard to believe?'

I tilt my head to one side, pointedly examining his buff physique. 'You look like a meat eater.'

He grins. 'I guess that's a compliment?'

'It is.' I lift my burger from the box, inhaling the aroma gratefully. 'You're not going to be offended if I eat this in front of you?'

He pulls a face. 'I brought it over here, didn't I?'

'I know. Some people can be sensitive about that kind of thing.'

'We don't know each other that well, so let me just tell you, I'm not really sensitive about anything.'

I open the box, and bite into the burger. It's delicious. Beef, bacon, cheese, tomato, pickle, lettuce on a brioche bun. And I'm famished.

'So why?'

'Why what?'

'Why are you veggie?'

'My mom, mainly.'

'She doesn't eat meat?'

'Yeah—well, she doesn't eat anything,' he says, and then covers the admission with a smiling shake of his head. 'She prefers to get her nutrients in the form of fermented potatoes and juniper berries.'

It takes a second for his meaning to sink in. Vodka and gin. 'She's an alcoholic?'

'She drinks to excess,' he says, frowning. 'And she

goes to rehab when she wants to dry out. Yeah, I guess you could say she's a high-functioning alcoholic.'

'I'm sorry,' I say seriously, taking another bite. 'That must be hard on you.'

'Yeah, mostly because she's just hard work.' He shrugs his shoulders. 'And she's alone, so I feel kind of responsible for her.'

'You've got brothers though, right?'

'Two, yeah. But they're on my dad's side.' He hesitates a little, then shrugs. 'They're pretty good with my mom, but they're not going to drop everything if she needs to get her stomach pumped.'

'And you do?' I murmur sympathetically, wondering at the urge I have to stand up and go and sit in his lap, to be closer to him.

'From time to time.'

I'm sorry for him, for that kind of worry. My parents might wish that I'd play it safe, that I'd be less aspirational and more content with a sensible job and quiet life, but they're still my parents—and they've never once made me feel like I had to parent them; they've never given me a day of worry.

'She's got staff. Housekeepers, a chef, tennis coach; it's not like I'm the only person who's going to be able to help her. She lives in LA, so I'm not even within easy reach of her.'

'But you're her only family.'

He nods, polishing off his burger in record time then reaching for a soda can. He has to lean past me to get it and spontaneously I reach up, bunching his shirt in my hands and kissing him.

I like kissing him. I smile against his lips then ease back into my seat.

'So, real estate, huh?'

I nod.

'How'd you get into that?'

I tilt my head to the side a little, thinking back. 'Partly happenstance, I guess. I studied business at university. One of my lecturers offered me an internship at his commercial property firm. Turns out I had a knack for it.'

'So you went out on your own?'

I nod. 'I met Gareth. He was the romantic—obsessed with the idea of matchmaking people to places, the beauty of forging connections.' I can't help the roll of my eyes.

Jagger laughs softly. 'That's not your view of it?'

'God, no. I can see the commercial value in buying and selling, in matching the right investor with the right property. Most of my clients want to make money, to see a return for their investment. I like to find them properties that will meet those needs—and, of course, to find investors who have the means to buy the properties I list.' I shrug. 'It's more a mathematical equation for me than a notion of matchmaking.'

I take a bite of my burger, chewing thoughtfully. 'But Gareth's vision helps with the marketing side. We were a good team.'

'Were?' His eyes narrow speculatively. 'I thought you still worked together? I'm sure I've been dealing with him on email.'

'Yeah.' I swallow, looking away. 'But not for long.

I plan to buy him out if I can.' I look away, my gaze focusing on the modern abstract art on the white wall opposite, not telling him that this sale is one of the key ways I'm going to achieve that.

Gareth's married now.

The wedding reception's probably on its way to concluding. I swallow past the lump in my throat, bringing my gaze back to Jagger's face—his Hollywood-handsome face. And I smile because spending my ex's wedding night with a guy like this is not exactly the worst fate I can think of.

'So you're like a gazillionaire?'

He laughs, shaking his head. 'Is that a thing?'

'Yeah. It's a term I just made up. For someone who happens to not only be a multibillionaire but also has oodles of personal charm to their name.'

'Is that a fact, Miss Llewellyn?'

I tsk. 'It's after dark, Jagger. I'm just Grace now.'

'Grace.' He says my name on an exhalation. 'You could never be "just" anything.'

My chest swells with pleasure at his praise. 'You don't need to flatter me. We've already struck our deal.'

He grins. 'And compliments aren't part of that?'

I shrug. 'They don't hurt, but they're not necessary either.'

'You're…'

'Yeah?'

'Just…not like anyone I've ever met.'

More tummy-swelling pleasure. 'Thanks. I think.'

'It's a compliment. Except you don't like compliments.'

'I didn't say I don't like them. Just that I don't need them.' I stand up, hitching my toga sheet up higher so I can straddle him in his chair, desire throbbing between my legs when I feel his cock already growing hard beneath me. 'I'm confident enough without.'

His eyes show a speculative gleam. 'I'm glad you're not letting your ex take that away from you.'

My heart snags a little. 'Oh, it hurt. It hurt me plenty. But he fell in love with someone else. What was I meant to do? Force him to stay? Force him to fall in love with me? He didn't love me, Jagger. That's all there is to it.'

We're quiet for a moment. The words hang in the air, not exactly sad but reflective. 'I think love,' he says slowly, dislodging the toga from under my arms, loosening it so my breasts are naked, at his eye height, 'is a big lie. I think it's something we tell ourselves we need, or maybe it's a message that's sold to us from when we're young—Disney movies, fairy tales, even fucking *Die Hard* is a love story at its core.' He kisses my shoulder and my breath catches in my throat. 'What if there's just this? Sex and laughs. What if that's what we should all be looking for in life? Great sex, fun, pleasure. Isn't that enough?'

There's an emptiness in my heart, an emptiness Gareth carved out when he walked away from me, and the emptiness expands a little at the picture Jagger's painting because I'm not sure I want to live in a world without the possibility of love. 'Aren't you a little young to be so jaded?' I opt for teasing, hoping it covers my own expanding ice chip.

'Twenty-nine years and I've had four stepmothers, two stepfathers, and now one ex-wife. You think that doesn't qualify me for a place at the jaded table?'

'That's a lot of failed marriages,' I say, still striving for teasing.

'Proof that love sucks.' He drops his mouth to my breast, rolling his tongue over my nipple, then lifts his mouth to mine. 'Sex is so much better than love.'

He stands up, lifting me easily, so easily, and like this, cradled against his naked torso, with his mouth moving over mine, I have to say I agree with him. Sex isn't just better than love. At this moment I'd have to say sex is the be-all and end-all of life—the reason for being. At least this sex, with this man, on this night is.

CHAPTER SEVEN

'WHAT'S THIS?' I run a finger over his tattoo, tracing the letters which, now that I'm close enough to see properly, I realise are Greek.

ο Δίας

His eyes are heavy but he blinks at me before pushing up on one elbow. 'A bet gone wrong.'

'Yeah?' I lean forward, pressing a row of light kisses over the ink.

'Mmm. A brotherly dare.'

'What does it say?'

'You really want to know?'

I blink up at him. 'Kind of why I'm asking.'

'It says Zeus.'

'Zeus? As in the king of the gods? Zeus the Greek god?'

'Yeah.' He laughs softly, running his hand to his hip bone, where a lightning bolt spreads towards his thigh. 'And the symbol for Zeus.'

'Is this when you tell me you have a God complex?' I look up at him, a smile twitching on my lips.

'This is the part where I tell you I got blind drunk on my twenty-first birthday and talked my brothers into getting inked.'

'But why Zeus?'

'That was Holden's idea. We're three half-brothers. He talked us into getting Zeus, Poseidon and Hades. Greek gods who were brothers.'

'And you're Zeus 'cause you're oldest?'

'I am oldest,' he agrees. 'But no. I'm Zeus because I run the construction part of our family business. The skies. Theo's Poseidon, that's the god of the sea, and he's in line to inherit the shipping and logistics operations.'

'And Hades?' I ask, my smile spreading at this family bond.

'That would be Holden,' he says, a small frown crossing his face. 'He's only three months younger than I am,' he says with a shake of his head, watching as I do the calculations.

'That's…unfortunate for your father.'

'Yeah.' He lifts a finger to my shoulder, running it over my flesh. 'You could say that.'

'So your dad cheated on your mum?'

'Oh, dozens of times, no doubt. But, so far as we know, Holden was the only kid he had 'cause of an affair.'

'But he's been raised with you?'

'Like a brother.' He nods. 'After Mom left, Holden moved in. We shared a room, a nanny. We're more like twins than brothers.'

'So why'd he draw the short straw?'

'He chose it.' He shrugs.

'Why?'

'He runs our casinos,' Jagger says, the words thoughtful and hesitant. I feel like he's holding something back, like there's something he's not telling me. And if this wasn't just sex I'd ask him. If I thought he'd still be in my life in a week's time I'd ask him.

I'd pry open that mysterious revelation, unpicking it for what titbit I could. But this is our second night together of a total of four. Just sex, just fun.

'I'm thinking maybe there was probably another Greek god that would have been more appropriate for you,' I say, pushing up, straddling him so I can run my fingers over his chest. I drop down, kissing the corner of his mouth, then lifting up just high enough so I can look into his eyes.

'Yeah? Who's that?'

'That would be Eros.'

'Remind me?' he prompts, his eyes teasing.

'The god of sensual desire,' I say, flexing my hips.

He grabs my wrists and rolls me, pinning me back on the bed, pushing into me, hard and huge, so I groan as satisfaction spirals through my gut. 'I think that might be more appropriate for you, Grace.' He drops his head forward, kissing the underside of my breast. 'Maybe you could get that tattooed right here?'

I laugh, shaking my head. 'That would hurt.'

He thrusts into me again, hard and fast, and pleasure is like starlight on my eyelids. I moan, digging my fingers into his back, and he's pushing into me again.

'Only a little bit.'

I don't believe him.

'And only for a minute.'

I don't believe him but I'm shifting out of this earth, finding my place in another. Pleasure is like a lightning rod, like the lightning on his hip, and it's cleaving me in two.

'Liar,' I moan, lifting my head up, seeking his lips as I come, hard, completely, wrapping my legs around his hips, burying him deep in my body.

But he's not a liar. He's completely honest—I love that he's being so frank with me. Not a hint of this is masquerading as anything that it's not. This is no-frills fucking—and it's exactly what I need.

I leave just after one. Grace is fast asleep, her breath heavy, her beautiful body naked, so that I watch her while I dress, pretty much unable to tear my eyes away, and then lift the sheet up to cover her. Despite the warmth of the day and evening, the night has come in cool, the humidity has dropped, and I don't want her to wake up uncomfortable.

I grab the rubbish on my way out, pushing it quietly into the waste bin in the corner before taking the lift to the second floor and going into my own hotel room. It's identical, except mirrored.

But it's close enough, so I can lie in my own bed, staring at the ceiling, imagining that I'm still in her room, that I can reach out and grab for her in the morning, like I wanted to yesterday, when I woke up in Sydney and needed to bury myself in her more than I can say.

I already feel the stirrings of desire; my cock's ready for her again. But we have a deal—soon it'll be morning and we'll be working again. I'm not messing around with this—I do actually need to spend these three days appraising the course, seeing if it's the right investment for me. I can't let fucking around with Grace distract me. Extending the trip's not an option.

So for now we'll sleep, in our separate but similar rooms, and in the morning she'll be Miss Llewellyn again.

I fall asleep with a smile on my face.

I wake up, disorientated and sore all over, but sore in the best possible way, as physical reminders of his possession strafe through me. I sit up, looking around. No Jagger.

There's a note, though, on the side of the bed he slept in last night.

Thanks... You were great. Zeus.

It makes me smile in a way that stretches my lips and makes my cheeks hurt. My phone buzzes with a call and I reach for it, and the smile dies.

Gareth.

A couple of weeks after we broke up, Penny changed the photo of Gareth on my phone. Now, when he calls, instead of the photo taken the day we signed the lease on our new offices, smiling, side by side, I get a purple cartoon picture of the devil.

I'm still weirdly disorientated, but it must be early because my alarm hasn't gone off yet. Why the hell is he calling me?

I swipe the phone to answer. 'Hello?'

My voice sounds shitty. Good. The guy got married yesterday, after all.

To someone else.

'Hey, Gracie.' I hate that he still calls me that. I stiffen in bed.

'What is it, Gareth?'

'Sorry I didn't check in with you yesterday. I didn't get a chance.'

'Why the hell would you have checked in with me yesterday? I was fine, Gareth. Completely fine. I know you're waiting for me to have some kind of breakdown or something but I don't give a shit that you're getting married. That you *got* married.'

He's quiet for a couple of seconds. Then, 'I meant just to see how things are going with Ryan.'

'Ryan?' It takes me a second to connect the dots. 'Oh, Mr Hart.' My own heart does a little triple step and then my tummy whooshes like I've just crested over the top of a roller coaster and I'm pitching back to earth. 'Fine. Why?'

'I kind of threw that to you, I know. Do you have everything you need?'

I lie back against the pillows. 'Of course I do, Gareth. I'm not an idiot. I've read the documents. I can sell this place. It's a good fit for him.'

'I'm glad you think so.'

Silence.

I open my mouth to offer something tactful, to end the call.

'I thought about you yesterday.'

Emotions zip in my chest.

'What?'

'It was strange. Not having you there.'

Something like sadness gives way to something like anger, and then a bubbling hysteria lurches to the fore. 'It would have been wildly inappropriate for me to come to your wedding.'

'No, it wouldn't. You're my friend, Gracie…'

I shake my head. We've had this argument before. 'I'm thousands of kilometres away. Can we not do this now? Besides, it's your honeymoon. Why the hell are you calling to tell me you *thought* about me? On your wedding day?'

'I just wanted to know you're okay…'

'I'm fine.' I glare at the kettle across the room as though it's personally done me a great wrong. 'You don't need to worry about me. Just go back to your honeymoon and your wife and don't call me again.'

I disconnect the call, wincing because actually we generally do a much better job of being professional and polite to one another.

But his wedding was yesterday. It's too fresh.

I push out of bed, showering, and when I step out onto the tiled floor I stare at myself in the mirror.

And stare.

Because my body is marked all over with signs of the way I spent last night. Scratches at my hips, stubble rash on my breasts, a hickey on my shoulder.

Holy crap.

I lift a finger and trace it, a smile throbbing on my lips. Flashes of memory spear through my mind. The way he sucked at my flesh, right there, as he moved inside me, our bodies locked together.

The way he walked into the hotel room and I pounced on him—it's never, ever been like that for me. I like sex. I love it. But I can live without it.

Except with Jagger. Even now, looking at myself in the mirror, remembering the way he went down on me last night, the way he took my body last night, remembering the way he kissed me on the plane... I want him with an intensity that blows my mind.

Disappointment almost leads me to swear into the room because I have a full day to get through first, and this one is big. There are meetings between the CEO of Karakedes Corp and Jagger and I expect they'll take all day, going over the basic operations of the course, the accommodation, the maintenance. Everything.

I can't be thinking about how badly I need him between my legs.

I flick the coffee machine to life and wait impatiently for a cup to fill. I drink it, reading the brief, reminding myself of the details so that I'm in command of the pertinent facts.

But Christ! Between Gareth calling me and Jagger fucking me until I was pleasure personified, I have no idea how I'm going to keep my head today.

Except I will because it's what I do.

I've worked too hard and have too much to prove to let anyone derail me.

I pull on my suit—navy blue trousers and a three-quarter sleeve jacket with a pale blue blouse, and a pair of cream stilettos that give me an essential couple of extra inches. I try not to think about how I'll get out of my suit later today. I definitely don't need those images in my mind right now.

I grab my leather document wallet and slip out of the room, double-checking I've got the key card before I pull the door shut. He's in the restaurant when I stride in and my tummy does that funny loop the loop thing again.

I fight the urge to lift a hand to it, to quell that response.

He's reading a broadsheet newspaper, one leg crossed lazily over the other. He's wearing jeans and a linen shirt, looking part hippy, part… I don't know. Sex god? Rock god? Something god. God of all gods?

I want to storm across the restaurant and throw him to the floor, climb on top of him and… Heat darkens my cheeks. I blink it away, grabbing the attention of the hostess by lifting my hand in a small wave. I gesture to another table across the restaurant and when I look back he's watching me, casually reclined in his chair, eyes burning with intensity, and I just *know* he's having all the same thoughts I am. I nod coolly and follow the hostess to my table a little way across the restaurant. The Coral Sea glistens in the morning light, spectacularly azure, endlessly inviting on this steamy, warm morning, but I resist looking at it because to do so would require me to look beyond Jagger and I'm not so sure I have the willpower right now to resist looking *beyond* him at all.

He's like temptation and eye glue.

I order a coffee and some scrambled eggs then reach into my bag and grab out the agenda for today's meeting. I know it back to front and sideways but extra prep never hurts. Besides, it's better than sitting here refusing to look in Jagger's direction.

My coffee arrives; I don't look up. But the waiter's shadow remains and so, with a small frown, I tilt my face and have to dig my fingernails into my thigh to stop from gasping. Gasping!

Actually gasping, like some kind of 1920s starlet.

'Mr Hart—' I reach for my coffee, lifting it to my lips without dropping my eyes from his face '—how are you this morning?'

His smile is really more of a smirk. And so sexy. Fuck. His shirt is unbuttoned at the collar and I can see his neck, his throat, the hint of his shoulder and chest. Did I mark him like he did me? Without realising it, I lift a hand and touch my shoulder, where the hickey he gave me sits.

'Fine.' He nods slowly. 'How did you sleep?'

My pulse ratchets up a notch and delicious longing flickers inside me. I lift my coffee to my lips to buy time, sipping it slowly. 'Fine,' I say back after a moment. 'I slept fine.'

He says nothing, just stares down at me for several long beats, and my fingertips pulse with a desire to lift up and run through his hair. I curve my hands around my coffee cup and bring my mind to the work at hand. 'Orion Karakedes will meet us in an hour. He's incredibly nice, and willing to answer any questions you have—he'll have his accountant there for financial queries. And of course I'll be able to answer anything property or contract specific.'

'Naturally.' He moves ever so slightly closer. If I moved my legs a little, they'd brush against his.

I jam them together, staying put. 'Is there anything you need before the meeting?'

I don't mean it as anything other than a straightforward business proposition, but his eyes narrow almost imperceptibly and his smile shows just what he needs—it just so happens to be what I need.

He drops down, on the pretence of studying the documents spread before me. 'What I need is to bury my head between your legs—' he lifts his head, to see the effect of his words; heat blooms in my cheeks '—Miss Llewellyn.'

I bite back a small moan of agreement because I would *love* him to go down on me right here, right now. I would love to throw caution to the wind and push him into a quiet corner and fuck him right this minute.

Obviously, I don't. I lift my wrist, checking the time. 'I'll hold you to that, Mr Hart.'

I reach into my handbag and pull out the spare key card for my room. 'Twelve hours and counting.'

His eyes flare and he straightens, his smile contagious. 'Deal.' He turns then, walking away, and my heart pounds hard in my chest. I don't realise until a moment later that I'm holding my breath. I expel it on one long, warm exhalation.

Twelve hours.

Hurry up, time.

I wouldn't have said I'd underestimated her. I just hadn't expected Grace to have such an encyclopaedic knowledge of not only the golf course but also the laws governing resort operations, golf club licencing, not to mention the marketing measures that are working for the club, and the details of its most profitable membership base. As the day drags on I make it my mission to find questions to which she won't know answers—just for my personal interest. I'm fascinated by how well she's prepared for this meeting, a fact that is obvious given how completely she's able to deal with all my enquiries.

'The membership dropped significantly in 2007 through eight financial years,' I remark, scanning the documents.

'The global financial crisis saw a twenty per cent dip across all luxury products and services,' she fires back immediately, her eyes sparking when they meet mine. 'You'll see membership numbers increased on the original figures by 2011. Allowing for reciprocal member fees, the course has seen a seven per cent revenue increase in its membership base year on year.'

I make a note of it, my business mind working even when ninety per cent of me just wants to tell every suit in this room to get out so I can lift her onto the conference table and fuck her senseless.

She leans back a little in the chair, her expression focused, but her eyes meet mine and one corner of her lips lifts, just a fraction, just for a second, but it's the sexiest, flirtiest smile I've ever seen. My cock throbs.

'Thank you, Miss Llewellyn. That makes perfect sense.'

'I'm glad, Mr Hart.' She nods, turning her attention back to Orion Karakedes.

Three more hours. Three hours of detailed cost analysis, examining the insurance scheme; every single bit of information I could want to make this decision is right in front of me.

Three more hours and finally I'm up, shaking hands, nodding, telling Orion I'll let him know in a couple of days. Thanking him for his time, being so patient when I am bursting with needs that absolutely require satiating.

Grace excuses herself and my eyes follow her to the door, daring her to turn around, compelling her not to leave. Not yet. Fuck.

At the door she spins, her eyes meeting mine, a smile hovering on her lips, a promise on that beautiful mouth. My groin squeezes.

I wrap the meeting up as soon as I can, declining the offer of a sunset drink in the penthouse, even when I probably should avail myself of every opportunity to survey the investment.

I stalk out of the meeting room and jab an impatient finger into the lift call button. I stand like a rock as I ride it up to her floor and then finger the key card in my pocket, where it's been all morning since she slid it across the breakfast table to me.

I read the numbers as I stride along the corridor and finally, at her room, I slip the key into the locking mechanism and push the door open.

It occurs to me, once I'm in the room, that I probably should have knocked. But I'm not thinking straight. I'm not thinking at all.

'Grace?' I call, moving into the tiny room, a frown on my face. I hear the shower running and jerk in that direction. Now I do knock, once, hard on the bathroom door, before pushing it open. And freezing.

She's in the shower, lathered up in soapy bubbles, wet and shiny all over, her breasts pert, her nipples tight, her stomach flat, her butt cheeks so gorgeous, and I groan because desire is flooding my body. Desire and a need for possession that almost bowls me over.

I strip my clothes, my eyes holding hers, and she runs her hands over her body, gliding fingertips to her breasts, palming them, so my dick pulses in my pants as I strip them from my body.

Her hands run lower and she tilts her head back as her fingertips find her sex, brushing over it while I watch, touching herself, and my hands ache to swap with hers. Yet I'm transfixed, watching her as though my survival depends on not looking away.

My body reverberates with need. I stand there, naked, and she rolls her head forward, moving her fingers faster, and her breathing gets louder. It galvanises me into action. I take the three steps necessary to bring me to the shower screen and pull it inwards, stepping inside and pressing my body to hers, pushing her back against the tiles, and my lips seek hers, my tongue pushing into her warm, moist mouth, my hands wrapping around her hips, curving around her butt. I kiss her until I can't think straight, until I can breathe again, I kiss her until she's moaning my name into my mouth, her fingers scratching my sides, and then I drop down, crouching in front of her, water dousing my head as I roll my tongue over her seam, flicking her clit until her knees buckle and it's only my hand at her hip holding her upright.

'Finally,' she groans, her fingers tangling in my hair, her body totally supplicant to this unearthly, raging pleasure.

'Finally?' I suck at her clit and she swears, her nails digging into my scalp.

'The plane.' The words come out tortured, just a suffocated invocation.

'Ah.' I smile, pulling away from her, kissing my way up her body, palming her breasts with sheer relief. 'You have no idea how much I wanted to do this today.' I bury my mouth at her shoulder, finding the mark I made the night before and sucking on her flesh again.

She whimpers, her body quivering with desire. I reach behind her, shutting off the water, and lift her slippery wet body up in my arms, stepping out of the shower, uncaring that we're both soaking wet. I carry her to the bed and drop her in its middle. Seconds later, I've donned protection and I'm spreading her legs, staring into her eyes as I drive into her still-throbbing core.

She shudders and lifts her legs, clamping them around my waist, holding me deep inside her, but I grab her calves and lift her legs higher, over my shoulder. My name on her lips, my name fevered in her mouth, is a sound I will never forget. I drive my hard cock into her now and each time she cries my name she breathes it into the room and it stitches deep inside of me, cementing this desire as some kind of integral life force, something bigger than I've known before.

This feeling, this explosion, this moment—is perfection.

CHAPTER EIGHT

'CLEARLY YOU CAN'T sleep here.'

My breath is still strained, my body feels as though
he's blown me apart, cell by cell, and I'm still in the
process of reforming myself to resemble a human. His
words come to me from a long way away.

'Huh?' I couldn't have told you, for a million dollars, what the time is.

'We've destroyed the bed,' he says, grinning, so my
tummy squeezes because his smile is both sexy and
devilishly handsome, sweet and…addictive. The words
run through my veins like ice.

'Huh?'

He laughs, dropping a finger to my nose, tracing
its length before dropping it to my lips and running it
over the tip. 'Is this the same woman who threw P & L
spreadsheets at me all day?'

My brain is still sluggish. With effort, I bring myself fully to the moment and realise he's right—this
bed is saturated. It's not going to dry out in a couple of
hours. 'Whoops.'

'Whoops.' He runs his finger lower, over my chin,

swirling it around the divot there, then tracing it over my throat, pressing his fingers to my racing pulse point.

'Have you eaten?'

'Since half an hour ago?'

He shrugs. 'Room service…'

'No. I came straight back to my room and had a cold shower,' I quip.

'How'd that work out for you?'

I shake my head. 'It didn't.'

'I'm glad I got here when I did then.'

'A minute later and you would have missed out on the party altogether.'

His laugh is throaty. 'Heaven forbid.'

He pulls up from the bed, standing for a minute, just staring at me like he's committing me to his memory.

'I just wanted to pick you up and fuck you on that conference table today, you know.'

'Funny, I was having the same fantasy,' I say honestly.

'I wonder what Orion Karakedes would have said…'

'I'm not sure he would have cared, so long as it didn't affect your interest in the property.'

He laughs. 'Damn it. Now I'm kicking myself for not acting on the impulse.'

'You couldn't,' I say, wide-eyed, scrambling to my knees, on the edge of the bed, pulling him towards me, his body still damp from the shower, naked for my touch and inspection. I flick one of his nipples with my tongue and feel his ragged inhalation beneath my mouth.

'Oh?'

'Daytime.'

'That's right. We're sexual vampires.'

I smile against his hair-roughened chest, moving to the other nipple, biting it gently.

'Uh-huh. Per the terms of our agreement.'

'But it's night-time now.' His voice is gruff.

'Yep.'

'So you're mine. Right?'

My heart does a funny little flip-flop in my chest. 'I'm mine,' I say with a wry glance at his face.

'Oh, no, Grace. Between now and dawn, you're *all mine*. Every little bit of you. And I intend to make the most of it.' He pauses meaningfully. 'Per our agreement.'

My pulse ratchets up a gear. 'I think I like the sound of that.'

'I kinda hoped you would.' He brushes his lips over mine. 'But I'm starving. Dinner first?'

It's still early evening. It makes sense to eat. 'Room service?'

He laughs. 'Definitely. But my room. I want a bed within reach that's not such a swimming pool.'

I nod. 'Fine by me.'

His room is exactly the same as mine, but flipped. I stroll into it, looking around, and perhaps my confusion shows because he smudges a thumb over my perplexed smile. 'What's up?'

'How come you stay in tiny hotel rooms?'

'I have to sleep somewhere. You think the street would be better?' He's being deliberately vague.

'I mean instead of somewhere more high-end.'

'Why would I?'

'Because you're a gazillionaire,' I remind him, smiling, dropping my handbag to the floor inside his door and padding to the small balcony that overlooks the edge of the golf course and, beyond it, the ocean. The smell of salt hangs in the air, tropical and breath-taking.

He's right behind me. 'A bed's a bed,' he says simply.

I turn around, bracing my elbows on the railing, regarding him thoughtfully. 'You don't like the trap-pings of wealth?'

'I don't like wasting money on crap I don't need.'

'You have a private jet.'

'That's necessary.'

I laugh. 'Really?'

'Sure. I fly a lot. I need a plane that can be at my disposal. I work on the plane. Entertain. It suits me.'

'But extravagant hotel rooms…'

He shakes his head. 'I have homes in the cities I travel to regularly. When I'm on the road I just need a bed. A gym in the hotel. That's it.'

I admire his attitude. Having known a lot of people who value status symbols over just about anything, it's refreshing to talk to a guy with a serious fortune in the bank who's happy to live like a normal person.

'What's your house like?' I ask out of curiosity.

He traps me with his hands, one on either side of my body, and I like the feeling.

'A penthouse.' He shrugs. 'Big. Glass. Open. Easy.'

'Why not have something smaller?'

'I spend a lot of time at home. I like the space.'

It makes sense.

'Plus, Brinkley really takes up most of the room.'

'Brinkley?'

'My dog.'

My heart does something dangerously soft and mushy. 'You have a dog?'

'A golden retriever.' He nods.

'Aww…'

He laughs. 'What?'

'I just didn't picture you as a dog person, but now you say it I can totally see it.'

He grins. 'I am indeed a dog person. Whatever that means.' He moves away, coming to stand beside me but looking out at the view. 'You got one?'

'A dog? Nah.'

He grins slowly and my heart flip-flops. 'You're not a "dog person"?'

'Oh, I am.' I shake my head. 'I've always had dogs. I left Harrison behind when I moved to Sydney and it was the hardest thing I've ever done.' Tears thicken my throat.

'Why'd you leave him?'

I turn around, facing out to the ocean, my body beside his. 'He was too old to rehome. I left him at Mum and Dad's—they have a big, beautiful property with bunches of avocado trees. He spent his days running around and eating the fruit whenever it dropped to the ground.' I shake my head fondly at the memory. 'I always thought I'd bring him to Sydney, but then I met Gareth and he's allergic…' My voice tapers off as I draw in a fortifying breath. 'Harrison died last Christmas.'

'I'm sorry.' He says it with the sympathy only a dog owner can feel. I nod curtly, but inside my heart is shattering.

'He was fifteen, and arthritic.'

'Doesn't make it suck any less.'

I shake my head, lifting my eyes to his. 'Nope.' Something passes between us. A surge of warmth or understanding, something that flutters in my gut. I rip my gaze away, focusing on the golf course.

'Do you know why it's called Silver Dunes?' I murmur, my eyes chasing across the course, finding the sand dunes one by one.

'Nice name?' he says light-heartedly.

I pull a face. 'Sure, that's part of it. But no, actually. It's that bunker there.' I point across the course. The twelfth hole is only partly visible, just the edge of the bunker shimmering from this angle. 'On a clear night like this, the moon hits it and the sand looks like starshine. Can you see it?'

'No,' he says with a slight laugh. 'I see dark rolling hills and pale sand bunkers.'

'Look, though,' I persist. 'Can't you see it? It's kind of magical.'

He angles his face, so close to mine I feel his breath against my jaw. 'It's not the most transfixing thing I've seen tonight,' he says simply and my stomach squishes and turns.

I bite down on my lower lip, stilling my smile, my pulse.

'Are you hungry?' he asks, the question soft.

I nod, even though my tummy is in loops and probably not capable of eating much. It's been a long time since lunch. 'Sure.'

'Happy for me to order something?'

I nod. 'Yeah. Whatever you're having.'

He pulls away from me and I feel his absence almost instantly. I stare out at the golf course, but he's back a second later. 'Your phone was ringing.' He holds it out towards me and I look towards the screen.

Gareth.

Jagger watches me for a moment, his eyes latched to mine, and then he turns on his heel, heading back into the modest hotel room, lifting up the room phone and speaking in his husky, sexy American drawl. I pull the glass doors shut, separating us and, with a heavy sigh, press Gareth's name in my phone.

I don't want to talk to him. Frankly, I wish he'd get stuffed. But we're business partners and I'm not going to let the fucked-upness of our personal lives get in the way of business.

'Gracie.'

I dig my nails into my palms. 'You called?'

'Yeah. Hang on a second.' There's a scratchy noise, sounds like he's covered the receiver, then his mumbled voice and the closing of a door. 'You there?'

I count to five. 'Did you want something, Gareth?'

'How did it go today?'

I count to ten. 'Why are you checking up on me so much?'

'It's a big deal,' he says straight away. 'I feel like I left you in the lurch with no support…'

I count to fifteen. I resist the urge to point out he

left me in the lurch when he walked out on our relationship and proposed to another woman. 'I've got it,' I say firmly. 'I know what I'm doing.'

'I know that. I just feel like I should be there...'

'You're on your honeymoon,' I snap, wishing I'd counted a few seconds before answering. I soften my voice. 'And I'm all over the material. There's nothing unfamiliar to me here. It's just another property, another deal. It's what I'm good at.'

I hear the doors slide open behind me and turn, facing Jagger as he saunters onto the small balcony.

'What's the investor like?'

He walks towards me purposefully, a glint in his eyes I can't understand. His hand finds the hem of the floaty dress I pulled on before leaving my hotel room, lifting it up my legs, his fingers glancing across my pussy—naked, because why bother with underpants when I know we're going to come together again any minute?

'He's smart,' I say as Jagger's fingers separate my seam.

'But is he interested?'

He slips a finger deep inside me, his eyes laughing, crinkled at the corners as I bite down on my lip.

'In the golf course?'

'Yeah. And the resort. The whole deal.'

'I don't know.' The words come out strained. He lifts his spare hand and presses a finger against my lips, urging me not to moan as he moves his finger deeper inside me and then pulls it out, thrusts it in again, as though he's fucking me. My hips buckle, pushing me forwards.

'You must have a sense...'

My breath escapes on a sharp hiss. 'I think the course is an incredible investment and he's smart and mon-eyed.' He drops his hand from my mouth and lifts it to cup my arse, digging his fingers into my flesh, pulling me forward, against his hard dick. I have to bite down hard on my lip to stop from groaning.

'So he'll buy it?'

'I don't know.' The words quiver.

'Are you okay, Gracie?'

'I'm fine, Gareth. I have to go…'

Jagger shakes his head, drops his mouth to my other ear and whispers, 'Don't hang up. Not yet.'

My heart rushes against my ribs.

'You sure you're okay?'

I nod, then realise he can't see me. 'Fine.'

'I'm going to make you come while you're on the phone to him,' he whispers in my ear, and my blood bursts through my veins.

I jerk my head away, my eyes lancing him, and he grins then drops to his knees once more, his mouth some kind of voodoo magic. I'm already at fever pitch and the second his tongue slides along my sex I feel the first tingling hint of explosion. I grip the railing tight.

'You've got a busy day tomorrow. Did Bianca send you the run sheet? Snorkelling in the morning, followed by lunch, then a game of golf in the afternoon. I know you're shit at sport but he's meant to be a keen player—supposed to be almost pro level. I'm sorry to miss it, actu-ally,' Gareth drones on, but I stopped listening eons ago.

Jagger lashes me with his tongue, the warmth of his

breath and the pressure of his mouth making pleasure roll through my veins until I can no longer keep quiet.

'I got it,' I moan. 'I have to go.' I fumble, disconnecting the call, then grip the phone tight in my hand as Jagger pushes me over the edge.

'I said not to hang up,' he murmurs as I come against his mouth, as I forget where I am, who I am, what I want in life.

'Couldn't…stay…quiet…'

'Good,' he purrs. 'I like you noisy, Grace. I like you screaming, in fact.'

I don't feel even a hint of embarrassment. I'm riding a wave of complete pleasure, total euphoric release. 'Don't stop,' I beg, staring up at the sky. 'Please, don't stop.'

'All night long, remember?' He doesn't say anything else. He uses his mouth to play my body, to fuck me with his lips, and I cry his name out at the top of my lungs as I spin wildly into an abyss from which I have no idea if I can escape.

'Why did you do that?' I ask when I can speak again.

'Because I like making you come,' he says simply, standing, straightening my dress. 'In fact, I fucking love making you come.'

Pleasure makes my smile broad. 'I meant, why did you do it while I was on the phone?'

His eyes flash for a second with something darker, something more hard-edged. 'Because he'd hate it.'

'He didn't know.'

'Sure. But you knew.' His arms encircle me. 'And I knew. And I like the idea of that.'

Something turns over in my gut, because I do, too, but it's petty and juvenile. 'I'm over him, you know,' I say seriously, determinedly.

'Sure you are.' He laughs softly.

But his cynicism angers me—I've fought too hard to put Gareth behind me to have anyone doubt it now. 'I am,' I say firmly. 'He's married to someone else.'

'That doesn't mean you're over him.'

'Hello,' I say with a forced smile. 'Have you been with me the last couple of nights?'

'Yeah. And you fuck like you're trying to forget. I've been there. I recognise it.'

Something like panic flares in my chest. 'You're wrong.'

'No, I'm not.' He lifts a hand, strokes it over my hair, but I jerk away. He takes a step back, not crowding me. 'But you'll get over him eventually. He doesn't deserve you.'

'I *am* over him,' I insist. 'You don't understand.'

'Sure I do. He jerked you around, promised you the world, then left you for someone else.'

'It's really not like that.'

'No?'

'No.' I shake my head. I turn away from him, staring out at what I can see of the twelfth hole. 'It's not him. It's *me*.'

He's quiet. The moon dips behind a cloud, darkening the course momentarily.

'He told me he didn't want to get married. When we first started dating, I mean. He said, "I'm not into marriage. Don't believe in it". And I was okay with that. I didn't really care, to be honest. I had no idea if I'd even be with him in a month's time. Marriage was nowhere on my horizon. But then we were still together a month later, and a month after that. Six months later. A year later. And suddenly I felt like I'd closed myself off to a whole world that maybe I did actually want to be a part of.'

'Did you talk to him about it?' The question is asked with clinical precision, the same businesslike professionalism he brought to the conference room earlier today.

'Sure. Once. He smiled and told me he loved me but that he hadn't changed his mind. Marriage wasn't for him.'

'I see. And you said…?'

'I said that I didn't really care, even when I did.' I shake my head. 'I told myself I was being stupid, that marriage is just a certificate and the option of changing your name—which you can do anyway. I told myself it didn't mean we wouldn't spend the rest of our lives together, wouldn't have kids together. Wouldn't be together, just like a married couple. I told myself loving someone was about accepting all their unique quirks and foibles, and this was one of his.'

I suck in a gulp of salty night air. 'Then we broke up and he got engaged to someone else and I realised he did believe in marriage.' My voice is raw. 'He believed in it. He wanted it. He just didn't know that until he met someone who made him want it.' I angle my face to Jagger's. He's watching me with a guarded intensity that strips me raw. 'He just didn't want me.'

He compresses his lips, his eyes scanning my face.

'I showed him all of myself, and he walked away. And I gave up all of myself—I gave up what I wanted in life, and love, because he asked it of me, and he walked away from me. I don't still love him, Jagger. This isn't about him. It's about how he made me feel—how I *let* him make me feel.' I tilt my chin a little, even when I'm sure my eyes are awash with all the hurt my heart carries.

'Compromise in a relationship is important,' he says finally. 'And caring for someone enough to give them what they need, to sacrifice in their name, is the only way a relationship can work.' He rubs his hand over mine on the balcony. 'He just didn't want to sacrifice back.'

'He did for her.'

He expels a sigh. 'Maybe. Maybe not.'

'What do you mean?'

'He's calling you from his honeymoon. Do you think he's giving her everything she wants?'

Something like anxiety swirls through my gut. 'I'm not getting involved in some weird love triangle. He's married…'

'Sure. I'm just saying he sounds like the kind of egotist who likes to make women feel a little insecure—to make himself feel better. Denying someone what they want is one way to keep the upper hand in a relationship, right?'

'I guess.' I shrug. 'I hadn't thought of it like that.'

'Do you need to speak to him while you're here?'

'No.'

'Do you need his business input? Because you seem to know everything about every blade of grass and grain of sand on this island…'

I smile unconsciously at his praise. 'I do.'

'And your buyer is very, very impressed...'

Pleasure and pride swell inside of me.

'So he's calling because he misses you, or he likes the idea of her being jealous. Either way, he's a fuckwit.'

I laugh softly. 'Yeah, he is.'

'And now you'll always know you had kinky sex while he was pining for you...'

I shake my head a little. 'I don't think that's the case...'

'We'll see.'

From inside the room a knock sounds. My tummy gives a low grumble, right on cue. He grins at me. 'Dinner.'

I slip inside behind him, wondering if he's right. Wondering if Gareth's calling because he wants to make his wife jealous. Wondering if he's calling because he regrets leaving me. Knowing with one hundred per cent of myself that I don't care either way. I was devastated when we broke up, I hated how unlovable I felt, how completely unworthy of anyone's love, and then I hated him for having that power over me.

Right now, the only man I have any time for, the only one I have interest in thinking about at all, is the gorgeous specimen holding the door open for the hotel waiter. He signs the cheque and we're alone again—and suddenly the fact we have two nights left together is like a spark igniting in my bloodstream.

Precious minutes and hours and then nothing—and I'm going to make the most of what time we have left.

CHAPTER NINE

WHEN I WAKE up it's with dawn light creeping into the room, through the open balcony doors. The day is already warm. I lift myself up, my eyes dragging over his sleeping body, a satisfied smile curving my lips.

I am laced with pleasure and contentment. Shifting just a little, I pull out of bed, checking the time on my phone. It's still early—in the fives. Biting down on my lip, I tiptoe into the bathroom and splash water on my face, finger-combing my hair over my shoulder before turning around, leaning into the doorjamb, staring back into the room to where he still sleeps. My clothes are folded neatly on the chair to my left—him, again. I reach across, picking them up, dressing silently, my eyes frequently straying to his sleeping form.

This is one of the strangest turns of fate in my life. Who would have thought the meaningless one-night stand I picked up on the eve of my ex's wedding would turn out to be a client? No, that he'd turn out to be Jagger. Smart, kind, insightful, seriously hot Jagger.

I walked out of his hotel room in Sydney with no intention of seeing him again, and I know I wouldn't

have regretted that. I know that was the obvious decision—why stick around until morning? Sure, more sex
maybe, but then that awkward conversation, the hedg-
ing around swapping numbers—and if he hadn't asked
for my number?

That same feeling of being unwanted would have
crested over me. Instead, I got to walk away on my
terms, in my own time.

Just like I would at the end of this trip.

Okay, he'd be walking away too, or flying away on
his swanky private jet, but we'd both be turning our
backs on each other, and this, by mutual consent. No
going out on a limb, asking for more, wanting an impossible dream.

This isn't like with Gareth. He said one thing and
meant completely another. He didn't listen to what I
wanted; he made no efforts to accommodate my wishes.
Just like Jagger said last night, Gareth was unwilling to
compromise for me. It was all me giving, all the time.
My anger is self-directed.

When did I become that woman? When did I let myself give up on my own wants and needs?

A smile curves my lips, a smile of feminine power
and wisdom, because I feel strong and confident, I feel
safe. I feel like my place here is clearly defined. I feel…
everything.

With my smile growing, I remember the way he went
down on me in the jet, the way he left me hanging,
so overloaded with desire for him I could have wept.
Flames burst in my bloodstream. Quietly, I tiptoe to his
side of the bed and pull at the sheet, easing it off his

body so he lies there, my naked Zeus, powerful, muscular, handsome—mine. For now, at least.

Careful not to wake him—yet—I drop my mouth over the tip of his cock, circling it. In his sleep, he makes a groaning noise. I smile, and then grip his base, bringing my mouth down his length. He grows hard as I move my mouth up and down, and when I lift my eyes up the length of his body, flashing over his flat chest to his chin, stubbled and square, he's pushed up on his elbows and is watching me with eyes that are not even remotely sleepy.

I flash him a quick smile before sucking him deep inside my mouth, so his tip hits the back of my throat, and he lets out a low moan, a rough sound, and I move faster, harder, my fingers curling around his base, squeezing him as my mouth drives up and down. Power thrills in my veins as I feel him throb in my mouth and a drop of his seed spills into me.

'Jesus, Grace…' He drops back on the pillow. 'Don't you fucking stop…'

I roll my tongue over his tip and pull up slightly. 'I'm sorry, Mr Hart, but I think you'll find it's daytime…'

He blanches, pushing up once more, glaring at me. 'You're kidding?'

'Oh, no,' I say sweetly, standing up, moving towards his head. 'And we have a deal, remember?'

'Fuck the deal.'

I laugh softly. 'But how will you know I'm a woman of my word?'

He sits up straight. 'Come here,' he growls, pulling for my hips, and I laugh, shaking my head, pulling just out of reach.

'We have a deal,' I purr, scooping my handbag up off the carpet and moving towards the door. I turn my hand over the knob, throwing a glance over my shoulder. My eyes lock to his and heat sizzles in my veins, making me want to go back to him, to give in to temptation—to hell with whatever we've agreed. 'Don't worry, Jagger. Only fourteen hours to go.'

His eyes narrow. 'You're going to regret playing with fire.'

I laugh. 'Probably.' I blow him a kiss. 'But I don't right now.'

'So that was payback for the flight, right?' He leans closer to me, his breath warming my cheek. I tilt my head towards his, smiling as though butter wouldn't melt, even when my heart is notching it up a gear and I have been fighting an urge to just *stare* at his pretty body since we left shore fifteen minutes ago.

'Do you really think I'd be so petty?'

The boat takes us farther out into the Coral Sea, the snorkelling instructor up the bow with most of the other members of this small group. The resort's branding is across the side of the boat.

'I don't know if it's petty.' His eyes flicker across my face. 'But I was hard for twenty minutes after you left this morning. I can't stop thinking about you.'

My heart explodes. I lift my eyes heavenward. 'Still daytime.'

He nods with mock seriousness, extending a finger and pressing it to my wet-suited knee. 'Eleven hours, right?'

Flames leap through me. I lean closer. 'And counting.' I reach for his finger and lift it off my knee, placing it squarely back on his. His eyes crease at the corners with the force of his smile and I am warmed from the inside out.

'I feel like I could have learned a lot about the island from my bed.'

I shake my head. 'Quiet. You're going to love this.'

'Sightseeing?' He raises his brows.

'How else can you experience your investment as prospective tourists will?'

'By you telling me about it? From reports you've read? Preferably naked?'

I shake my head to clear that vision from my mind.

'And I still haven't agreed to buy this place, Miss Llewellyn.'

Uncertainty lurches dangerously in my gut and something like storm clouds must pass over my expression because his own face becomes serious. 'You know that's a decision I'll make on business merit alone, right?'

'You mean do I think the fact we're sleeping together will lead you to invest tens of millions of dollars?'

'I mean it's a business decision,' he fires back softly.

'And I'd never try to influence you with anything other than the common-sense appeal of this. Trust me, Jagger. I'm good at my job. I'm great at it. I have an instinctive sense of what properties are right for which investors and you're not going to find anything better than Silver Dunes.'

A muscle jerks in his cheek. 'I don't know if I believe

in that kind of declarative statement. But I do believe you think this is a good buy, and that you've made that decision from your experience and knowledge alone.'

My breath gains pace. 'You know Karakedes Corp is technically my client,' I say, dropping my eyes. 'I work for them. Whether it's you or someone else, my job is to get them the best buyer, the best price, the most favourable terms for my vendor.'

He moves infinitesimally closer. 'Yes.'

'So don't think the fact that you're all Eros the Spectacular means I'll give you an easy deal when we sit down to negotiate.'

'If,' he offers as a rejoinder, and now he moves his lips to my ear, speaking right into my soul. 'And we won't be sitting down to negotiate, Grace. Not unless it's you sitting on my dick, anyway.'

Heat blooms in my cheeks. I don't move away, though. Being close to him like this, our bodies practically entwined, even when there are people around and the sun is out, is alluring and hypnotic.

'I look forward to it, sir.'

'Not as much as I do. I've been told I drive a very hard bargain…'

I want to respond with a flirtatious rejoinder but this is business, too, and what I just said a few seconds ago holds true—Karakedes is my client. 'They won't go lower than the asking price. I believe Bianca made that clear in her emails to you. That wasn't a starting price for negotiations. If you're planning to lowball them, you might as well tell me now and I'll save us both a lot of time and energy and put a stop to this.'

'When we're having so much fun?' he teases, perhaps not realising that I've swapped out of flirty, take-me-to-bed personal and I'm all business now.

'Fun is beside the point.' He straightens, his gaze intent now. 'I'm not messing around here, Jagger. If you're going to dick me around, tell me, because my client has a right to know. And I have a right to know, to get back to work finding someone else who's interested in this once in a lifetime opportunity…'

'Are we talking about the golf course or you?'

I glare at him. 'I'm talking exclusively about the golf course now.'

His frown is just a flicker of his lips. 'You're pissed?'

The last thing I want is to seem like I'm churlish and petulant—like my emotions are in play here. 'I'm…no. I'm just… I need to know if you're planning on stuffing me around because that's not going to work here.' Panic is surging inside of me, though. I struggle to cover it. 'Something my office made clear before embarking on this inspection.'

'They did,' he agrees with a nod. 'Irrespective of that, if I make an offer on Silver Dunes, it will reflect what I believe the property's worth.'

'You don't think it's worth what we're asking?'

He's quiet for a moment, his eyes skimming over my face, and then he smiles, a smile that reaches into my heart and squeezes it tight. I love his smile, the way the light dances in his eyes and his skin crinkles at the corners. It's a smile that changes his face completely. He leans forward conspiratorially. 'I didn't say that.'

My heart turns over.

'I'm evaluating it. I'm thinking. And when I'm ready, if I decide it'll be a good addition to my portfolio, I'll make a fair and reasonable offer.'

I wish I had another buyer lined up to coerce him into acting faster, but alas, properties like this are tricky to sell—to find buyers with the necessary means who are interested in this kind of investment takes time.

The boat slows down and the tour operator runs through the safety guidelines. I have butterflies in my stomach—the good kind, and the bad kind. I don't know why, but it hadn't occurred to me that he might not buy the resort. My need for the commission overtook every modicum of restraint I would usually employ. Crap.

What if he doesn't?

My stomach lurches. Because I can't keep working with Gareth. I need to buy him out. I could borrow— not the whole amount though. My parents are way too risk-averse to help—even if they could lay their hands on the kind of cash I'd need. Maybe Gareth would sell it to me in instalments?

Only…*no.*

I don't want that. I want a clean break. There's only one other option before me. To sell. Gareth came into this with more money behind him; he could buy me out.

I curve a hand around the boat railing, staring at the ocean as that reality expands before me. My throat thickens with unshed tears; I want to push that away, I want to push that idea off the edge of my mind.

I've worked so hard to make this business a success. In the face of my parents' disapproval and scepticism,

I worked hard, I did everything I could. How could I have known Gareth would do what he did?

'You ready?'

He stands beside me, the sun bright just behind his head. Even in the enormous scuba goggles, I find him ridiculously attractive. 'Yeah.' I am ready. Ready for anything. Whether he buys or not, one way or another, I have to get out of this business.

And I will.

'Okay, Grace! Go!' The instructor's behind me. I hold my nose like he's taught us, stepping off the side of the boat. Once in the water, I turn around and wave up at him, showing I'm okay, then put my mask in place. A second later there's another splash. Jagger's right beside me.

I lift up, looking at him, and he waves right at me.

I wave back. My insides tremble. He points towards the water, his thick brows lifted above his mask.

'Ready,' I say, the word swallowed up by the plastic of the scuba mask. I kick my flippers to stay afloat then duck-dive, so I swim along the water's surface.

Beneath us, there's the most incredible coral reef, the colours so bright it's hard to believe it's natural. Orange, turquoise and the brightest pink you can imagine dazzle with white shimmering sand beneath. It's so cool down here, unlike on the boat, where the sun was unrelenting.

Something big emerges from behind the coral and I make a bubbling noise of delight as a big stingray swims right past us, followed by a much smaller one. A little line of crabs march sideways to get out of its way.

Jagger, beside me, grins. I smile back then turn in another direction, moving around the coral reef, wondering why I've never done this before. It's so incredibly beautiful, and so close to home—I should have made a point of seeing this earlier in my life. Still, better late than never.

It's strange being here with Jagger. Knowing him to be temporary in my life doesn't change the fact that I'm glad it's him—I'm glad he's experiencing this with me.

There's a shipwreck a little way from the group and we swim towards it, signalling the instructor as we set off.

Jagger is always close by, always at my side.

As I swim close enough almost to touch the bow, wondering at the people who rode this craft, who were on board when it sank to the bottom of the reef, Jagger puts his hand over mine and, despite the fact we're in the water, I feel fire and flames arcing through my bloodstream, heat coursing into my cells, setting me alight. I turn my hand over, linking my fingers to his, my eyes lifting to his. I can't see much—the water and the masks do a good job of concealing our faces—but, close to him like this, I want to kick my way to him, closing any distance, moulding our bodies together. I want to dig my hands into his pants and feel his cock, pull him closer, push him inside of me. I am alight with need.

He squeezes my hand and begins to kick to an upright position.

I surge with him, our hands still intertwined when we break the water's surface and into the air a moment later. He rips his mask off and now I see his eyes and they're so full of complex, tangled thoughts and wants that my breath feels thick in my lungs.

'You okay?' he asks, reaching out and removing my mask, keeping it hooked over one finger, with his. Our hands are meshed. My stomach feels loopy. This time tomorrow we'll be on a flight back to Sydney.

Something like doubt clamps at the edges of my gut. 'Fine.' My smile is over-bright. 'This is amazing, right?'

'Yeah,' he admits, looking around.

'And to think it could all be yours for the bargain price of sixty million dollars...'

He laughs, pulling me closer, clamping a hand around my waist. My eyes flare wide and I long to surrender to this. 'Small change.'

The thing is, for him, it pretty much is. I bite down on my lip and his eyes drop to the gesture; my heart hammers.

His eyes are heavy on my face and, even though he's not kissing me, phantoms, ghosts, memories of previous kisses and intimacies throb through me, the recollections so powerful they feel real.

'How many hours?' he asks, running his hand over the side of my breast. I groan softly.

'Too many.'

He lifts his head up, looking at me. 'We could always... renegotiate the terms of our deal. Cancel the day and go straight back to bed...'

God. I want to. And that in and of itself is a red flag, because this is the most important deal of my career. 'But you're not a man to go back on his word,' I say softly. 'And this means too much to me to ever worry I stuffed it up.'

His brow furrows as he takes those words in but,

before he can respond, a whistle sounds from the boat. We look in that direction to see the instructor waving the 'come in' flag. I pull my hand away from his and smile. 'Let's go, Mr Hart. There's plenty more in store for you today.'

'You need your legs a little further apart.' I stand behind her, wanting to scrap this game of golf, throw her over my shoulder and drag her to the nearest damned bunker, just like I've been wanting to all damned day.

This means too much to me.

I gather Grace's assistant organised this day to show me the charms of the resort. Pity I can't see past the charms of Grace's arse. And her breasts. And her laugh. And her stories.

I bring my hands around behind her, holding the golf club over her hands, my arm brushing her breast as I guide her swing. 'Good,' I murmur into her ear. 'And now strike.'

She brings the club down and misses the ball, then laughs.

I laugh with her. 'Once more.'

'What am I, up to like a hundred strikes?'

'It's a practice round. We won't tell anyone.'

She spins in my arms, her smile contagious. 'Now, now, Mr Hart, I'm not a cheat.'

'Of course not.'

'How about you play and I'll watch?'

'Oh, believe me, this is much more fun.'

'But I suck. I mean, I really, really suck,' she says with a quirk of her lips.

'You have other talents that compensate.'

'Yeah? Such as?'

It's been a huge day. We were on the reef for three hours, then in the restaurant for lunch with Orion Karakedes. I could have done without it, to be honest—Grace was back in business mode, so sexy and in control, so incredibly intelligent—but I didn't want to hear about the historical expansion of the resort, nor the design of the golf course. Everything can be put in a report—a report I can read later.

The time is ticking—no, it's rushing—and soon Grace will be gone, I'll be gone, this will be over. I'd rather not have wasted ninety minutes sharing a table with Orion Karakedes.

She went back to her room after lunch for an hour and I fought an urge to follow her, to knock on the door and tell her to scrap the afternoon. I had work to catch up on anyway, emails that couldn't wait. Golf, though, seemed like a torturous prolonging of our day.

Now, however, her body so close to mine, her butt pressed against my cock as she tries to perfect her swing for the hundredth time, I think I'll never play a round of golf without wishing Grace was with me—lousy swing included.

'Good,' I murmur as she brings the club up again. This time, when she draws it down, she chips the ball nicely and it sails down the fairway.

She watches it and, despite the fact it hooks left and lands wide of what could be considered a fair placement, she jumps up and down in excitement.

'I did it!' She's so damned excited, so proud of herself, my gut rolls and I nod, returning her beaming smile.

'Yeah, you did.'

'And I thought this would be hard.' She laughs, sliding the club back into the bag.

'Your go.'

I arch a brow. 'Sure.' I line up my tee and swing at it, knocking it down the fairway and onto the green.

She pouts. 'So, you're really good at this.'

I nod. 'Yeah. I've had a lot of practice.'

I choose an iron for her and we walk towards her ball. 'The country club.'

'Yeah.'

'Was it like this?' She sweeps her hand, gesturing to the course.

I stand still, my eyes following her movement. The hills roll gently in every direction, the sky is a bright azure blue and the ocean glistens just beyond the course, spectacularly turquoise and inviting. This morning I saw colours I didn't know existed in the corals on the bottom of the reef. Knowing that's out there, this ancient, exotic wilderness, calls to something inside of me.

'No.' My voice is gruff. I clear my throat. 'I've never seen anything like this.'

When I flick my gaze to her face, there's a knowing—and somewhat smug—smile hovering on her lips.

'Don't,' I say. I laugh, though, and resist an urge to pull her into my arms and kiss her. Helping her golf swing is one thing—but we're still technically in the 'professional' part of our time together.

'Don't what?'

'I can think a place is stunning without wanting to buy it.' Just like I can think a woman is the most fascinating, beautiful creature I've ever spent time with and be willing to walk away at the end of three days together.

The thought comes out of nowhere but I hold onto it, reaffirmed by the sense it makes.

'I know—' her grin doesn't drop '—but you will.'

Her confidence is sexy. Hot. Addictive. 'What makes you so sure?'

'You're buying up properties just like this.' She shrugs. 'You have the cash. And there's nothing like it on the market. Hell, there's nothing like it out there. You'd be crazy to let the opportunity go by.'

She's talking about the golf course but something stutters a little in my chest. I nod, pointing towards her ball. 'You got this, or do you need me to help?'

She shoots me a droll look. 'I think I can manage.'

She does—after four missed swings.

It putts onto the green. She lifts a hand for a high-five. I return it, fighting myself the whole time, not to drag her into my arms right here.

'Who screwed you over?' she asks as we move back to my ball.

'Huh?' I'm jarred out of the moment, lifting my gaze to her face. 'When?'

'On the plane over, you said I'd been screwed by an ex, you'd been screwed by an ex, so we should just screw each other.' She lifts her eyes to mine. 'Who's your ex?'

I forgot I said that. I don't particularly want to think

about Lorena right now. The green darkens as a cloud moves overhead, blocking the sun.

'Come on. You've psychoanalysed Gareth. Let me do the same.'

'I don't need your help to psychoanalyse Lorena.'

I don't even like saying her name aloud.

'Did she cheat on you?'

My hand grips the golf club tighter. I swing for the ball—too hard. It sails past the hole.

'No.'

'You're still angry with her.'

It's not a question. Grace is seeing into my soul in that way she has—that way I don't completely like.

'No.'

'Sure. You sound the complete opposite of angry.'

My laugh is humourless. 'My divorce came through just over a week ago. I'm allowed to still have feelings about that.'

'Feelings for her?'

The question is flat, her voice almost a monotone. That's what tips me off—she's trying too hard to smother everything out of her tone. I shoot my eyes to her, a frown on my face. Her expression is as blank as her voice.

'Not good ones.'

She stares into my eyes for a long time and I don't look away.

'Why? What happened?'

She turns to the golf course, eyeing up the positions of our balls. We begin to walk back to the buggy.

She sighs. 'Okay. Let's start with easier questions. How long were you married?'

'A year.'

She stops walking. 'Just a year?'

Without knowing it, she's echoed my biggest criticism of myself. 'About eleven and a half months too long,' I quip.

'But you married her. So you must have loved her. What happened?'

'Haven't we already decided love is juvenile?'

She frowns. 'Love at first sight, maybe. But love? I don't think that's in the same category.'

Her eyes show defiance and hope. I hate crushing her spirit in a way. 'Give it time, Grace; you'll earn your cynicism. A few more Gareths and you'll get there.'

She shakes her head. 'I doubt it. Even in the midst of that, I understood. He just didn't love me. But he loves Alicia. Love is real, it's out there, just not for us, not for him and me.'

'You loved him, though.'

She considers that for a moment. 'I guess there's lots of different types of love,' she says after a while. 'I did love him. It was a slow-building love—the opposite to love at first sight. I trusted him and I liked him, way before I loved him. I honestly thought he was the safest person I could invest my time with.'

'Sounds…clinical rather than romantic.'

'That suits me,' she says with a nod. 'I've always been someone who'd rather think than feel. I *thought* I'd found my way to someone who was a safe bet. We were on the same page with business, life, philosophy, politics. We made complete sense.' She shrugs, her shoulders slender. My eyes drop a little lower, to the swell of her breasts revealed by the white cotton T-shirt she's wearing.

'Growing up—' I put our clubs back in the bag and wait for her to climb into the buggy before swinging in beside her '—I had proof, again and again, that believing in love and "happily ever after" is just about the stupidest thing you could do.'

'Your parents?'

'My parents, and the litany of step-parents I briefly knew. I could fill a library with the arguments I heard. My dad wasn't an easy guy to live with. Bombastic, a heavy drinker, a womaniser—rapier sharp, quick-witted, untrusting and untrustworthy. He made an art form out of icing people out, pushing them away. And he had a team of fantastic lawyers who drew up iron-clad prenuptial agreements so he never paid out more than a million to each wife.'

'But he loved you?'

Strangely, given how accepting I am of the facts, I feel emotions I haven't grappled with in a long time. Hurt and pain. I shake my head, pushing them away. 'Not really. Adrian Hart didn't truly love anyone.'

'I'm sorry,' she says softly. 'That must have been hard to live with.'

'You get used to what you know. I didn't realise until I was a teenager that other people didn't have a revolving door of parents and new siblings to contend with.' Her face is in profile as she concentrates on driving us towards the green. 'I swore my life would be different, that my marriage would be different.'

She shifts her gaze to me briefly, slowing the cart to a stop. 'Do you regret divorcing her?'

'I regret marrying her.'

Perhaps the degree of ice in my words cuts through her because she frowns and I understand why—I remind myself of my father in that moment and the thought turns my stomach.

I'm nothing like him.

'What happened?'

The year of marriage to Lorena flashes through my mind and I shake my head with rueful frustration. 'It was a shitshow from just about day one.' I clench my jaw, not wanting to think about it, let alone to go back. 'My brothers hated her—Holden especially. That should have been my heads-up. I just never saw what they did.'

'And what was that?'

'A money-grabbing, lying bitch.'

The vehemence of my proclamation makes her reel a little.

'You probably think I'm being a bastard.'

She shakes her head. 'You're not like that. I'm just wondering what anyone could do to make you so angry.' She lifts a hand to my chest and it's not a professional touch; it's something else. It's comforting and kind. Sympathetic. My heart closes over. My marriage was *my* mistake. I don't need anyone pitying me. I should have been more careful.

'We had a prenup,' I say guardedly. 'At my father's suggestion.'

'Naturally.'

'She got a million-dollar bonus per kid.'

'Seriously?' Grace's disapproval shows.

'It's standard, apparently. I didn't take any interest in the terms—I only found out months later that Lorena did. She was at my lawyer's every day, her lawyers in tow, demanding all sorts of provisions and bonuses.'

Grace is quiet, but I see judgement in her eyes and it warms me inside.

'I didn't want kids. Not yet. Now I realise I probably just didn't want them with her. Maybe alarm bells were going off the whole time and I was so determined not to be like my parents and their failed marriages that I refused to heed them.' I shake my head, reaching for a golf club and handing it to Grace.

'So you didn't get pregnant?'

'No. But when I told her I wasn't ready she withheld sex. She'd use it to try to blackmail me into agreeing—she knew I'd never cheat.' My smile is wry. 'And that I didn't really want a sexless marriage. She tried to get our prenup changed so she'd get her baby bonus sooner. I just had no idea she was after cash. I would have given her money— I would have paid her off as a test if I thought it'd work.'

I'm nauseated by the conversation, by the reality. 'She threatened to leave me unless I either gave her a million bucks or got her knocked up.'

Grace's indignation shows in her face. 'Bitch.'

I laugh at how unnatural the word sounds coming from her lips. 'Yeah.'

'What did you do?'

'Gave her our home and three million dollars, in exchange for a quick, painless divorce. I told her I never wanted to hear from her again.'

'So that's it?'

'Not quite. She tried to take Brinkley.'

'Your dog? She didn't!' Grace is outraged. 'I can't believe it! Why would someone do that?'

'She wanted to hurt me, in the end. She was furious I wouldn't just give her what she wanted.'

'You gave her a fortune.'

I pull a face. 'Not really. Not compared to my worth. I guess she thought I'd crumble, have kids with her, and she'd have access to everything I own for ever.'

Her eyes show outrage. I feel a connection between us forging out of steel.

'It was a mess. We had shouting matches that would have shocked even my parents.'

'I'm glad you realised what she was like before you started a family together.'

'Yeah, me, too. I can't think of much worse than bringing kids up with someone I hate and despise on every level.'

She takes the club from me, weighing it in her hands.

'Maybe that explains why I'm not exactly a champion of love—be it love at first sight or a long-to-develop, slow, safe love.' I move closer to her so I can smell her vanilla-and-honey fragrance. 'But temporary white-hot sex with beautiful strangers?' I lift my brows, my eyes sparking with hers. 'There's nothing bad that can come from this, right?'

CHAPTER TEN

'WHAT'S UP, LADY?'

I smile at the sound of Penny's voice. 'Oh, you know, nothing. You?'

'Work. Work. More work.'

'Same.'

'Yeah, but my work involves teaching recalcitrant ten-year-olds in inner-city schools how to not punch each other. Yours is at least in the lap of luxury in the Whitsundays.'

I run my fingertip over the balcony railing, checking out the time on my watch for what feels like the hundredth time. The sun is still high in the sky—night-time is a while away.

I'm tired—scuba diving, a long business lunch and then a round of golf and my body is exhausted. And yet... I'm also completely energised, ready for the night ahead, poised for Jagger.

Jagger.

'It's not as simple as that,' I say, biting down on my lip.

'Why? God, don't tell me Gareth's reared his bastard head?'

'No.' I shake my head. 'It's not Gareth. It's…you know that hot American from the other night?'

'Jaggerrrrrr.' She purrs his name and my pulse threads through me.

'He's also my very, very cashed-up potential investor.'

'Shut up! He is not!'

'Yeah, he really is.'

'So you slept with him and now you're trying to get him to buy a multimillion-dollar property?'

'Yes.'

'I did not see that coming.'

'You and me both.' I tighten my fingers around the railing.

'He's up there with you now?'

'Not right now,' I mumble.

'But he's on the island. And you're staying in the same hotel?' Penny laughs. 'Well, that's just the gift that keeps on giving. I hope you're taking full advantage of that fabulous body of his…'

My cheeks feel warm. 'He's my client.'

'And you're two consenting adults. What's the problem?'

'I… There's no problem.' Except there is. I can't put my finger on it but something feels… I don't know. Complicated.

'You sound worried. Is he giving you a hard time?'

I shake my head, smiling a little because I wonder if Penny would leap straight onto a flight and come to my rescue if he was. 'He's great. He's…' Really great. He's charming and funny and smart and I love spending time with him. Danger lurks on the peripheries of my mind. 'I think it's going well. I don't know if he's going to buy it, though.'

'I thought he was pretty much a done deal?'

'Yeah.' I nod jerkily. So did I. 'But you know, nothing's definite until it's all signed.'

'You're great at this. If he's not convinced, convince him.'

'I'm trying.'

'Use every tool at your disposal,' she jokes—and I know she's joking, but protective hackles rise in my body. The memory of his face when he told me how his ex-wife had seen him only as a bank balance fills me with rage. I could never do that. He has to decide what he wants to do with this place, and it has to be based on his own business interests. I can't pressure him or force him.

I can't do my job. Not effectively.

My stomach drops because I was an idiot to think I could keep business and pleasure separate, to think this wouldn't somehow bleed into our working relationship. We've been sleeping together a few days and I know I can't ever have him wonder if I took advantage of this.

'Listen, Gracie, make the most of him while you've got him. The property stuff will sort itself out. Relax. Don't overthink this.'

I murmur my agreement with no intention of listening to her. I should have thought it over sooner—I should have realised there was danger here.

A knock sounds at my door. I turn to look into the hotel room in time to see Jagger pushing the door open and my chest hurts like it's been cracked open, right down the sternum.

'Pen? I gotta go.'

'Call me later. Let me know how it's going.'

'I will. Love you.'

I disconnect the call, but don't move inside. He's changed into a pair of beige shorts and a white shirt, with flip-flops on his tanned feet. His hair looks blonder now than when we first met—a few days in the sunshine have also darkened his tan.

'Gareth?' he prompts, stepping onto the balcony, so I roll my eyes.

'No, Penny. Checking up on me.'

'Ah.'

He comes to stand right in front of me, his body so close I can feel his warmth.

'I've been thinking,' I say, lifting a hand to his chest to keep him at a distance. 'Once we get back to Sydney, I think you should deal with Gareth. If you want to make an offer.'

His frown is just a flash across his features. 'Why?'

'After what you said today, about Lorena, I'd hate you to think I was taking advantage of this—of us—to get you to pay more than you want to. I can't do my job effectively with that in my mind. I'm a sales agent, I need to *sell* the property to my buyer, but I don't feel comfortable putting the hard word on you. Not now, not after the last few days.'

He frowns. 'Why?'

'Because. You're not just a client. An investor. You're someone who's…'

'What? Fucked you sideways?' he prompts. 'We talked about this. Sex has no bearing on my decision. I'm only going to offer what I'm prepared to pay...'

'And if the offer's not high enough, I need to be able to tell you that and not worry you think it's because we slept together, that I think I have some special way of pressuring you or whatever.'

'Sex is sex. We both agreed to the boundaries of this from the start. Why would you pressure me? What do you stand to gain from this?'

'Other than a big fat commission?' I prompt, and he shrugs.

'Sure. But if I don't buy it, someone else will. You'll get that commission one way or another.'

My smile is weak. He sees through it.

'But you want the commission now?'

I open my mouth to deny it, but then nod. I'm not a liar. I'm not going to lie to him. Besides, there's nothing unreasonable about my position. 'Yes. See? It's over-complicated.'

He shakes his head. 'I disagree. You want the commission, fair enough. I'm sorry to seem cold-hearted, but that's still not going to sway me. I'm too good at what I do to let anything like that come into the equation.'

I should feel relieved, but I don't. It's like he's scratching sandpaper over the ventricles of my heart. 'It's better if you deal with Gareth.'

'I don't want to deal with your fuckwit ex.'

I hold his gaze determinedly. 'He's great at his job.'

'So are you.' He glares at me. 'Sell me on this place,

Grace. Sell me on why I can't live without the golf course. Sell my on why it's a standout investment I can't turn my back on. Do everything you can to make me buy it, to pay the price you want. Don't think for one second I'll let anything personal factor into my decision-making.' He drops his head closer to mine, his eyes intense. 'Don't think I won't walk away if you try to push me onto that idiot Gareth.'

I curl my fingers into the warm cotton of his shirt, gripping him, holding onto this reality a moment longer, before he slips through my fingers. The sun is warm on my back but I feel ice-cold.

I don't know why I feel so wishy-washy, so uncertain, so unclear. It's not like me. As with all things in the last six months, I blame Gareth. I blame him for making me feel like less of a woman, less of a lovable person, than I ever have. I blame him for letting me open myself up, for inviting me to show him all of myself and then turning his back on me.

'You'd be cutting off your nose to spite your face.' My words are thick, coated with emotion. A small frown mars his expression.

'I want the resort,' he says finally. 'I'm going to make an offer on it.'

Relief bursts in my gut, but it's short-lived. 'What will you offer?'

'I haven't decided yet.'

His expression shows concentration and concern. It's the latter that worries me. He's analysing me, this, and treating me with kid gloves. Because we've slept together. What an idiot I was for thinking I could keep the business out of bed!

'I need to review the financials you've given me. The offer I make will be fair, based on what I think this place is worth. You'll take it to Orion and he'll accept, because he's not an idiot and he'll know a buyer with readily available funds is worth more than the promise of a future sale for a few extra mill.'

He's probably right. I've sold enough properties to know it's never black and white—the smallest details can convince someone to sell. Besides, my job is to get this over the line. But what if my relationship with Jagger is part of why I push Orion into accepting this deal?

The ethics of this situation are no longer clear. Or maybe they are, maybe I see them with absolute clarity and I know what they're telling me to do. But I don't need to tell Jagger that. I'll work out how to make this okay once he's gone. Once this is over.

For now, we have one night left. One humid, sultry night.

'What do you think?' My voice catches a little in my throat, hoarse with desire. I turn my head to the side, towards the beach. 'Another hour before sundown?'

His gaze follows mine. 'I'm prepared to relax our rules on this last night.'

My lips twitch. 'Rules are rules, Mr Hart.'

His groan is a gravelly sound from deep in his gut. He drops his head forward, pressing it to mine, and I breathe in deeply. He's an intoxicating mix of woody soap smell and something that's just him. It hits me in the gut—the memory of our first night together, when

I just wanted to fuck some guy, when I wanted to put Gareth's wedding out of my mind.

And now?

There's so much less real estate for Gareth in my head.

'If you're determined to torment me,' he says, brushing his lips over mine then pulling away, 'why don't you throw on your swimmers and we'll check out the pool?'

My smile is sceptical. 'That doesn't sound like something a commercial sales agent would do with a buyer...'

'Oh, it would be purely professional, Miss Llewellyn, I promise.'

'And you're a man of your word.'

He takes a step back and draws his finger over his chest. 'Cross my heart.'

He crosses his heart and my own heart reacts, my own heart jumps. My own heart reminds me it's there, inside me, a part of me, feeling what I feel, wanting more than I've considered I might want.

My own heart is going to cause me problems, I think.

As soon as I get to the pool his plan takes on a new level of deviousness. The sun is still giving off warmth and light, ergo, it is daylight, and yet...watching Jagger Hart stroll around the pool in just a pair of black board shorts, his chest wet from where he's presumably already been swimming, desire is a torrent in my bloodstream.

There is power here, an inevitability, a push, a pull, a need, a want.

I had no idea I could be self-conscious until this moment as he strolls towards me, a smile on his face, his handsome face, his eyes swarming with thoughts that make it impossible for me to think straight. I brought a utilitarian one-piece for this trip. Hey, when I packed a few mornings ago I was exhausted from a night with Jagger, and I didn't exactly know I'd be spending three days with someone like him, wanting to seduce and be seduced…

I brought bathers for the pool inside, figuring I might want to do a few laps one morning.

But when I lift my arms to slide my loose T-shirt from my body, heat throbs from Jagger to me. His eyes follow the action, up my arms, over my head and then, as I bring my arms to my sides, he stands right where he is, letting his gaze trickle over me slowly, so slowly.

My breath escapes on a sharp hiss. His smile is weak.

'I made a promise,' he says quietly, taking a step towards me. My heart scrunches. I bite down on my lip and just stare at him.

'Tell me it doesn't matter,' he says softly, his eyes pleading with mine. 'Tell me you're Grace now, and I can touch you.'

But I can't. I really can't. Fun, carefree fun, has become something else. There's danger on the horizon; I can feel it. It's settling in my soul. So I shake my head and force a smile to my face, reminding myself that not once did I let Gareth see me cry, reminding myself I am a master at hiding how I'm feeling until I'm alone to process things in private.

'I'm sorry, Mr Hart.' The words come out so husky I might as well have invited him to strip me naked right here. 'This is a business meeting.'

He groans and lifts a hand, running his fingers through his hair. 'I'd better get in the pool then because this situation is hardly PG.'

He flicks his eyes down and I follow, my breath snagging in my throat to see his hard dick, visible in his shorts. Desire snakes through me.

'You're not the only one who keeps their promises,' I say, sauntering past him, my heart beating so fast and loud I can't believe he can't hear it.

'Oh, yeah?'

At the edge of the pool I angle my face to his. 'I meant what I said this morning.' I lower my eyes to his cock. 'That was just the beginning.'

I hear his muffled sigh as I dive underwater, smiling to myself as I push to the other side of the enormous pool.

I hear his splash behind me and, just like when we dived this morning, he comes up beside me, but this time, without the masks, I can see his face, I can see his beautiful face, and I can hardly look away. I burst up, out of the water, my breath coming hard, my lungs burning. I reach for the side of the pool, laying my fingers over the coping, just looking at him.

I look at him and I wonder about the man I met at the bar, the connection I felt, even when I knew it would just be sex. I look at him and I see him through the filter of what I know now, I see the man who escaped a disastrous marriage, I see a man who had his heart broken again and again, each and every time his parents split with new partners. I see a man who, from the outside, appears to have it all. I see a man who must wonder if women are only ever interested in his bank balance. I stare at him and I see a man I want to see more of.

I see a man I'm not so sure I can walk away from, a man I don't think I *want* to walk away from.

He stares at me while I stare at him, and I wonder if he sees me for who I am. I wonder if he sees a woman, a strong woman who's fought hard to get where she is in life, who's terrified of putting herself out there again, only to be rejected. I wonder if he sees that, beneath what I show to the world, there's a woman who had her confidence shattered six months earlier, who takes nothing for granted but still wants to fight for her dreams.

I wonder if he knows that somehow, at some point in these last few days, he started to become one of those dreams.

For several long seconds we stare at each other, and then a kid throws a ball that skids between us, splashing me, waking me from the trajectory of my thoughts, like a light-bulb moment except with water and laughing. I kick back from Jagger, a smile on my lips, and float away while he scoops up the ball and tosses it across the pool.

When he comes up beside me again I'm ready. 'The pool is the hub of the accommodation,' I say.

He takes a second but his expression sobers and he nods with mock seriousness. 'Tell me more, Miss Llewellyn.' He tosses a glance over his shoulder, though, towards the setting sun. The sky is morphing from brilliant blue to an equally stunning shade of purple and orange. 'Tell me while you can.'

My stomach rolls at the promise in those words,

but I don't betray a hint of how hard I'm finding it to focus. 'The pool itself was built in the late '90s, in the lead-up to the millennium celebrations. The designers developed it with the coastal views in mind, intending to capitalise on the spectacular location of the resort.'

'Quite,' he drawls, treading water beside me, his powerful legs kicking easily. The sun drops lower; the sky darkens.

'The original pool,' I continue, swallowing my smirk, 'was at the back of the building. Built in the '20s, the full grotto-inspired construction was demolished in the '70s, when modern amenity was valued above...follies.'

'A shame,' he says, and I don't know if he's being serious or not. 'Do you know this much about every property you sell?'

He's watching me intently and my pulse fires in my veins. I wonder that my veins haven't yet given out because this—the way this feels—is putting my body under all kinds of new and different strains. 'Of course I do.'

'You don't think that's...obsessive?'

'I think it's professional,' I fire back, flashing him a quick grin.

'Ah. That word again.' He looks over his shoulder once more. Lower, lower, with gaining momentum, darkness looms.

'Believe it or not, you're one of my least demanding clients,' I say, moving infinitesimally closer to him, drawn to him by the impending night, by the certainty our time is almost upon us.

'Then I'm not working hard enough,' he murmurs.

'I feel like I've asked plenty of you since we got here.' He's not talking about work.

'And given me plenty in exchange.' My voice is breathy. I move away from the double entendre. There can only be a few moments left. Perhaps it's silly to put such stock in an arbitrary delineation but, having given all of myself once before, to someone who found it so insultingly easy to turn his back on me, on all that I am, all that I offered, I take comfort in the idea of being able to hold fast to our intentions. Even as my own are crumbling around me.

'Our company became one of the most prominent bespoke commercial realtors in Sydney in an incredibly short time.' Pride tinges my statement. 'We can't compete with the Duncan & Greys or Matmouths—they have thousands of agents worldwide. But what we do is niche, personalised and tailored to each of our client's needs. We don't waste time—a buyer's or vendor's. Everything we do is deliberate and nuanced.'

He's speculative again, sifting through my words and seeing things that I didn't intend to show. 'You love what you do.'

It's not a question, but I nod. 'Yes.'

'So what next, for you?'

I frown. 'What do you mean?' Darker, darker.

'Gareth comes back from his honeymoon, and you keep working together? Side by side?'

'No.' I shake my head. 'I doubt it.' I don't realise at first why I fight an instinct to tell him about my plans to buy Gareth out. Only comprehension dawns almost immediately. Jagger is integral to that plan—but he shouldn't and can't know that. I'm already worried that we've blurred lines and muddied the waters of what should be a straightforward commercial transaction. I can't add another layer of complexity to that.

'You'd walk away from your business?'

The question surprises me, for the simple reason I hadn't admitted the possibility that I might be the one leaving the company. I shrug my shoulders now, uncertainty shifting through me. 'If I had to.'

His eyes are thoughtful. 'And then? What would you do instead?'

'I'd travel,' I say with a twist of my lips. 'I always wanted to, you know. Sydney was only ever supposed to be a stopgap.'

'On your way to?'

'New York.' I sigh romantically but then, when he doesn't say anything, I have a lurching sense inside, like he might think I'm hinting at wanting him to invite me or something. So I rush on. 'London. Tokyo. Just anywhere. See the world, experience it, enjoy it.' I lift a hand to the ends of my hair, toying with them thoughtfully. 'We didn't travel much, growing up. My parents were always saving, saving, saving—they liked to have money put aside for any number of rainy days.'

'And you wanted to?'

'I wanted to travel.' I smile. 'I watched *Sex and the City* and fell in love with Carrie Bradshaw's New York. I've gone on holidays, I've seen some of the world, but if I didn't have the commitment of the business, I'd probably take some time and evaluate what I want to do next.' I shrug. 'It's all academic, anyway.'

He mulls that over. The sun is almost gone. The lights in the pool brighten a little.

'You're so good at this,' he says thoughtfully. 'It would be a waste to walk away from it.'

Pleasure fires through me. 'I don't plan on walking away from it. Yet.'

Something flickers across his face, an emotion I can't fathom, but then darkness falls—like magic, like a switch has been flicked and the lights of daytime have been turned off, or the curtains have been raised, showcasing the night.

Jagger pounces, like some kind of tiger and I'm his prey—his oh, so willing prey. He pushes through the water, bringing his body to mine, surrounding me, encapsulating me, and I feel his body, the hardness of him against the softness of me, and the heart that has been whispering seductive demands for the last few hours begins to roar, shouting at me to stop being so obtuse and take notice of what's going on.

'The pool is very impressive, Miss Llewellyn,' he says, looking straight into my eyes, so my heart shouts even louder, begging to be heard above the din of my desire and the rushing of my heated blood. 'But I think I've seen all I need to now.'

'Are you sure?' I can't resist teasing. 'Because there's a lovely walk we could do, to the silver dunes…'

His eyes flare and he pushes me gently through the water so my back connects with the edge of the pool and his whole body traps me there. His eyes lock to mine and there is fierce determination in his gaze. 'If we don't go upstairs right now I'm going to ignore the fact there are families all around and strip you naked right here.'

Pleasure pounds against me; my heart fails.

'I just have to send some emails,' I say, my smile making it obvious I'm joking.

He grins but dips his head forward, sucking my lip between his teeth before dropping his mouth to my shoulder, where the darkness of his kiss lingers. 'I'll make you pay for that, Grace.'

I tremble as his hands creep inside the elastic of my bathers, curving over my naked arse. 'Do you promise?'

He lifts his head so his eyes meet mine and when he nods I feel the force of his promise, his guarantee, and I feel as though I've stepped off the edge of the world. I have no idea if there's any kind of safety net; I'm in free fall, but Jagger's there and somehow that makes it all right.

I follow him as he steps out of the pool, with the worrying certainty I would follow him anywhere he asked me to…

CHAPTER ELEVEN

SHE WATCHES ME as she strips her bathers from her wet, shining body, her eyes holding mine with some kind of challenge and promise mingled in her gaze. A challenge I can't answer because I don't understand it. I watch her strip her bathers from her body, down her legs, over her feet, feet that—as a sign of how much I want this woman—I find completely erotic.

She crouches down to lift her wet bathers from the carpet and, still watching me, carries them towards the bathroom, hooking them over the shower screen. I watch but I do not move. I don't move because I'm not sure I can. My feet are planted to the ground, my dick growing ever harder, my whole body alert and ready.

She woke me up by tracing the outline of my cock with her tongue and ever since then I've been tense, aching for her, aching to dip myself inside her, to feel her mouth, her flesh, her body absorbing me; I've been anxious to own her, all of her.

Her eyes are locked to mine as she moves back towards me, the only light in the room coming from the subtle lines that run across the cabinets. I have an urge to flick every light in the room on, to light her up, to fill this room with white so I can see her properly, all of her, every line, every indent, every mark, so I can see her face as I possess her, see her pleasure wrap through her, see her face as she breaks apart.

Her fingers on my hips are tentative. She slides them into the waistband of my bathing shorts and pushes them down my hips, still looking at me, looking at me as she bends down, crouching slowly, bringing the shorts to the floor and staying where she is, at my feet, her eyes on mine.

My dick is right there and deliberately she moves her attention to it, and I hold my breath. I hold it until I may possibly pass out. I still hold it when she brings her mouth to my tip and runs her tongue over me. I hold my breath as she widens her mouth and her eyes lance mine as she takes me in, deep, as deep as she can. I feel the back of her throat and now I release my breath in one sharp hiss, an expletive somewhere in there, too. My hands twitch by my sides. I hold them there, even when I want to lift them to her hair, to feel its wet ends in my fingertips. I stand there, legs apart, watching her move her mouth up and down my length, her breasts jerking with each movement, the curve of her arse visible to my devoted inspection.

Her hand lifts up, finding my balls, and she holds them then moves to the base of my cock, squeezing it as her tongue licks my tip again, and self-control—something I pride myself on—wanes. I shudder as I almost spill into her mouth and I pull back, not ready

to come, not ready to end this. As fucking amazing as
her mouth is, I need to be deep inside her sex right now.

Right now.

I swear again and reach for her, lifting her under her
arms, higher, wrapping her around my body and pushing her against the desk, a narrow piece of wood locked
to the wall. It's just enough space to give her arse some
purchase. I thrust into her hard and she cries out, digging her nails into my back, but she shakes her head and
says my name in a way that is serious—serious enough
to pause me even when I'm so close to exploding.

'Condom,' she grunts, her hands running over my
chest like she can't stop touching me.

Fuck.

Condom.

'I'm sorry.' I am. I *always* practise safe sex. I spin
away, moving with alacrity to the side table and pulling
out a rubber, sliding it over my length. Even that motion makes me jerk and spasm and I grind my teeth—
no way am I going to tip myself over the edge. I need
more of her and I need to see her come, I need to feel the
force of her orgasm. Within seconds I'm back, spreading her legs, dropping my mouth to hers and kissing her
as I thrust deep inside of her, balls-deep, and her tight
muscles squeeze around me, promising me heaven on
earth, promising me a delivery to some kind of magical, mystical bliss.

'I love this,' I groan into her mouth, and she stills
before kissing me back, harder, fiercer, and pushes her
body forward, so I lift her up off the desk, kissing her,
my cock deep inside her, carrying her to the bed where

I drop her down and fuck her as though this is my purpose on earth.

I hold her as she comes, crying my name at the top of her lungs, and I laugh even when I'm burning up with pleasure, I laugh because her passion is unbelievable, and because it reminds me of the first night we were together when we both lost our heads completely.

That night—when I thought I'd never see her again. The way I woke up and reached for her and felt a kind of murderous rage at her desertion.

My smile spreads as finally I give in to my body's needs and push into her and hold myself there, riding the wave, coming hard. I had no idea it wasn't the last time we'd be together. I had no idea I'd have three more nights of her, of this.

And this, our last night, is one I'm going to make count. Day will break and this will end, but until then there's me, her and the perfection of this kind of arrangement. No strings, no promises, no future, no hurt.

It's late. Or early. Some time near three. I'm exhausted. So tired I might almost be delirious, and yet I can't sleep. My eyes are heavy…my mind is overactive. Jagger, beside me, is silent, his body still, save for the regular rise and fall of his chest.

Am I stupid to still be lying here?

Should I go back to my room?

Maybe.

But hours remain, and I don't want to squander them when I'm not absolutely certain what I need to be doing.

I push up quietly, sliding out of bed, moving to the

kitchenette near the front door. Gently, I lift the kettle off its base, shaking it for water. There's enough. I replace it and flick the button.

'Can't sleep?' His voice rumbles towards me, so sexy, breathing through my bones and body into my cells and blood, my DNA.

'Nope.' I turn around, a smile on my lips, but it's a smile that feels heavy and somehow sad. 'I guess I had all the sleep I need.'

A muscle jerks in his jaw, like he's grinding his teeth, and the silence that falls isn't companionable so much as it throbs with awareness. Maybe it's the direction of my thoughts, perhaps it conveys itself in my body, because there's an awkwardness that only the uncertainty of the morning can explain.

Is it uncertainty, though? When we both know 'goodbye' is on the horizon?

I've been in relationships before that I know are going nowhere. I've been with men that I either like or desire but don't want more with than a casual fling. And I've never felt this sense of drowning, of suffocation, of being caught in the folds of time.

'Would you like a tea?'

He shakes his head. 'No.'

His eyes linger on my face. I turn away from him, put a teabag in a mug and slosh in water. I reach for a small pot of milk from the fridge.

'If you were to buy the resort,' I say thoughtfully, not sure where the question comes from but knowing I need to ask it, 'how involved would you be in the running of it?'

I don't look at him because, as I ask it, I hear the question and I know what it sounds like—as though I'm looking for more from him than either of us ever agreed to.

'I'll oversee all aspects.' Something like hope lifts inside me. 'From New York.' He says the last three words quietly, and I'm sure he knows that my hopes have been pinned on him becoming, somehow, for a while, more local, more accessible to me.

I've been burned by Gareth, burned by love. I have no way of articulating what I would even do if Jagger were to start spending more time here, in Australia. I know only that the door would be open, that possibilities would be there.

Possibilities for what?

I don't want a relationship. I have to get my business sorted—the last thing I should be thinking about is any kind of ongoing situation with Jagger.

And yet...

Tomorrow we'll fly back to Sydney, and then what? He'll jet out of my life? Sure, we'll have to negotiate the contracts, but he'll never touch me again? Kiss me again? Fuck me like his life depends on it?

It makes no sense, even though I know it's how it has to be.

'So you'll have someone here, locally?'

His frown is barely detectable in the soft lighting of the room. 'I'll move my global director of operations out here for a few months to get a feel for it.' He shrugs. 'She'll appoint the corporate and management team.'

It's all so sensible. So final.

I try to take comfort from the fact he's talking more definitely about the purchase—I *will* move, not I *would* move. That bodes well for the sale, at least. If I can't have Jagger, *not that I want him*, I can at least comfort myself with the company that has years of my blood, sweat and tears poured into it.

'Come back to bed.' He pats the space beside him. I follow his gaze, my heart pumping faster, moving blood around my body as best it can. I have a thousand questions, thoughts that need to find expression, but none are more imperative than my body's need to be with his. To fuck him, yes, but also to fall asleep tucked in the crook of his arm, so close I can feel his heart beating in time with my own.

The morning light in this part of the world is different to my own. New York sunrises have more pink and more haze. There's something dramatic and clear about the way the sun bursts over this ocean, casting glitter and light on its aquamarine surface. As dawn gives way to full-blown morning, I turn to look at her one last time.

She's fast asleep, her hair curved over her cheek, her breathing rhythmic.

My stomach tightens; our time is almost up.

She'll go back to Sydney this morning and I'll head back to the States, to New York, to Brinkley, my life.

I run my eyes over her body, savouring every dip of her flesh, every curve and undulation. I let my mind absorb every detail, committing her to memory, because once my jet takes off and I leave Australian air space, this is over. Done with.

No more Grace Llewellyn.

And I hate that.

I hate the idea of walking away from her. I hate the idea of never seeing her again. And you know what I hate most of all? The idea that some other guy's going to see her, meet her, make her laugh in that way she has, so sweet and sexy. That some other guy's going to peel her clothes from her body and make love to her, make her scream his name.

But this feeling of possession is just that—and it's beneath me, and not worthy of her. She *deserves* to meet a great guy. Someone who believes in marriage and all the shit someone like Grace should have. Someone who'll make her realise Gareth was an A-grade arse-wipe to choose someone else over her. Someone who'll make her feel like she deserves that perfect future.

Someone who believes in perfect futures—the opposite of me, then.

It's a sticky, warm day, the humidity causing my cotton dress to stick to my back. I sip my coffee, barely tasting it.

I'm numb.

I've made myself numb.

Since we left the room half an hour ago, pretending like everything's normal, coming down to the restaurant for breakfast and coffee, I've been biting back what I want to say. I've been tamping down on a ridiculous urge to ask him to stay. A while longer. Just a little while longer.

And you know why I don't?

Because I know it won't be enough.

I don't want him to stay another week. Or another month. I don't want there to be a time limit on this.

It scares the crap out of me to think I want anything from Jagger because we had a deal, and it was so simple. So very simple! Sex: easy, walk-away-when-we're-done sex.

I sip my coffee again, my heart splintering.

I feel like I've wasted so much of our time together. My insistence that we stick to work during the day seems juvenile now, and so limiting. Because there's so much more I want to know about Jagger! So much I held back from asking because I told myself questions didn't belong in a temporary relationship.

I lift my eyes to his; he's watching me.

My heart feels like it's got a stitch, right in the middle.

I don't want you to go yet.

The words rush through my brain, my mouth, but I don't utter them and I think, as the world descends further, faster, that I know why. Gareth walked away from me like I meant nothing to him—like our two years together meant nothing.

And Jagger's going to do the same. It's only been a few nights, but this—what we share—is so different to anything I've ever known. This kind of connection is powerful and seducing, completely drugging.

But if he doesn't feel it too, then it's just the same as what happened with Gareth. He's just another guy I want more from than he's prepared to give. He's just another guy I care for more than he cares for me.

My stomach rolls.

'You okay?'

I'm not. I don't just want *more* from Jagger than he's willing to give—I want all of Jagger.

I've fallen in love with him. I have no idea how or when, nor how damned stupid I could be, but, somewhere between the sex and the Greek god tattoos and the sex and opening my soul to his inspection, I've fallen in love with the guy I thought I agreed just to have casual sex with.

And I'm almost positive he doesn't love me back.

It's Gareth all over again, but so much worse.

I swallow, the sting of tears on my eyelids coming at the worst possible time. No way will I give in to them! I dip my head forward, blinking furiously, then force a smile to my face.

My heart cracks.

His eyes drop to my mouth and then he looks away, a muscle jerking in the base of his jaw, his expression tight.

And something like hope bursts through me. Is it *possible* he feels the same way I do? That this, us, our time together, has come to mean more than he thought it would?

Is it possible he feels the same way for me?

And now the world is wildly off its axis, and there's a humming in my ears that demands attention.

He shifts his head, angling it back to me, and swallows, his Adam's apple bobbing with the movement.

'I'll have my lawyer be in touch with an offer by the end of the week. Will that work for you?'

The world stops spinning. His words come to me as

if from a long way away. I frown instinctively, taking a minute to catch up.

'I…thought you were insisting on negotiating with me?'

He shakes his head slowly. 'I'll offer what they're asking. There's no need for negotiations.' His smile doesn't reach his eyes. 'You've done an excellent job, Grace.'

His praise doesn't even touch the sides of my heart. I stare at him, the finality of his words cutting through me. Panic makes breathing difficult.

'Thank you.'

He's going to leave. I'm going to catch a cab to the airport and he's going to fly out later, and I'm never going to see him again.

Darkness descends on my mind; hope gives way to grim acceptance. This is what he wants.

And what about what I want? My heart is insistent, becoming enraged. I told Gareth I didn't care about marriage, even when deep down I did. He left me and got engaged to someone else and I told him it was fine, we could keep working together, when it wasn't. How is it that someone like me, who's so determined and *good* at what I do professionally, is so bad at the personal life stuff?

I don't want Jagger to go.

I don't want him to leave.

I want him to choose to stay.

But if I don't at least tell him how I feel, I know I'm going to regret it for the rest of my life. And I'm done with regrets, with wondering and worrying.

'Jagger…' I place the coffee cup in the saucer and shake my head. It isn't the time and place for this. 'Can you come to my room when you're done here? I'm just going to go up and get a head start on packing.'

He frowns. 'You've hardly eaten.'

'I just wanted a coffee.' I stand, scraping the chair back. 'See you soon?'

His eyes pierce my soul for a long moment and then he nods, just a jerk of his head. 'Ten minutes.'

Ten minutes. Great. I feel like the executioner's blade is inching its way downwards—all that's left is for me to be brave and accept that soon my head may be rolling away.

CHAPTER TWELVE

'WHAT IF YOU don't go back to New York today?'

Wow. Okay. So I thought I'd at least let the door to my hotel room shut before blurting it out and, going by the look of complete shock that crosses his face, I should have prefaced this with a little softening pre-amble.

I didn't.

The words are out there and I have a plane to catch. Life's too short to delay. I'm not going to be the same woman I was with Gareth, pretending I was okay with something that really I wasn't.

'As opposed to?' he asks guardedly, watchful. Wary.

Shit.

Wariness is not good. It doesn't exactly scream, *Hoorah! Let's be together for ever.*

I take a breath, trying to compose my thoughts. 'What if you were to stay in Sydney a bit longer?'

He lifts a brow, saying nothing, waiting for me to fill the silence.

'And what if I were to come to New York on my next holiday? And then you were to come back here for a while?' He's looking at me like I'm asking him to sacrifice his mother to the devil.

I want to curl up in a ball and disappear, but I've come too far. 'What if we were to go back and forth a while? And talk on the phone. And keep having sex. And keep being in each other's lives. Not just sex, but everything. What if we were to actually see what this is, beyond just a few nights?'

He swallows, standing completely still, his eyes running over my face.

'What you're suggesting sounds a hell of a lot like a long-distance relationship.'

I nod once. 'I guess it does.'

His eyes soften. There's sympathy in his expression. Not joy. Not delight. 'Neither of us wants that.'

'Oh, really?' I prompt, my smile lacking humour. 'I thought that's exactly what I want, hence the fact I've brought it up in this awkward as arse conversation.'

He laughs then, but it's more a sound of rebuke.

'This has been more than I expected, Grace. Sleeping with you… I mean, it's blown my mind. I love being with you. But we both knew what we wanted. It's been great.'

'But now it's over,' I finish for him, wondering if saying the words should somehow make it easier to accept.

He compresses his lips. 'Don't do this.'

'Do what?'

'Act like we both didn't know it was coming to this.'

'I did. We both did. I thought I just wanted…a few days. Fucking you, forgetting him.'

His jaw tightens.

'But the idea of never seeing you again is making me feel ill. You can't say you don't feel the same.'

He shakes his head, looking past me and, even though he's not speaking or reacting, he's angry—I can just tell. 'Do I want to see you again?' He drags his hand through his hair and then looks at me, his eyes brimming with frustration and impatience. 'Sure. I want to see you again.'

My stomach scrunches.

'I want to cancel my flight and drag you to bed right now, fuck you until I can't see straight, listen to you shouting my name, listen to you come, watch you die a thousand deaths of pleasure.' He shakes his head. 'But then what? What next? When does it end?'

Be brave. 'Who says it has to end?'

He swears under his breath. 'That right there's the problem. You want the happily-ever-after fairy tale—and you deserve that—but I'm not the guy to give it to you. I'm not that guy.' He says it again, emphatically, shaking his head for added conviction. 'I've probably never been that guy and, even if I was, even if there was a shred of me that believed in all that crap, my marriage woke me up to the real world.'

'I'm not your ex-wife.' My voice trembles a little. 'I don't want your money. I don't want anything except *you*.'

'You want me to give up my life and move here, to be with you. You want me to be someone who believes in weddings and marriage and babies and growing old together, swinging on some porch seat.'

A fine blade seems to be jabbing under my ribs,

running along the edge of my heart. 'I want you to be that—for me.'

His eyes narrow. 'You want me to be what your ex wasn't.'

'He *is* that guy.'

He shakes his head. 'You want me to make you feel better about yourself. You want to think *someone* wants to marry you.'

'Christ, Jagger, I'm not expecting you to propose. I'm not suggesting we get *married*. I'm just saying I don't want this to be over.'

'But you want marriage, babies, the works. And I'm telling you, I'm not capable of giving that to you.'

And it's like my skin is being ripped off my body because he's saying exactly what Gareth said, before he fell head over heels in love with someone else and married her.

Jagger is saying he doesn't want to settle down, but is it really just that he doesn't want to settle down with me?

Tears sting my eyelids now. 'Why not?'

'Pick a reason!' he snaps, and then softens his voice. 'I don't *want* that, Grace.'

'Not with me?'

'Not with anyone.' He moves closer, bringing his body to mine, his strong, powerful body. 'You're an incredible woman. I have loved getting to know you, and I wish you every bit of success in this world. I want you to get everything you want in life—your business, your future with some guy who shares the same dreams you do.'

'But that's not you.' I nod slowly.

There's a pause, a tortured beat, and then a shake of

his head. He drops his forehead to mine and a sob escapes from me before I can stop it.

'God, Grace, don't,' he pleads with me. 'Don't cry. Don't let me be the reason you're crying.'

I shake my head, denying it silently.

'The last thing I want is to hurt you.'

'You haven't,' I groan truthfully. 'This isn't your fault.'

His lips are so close to mine. My body is charged with some kind of electrical energy. I keep my eyes shut, trying to level off my breathing.

'I'm an asshole.' He drops his mouth, buzzing the words to mine. 'I should never have let this happen.'

'It's not your fault.'

'I knew this wasn't just sex. I knew it was more than that. I should have kept it to one night. The second you got on my plane, I should have controlled this situation.'

If it's more than just sex, how come he's still pushing me away?

'I don't want to get involved with anyone, least of all you.'

'Why not?'

He reaches up, disentangling my arms, arms I didn't even realise I'd wrapped around his neck.

'Because I don't believe in love,' he says stiffly, his eyes rebuking me silently. 'I think it's just a construct, something we're told to strive for that exemplifies the pinnacle of human togetherness. I think *sex* is as good as it gets, as honest as it gets.'

It hurts, but it's something.

'Then stay for the sex,' I say simply, moving closer to

him, knowing I'm compromising more than I can probably bear, but that it's better than losing him altogether. 'Stay because the sex between us is like something elemental. Stay because you want to keep sleeping with me.'

'And you'd be okay with that?' he prompts, his eyes scanning my face, calling me on the weakness in my plan, on the fatal flaw to what I'm suggesting. 'You'd actually accept that kind of relationship?'

I open my mouth, then close it again. 'I don't want to lose you.'

His eyes shut. 'I'm not yours to lose.'

God. It hurts. So badly. I stagger backwards a little, spinning around to cover the involuntary movement.

'And I'm not going to be some other guy who uses you for what he wants. I was very clear about all this from the beginning.'

He was. Panic is making it hard to breathe. 'I know.'

'And so were you. This was just a few days' fun, before we get back to the real world.'

'Not to me.' I whisper the words.

'What?'

'Not to me.' Braver this time, louder. 'I fell in love with you, Jagger.' I spin around, my gaze defiantly latching to his. 'I fell head over heels in love with you, somewhere in these last few days. So go back to New York if you want to. Get on your private jet and fly off into the sunset or whatever, but don't kid yourself that we're just two people who've been sleeping together.'

He groans softly, rocking back on his heels, his expression sheened with emotions I can't comprehend. 'We're not.'

Thank God.

'But sex is all I want, it's all I can give. I like you, Grace. I think you're… Fuck. I think you're amazing. I am blown away by your determination, your grace, your courage, your strength, your brain—your mind is unbelievable. I love talking to you, laughing with you. I want to punch your fuckwit ex for what he did to you. I know it's not just sex between us. But I'm no more… interested in a relationship than I was a week ago. And I'm sure as hell not any better suited to one.'

'I think you're being too hard on yourself,' I say, desperate for him to relent. 'I think you'd make an amazing partner. Boyfriend, fiancé, husband—whatever. I think you're not your dad or your mum, and that you shouldn't let your ex-wife define you. So your marriage ended. It was a mistake. Your brothers knew it; they tried to warm you. You learned the hard way. Are you going to insulate yourself from the likelihood of any happiness, going forward, because it carries with it the possibility of regret?'

'Stop psychoanalysing me,' he grunts, shaking his head. 'You don't know anything about me.'

'Bullshit,' I drawl. 'You're an open book to me now, Jagger. I've seen all your secrets and wants. I *know* you. You don't get to wind back the time we've spent and act as if we're two strangers.'

'I'm not.' He's angry. His voice is loud. 'I'm not trying to diminish a damned thing. I'll give it to you—I'll give it to you that these last few days have…defied every single one of my expectations. *You* have defied every one of my expectations. But that doesn't change who I am and what I want in life.'

'And you want to be alone?'

A muscle jerks in his cheek. 'I want to be alone,' he agrees after a beat too long.

'Apart from one-night stands with women you're never going to see again.' God, the idea of that sickens me now. He's mine. I can't abide that notion.

'Yes.' He glares at me and, even though we're not touching and a room full of acrimony separates us, I feel his racing heart as though each beat is causing reactions in the atmosphere. 'Is that what you want me to say, Grace? That I'm going to go back to New York and fuck someone else? That I'm going to take some other woman to bed to forget you?'

I draw in a breath—it burns my lungs. Tears spring to my eyes and I see recognition cross his face, recognition that he's gone too far. He swears and moves his strong, powerful legs, striding across the room and bundling me up, lifting me to his body, kissing me, tasting the tears in my mouth.

'I'm sorry,' he says against me, but I don't know what he's sorry for. That I fell in love with him despite every caution not to do so? Or because he was speaking the truth a second ago? Because his beautiful body is going to belong to someone else in a matter of days. Because I'm not losing him—it's so much worse than that—I never really had him.

He kisses me as though both of our futures are depending on this kiss. His is a kiss of atonement and mine is one of dreadful acceptance. Of weary comprehension.

I fell in love with another man who doesn't want me,

but this is so much worse. Where Gareth and I made some kind of calm, rational sense, where I *liked* Gareth and cautiously discovered what I could about him before deciding I *loved* him, it wasn't like that with Jagger.

This wasn't a conscious decision. Rather, it stole upon me. He breathed into my body when I wasn't watching, like a spell or a curse, and he's become a part of me now. So that even when he leaves and I'm alone again I think he'll always be a part of me.

But that won't stop him from leaving.

I kiss him goodbye and then wrench my head away, putting space between us with a guttural cry.

'This was so much more to me than sex.' I say it because it's true and because, no matter what happens next, I want him to understand that I truly fell for him, that my love is genuine. 'I fell in love with you a little bit more every time we were together. Every movement of yours inside me, every kiss, every shared breath. I fell in love with you when you told me about your brothers and your parents and your ex-wife, about your life in New York and Brinkley.' My voice cracks. 'I fell in love with you while we dived in the reef, when you tried to teach me to play golf—badly. I fell in love with you when I was determined I wouldn't, when I was absolutely certain I was done with love. At least for now. I fell in love with you because something about this, about us, is bigger than what either of us *want*. I fell in love with you because I had no choice.'

He stares at me for several long, painful seconds.

'I think you love me, too,' I surprise myself by saying, soft condemnation in my words. 'I just think you're either too stubborn or too afraid to admit it.'

Silence.

Heavy, painful, accusing silence.

'You're wrong.' His expression shifts and I don't know if he's lying to himself or if I'm completely mistaken. 'I think you're amazing, but that's not love.'

'You say you don't believe in love, so how do you know?'

'Because I know it wouldn't feel like this.'

I'm being sliced in two.

'I've done all this before, Grace. I've looked into a woman's eyes and smiled and told her I loved her, swore I'd love her for ever. In front of my friends, my brothers, everyone I know, I've pledged to be with her until death us do part. And it fell apart. I've done this. I've looked into a woman's eyes as she told me she loved me, as she told me she'd always love me. And it was all a crock of bull. So don't stand there and expect me to be jumping for joy because you're saying you feel… that. For me. I don't want it. I don't want this. We had a deal, remember? Sex. Easy, no pain, no emotions. Sex.'

I remember. I remember even when it's killing me.

Gareth walked away from me like I meant nothing, and Jagger's telling me exactly the same thing.

I'm not enough to stay for. Not enough to even *try*. I feel his pain; of course I do. I feel his hurt, the fact he's had his heart broken, his trust crushed. But I'm not Lorena and if he doesn't see that, if he can't see how different I am to her and what we feel is to what they shared, then what hope do I have?

I tilt my chin defiantly even when I think all my bones are breaking into tiny, crumbling pieces. 'Then go.'

I glare at him, waiting.

There's silence.

'You don't need to go to the airport for another hour.'

I jerk my head in a tiny acknowledgement of his words.

'Don't let it end like this,' he growls, jamming his hands into his pockets. 'We've had too much fun for it to finish with an argument.'

'Fun?' I spit, the asinine description of what we've shared rankling more than just about anything.

'Yes, fun! Goddamned fun! Like we both wanted, like we both needed. What's wrong with that?'

Because it's not enough any more. The idea of having a no-strings fling with Jagger is so absurd, so hugely out of step with what we are.

'You think this is fun?'

'Not right now, I don't.'

I ignore him. 'You honestly think you're going to fly off into the sky and carry on your life? That you won't miss me, this, us?'

He stares at me and I feel the pain bursting through him, too. Damn it! I'd bet almost anything on him wanting to stay, on him being in love with me.

But he's too damned stubborn, his own past making admitting that impossible, and my own past making me too wary to push him. I'm done with men who don't truly want me as much as I want them.

He shakes his head slowly, and it's the final drop of

the blade. 'I'm sorry,' he says again, frowning, stepping backwards.

Fuck.

'Just go.'

He nods, his eyes locked to mine. 'You deserve better than me. Better than him.'

'Just go.' It's a plaintive whisper. I need him to leave so I can cry—properly.

I pull the door to my apartment shut and slump against it. I think it must be about eight o'clock. Maybe closer to nine.

My body is heavy, my mind more so.

Eleven days since I returned from the Whitsundays. Nine days since Jagger's lawyer emailed the contracts over. Eight days since Orion Karakedes accepted.

Five days since I offered to buy Gareth out of our business.

Four days since he agreed, even when he told me he didn't want this, that he didn't want us to ruin what we'd built.

Four days since I told him to stop being such an arrogant arse. I'm not going to ruin what we built; I'm going to make it stronger.

Better.

All on my own.

On my own.

I straighten, grabbing a glass of water as I pass the kitchen, collapsing on the sofa and staring at the television screen—it's dormant, the pixels resting. I can make out my vague reflection, the pale suit I wear today showing like a smudge, my blonde hair like gold.

Eleven days since Jagger walked out of my hotel room and I slumped to the floor, the reality of my situation abundantly clear.

I did love him.

I loved him in a way that was shredding my soul to bits, that was burning me inside, that was making me feel like I couldn't stand up straight.

This is so different to when things fell apart with Gareth. If there's one thing to be grateful for in this mess, it's the realisation that what I shared with Gareth wasn't love. Not the kind of love that reaches inside of you and rearranges who you are. Not the kind of love that breathes fire into your cells and freedom into your bones.

Is that what I had with Jagger?

I close my eyes, blocking out my doppelgänger, my apartment, my life, my *now*.

I did.

It was.

It really was.

His failure to understand that doesn't change what we felt. His inability to love me doesn't make the love I felt any less real, any less potent.

It's love.

I love him.

I love him, but that's not enough.

He doesn't love me—not in the same way I do him. Because on no planet, at no time and in no way would I have ever been able to walk away from him like he did me.

I would never have been able to turn my back on him, to see his face crumple, to hear his proclamation of love and act as though it changes nothing.

I would never have compared him and me to me and Gareth. The idea that he told Lorena he loved her, that he said to her what he might have said to me, that he felt for her what I wanted him to feel for me?

Repugnant.

He didn't love me. He doesn't love me.

I don't doubt he's been with another woman since me. Someone else has worshipped at the altar of Zeus, has lost her mind to his prowess and power. It's been eleven days, and he's Jagger Hart after all.

Nausea surfs my insides. I ignore it, rolling onto my side and squeezing my eyes closed. And, just like every night since I got back to Sydney, I sleep like the dead.

I sleep until dawn and then I go into the office despite it being Sunday and I focus on work, on my future—on a future that is just about me—and I force myself not to think about Jagger.

Not to think of him, not to wonder about him—to remember that he walked away from me just like Gareth did.

I force myself not to think about the fact I looked my nightmare in the face—and lost.

CHAPTER THIRTEEN

'YOU SAID IT'S GOOD?'

I blink, focusing on Theo, bringing myself back to the present. 'Yeah.'

'More than you expected?' He's staring at the golf course, the aerial shot showcasing it at dawn, the pale oranges and purples streaking across the sky.

'The property has a shitload of potential,' I say, my eyes shifting over the course, remembering Grace, the way her body backed into mine as I showed her how to swing the golf club.

But no memory of Grace is complete without the final one—the look of utter devastation on her face. Of destruction. Of brokenness. No memory of her can be enjoyed for its warmth and completeness when that hard edge of pain and hurt is right there, waiting to be remembered, to remind me what I did to her.

'I've heard good things.' Theo straddles the seat opposite me, his dark hair pulled up in a messy bun on top of his head. He hasn't shaved in at least a week and stubble has turned into a full beard. His Greek heritage is so apparent.

I mull his sentence over, but don't speak. I guess you could say I'm brooding. I've been brooding since I walked out of her hotel room, back to mine and slammed the door so hard a painting slid off the wall.

I flew back here telling myself I'd done the right thing. I flew back here so fucking angry at Grace for taking what we'd agreed to and trying to turn it into something else. I was livid! So fucking angry at her for changing the rules of what we were.

But also so in awe of her.

So in awe of how brave she was to admit how she felt for me, even when her heart was still so raw from that asshole Gareth. She did something I've never really been good at in my private life: she went way out on a limb, bracing herself for whatever my response was, knowing she needed to at least be honest with me.

She risked her own heart, even after what Gareth did to her.

And I walked away, just like I told her I would.

'You getting Samson to run it?'

I drag myself back to this conversation, to Theo, to this moment in time and try not to think about the fact it's been almost a month since I left Australia.

How is she?

Those words run through my mind every day, like a whispered invocation. *How is she? How is she? How is she?*

I wake up in the middle of the night, clutching at my chest, feeling like someone's punched me hard in the gut, winding me, robbing me of breath. And then I remember.

I'm not under attack.

I haven't been hurt.

I'm just missing Grace.

I'm missing her so much it's become a physical pain.

'Dude. What the fuck? You're miles away.'

'Samson, yeah.' I pour a Scotch. 'You want?'

He shrugs. 'Sure.'

I slosh some into a tumbler. It's good. Spiced, aged, heavy. I savour the flavour as it hits my belly.

'So?' Theo's watching me. 'What's going on?'

Defensiveness curls around me.

I can't talk to Theo about this.

About Grace.

I can't have him tell me I'm being an arse. Or telling me I did the right thing.

I don't need someone else in my head giving me their opinion on my life.

'Nothing.'

His laugh is throaty. 'Yeah, I can see that.'

Fuck. 'Get out of my head, Theo.'

'But it's such a fun place to be.' Sarcasm trips off his tongue easily.

I cradle the Scotch in my palm, staring out at Manhattan.

I wanted to travel. I watched Sex and the City *and fell in love with Carrie Bradshaw's New York.'*

'Samson'll probably want to revamp aspects of the club,' I hear myself say, like I'm my normal self, focused on business, totally unfazed by anything.

'Sure.' Theo's not convinced.

Great.

'This is about the wedding, right?'

I frown. 'What wedding?'

'Lorena's? I got the invitation last night.'

'Lorena's getting married?'

Theo's watching me like a hawk.

'To Thomas Scott-Moore.'

I laugh softly. 'They deserve each other.'

'He'll just have to get her to position his Zimmer frame before they fuck.'

I shake my head. 'He's worth a bomb.'

'That's all she cares about.' I nod slowly. Theo's right—but we've discussed Lorena's failings ad nauseam. 'I still can't believe you gave her such a generous settlement in the divorce.'

'It was worth it to make her go away.'

'Then Lorena's not the reason you're walking around like it's doomsday. So what's going on?'

'Nothing.' I'm impatient now. Talking about Grace isn't going to help. It's not going to cover over this hole that's developed in the region of my chest that makes me feel as though my soul's being drained into the sidewalk.

'Bullshit.'

He's like a dog with a bone. 'Have you spoken to Holden?'

Theo makes a noise of exasperation. 'Nice subject change.'

I don't smile. I can't. I stare out at the city and imagine Grace in it. I imagine her smile as she looks up at the high-rises on a night like this, with snow falling gently from the sky, swirling its way to the ground. I imagine the wonderment on her face, the look of amazement. I imagine lifting her up, holding her to my chest and kissing her right in the middle of Times Square, surrounded by noise and bustle and action in every direction.

I imagine bringing her to my penthouse, laying her on the crisp black sheets of my bed, her skin and hair so pale in comparison, and it's all I can do not to double in half. Needs and desire threaten to cut me off at the knees.

What I *need* is to get laid.

Katrina from downstairs would probably be up for it. But am I?

The thought of kissing another woman is anathema to me. Making love to one even more so.

It's Grace I miss. Grace I want to hold tight and lose myself inside. Grace I want to hear screaming my name at the top of her lungs.

But I can't go back into her life just because I want to fuck her. That wouldn't be fair on her.

'He's in Amsterdam,' Theo says after a moment.

The certainty that I've been a pretty average brother to Holden makes me cringe inwardly. 'He's okay?'

'I imagine he'll survive,' Theo drawls. 'He's gone into some kind of existentialist crisis about not being a true Hart.'

'Oh, for fuck's sake. Who gives a shit about blood? He's our brother.'

'Have you told him that?' Theo's eyes are intent when they lock to mine. Guilt rumbles through me.

'No.'

'You should. He's spent almost three decades believing we're his brothers and Dad was his dad and now he's grappling with this bombshell. His mother's dead, he has no idea who his biological father is and the two guys he thinks of as brothers aren't even related.'

'Bullshit. We'll always be his brothers.'

'I know that and you know that but he's having difficulty accepting it. He's brooding all over Keizersgracht, frankly wishing he hadn't been born.'

Silence descends, a silence of worry and sorrow. Our father made many decisions in his life that seem beyond comprehension. He was selfish and self-serving, so choosing to raise another man's son as his own makes very little sense.

I let out a breath. A breath of discontentment. Holden, Grace—it's all one knot in my gut and I can't see a way through any of it. Snow continues to fall, faster now, flurries dancing beyond this office, glimpsed through the enormous windows beyond.

'Anyway, why don't you show it to me?'

I turn around, having zero clue what Theo's talking about.

'The golf course.' His head is dipped, his eyes focused on the picture once more.

My body jerks with something like adrenalin and excitement. The very idea of going back, going to Australia, is like catnip. Because Grace is there. I could see Grace. Hell, she's the realtor selling the damned place. It wouldn't even matter if she didn't want to see me! I could make her come up and show Theo around and then, when we were alone…

What, asshole?

Get her to put aside the fact she gave you her heart and you ripped it into tiny pieces? Ask her to forget the fact she's in love with you, just because you want one more roll in the hay?

'I thought you were working on the Santiago deal?'

'Waiting on a building inspector's report.' He waves a hand through the air nonchalantly. The South American project is huge; Theo's been working on it for three years and he's almost got it over the line. 'It's going to be a week or so before I can do anything there.'

I don't have to let her know. We could fly in, have a look around and fly out. She never needs to know.

My dick jerks angrily in my pants and my stomach rolls with nausea and disgust. Is this what it's come to? Hiding out from a woman I really like just because she had the audacity to fall in love with me?

It's for her own good, though. All of this is for her own good.

'Okay.' The word's reluctant, but I nod. 'Just for a few days.'

'Sure, just for a few days.' He mock salutes. 'You're the boss, Zeus.'

I've seen him behind my eyelids every night, every blink. I've seen him in my memories, my mind's eye. He's imprinted in my field of vision somehow.

I've seen phantoms of him, memories of him, and yet, staring at the picture of him now, my whole body seems to lurch a little sideways.

I glance up, checking where we are. Only a couple

of blocks away from my meeting. I swallow, my gaze
dropping to the phone again.

I follow the official Instagram account for Silver
Dunes. Obviously. I mean, it just makes sense. When
I'm selling a project I get completely absorbed by it—
the operations, the marketing—everything. I need to
know all the details of the place in order to be able to
represent my vendors.

Scrolling through my feed without paying much attention to anything, I scroll past the picture initially. I've
seen phantoms of him a thousand times in the thirty-
one days since he left.

Thirty-one days of seeing him in my mind so often
that I want to slap my forehead just to get him out, just
for a moment.

At first I don't react. I barely register that it's *actually* him and not just an image my mind has thrown up.

I scroll a little backwards in my feed.

And my whole body tenses. Sweat beads on my brow
and my fingers tremble as I lift the phone closer to my
face.

Jagger.

I swallow. My throat remains bone dry. I press my
fingertips to the outside of it, holding it, as though that
will help, all the while staring at the picture. He's not
alone.

To his right is another man of a similar build but
different complexion. Where Jagger is tanned and fair,
with those spectacular green eyes, his friend is big and
muscular, dark, with a thickly stubbled jaw, straight
brows and an aquiline nose. His hair, which must be a

few inches past his shoulders, is pulled up into a messy bun on top of his head. He has tattoos running down one arm, like a sleeve.

J Ryan Hart and Theodore Hart, of Hart Brothers Industries, have spent the last three days discovering all that Silver Dunes has to offer. Be like a Hart and come play on one of the world's most highly rated courses. With this view—(swipe right)

I don't swipe right. I jam my phone back in my bag, my pulse firing out of control. 'Here's fine.' My voice is jerky. I pull cash from my purse and pass it to the driver, opening the door as soon as he's pulled to the side of the road.

I'm still a block from the meeting but I need to walk. I need to walk and calm down, to get my pulse back under control, before I have to be Grace Llewellyn again.

I have to get my head sorted before I can be the most professional version of myself.

My legs are shaking a little as I walk. I get to the corner of the street and then succumb to temptation, pulling my phone out and staring at the picture of him.

He looks…so happy.

My heart drops.

I study his face for any sign of the pain I've been feeling, for any sign that he's been even remotely miserable. There's none. He's tanned, relaxed looking, his hair close-cropped, his clothes impeccable.

I shake my head, sliding the phone away again, lifting my eyes to the intersection. Traffic zips past. I wait for a gap and then push out into it, walking across the road quickly, dipping my head forward.

I'm well prepared for the meeting. I know my stuff. You'd have to: bidding on the commercial sales for one of the hottest high-rises in town takes *nous*. Nous I have in spades.

But my mind isn't on the job.

Not one hundred per cent. Not like it should be.

I get through the meeting. My prospective client is the CEO of a French investment company. He's in his forties, I'd guess, with silver-grey hair, intelligent brown eyes and a nice smile. He seems impressed with my presentation but I'm pretty sure he's not sold.

I need to get him over the line. I want this job.

'Why don't we go for a walk,' I suggest, 'and have a look at the precinct? You can get a feel for some of the other businesses that are thriving here.'

He regards me thoughtfully. 'You have time?'

I realise then it's after six. I shrug. 'All that's waiting for me at home is a half-eaten pizza and a neighbour's cat I'm feeding.'

I smile to make it sound less sad than it is.

'Then that sounds like an excellent idea.'

We stroll through the CBD and I point out recent developments, which shopfronts have recently changed hands and why. I've made it my business to know the commercial landscape of Sydney back to front. I live and breathe this market. Any question he has I know the answer to.

And as we walk and talk I feel like it's closer to being

a done deal. I tell myself I can breathe easy. Landing this client means I'm okay. That I'm still the same person I was before Jagger. Before Gareth left the business.

It means I can do this on my own.

It's after eight by the time we're done. He suggests dinner. I demur. I can't. I can't sit across from another guy—even a client—and share a meal. I'm not ready.

I part company with him and catch the bus home, so tired I feel like I could sleep for a week. I read somewhere that exhaustion is a part of heartbreak. It's the body's way of putting you into a kind of semicomatose state until you've had time to heal, and that absolutely feels like what's happening with me.

I feel that. I feel completely drained of enthusiasm.

Ordinarily, I'd celebrate a night like tonight, but I just don't have it in me.

I'm asleep within ten minutes.

The photo is the first thing I think of the next morning, and it's with renewed irritation. Hurt. Annoyance. He's here, in Australia, at the golf course I sold him, and he hasn't got in touch. Is there a clearer way to show me that he doesn't want a bar of me?

That he doesn't want me?

I mean, I get it.

It's obvious. But it still hurts like hell.

The sunrise is spectacular.

I stare at it as the colours infiltrate the horizon, as pink bleeds into black and the stars twinkle and fade, dipping behind the ocean. There's a boat on the water, a trawler, far out, and even though it's a fishing ship it makes me think of the scuba cruise we did. It makes me think of her.

Grace.

She's everywhere here. Her name's on the breeze, tormenting me, scratching over my body, whipping me with remembered pleasure.

Grace is the air I breathe, the sky I see, the tightness in my body—a tightness that speaks of a longing for which I have no words.

And suddenly, staring out at the water we swam in, the ocean we looked on together, I can't not see her.

I can't be here, in Australia, so close—just a few hours from her, and not… I don't know.

It's selfish. Selfish as all fuck. And stupid, too, because it's been more than a month and maybe she's over me, maybe she's forgotten all about me.

The idea of that is like a knife in my gut.

Fuck.

I grab my wallet and head to the door, calling my assistant as I go, asking her to get the jet readied. It's only as the cab speeds towards the airport that I remember Theo.

Heading to Sydney for the day.

I send the text then switch my phone off. I don't want him to call. I don't want him to ask me why. I'm not ready to discuss it. I think I'm one sane conversation away from being talked out of this stupidity.

Or maybe he wouldn't even try. Maybe he'd chew me out for having left in the first place. I drag a hand through my hair, watching the scenery change outside my window.

The plane's ready when I arrive. I stride onto it, impatient now to see her. Grace is everywhere here, too.

I go into the conference room on autopilot, and see her as she was that first morning, sitting there telling me she'd need guidelines, that if we were going to keep sleeping together it would need to be on her terms.

From the beginning she knew there was danger here, and still she went with it. She was brave, right to the end.

'I fell in love with you, Jagger. I fell head over heels in love with you, somewhere in these last few days... Don't kid yourself that we're just two people who've been sleeping together.'

I hurt her.

I hurt her so badly.

The plane takes off. I stare out of the window, my body still, a rock settled heavily in my gut.

For the whole flight to Sydney, I swear I barely breathe.

I told Bianca I don't want to be interrupted. I have a bucket of coffee, a massive blueberry muffin and a mountain of work to do.

Nonetheless, a little before nine o'clock, my intercom buzzes.

I snatch it up without lifting my head from the brief I'm reading.

'I'm sorry to bother you, Grace.'

I purse my lips. 'That's fine.' My tone says it's not

fine. I've become a little less nice than I used to be. I think Bianca's great and I like her, but I just don't have a lot of room left for civility right now. Even Mum gets short shrift when she calls.

I'm just so tired.

'I have a Mr Hart for you.'

My body goes into a state of shock. Adrenalin floods my system, my mouth fills with the taste of metal. I sit up straighter, reaching my hand out for the phone. 'What line?' The question's breathy. I swallow. I don't want to sound breathy when I speak to him. I want to sound calm. Cool. Unaffected.

Over him.

As if.

'No.' Bianca's voice comes as if from an echo chamber. I surmise she's cupped the receiver. 'He's *here*.'

My heart slams against my ribcage. I swear I feel a rib actually shatter with the force of it. I stand up jerkily, awkwardly, running a hand over my stomach, my thighs, then lifting it to my hair.

'I… Give me a minute.' I replace the handset, pacing out from behind my desk, walking towards the window that shows a glimmer of Sydney Harbour in the distance. I breathe in. Out. In. Out.

Close my eyes and he's there. I see his face. I see him. I feel him like a ghost, wrapping around my body.

I expel a soft breath, trying to calm the flock of seagulls beating their wings against my stomach.

He's here.

Outside my office.

Thirty-four days after walking away from me, he's

back. And, no matter what's brought him here, nothing erases that. Nothing.

With that sobering thought I move across the room, pulling my office door inwards.

But hell.

I'd forgotten.

Not what he looks like, but just…the impact of him. It's more than his Hollywood-handsome face and powerful frame; it's all of him. He has this charisma that's completely compelling.

He's not looking my way. I have a second or two to fortify myself before he turns, his eyes immediately catching mine.

Lightning strikes.

With every single fibre of my being I concentrate on standing where I am, holding my ground, looking as calm as can be when inside I'm quivering.

It's early.

Did he stay in Sydney last night?

The question pops into my mind, out of nowhere.

I dismiss it.

'Mr Hart.' My voice comes out almost completely normal, but I have no doubt hurt shows in my eyes, despite all my efforts.

His expression shifts a little. There's a wariness in his expression, a tightness around his jaw. I look closer.

He's…different. Pale. He looks nervous.

Nervous? Jagger. No way.

'Miss Llewellyn.' His voice is gruff. It pours over me like treacle, stimulating my nerve endings rather than calming them. 'May I come in?'

I want to tell him *no*. I want to tell him to get lost. But of course I don't. With a tight nod I step backwards, gesturing towards my office. I step back even further when he walks past me so we don't touch, but that doesn't stop his woody masculine fragrance from assaulting my nostrils.

My stomach flip-flops.

I click the door shut, blocking out Bianca and the outside world.

He's watching me. Staring at me.

I swallow and move behind my desk, grateful for the distance and physical barrier.

Neither of us speaks, and the silence is profoundly heavy.

Finally, he moves towards me. I stiffen. 'What are you doing here?' The words are dismissive, brimming with my anger and resentment.

He stops walking, standing exactly where he is. 'I came to see you.'

Fuck.

'Well, you've seen me. You can go away again.'

His expression tightens. 'You're pissed.'

I open my mouth to deny it, wishing I could tell him I'm not. That I don't care one way or another what he does with his life. But it's a lie.

'Yes.'

He nods. 'Good.'

'Good?'

'Yeah. You should be pissed.'

I let my breath whoosh out of me. 'I'm so glad I have your approval.'

'I deserve it,' he says, moving a step closer. I glare at him, warning him not to circumnavigate the desk.

'You have no reason for being here,' I murmur, my stomach doing loop the loops, my insides churning. 'And I want you to go.'

His eyes flash with mine and I feel the force of his contradictions, the arguments he wants to wage. But he doesn't. He nods softly then takes another step towards me, bracing his palms on the desk, his body opposite mine.

'I will go, Grace. But first I need to talk to you.'

Alarm bells and hope war with one another. 'I don't want to talk to you.' I drop my gaze to hide the complex knot of emotions I'm navigating.

'Then let me talk,' he says softly, gently, his voice husky, as though he's been up all night.

But I can't do this. Twice I've let myself fall for guys who found it disgustingly easy to turn their backs on what I was offering. I'm not going to let him in again. Maybe I've finally learned my lesson?

'It's been thirty-four days,' I say quietly. 'What could you possibly have to say to me now?'

'Thirty-four days? Is that all?'

I jerk my eyes to his because he sounds as absolutely stunned as I feel. Like his time has been running as slowly as mine. But he has no right to feel like that! This was all his decision.

'You can't be here.'

He lifts a hand, running his fingers through his hair. 'I have to be here.'

I shake my head, making an impatient noise of frustration. 'Stop it. Just stop. Stop acting tortured. Stop acting like you're messed up by this. Just stop.' I come around from behind my desk, bringing my body toe to toe with his.

'You're in Australia. You came to play golf with your brother and then you've come to Sydney. Why? You want to fuck me again? For old times' sake?'

He stands completely still, staring down at me, and anger flashes inside my belly. I lift my hands, pushing at his chest, but he stays completely still. My fingers curl in his shirt and I lift up onto the tips of my toes. 'You want to fuck me right here, on this desk? Meaningless sex while you're in town?'

He's struck mute and I'm thrilled. Thrilled to have confused him, to have made him think. Thrilled to be firing questions at him he can't answer.

I make an angry noise as I crush my lips to his, and my kiss is heated by fury. I push him with my body as I kiss him, and he lets me, stepping backwards, sitting on the edge of my desk, his legs forming a triangle in which I stand. I push at his shirt, lifting it from his pants, my fingers touching his bare hips. 'Is this what you came here for?' I grunt, pulling the shirt so a button flies across the room.

'Grace…'

But I don't let him speak. I don't want him to speak. 'Just shut up!' I say. 'Don't say anything.' I'm crying, salty tears running down my cheeks. 'Just don't talk.'

His breath is raspy, loud, tortured. I don't care. I flick his jeans open, pulling his cock out of his pants, glaring at him, daring him to stop me as I run my hands over its hard length.

'Fuck. I did not come here for this.'

'Shut up,' I say again, so angry, so dark. I kiss him again, using one hand to dislodge my underpants and push them down my legs.

I scramble up onto his lap and now I stop kissing him, I glare at him as I straddle him and take him deep inside me, crying hot, stinging tears as he fills me up. It is madness and it is perfection.

It is some kind of earthly coming together. I stare at him, my pained eyes locked to his as I move my hips. His expression shows me so much but I blot it out. I don't want to think about what he feels or wants. I don't. This is about me.

I'm so damned angry.

I dig my nails deep into his shoulders and then I'm coming, so hard, so fast, so completely. My orgasm spirals through me and I tilt my head back, groaning quietly, keeping my voice low as pleasure arrows through my nerves.

I feel like I've been flooded with blinding light. I am glittering silver.

My lungs work hard to keep air pumping through my body and then I lift my head up, looking at him once more.

'Is that what you came for?' I ask, despite the fact he hasn't come. That doesn't seem relevant.

A muscle jerks in his jaw.

And now, with him still so hard inside me, I'm sickened by what I've just done, by whatever madness has driven me to this. I lift up off him, climbing awkwardly off his lap, off the desk, placing my feet on the floor and turning away from him while I smooth my skirt down. 'Is that what you came for?'

The words come out mangled by sadness.

'No.' A single, gruff response.

But he doesn't say anything more and I spin around to face him, my expression stiff. 'Just go, Jagger. Just get out of here.'

'No.'

The word is like a whip, cracking through the room.

'I came here to speak to you, and I'm not leaving until I've said my piece.'

I shake my head. 'You honestly think you have any right to hold me hostage?'

He stands up, zipping his pants up, leaving his shirt unbuttoned so my eyes chase his tattoos hungrily, before I can stop them.

'The day I got married was the happiest day of my life.'

Great. Just what I needed to hear. I cross my arms over my chest, my heart withering inside of me.

'I stood up there and said my vows and I felt like this huge weight was being lifted off my shoulders. I'm nothing like *him*. Nothing like my father. Because I'd met someone I intended to spend the rest of my life with and I had the wedding to prove it! I stood there and I felt like I was finally dodging my destiny or fate or whatever the hell you want to call it.'

I spin away from him, furious at him and even more so myself, because I'm listening, waiting for him to continue with ill-concealed impatience.

'Curse, maybe,' he continues with a tight smile in his voice.

'I don't care,' I whisper, hollow.

'But a wedding doesn't prove I'm not like my father. A wedding doesn't exemplify the kind of man I want to be.'

I stare out of the window at Sydney, my heart and soul splintering apart. 'You know who I want to be?'

I don't say anything.

'I want to be a man who fights for what he wants. I want to be a man who reaches out and grabs what matters in this life with both hands, never mind the fact I'm scared shitless of losing you. I'm not my father. I'm not someone who's going to spend his life getting married to women I don't love. And I'm not going to spend my life running from love.

'I loved my ex. I thought I did, anyway, until I met you and finally understood what love is. And it's not something you do to prove a point. You don't love someone—marry someone—to show the world you're better than your parents. Love is private, personal, between two people. Love is me waking up every single damned night since I left, reaching for you, realising you're not there, that you're on the other side of the world, so far out of my time and reach. Love is feeling like I've been shot in the heart, the head, the chest, every single day I have to get through without a hope of seeing you.'

I am frozen to the spot and shaking all over.

'Love is realising I have made the worst mistake of my life in letting you go. Knowing I hurt you in a way you might never forgive me for, and still coming to see you because I can't not. Love is knowing I can't go another minute without telling you how I feel, without telling you I want to spend the rest of my life with you.'

I swallow convulsively; tears sting my eyes.

'Love is this certainty I have in my gut, like a rock, right here, that tells me if I walk out of here without making you understand that you have become my reason for being, the highlight of my life, the sense of everything I want in this world, I will never forgive myself.'

I sob, my feelings ricocheting inside of me like jelly.

'Love is all I can think when I think of you, Grace, and I think of you all the time.'

I turn to face him slowly, and see the truth in his expression, the raw honesty and vulnerability on his handsome features.

'I thought getting married to Lorena would prove to the world I'm different to him. But the truth is, what my dad never did was find that one person who made him happy. That one person who was a match for him in every way. Maybe he didn't try. Maybe he just didn't get lucky like I did. But now that I've found you I'm not going to let you go, Grace. I can't.'

I lift my fingertips and dash my tears away.

'I have no right to expect anything of you.' He speaks slowly, as though I'm a wild horse and he's trying to tame me. To gentle me at his approach. 'I didn't come here today to ask anything of you except this.'

I wait, holding my breath. When he doesn't speak I lift my eyes to his. 'What?'

'I'm in love with you, Grace. I'm so completely in love with you I can't think straight. And all I want is a chance to show you that. To do what I should have done thirty-four days ago in that hotel room.'

'And what's that?' I whisper thickly.

'To tell you that you are the most incredible woman I've ever known and that I don't want to live another day without you in it. To tell you that I look at you and see the only future I could ever want.' And, emboldened, he strides towards me, his strong hands cupping my cheeks. 'To tell you that I will love you, worship you, adore you every single day, for the rest of our lives.'

But it's too much, and somehow not enough. I step back, wrapping my arms around my torso. 'I can't do this.' I shake my head, infusing my words with strength when I feel like jelly. 'Twice I've felt this pain, I've been walked out on, and I can't… I can't do it again. You… I told you I loved you and you said, to my face, that this was just sex. And you disappeared, into thin air. Do you have any idea what it's been like for me, this last month? You disappeared like I meant nothing to you.'

'You mean everything to me.'

I shake my head so hard and fast my hair whips my eyes. I disentangle it from my lashes without missing a beat. 'You meant everything to me and I told you that, and you cut me off. How dare you come back here and act as though that's okay?'

'It's not okay,' he groans, stepping towards me again. 'It's not okay, and I'm so disgusted by what I did to you. You opened yourself up to me, you chose to love me and to give me all of yourself and I treated you just

like he did. Worse. Because what we shared shouldn't
have even required words—you and I were both there.
We both knew how special it was. But when you said
that you loved me, that you wanted me to stay, I freaked
out. I freaked out, Grace. And I'm sorry. I am so sorry
that in that moment I let a ludicrous paranoia stop me
from seeing things clearly. I've spent my adult life running so hard from the man I thought I was destined to
become. The idea of meeting and falling in love with
a woman a week after my divorce came through? It
made me crazy.'

'I get it,' I whisper, shaking my head. 'But it doesn't
change the fact that you hurt me.' I sweep my eyes
closed. 'I trusted you not to be that guy, and you were.'

And then his hands are on my cheeks again, holding my face up to his, and I feel his fear and panic and
truth and my heart twists in my chest.

'I'm not that guy.'

A sob jams in my throat. I swallow it back.

'I am in love with you, Grace Llewellyn. I have spent
thirty-four nights feeling as though I'm in some kind of
hell. All I'm asking for is a chance. A chance to prove
to you that I can be trusted. A chance to show you how
much I love you.'

His words roll through me like sunshine in winter.

'I'm not saying we have to get married,' he adds,
dropping his head and inhaling the fragrance of my
hair, so that I whimper a little. 'Not now, not ever; that's
up to you. I'm just asking you to let me take you out.
To date you. To love you. To show you that I will never
leave you again.'

I'd dated Gareth for two years and one morning he told me he didn't love me. Gareth—who seemed the safest choice of companion on earth.

There are no guarantees in life. But there is passion and love and in this moment, looking up at Jagger, I feel every single part of me lock into place.

'I'm in love with you,' he says again, simply this time, and comprehension shimmers like blades of reflective glass, beaming the truth into every part of my body. Because love *is* simple.

He was overthinking it. I was overthinking it. I lift my hand to his heart, feeling the good, solid thumping there, and a smile shifts across my lips. Because I hold his heart in mine, I know I do. I hold his heart in mine and I suspect it's going to stay there for the rest of my life.

'Okay, Mr Hart. You've got yourself a deal.'

EPILOGUE

'Is that coffee I smell?'

'You'd better believe it, Miss Llewellyn, but you're going to have to open your eyes if you want to drink it.'

I blink, looking first to my clock, to verify that it is actually daytime, then in the direction of Jagger's voice. And my heart stutters against my ribs, slamming into the wall of my chest. It's been six months since he showed up in my office that day—six months since he prised open my withered heart and taught it to risk again.

It's been six months of smiles and laughs and unbelievable sex, of hand-holding and sitting up late talking about politics and life, the universe and our place in it. Six months in which I have never, not once, regretted my decision to leap off the edge of this cliff—Jagger by my side.

'Isn't it Sunday?'

Jagger's smile is so sexy, and so full of excitement. 'Yep.'

'Why are you waking me up at dawn?'

He laughs, the sound rich, pulling at my belly like a string of desire. 'It's eight o'clock.'

'Same thing.' I eye the coffee dubiously, torn between drinking it and falling back against the pillows and drowning myself in sleep once more.

'Don't even think about it, sleepyhead.'

He picks up the coffee and holds it out to me, his expression showing me he'll resort to other ways of keeping me awake if I resist. That thought alone is seriously tempting...

'We were up so late, though.' I pout, taking the coffee and sipping it, the hit instantaneous.

'Yep.' He grins, and my tummy flips. 'But it's a big day.'

'Why?'

'Because you made a huge deal last week.'

'Yes, and we celebrated that last week.' I laugh. The French company gave me the high-rise listing and I've sold ninety per cent of the office and retail space. It is a big deal and even I'm reeling at how much I've been able to achieve since Gareth agreed to sell our business to me.

'And,' he pushes, 'you're the undisputed queen of Sydney real estate, that's why. The newspaper says so. See?' He drops a paper to the bed—I didn't even realise he was holding it but then again, I'm sleep-addled and hot-boyfriend-addled. It's the real estate section and my photo is on the front.

'Oh, my God.'

'I know.' His pride is almost better than this article. Almost, but not quite.

'Seriously?'

'Evidently.'

'This is unbelievable.'

'No, Grace. It's completely believable, and absolutely

deserved.' He leans down and then kisses the top of my head and, out of nowhere, tears clog my throat. Because that's so like Jagger—one minute he's driving me crazy with early wake-ups and the thread of desire that is always pulling me to him, and the next he's filling my soul with sunshine and mermaids and promises that I might have thought were too good to be true if he hadn't spent every minute of every day showing me that Jagger's promises are always true.

'Read it,' he says, pride thick in his voice. 'And then get ready. We're going out.'

'To where?'

'Breakfast on the water?' I look towards the harbour on autopilot. Sydney is sparkling today, just like my mood, and Jagger's yacht would be the perfect place to be. We love his boat—it's not like the kind of thing you'd expect a mega billionaire to have. It's on the small side, though inside it's been fitted with every mod con. He might hate overt status symbols, but he likes the idea of being able to sail off into the ocean from time to time, knowing he can get back safely.

'Sounds good.' I drop my attention to the newspaper, scanning the article, contentment settling around me.

'You've got ten minutes, Sleeping Beauty.'

'Make it eight.' Why wait? Now that I'm awake, I want to roll up my sleeves and enjoy every minute of this day.

Jagger turns on his heel and pads out of our bedroom. I read the article quickly and I'm just pushing out of bed when he strolls back in, a goofy smile on his impossibly handsome face.

'That was only four minutes.'

'I know.'

'So?' I put a hand on my hip, grinning even when I'm trying to be pissed off at him. 'You owe me four minutes.'

'Actually, I owe you a lifetime,' he corrects and leaves again.

I laugh, even when my heart is beating double tempo.

I shower in one minute and pull on a pair of jeans and a cashmere sweater, smiling at the feeling of a paw on my thigh. Brinkley isn't technically supposed to be in our room. That's Jagger's rule. But on the few occasions I've been too busy to travel with Jagger and Brinkley's been here alone with me, I've caved completely and let Brinkley sleep at the foot of our bed.

He knows I'm a soft touch.

'Hiya, boy.' I abandon my attempt to tame my hair and crouch down, running my hands over his fur. 'Your daddy's going to be cranky if he sees you in here.'

Brinkley buries his head in my stomach and I smile.

'Don't worry. I'll explain.' I ruffle my hands at his neck and feel something hard catch my fingertips. His collar is on—I spin it around, checking for obstructions, and I can only frown when I find a bright red ribbon tied there. I look closer and all of my breath explodes out of my body. Because, tied carefully to Brinkley's collar, is the biggest, most beautiful ring I have seen in my entire life. Two diamond bands are snaked together, plaiting the full circumference of the ring. It's sparkly but simple and elegant, all at once.

My fingers are shaking a little and I look up, on autopilot.

Jagger is standing in the door frame, watching us, his eyes shining with emotion. 'I told you, we're celebrating.'

I can't speak. I stare at him and then look back at the ring, none of it making sense. Brinkley nuzzles in closer to my side and my heart explodes because I never thought I could love anyone again, and here I have the most beautiful man and puppy in my life.

'Jagger...'

'I meant what I said, Grace. I owe you a lifetime.' He closes the gap and lifts me to my feet, his eyes scanning mine as if there's even a remote possibility I might say 'no.' 'You have brought meaning to my life and happiness to my soul. You are all the parts of me I didn't even know I was missing. You're my Aphrodite.'

A sob bursts through me. 'Jagger...' I shake my head, lost for words.

'Don't say no,' he pleads. 'Don't say anything. Just know that one day, when you're ready, this is what I want. No prenup, no lawyers, just you and me and my certainty that for the rest of our lives we belong together.'

I laugh then. 'I'm not saying "no"! I'm saying yes, a thousand times over.'

His eyes widen.

'You must know how I feel about you,' I murmur. 'And if I didn't already love you to bits, this ring would definitely seal the deal,' I tease, looking down at the stunning choice.

'You don't want something...bigger? I looked at others but this just seemed...'

'Perfect,' I finish his sentence, tears filling my eyes. The two strands are perfectly wound together; the ring needs both to hold its shape. 'It's like us.'

'That's what I thought.' We stare at each for a moment, just two people smiling so much our cheeks hurt. 'So that's definitely a yes?'

I laugh. 'Yes! It's unequivocally a yes, Jagger.'

His laugh is husky and gravelly. 'I'm glad. Although I definitely had other ways in mind if you needed extra convincing.'

'And you know, I just might,' I murmur, handing the ring to him so he can slide it onto my finger, our bodies cleaved together.

It fits perfectly and we both look down at it, smiling, for several beats. Pleasure, happiness and contentment are tying bows inside my soul, but there is lust and hunger, too, a beating drum demanding my attention.

Brinkley rubs against my leg and barks, trying to nudge between the two of us.

'Down, boy.' Jagger grins. 'I saw her first.' He's joking, but the words embed deep inside of me, because I'm in Jagger's heart and I'm in Brinkley's heart and I know how lucky I am to have found my place there, an integral part of both their worlds.

'And you're about to see a whole lot more of me.'

Only Jagger shakes his head, his expression rueful. 'I'm afraid we have some place to be, Miss Llewellyn.'

'It can wait.'

''Fraid not.'

'Why? Where?'

'Your parents are on the yacht, as we speak, desperate to toast us…'

'My parents?'

'I didn't really think I could tell your father I was planning to propose without inviting them down here…'

'You spoke to my parents about this?'

'Hell, yeah. I'm old-fashioned. Not so old-fashioned to think you'd ever marry me if you thought I'd asked someone for permission, but enough to know this shit matters to parents. Or to your parents, at least.' He grins and my heart turns over in my chest.

Because he really is perfect—for me.

'I'm going to take this as an IOU,' I say sweetly, lifting up and kissing his lips slowly, falling into his arms and staying there for a moment because it's the only place I want to be.

'And you can spend every day for the rest of our lives cashing it in.' He grinds his hips against me and pleasure shoots into the pit of my stomach.

Every day for the rest of our lives sounds pretty damned perfect.

Meanwhile, in New York City...

I stare at the text message with the same sense of cold disconnect that has dogged my steps for eight months, since I learned that the man who raised me is not my father. Since I learned that my mother, may she rest in peace, lied to me, lied to him, lied to my brothers. All my life is a lie—every single shred of it.

I am not Holden Hart, I am Hades, the darkness, the devil.

She said yes!

Jagger's happiness would have meant the world to me once upon a time, but not now. Nothing means anything.

I throw the Scotch back, the burn against the back of my throat as familiar to me as breathing.

Jagger's getting married. The man I've thought of as a brother all my life has fallen head over fucking heels in love, whatever that means, and is going to start a family of his own.

And I won't be a part of it—I don't belong, not really. I'm a Hart in name only and the sooner they start to accept that, the better.

Across the room, a woman smiles at me, slow and languid, and I contemplate picking her up. I could do with a good fuck. Not sure my head would tolerate the movement, though. I think I'm on about seven days straight of being hammered.

I look away, back to the phone as it buzzes once more.

You're my best man, by the way.

I groan, dropping my head into my hands. I want to tell him to fuck off, he's dreaming, because I'm not really his brother, not really a Hart, and I'm no kind of best man.

I am not Holden Hart any more. I am the darkness, I am the devil, I am Hades and always will be…

* * * * *

COMING SOON!

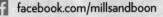

MILLS & BOON

THE HEART OF ROMANCE

A ROMANCE FOR EVERY KIND OF READER

MODERN

Prepare to be swept off your feet by sophisticated, sexy and seductive heroes, in some of the world's most glamourous and romantic locations, where power and passion collide.
8 stories per month.

HISTORICAL

Escape with historical heroes from time gone by. Whether your passion is for wicked Regency Rakes, muscled Vikings or rugged Highlanders, awaken the romance of the past.
6 stories per month.

MEDICAL

Set your pulse racing with dedicated, delectable doctors in the high-pressure world of medicine, where emotions run high and passion, comfort and love are the best medicine.
6 stories per month.

True Love

Celebrate true love with tender stories of heartfelt romance, from the rush of falling in love to the joy a new baby can bring, and a focus on the emotional heart of a relationship.
8 stories per month.

Desire

Indulge in secrets and scandal, intense drama and plenty of sizzling hot action with powerful and passionate heroes who have it all: wealth, status, good looks…everything but the right woman.
6 stories per month.

HEROES

Experience all the excitement of a gripping thriller, with an intense romance at its heart. Resourceful, true-to-life women and strong, fearless men face danger and desire - a killer combination!
8 stories per month.

DARE

Sensual love stories featuring smart, sassy heroines you'd want as a best friend, and compelling intense heroes who are worthy of them.
4 stories per month.

To see which titles are coming soon, please visit

millsandboon.co.uk/nextmonth